IT'S MY PARTY

IT'S MY PARTY

MIDDANG3ARD™ BOOK THREE

RAMY VANCE

MICHAEL ANDERLE

THE IT'S MY PARTY TEAM

Thanks to the JIT Readers

Jeff Goode

Dave Hicks

Diane L. Smith

John Ashmore

Dorothy Lloyd

Kelly O'Donnell

Deb Mader

Jeff Eaton

Misty Roa

Larry Omans

If I've missed anyone, please let me know!

Editor
The Skyhunter Editing Team

LMBPN Publishing
PMB 196, 2540 South Maryland Pkwy
Las Vegas, NV 89109

First US Edition, September 2019
ISBN (ebook) 978-1-64202-434-0
ISBN (paperback) 978-1-64202-435-7

DEDICATION

This book is dedicated to the wee monster growing in my wife's belly at the moment of this book's publication. I can't wait to meet you!

—Ramy Vance

To Family, Friends and
Those Who Love
to Read.
May We All Enjoy Grace
to Live the Life We Are
Called.

— Michael

1
____

Six riders atop axbeaks crested the hill, the sun beaming on their backs.

The sun hung in its midafternoon arc. Butterflies and bees were swollen and tired, lounging on beds of pink and blue flowers with petals the size of quarters. The wind blew through the blades of grass that stretched skyward as if in prayer or exultation. With the appearance of the axbeaks over the hill, the air filled with the sound of whooping, screams, and shouts.

The axbeaks that appeared were thin, two-legged creatures with spindly legs, feathers, and sharp ax-like beaks covered in old bloodstains. They were each saddled and bore a rider. As they raced, the veins in their necks stood out and they shook their feathers to try to cast off the heat of the sun.

Suzuki rode toward the front of the pack of screeching birds. He no longer looked like the youth he had been only months ago when he first came to Middang3ard. Now his face was worn with the scars of the many battles he had survived. His loose leather armor was sweaty, and he wore a leather hood that cast a strong shadow over his face. A hand ax was ready in one hand, and he held a flaming fireball in the other.

He cast a furtive glance over his shoulder.

To his side rode Stew, who was working tirelessly to get his axbeak to move faster. Stew was at least a foot taller than Suzuki and much more muscular. His bare chest was covered in small scars, and his face was covered in acne more fitting for a teenager, a reminder of the life he had left far behind. He wore hardly any armor, only a kilt that was weighed down by two broadswords, an ax, and a belt of daggers.

The barbarian slapped his axbeak in the back of the head to urge it to move faster.

Sandy rode at Stew's side. Her hair was braided in an elaborate fishtail, and she wore long, flowing black robes that sported blue trim across her chest and around her wrists. She did not bother to hold the reins of her axbeak, but it responded to her commands, regardless. A massive tome levitated in front of her, and she flipped through its pages rapidly.

These were the Mundanes, and they rode with the fury of those who have been chased for far too long.

Along with them were the Horsemen.

Behind the six human riders came a host of others in pursuit, bestial creatures intent on murder and mayhem. There were gray orcs whose skin hung loose from their bones, their eyes red with rage, their teeth sharpened nearly to dagger-like razors. Their muscles flexed under their skin as they snapped the reins of the wargs they rode, which were massive wolf-like creatures.

Their steeds, if you could call those monsters by such a lofty term, were disfigured, their massive heads far too large for their bulky, muscular bodies. Foam dripped from their mouths as they dashed forward like manic creatures pulled from a nightmare from whence few ever awaken.

Goblins rode beside the hulking orcs. They were smaller, yet no less bloodthirsty. Their beady eyes looked out from under armor too large for their slim forms, daggers gripped firmly in their hands and teeth. They resembled pirates.

Many of them rode wargs as well, while others sat atop smaller wolves that they kicked and chided to move. The goblins foamed nearly as much as the beasts.

Toward the back of the swarm of savage monsters were giants, massive human-like beings with slack jaws and dead eyes that lumbered dumbly after the hellish gray orcs comprising the bulk of the riders.

They totaled nearly fifty, and the Dark One's forces rode with a speed that could only come from the madness of bloodlust.

Up ahead, Suzuki checked over his shoulder again.

The Dark One's forces were gaining. It was as if their wargs were spurred on by the hope of blood, their jaws already gnashing at the thought of a fresh meal.

"We are so fucked," Suzuki shouted as he kicked his axbeak in the side to make it speed up. "Like, fucked-fucked. Like, grossly outnumbered and gangbanged into submission kind of fucked."

The man riding on the left side of Suzuki laughed. José's heavy silver armor glinted in the sunlight. His armor wasn't as rudimentary as the Mundanes'. It appeared to have been lovingly crafted, and there were small additions and upgrades such as his knuckles, which were outfitted with magical spikes that flickered, emitting little sparks of energy. A massive broadsword and shield hung from his back.

"You've never survived a gangbang," José shouted, the joy of the chase obvious in his voice. "Everyone should have one good gangbang before they die."

The woman at José's side, Diana, shrugged her robed shoulders. Her robes were similar to Sandy's yet, somehow, completely different. They appeared to be softer and more durable at the same time. She held a wand lightly in her hand and glanced cautiously over her shoulder at the approaching horde.

"I'm not sure everyone enjoys being gangbanged, José," she countered. "Some people enjoy singular intimacies."

The last of the six riders looked somewhat out of place among the others. Chipmaster, or Chip, wore very loose leather armor, but what she lacked in traditional armor, she made up for with a dazzling array of upgrades.

A pair of heavy goggles hung around her neck, and her arms were covered with what could only be described as a hybrid between magical gauntlets and a mechanized buzz-saw launcher.

She held her axbeak's reins so tightly that her hands were white. Her face lacked the joy of her other party members, the Horsemen, and she appeared ready to vomit.

The Mundanes and the Horsemen rode down the hill as the horde of villainous creatures chased them. There was still a fair amount of distance between the two groups, but Suzuki realized it was growing smaller by the minute.

"We're not going to be able to outrun them forever," Suzuki shouted.

José drew his sword, pulled on the reins of his axbeak so that the creature turned a 180, and rode toward the orcs. "Well, let's give the fuckers a reason to slow down," he called over his shoulder.

Stew smacked his axbeak and pulled the reins so that he

too turned and chased after José. He was smiling widely as he unsheathed one of his short swords. "This guy is out of his fucking mind." Stew laughed.

The rest of them turned around and headed toward the screaming mass of the Dark One's forces. Suzuki wondered what José was planning. They were grossly outnumbered and running straight toward the enemy.

Suzuki pulled up his HUD, the small visor that helped him manage his inventory and get a general read on the world around him. He looked from his companions to the horde.

His HUD read that they had a 2% chance of victory.

Suzuki caught up with José, who was rushing headlong toward the fight. "What's the game plan?" Suzuki asked.

José pointed his sword at the orc leading the rampage. "That one," José growled. "All we need to do is take him out and they'll be confused. We kill that fucker, take a couple more as we retreat, and we'll put a good amount of distance between us and them for a bit."

"You hear that?" Suzuki shouted to his party. "Everyone tag a man. José's gonna go for the leader."

José shook his head. "I am? No way. You see how big that fucker is? You and me. We're taking him out."

Suzuki's eyes narrowed as he looked at the lead orc. He was small...for an orc. For a human, he was positively massive, but among his own kind, he hardly stood at shoulder height for the average orc. "Oh, come on, he's not that big."

"That's Ulrag. I've been fighting that bastard for the last two years. His personality is really what's big. And it's that winning personality that usually ends up killing people. So be on your game."

"And what about the rest of them?" Suzuki asked.

José chuckled. "Oh, ye of little faith. My guys got this one. It's a freebie. Try to keep up in the future."

Diana and the Chipmaster were riding very close to each other. Chip reached out and grabbed Diana's reins as Diana shakily stood to her feet, balancing herself precariously on the thin back of the axbeak. She waved her wand around, eyes closed, muttering something under her breath. Above, black clouds were gathering.

Chip scrambled to keep hold of the axbeak's reins as it tried to buck Diana off.

"Hey," Chip called to Sandy. "You might have fun with a fireball or two, but you gotta behold the splendors that my girl be working with. The whole natural world her domain."

Diana opened her eyes as she grit her teeth. "Not quite," she managed. "This one's gonna take a lot out of me, so y'all better make sure to clean up the pieces and not waste it!"

The clouds continued to darken and mass as the orc horde drew closer. The six riders were going to crash into the orcs at any second.

There was a loud boom of thunder and a giant lighting crack. A bolt of lightning sizzled through the air and struck the middle of the orc horde, sending bodies flying and burning through the air. Many of the orcs and goblins were thrown from their wargs as the animals scattered among the scorched earth and burning grass.

Sandy looked in awe at Diana, and then stared at the destruction she had caused with something akin to love.

The riders connected with the first line of orcs and goblins. It was difficult to see what happened, but by the time Suzuki got to his feet and drew his sword, the field was already drenched in blood.

Ulrag pulled himself up from the bleeding warg at his feet. He stomped the warg's head in a vicious, thoughtless move. He was staring at José as he slowly walked toward him.

All around the few orcs and goblins who weren't completely disoriented were already sizing up their prey.

José pulled his shield from his back and drew his massive broadsword. The sword's edge fell to the ground with a heavy clunk. It looked too large to even be wielded by three men. "Tag 'em and bag 'em, boys," José shouted.

Ulrag was an orc of orcs. Now that he was on the ground, Suzuki could see that he was easily seven feet, his body a walking tapestry of pain, his eyes set and his mouth chewing in anticipation of the flesh he was going to tear. "José." Ulrag sneered. "You do me and my horde a disservice. We will not fall so easily."

"Fuck off and let's tango, buddy." Then he said to Suzuki, "Come on, kid. Let's kill us an orc general."

Ulrag, José, and Suzuki rushed at each other. José lifted his claymore with hardly any effort, the massive blade sailing through the air as Ulrag pulled two broadswords and blocked the attack. Ulrag kicked José in the chest, José barely having a moment to lift up his shield to absorb the blow, which still pushed him back a few feet, his boots sinking into the ground from the force of the attack.

Then Ulrag turned his eyes to Suzuki.

The attacks came faster than Suzuki could have been prepared for. All he could do was try and sidestep Ulrag as his blades cut through the air, each time barely missing Suzuki. *Holy shit, this is how I'm going to die,* Suzuki casually thought as he jumped back from an attack that would have disemboweled him.

Suzuki had fought orcs before. Scores of them, actually, but something about this orc was off. He moved with a precision and cut-throat speed that Suzuki had never seen before. Maybe the orcs he had seen before were just grunts. Maybe the Dark One was taking a real interest in the Mundanes now.

The Dark One.

That was the name Suzuki heard over and over since he was first drafted into the insanity of Middang3ard. The powers that be, mostly a wizard moonlighting as a video game designer and CEO, had spent hundreds of years preparing the human race for the coming of the Dark One. That's the line that Myrddin had fed Suzuki the day he had been whisked away from a New York skyscraper and dropped into Middang3ard's boot camp.

Suzuki's whole world had been turned upside down. In a matter of minutes, everything he had thought about reality and fantasy had been pulled out from under his feet. Then, only a couple weeks later, he was dodging axes and fireballs from a host of creatures intent on his death—all in the name of saving the realms from the Dark One. Suzuki still had no idea what the Dark One even looked like. The closest he'd come to seeing the enemy was coming into contact with someone known only as the viceroy.

Needless to say, Suzuki's life had gotten weird—that very same life that he was very aware could end with a miscalculated step.

Now is not the time to be thinking, Suzuki thought to himself as he flung himself out of Ulrag's incoming attack.

Suzuki skidded across the grass as José leapt through the air and brought his sword down on Ulrag, who tossed up his sword to deflect the attack. The two stood, locked in a stalemate, glaring into each other's eyes, waiting to see who was going to crack first.

This was an opening. Suzuki concentrated and called his familiar, Fred, an irate eldritch imp who lived in a pocket dimension in Suzuki's head, and used the demon's magic to enchant his ax with fire. Then he hurled his ax and watched it sail through the air and sink into Ulrag's chest.

Ulrag screamed in rage and pain and fell to his knees. José kicked Ulrag in the chest, jamming the ax farther in, spun, and lobbed off the orc's head. José wasted no time in celebration. He turned, grabbed Suzuki, pulling him off running toward their axbeaks. They both leapt onto the fowl's backs and José took off without looking back.

Suzuki hesitated. "Hey, what about them?" Suzuki called to José.

José tossed a dagger that landed square in the chest of a goblin as he turned back to Suzuki. "Do you have to babysit your party or something?" José teased. "Go get 'em if you have to, but we need to put some distance between us."

Suzuki reached out to Fred and felt the imp unfolding in his mind. It helped if he imagined Fred, a smallish demon with red scales that bristled anytime he was spoken to, especially if it was by Suzuki. "Hey, Fred, can you let the other familiars know that we have to get out of here?" Suzuki asked.

There was a long pause and finally Fred replied. "Yes, human."

Suzuki knew that he could trust Stew and Sandy to catch up. They were both capable and had saved his ass multiple times. Still, it felt weird to just get up and leave them.

The party wasn't supposed to be split, even if it was for a few moments. Suzuki turned and instead of following José, rode back toward where he thought Sandy and Stew were. It didn't take long to spot them.

Stew was on the ground, holding down a goblin. The goblin was spitting in Stew's face, trying to escape Stew's massive body, ineffectually slashing at Stew, who brought his fist down in the goblin's face before standing and driving his sword through the goblin's chest.

Standing, Stew wiped the blood off his face, and screamed. It was more than just an adrenaline rush, though. The air rippled with the force of Stew's voice, and Suzuki could feel the magic affecting him. He felt rejuvenated and bold. The goblins nearby scattered. Stew was getting pretty proficient at his barbarian spells.

Suzuki rode up beside Stew and watched the goblins turning tail. "Come on," he said. "We gotta get going. Let's put some more distance between us and them."

Stew nodded and jogged over to his axbeak, which was towering over a riderless wolf, hacking the thing to pieces. Stew jumped on top of the axbeak, grabbed the reins and took off after José. "Where's Sandy?" Suzuki called after him.

"With the Horsemen!"

The Horsemen were more than capable. Suzuki figured Sandy would be all right, but he still didn't feel comfortable leaving her behind with the horde of orcs and goblins. He scanned the battlefield watching the Dark One's retreating forces. The retreat wouldn't last for long, though. Stew's spell was going to wear off soon enough, and the orcs would get their courage back.

A few feet away, Suzuki spotted Chip, Diana, and Sandy. They were easier to spot than Stew because of the ring of fire surrounding them. Sandy was floating above the circle, nearly ten feet in the air, her book levitating in front of her.

Sandy raised her hands, and burning runes and sigils appeared in her palms.

The fire circle exploded, sending a wall of flame

scorching the field, cutting the orcs off from the Mundanes and Horsemen.

Sandy floated back down to the ground as she and the Horsemen jumped back onto the axbeaks. They rode toward Suzuki. "Aw, were you worried about me?" Sandy asked as she caught up with Suzuki.

Suzuki shrugged and pulled on his axbeak's reins so that it turned and rode away from the fire and toward José and Stew. "Never split the party," Suzuki replied. "Remember?"

"You just don't want me having too much fun. I can see it in your eyes. Terrified that we're going to kill everything before you get a chance to. Party pooper."

Sandy and the Horsemen took off after José and Stew. Suzuki brought up the rear, checking over his shoulder again to see how the pack of the Dark One's degenerates were faring with the wall of flame expertly provided by Sandy and Diana.

No matter how long he had known Sandy, he never quite got used to how giddy she was about violence. When they had been playing online together, Suzuki had just assumed that it was part of the roleplaying. Being out in the real Middang3ard had completely changed his mind. Sandy was a totally different person out on the battlefield. He rarely heard her laugh as joyfully as when she was arms deep in the entrails of the enemy.

Axbeak feet flew across the plains as the Mundanes and Horsemen pushed their fowls to the limit. The fires behind them were already starting to burn out. The orcs, goblins, and giants would be after them again soon. Luckily there seemed to be enough space between them that it seemed possible that they might actually be able to slip away from the Dark One's small troop.

The inner fan boy was welling up. He had seen José a

handful of times and heard other MERCs, the paramilitary mercenary force raging war against the Dark One, talking about the Horsemen's exploits. They had always seemed so fantastic. Part of Suzuki didn't believe any of the stories to be true, but in the little bit of time that they had been traveling with José, they had already managed to be attacked by a small army, and José was handling the situation as if it happened once a week.

An ear-piercing screech broke Suzuki's concentration. He looked up in the direction of the noise and saw three harpies. The creatures had the bodies of emaciated, naked women and their arms were winged, covered in a patch of feathers.

Drool trickled from their mouths as they screeched, and each of the harpies held a goblin in their talons.

Suzuki pointed up at the harpies as he shouted, "Hey, guys! We got a little situation here."

One of the harpies dropped its goblin. The goblin sailed through the air, pulled out two long daggers, and landed on the back of José's axbeak. It jabbed one of the daggers into José's side. "Christ's fucking tits," José shouted as he elbowed the goblin in the face, sending it flying. "Chip, get my back for me!"

José stood atop his axbeak and stared up at the harpies flying overhead. He crouched low and then sprung into the air, flying straight toward the harpy that had just dropped the goblin. "Cry havoc and let loose the dogs of war," José shouted, his voice almost as giddy as a kid.

Behind the riders, the giants had made their way to the front of the horde. They were closing the most distance, their long legs giving them an edge over the others. Their rage-filled roars shook Suzuki from the inside out.

The harpies could be heard screaming from above. Even

though Suzuki knew he had to pay attention to what was going on around him, he couldn't help sneaking a peek at what José was doing.

One of the harpies had been lassoed by José, who was hanging from the rope tied round the harpy's neck. José swung back and forth on the rope, dragging the harpy down until he got enough momentum and flung himself through the air.

He crashed into the goblin clutched in the harpy's talons and his sword slid into the goblin's belly as he twisted away, flinging himself above the other harpy, slicing through its neck with a fluid movement as he rose and then fell, grabbing the last goblin, situating it under his feet so that he descended like some bizarre parody of a surfer, the goblin standing in for the surfboard.

The goblin splattered on the ground when José landed. José pulled his hair out of his face, looked down at the bloody mess he stood in, and chuckled. "Huh. Didn't really think that was going to work out like that."

Behind José, the giants were closing in. Suzuki didn't think José was aware of how close the giants were.

But as Suzuki was preparing to turn back, Chip, one foot on her axbeak and the other on José's, went screeching past him. "Heyo, bossman," Chip clamored as she tried to control the axbeaks, her face nearly green with sickness. "We got two giants gamboling in your general direction to acquaint your bones with the fleshy outer layers of your skin—"

"Goddamn it, Chip, what the fuck are you saying?"

"Two giants! I cut up one of them, you get choppy with the other!"

"Wind 'em up!"

Chip jumped from the axbeaks, sailing through the air toward José. "Catch me in yer big strong arms." She cackled.

José caught Chip but instead of putting her on the ground, he launched her into the air, drawing his sword, taking a knee and slashing the legs out from the giant coming up behind him.

Up above, Chip soared through the sky, taking aim with the haphazardly built buzz saws hanging from her arms. There was a loud clinking sound as her eyes went wide and two massive circular saw blades shot out from her wrists, neatly slicing into another giant's head. Chip fell down and José scooped her out of the air. "Aye, my many thanks for not letting me crack me ass," Chip said as she grabbed the nearby axbeak.

José and Chip sped away as the last giant looked on in confusion at its fallen comrades. The Horsemen's attack couldn't have taken any more than ten seconds.

It didn't take long before the two Horsemen caught up to the Mundanes. Suzuki didn't even want to bother looking to see how far away the horde was. If it was that easy for José and Chip to catch up to them, it wasn't going to take long for the horde to do the same thing.

This couldn't go on forever.

José was at Suzuki's right, smiling as, on the other side, Sandy cackled madly while lobbing fireballs, which exploded like small grenades. "You look like you could use a smile." José prodded Suzuki. "It's good to know that at least one of you guys knows how to have a good time."

Suzuki let the comment roll off his shoulders. He was far from having a good time. "We've only been riding for three days. We've only just crossed into the Dark One's territory and we're already grossly outnumbered," Suzuki retorted.

"So, what I'm hearing is that we're already having a fucking blast."

Suzuki groaned. "We can't keep this up. We need a plan

to get out of this."

"Hm...you are a very observant kind of downer," José said. "That's probably why your merry band of idiots is still alive."

"We are not idiots!" Suzuki protested.

Just as Suzuki spoke, Stew lost control of his axbeak and went speeding off in front of the rest of the group. The axbeak had seen something that it thought was obviously more important than listening to Stew, who was beating it over the head, trying to regain control.

Suzuki had to admit it: Stew did look pretty stupid.

Suzuki leaned forward and spurred his axbeak to catch up with Stew. José and the rest of them did the same. "Okay," Suzuki grumbled, "If we're so stupid, what the fuck is *your* plan of action?"

"Kid, I told you before, I'm just along for the ride." José wore a shit-eating grin as he spoke. "This is your rodeo."

"You're just going to talk shit as a backseat rider?"

José shook his head. "I wouldn't say talk shit so much as provide constructive criticism to lighten your ass the fuck up."

"How am I supposed to lighten up?" Suzuki asked. "We're being chased by a mob of orcs and goblins stronger than anything I've ever seen. And they have giants."

"Two fewer giants than they did before. Now get your shit together and calm down. What are we going to do?"

Suzuki racked his brain trying to come up with an option. All he could see was the terrain ahead of him and he knew what was behind him.

Just hills and plains.

He wasn't sure how long they stretched out, but he knew that if these were just flatlands, it was only a matter of time until the orcs caught up.

Making a stand was out of the question. Suzuki had noticed that Diana was holding back attacking after that massive lightning strike. This led Suzuki to assume that she had used a lot of mana for the attack. Even though it had been strong, it still hadn't been enough to stop the horde.

When Suzuki thought back to his attack against Ulrag, he remembered that his ax throw had just startled Ulrag. It had been José who had delivered the death blow.

Even though these were all just observations, Suzuki figured that the Mundanes still weren't strong enough to do too much damage. Even the Horsemen, who had substantially better gear, didn't seem too gung-ho at the prospect of a straight-up fight. *If only there was something that I could do to get a better view,* Suzuki thought. *Wait! Fucking got it!*

Suzuki reached out tentatively to Fred. Usually, he tried to cast magic without actually talking to Fred because it took time and, frankly, Fred seemed to delight in embarrassing Suzuki any chance that he got.

Hey, Fred, Suzuki said. *I need a hand. You remember that clairvoyance spell?*

Fred reared his head from within the pocket dimension. *I am not a goldfish,* Fred responded, irritation dripping like poison with each word.

What does that have to—

I remember.

All right. I need to cast it, but not ahead. I need to cast it from above. As high up as you can get it.

You want to see from the atmosphere? Fred asked.

Okay, maybe not as far as you can. Let's see...high enough that I can see in a ten-mile circumference from where I'm at.

So specific. I can see you have a basic understanding of geometry. You must feel quite accomplished with your wisdom at—

Suzuki pursed his lips. *Fred, now, please!*

Very well, human.

A portal roughly the size of a basketball opened in front of Suzuki. When he looked through it, he could see an aerial view of the fields. It was difficult to tell how far away the horde was due to the perspective, but it was easy to see that it was not far. Suzuki scanned what he could see of the field. His SD upgrade allowed him to cast the specific spell, but he still needed an upgrade to get a crisper view. This was all he had at the moment, so it was going to have to do.

Toward the West, there appeared to be a cave. *Perfect,* Suzuki thought. *Fucking perfect.*

Suzuki waved the portal away just in time to keep from crashing into Stew, who was still battling to get his axbeak under control. "Listen to me, damn it," Stew shouted as he veered off course again, barely managing to keep from sliding off the axbeak.

As Suzuki maneuvered away from Stew, who had practically become a wrecking ball, he shouted to the Mundanes and the Horsemen, "All right, everyone! We're going East. There's a cave and we can funnel these fuckers into it and take them out Spartan style!"

The two parties shifted their trajectory with Suzuki and José leading them. "Spartan style?" José asked.

Suzuki pointed ahead at the cave in the distance. It had a narrow entrance and appeared to extend far into what looked like a series of hills outlining a mountain hidden by perspective and clouds. "Yeah, you know," Suzuki started to explain. "Like the 300 Spartans that fended off the Persian army. Although, records show that the Spartans probably had more than 300 foot soldiers. However, the same principle of funneling your enemies into a kill tunnel still holds up pretty well. In theory, at least."

"Nice. Pre-Greco Roman battle tactics. You know your shit."

Suzuki beamed at the compliment. He nudged his axbeak in the side and took off toward the cave at top speed. Suzuki knew that Sandy and Stew both appreciated his tactical mind, there was no doubt about that, but neither of them seemed to know or care where Suzuki got his ideas from. It felt good to be given credit from someone who knew what it was that he was doing, to feel that kind of appreciated. It was even more impressive that it was coming from the top MERC.

The cave was quickly coming up, and Suzuki saw that it was indeed part of a large section of hills and mountains. This would work perfectly. Not only would it give the two parties a place to funnel the horde, but they would also have some space to lose any stragglers and make it harder to be tracked.

Once the Mundanes and Horsemen made it to the cave, they dismounted from their axbeaks and herded them inside. In the distance, the horde approached, climbing a hill. They stopped, searching. Then an orc who held Ulrag's head on a spike pointed in their direction.

"All right," Suzuki shouted, "Everyone into the cave!"

Stew, José, and Chip ran into the cave. Sandy and Diana stayed outside with Suzuki. "We should at least try to make them work for our heads," Diana said as she knelt down and started drawing symbols into the dirt with her wand. "Gimme a hand, Sandy."

Sandy drew her own wand and started to copy the arcane symbols that Diana drew. As the two wove the symbols into the earth, Suzuki could see the air vibrating with magic. Sandy and Diana finished and retreated into the cave. Suzuki followed. He noticed that as he crossed the threshold, his skin grew very warm for a second.

Diana noticed Suzuki looking at his skin with confusion. "You guys just use elemental magic, don't you?" she asked. "This is one of the reasons you need to have mentors. It's nice and fun to throw a fireball, but just think of the mayhem you can cause with a well-placed trap. First, they have to break past the physical barrier. Then they find out that breaking the barrier sets them on fire."

Sandy's eyes lit up at the prospect of burning orc flesh. "Fuck, that is so cool. I never would have thought of that."

Diana smiled. "Which is why you, my dear girl, need a diligent teacher. You and I are going to have a grand time on this quest."

Suzuki peered out from behind the magical barrier. He could see the horde in the distance, approaching. "Come on, we need to get farther into the cave before we take a break and figure out what else is going on," he said.

No one questioned his order.

Even the veterans seemed more than happy to let Suzuki lead the way, which he did. Ahead of them, the cave split into a dozen different paths. Suzuki choose one arbitrarily and the two parties went down it. He didn't feel it made much sense to agonize over the path.

There was no way to know where they were going. He didn't have enough time to check each pathway with Clairvoyance. The only criteria for the tunnel was that it wasn't too wide. He chose what looked like the thinnest tunnel and prayed for the best.

Outside, the orcs and goblins raced toward the cave's entrance while the Mundanes and Horsemen began to explore the inner workings of the cave. Neither was aware of what they were to come across.

2

———

The cave that the Mundanes and Horsemen explored was dark. Hardly any light from the cave's entrance made it down the tunnels. The cave smelled of moss and water, which meant that somewhere in here, there was a water source. But where? Suzuki wasn't sure. He couldn't hear any running water. All he knew was that the walls were some kind of flint and that he had never seen anything like it back home.

Chipping off a little bit of flint, Suzuki saw geodes glittering like diamonds. If there had been time, he would have explored the cave more thoroughly but, seeing as there were orcs trying to kill him and his friends, Suzuki was in somewhat of a rush.

No one seemed particularly bothered by this plan of action. They slowly made their way through the cave until they could find a place to set up and defend themselves. The tunnel that they were traveling down was wider than Suzuki had anticipated and he adjusted his plan accordingly, now he knew that Diana could lay traps. So could Sandy, with a little bit of guidance. This meant that if they found a small enough space, they could layer the room with traps to help thin out their enemies.

Behind Suzuki, Diana and Sandy were talking to each other in low whispers. Stew and José were also speaking with each other. Whatever Stew was saying was cracking up José. The tunnels were filling with José's deep boyish laughter. The others had coupled up, except for Chip.

The little bit of light in the cave was fading. Sandy pulled out her wand and cast an Illumination spell. A small orb of light floated up overhead and cast a dull blue hue over the adventurers.

"You gotta start stretching yourself," Diana said as she gently nudged Sandy's side. "We can sit down with Chip later and go over some of your SD cards. See how we can get your spells to be a little more...inspired."

Diana waved her wand, and the ceiling sprouted thousands of eyes that dazzled and flickered until they turned into what looked like tiny stars. The cave was nearly as bright as daylight now.

"That is so fucking sick," Sandy whispered as she stared up at the constellations painted on the cave's ceiling.

Diana nodded. "Creativity is the highlight of human magic. It's what sets us apart from the elves, dwarves, and halflings. You don't have to restrict yourself to what you read in books. All you need is a general idea and 'bam'! I'll show you all about it."

At Suzuki's side, Stew and José were talking softly to each other. From what Suzuki could gather, they were exchanging stories. He couldn't tell if they were talking about fighting or fucking, but whatever the topic, they both seemed riveted. Suzuki hadn't heard José laugh that much outside of a poker game or a battle. And it had been a battle. There was a part of Suzuki that had been worried that everything he had heard about José was nothing more than myth, the self-proclaimed greatness of one MERC telling stories that grew out of control.

Now, after seeing José fight, every doubt had left Suzuki's mind. The man had moved so calmly and seemed to delight in fighting. There was obvious joy, but it was different from what Suzuki saw light up Sandy's face. Sandy liked to make a mess and feed some part of her personality that she couldn't on Earth. Stew got excited because he liked to prove himself, at least that was what Suzuki suspected. José, though? Suzuki couldn't figure out what it was that made José a superhero on the battlefield.

Suzuki looked at José, whose hair was pulled back in a long ponytail, his scruffy beard with specks of dried blood. He could see why people called the guy Christ. He had the look of a prophet down, and he carried himself like he knew he was a savior. Suzuki assumed that was where the similarities ended. There weren't many stories in the Bible that involved orcs or magic-casting mages. Still, it didn't really matter. José was on their side regardless of what he was.

The adventurers continued to make their way through the star-covered cave, their shadows dancing like wild children across the flint stone. Farther and farther into the cave they descended. Finally, they came to an opening.

The slope of the ground they walked on had been worn into a kind of staircase. They descended and the cave opened up to an underground cavern. Stalagmites taller than José nearly touched the ceiling, which opened up in some parts and let sparse rays of sunlight shoot down and dance on the ground. There was an underground spring in the middle of the cavern. The water was clear as glass.

José walked over to the water and dipped his finger in. "This looks like as good of a place for a break as I think we're going to get," he said as he sat down on a rock nearby. "What do you think, kid?"

Suzuki didn't answer at first. He still wasn't used to being addressed as an equal. Even if he was being called "kid" all the time. *Does José even remember my name?*

"Does this match up to your high standards, Suzuki?" José repeated.

That snapped Suzuki out of his thoughts. "Yeah, yeah," he muttered, caught off-guard by seemingly having his mind read. "This is a good spot."

José stood, walked over to Suzuki, and flicked the water on his fingers in Suzuki's face. The warrior-mage stepped back and batted his eyes furiously.

Caught off-guard again.

Before they left the Red Lion, Suzuki had felt that José treated him like an irritating, brown-nosing student, and he couldn't blame him. Even when José was talking shit, it was hard for Suzuki not to gush with excitement at being spoken to.

Now Suzuki felt he was being treated like a brother. The change had been almost instantaneous.

Suzuki wandered around the cave, separating from the rest of the two parties for a bit. He wanted to see if there were any other entrances into the cavern. More entrances meant that the tunnels that they had seen before could connect. There were obviously entrances from above, the openings where the light streamed from, but they were a good way away from the opening of the cave. Unless the orcs had scouted the area already, they probably didn't know that there was direct access from above.

Still...something could probably be done about that.

Across the cave, Diana was waving her wand, which was shooting out small red sparks. "Come on," she shouted,

"Lunch is on." She waved her wand and a few boulders nearby levitated toward her. A tablecloth spread out over the boulders. Plates and cups appeared. Then she scrolled through her HUD inventory, selected an option, and food materialized onto the plates: a selection of various dried meats, cheeses, and fruits. The cups filled with ale.

Suzuki grabbed a plate and popped one of the pieces of cheese into his mouth. The cheese was funky, flavorful, and a little bitter. It smelled like old t-shirts, but Suzuki couldn't get enough of it. He rolled some of the cheese up in a few slices of cured goat and dug in. The cured meat was savory and melted in Suzuki's mouth. Something about the meat reminded him of waking up early in the morning, watching the sun rise over a green hill, the smell of fresh dew and past rains.

Whatever Diana had packed was substantially better than the morsels that Wendy, the barkeep of the Red Lion, had sent out with the Mundanes on their last few missions.

Stew said what everyone was thinking. "Hey, what gives? This is a shit ton better than the shit that Wendy sends us with. I mean, I can make it work. My culinary skills are...let's just say, bat-shit crazy. But this...this shit is amazing."

Candles appeared on the table as Diana waved her wand again. "Wendy is a saint," Diana explained, "who works her ass off. She's—"

"If she had an arse," Chip interrupted as she downed her ale.

"Shut it, Chip."

The brash warrior just smiled. "Just saying she don't have much of a storage compartment toward the rear. Ain't nothing wrong with a flat-butted vixen. My own arse leaves a little to the imagination, if you've ever taken a gander. Which I know you have."

"*Anyways*, I don't get my food from Wendy," Diana said. "The Red Lion is more like a hub for the newbies. Granted, we all like to get trashed there, but it's mostly to see what's going on with everyone else. There are MERC hubs all throughout the realm. Hell, you saw that we had two inns at the encampment. But like I was saying, they're mostly for the newbies. Wendy sends everyone off with some top tier shit. But we've been at this for a while. Long enough to know that we can do our own grocery shopping and take some of the work off of Wendy. We mostly get our food from elvish markets. José's partial to the food enchantments."

"Enchantments?" Suzuki asked.

"Yeah, you know how every bit reminds you of something, even if you aren't sure that you're actually remembering anything. That's the enchantment. Kind of like their wine but less...hardcore, I guess."

Suzuki took another bite of the cured meat. For a few seconds, the stress of being chased by the Dark One's forces dissolved. All that Suzuki was left with was a warm feeling in his stomach as a brief vision of himself sitting on a beach next to a windmill filled his mind. He could almost smell the salty sea breeze tickling his nose while he leaned back and felt the coarse, warm sand on his palms.

The vision vanished and Suzuki was back in the cavern. The feelings of contentment and comfort remained, though. Suzuki reached for a piece of fruit as José took a sip from his ale.

"Helps keeps the nerves steady," José explained. "All the near-death experiences have a habit of causing paranoia. Surprisingly, there's nothing worse than being stressed while you're trying to stay alive. This way you keep up your energy and morale. The elves were on to something. Been trying to get Wendy to start giving it a try. The recruits could use it. Most of you guys burn out after the first month. How long've you been here?"

Suzuki shrugged his shoulders. Time had practically lost all meaning since he'd come to Middang3ard. He didn't have a calendar. Besides that, so much had happened that he felt caught in a whirlwind. He had no idea when he had been whisked off to Middang3ard. His first mission hadn't been long after that. The only period of time that had stood out was Beth's capture. That was a little over two weeks ago.

Beth hadn't drifted into Suzuki's mind in a while. Or was it that she never left his mind? Since Beth had been drafted into the army, she had existed only as regular voice and video messages. When Suzuki joined MERC, it was only so he could get closer to Beth. Then she had been captured. Since then, everything that Suzuki had done was to save Beth. That's why the Mundanes and the Horsemen were sitting in a cave, hiding from orcs, decompressing with an elvish charcuterie plate.

It was all to save Beth.

The rest of the meal continued in relative silence. Each of the adventurers was caught up in the mini false memories, far off gazes resting on their faces. Suzuki wondered what each of them was imagining. Back when he had first tried Elvish wine, the stories that were crafted into the wine were the same for everyone. This felt a little different. This felt like it had been tailored just for him.

Once they were finished eating, Diana waved away the food. "All right," she said, "equipment check."

Diana pulled off her HUD, as did José, and handed them to Chip, who took a seat on a rock before taking out a pair of pliers and a soldering iron.

Suzuki had been trying to peg the Chipmaster down

since José had told him that she was coming on the quest as well.

Spending any time around José, it was obvious what his role in his party was: tank. It wasn't often you saw a party leader tanking, but José seemed to have worked out a system.

Diana was also pretty obvious. She was the party's mage. She didn't seem to deal with buffing so much as strategic offense.

The Mundanes party was fairly straightforward in that way as well. Suzuki was a battle mage. He tried to blend his melee approach with offensive magic. He'd taken a special liking to fire magic.

Stew was a tank. All Stew had ever been was a tank, stretching all the way back to their first time playing with Beth, before Sandy had joined the party.

And Sandy was a mage. She hadn't seemed too excited for the role when they had first started gaming together and Suzuki always assumed that she had only accepted it because it was the role that the party needed her to play. That had changed since they had come to Middang3ard. Not only did Sandy seem to have a knack for magic, but she was compulsively reading and expanding her under-standing of the craft.

All that being said, Suzuki couldn't place Chip. He'd only seen her a handful of times, usually when the rest of her party was out on a quest. She was usually at the Red Lion, huddled in some corner, tearing apart HUDs or other electronic devices.

Technology wasn't a huge part of Middang3ard: almost everything was done magically. That's why Suzuki had been surprised that Chip always had her hands on a new piece of tech. Other than upgrading her party's equipment, it was difficult to tell exactly what she did. She didn't seem all that comfortable in a fight.

It didn't take Chip long to finish working on her party's HUDs. She tossed them back to José and Diana and then motioned for Sandy and Stew to hand theirs over.

Stew removed his HUD and gave it to Chip. "I don't think you have to worry about ours," Stew said. "We haven't really got shit on them."

Chip removed the HUD's paneling and hit a button that caused the HUD's SD cards, the upgrade nodules for the HUDs, to pop out.

"I take a kind liking to your professional musings," Chip murmured, "but I do think that your headpieces have a little bit of personality that could be brought out."

Chip pulled down her goggles and peered into the inner mechanics of the HUD.

Sandy came up and stood next to Suzuki as she watched Chip work. "A little bit odd, isn't she?" Sandy asked.

A spark popped from Stew's HUD and a giant geyser of fire spouted out for a second before Chip was able to pat the flames down.

Suzuki instinctively touched the side of his HUD, imagining his exploding from something Chip had done to it. "Yeah," he agreed. "Just a little bit."

Chip turned Stew's HUD upside down and welded something into the visor. Then she shut up the HUD and handed it back to Stew.

"It looks like you got a pretty standard Critical Hit SD in there," she explained. "Now these standard pieces are a wee bit underwhelming, to say the least. Ye already know where the pointy part goes, aye?"

Stew tried not to look too confused as he fumbled for his

words. "Uh...yeah...the sharp point goes in the body," he said.

"Exactly. Heads have brains. Big knives work really well, with the pointy part to get to them good ol' gray parts. So, I found a way to make your upgrade all nice and shiny. A good and proper upgrade. Now, I got this piece set up so it'll give you a nice little peek at unknown crits. When you hit one of these little buggers, it'll over clock the HUD, send a jolt to your already impressive muscles and whamo! You'll be stabbing twice as hard. Read out will pop up on your HUD to give you a good idea of where to get stabby. Sound manageable?"

"Uh...yeah, that sounds pretty fucking great."

"Get ye swing on, chap. Just pay attention to the readings. It'll be all bright and hot where you supposed to get all killy. All right, tall, dark, and murderous, step right up."

Sandy couldn't seem to tell if Chip was talking to her, so she approached cautiously. She removed her HUD and handed it to Chip gingerly as if she were afraid that Chip were going to do some irreparable damage.

The way that Chip handled the HUD was frightening. She tossed it into the air, caught it with her pliers, and through some kind of mechanical wizardry, broke the HUD into a thousand pieces that floated, suspended in the air.

Sandy's eyes widened as she marveled at the artistic display of gears, microchips, and microscopic pieces.

Chip peered at the gutted HUD and hummed to herself. She walked a few circles around the HUD and prodded a gear or microchip here and there. Then she prodded a few microchips, reached into the floating galaxy of technology and started to rearrange the whole thing by hand.

The process hardly took any time, and she handed the HUD back to Sandy when she was done.

"All right," Chip said. "Your SD cards are already on the up and up. I popped open your little guy and reset your mana usage. You have been blowing through a fair amount of it a little too quickly. Gotta little trick you might like. Switching between your staff, wand, and hands will give you a little bump on the ol' recharge. Chain 'em together and you'll get some nice synergy. Extend your mana as long as you're chaining your magic usage. Sound spiffy?"

Sandy accepted her HUD back from Chip. "Holy shit," she exclaimed. "That sounds amazing!"

"Figured it'd be similar enough to your VR tricks, am I right?"

Sandy was positively beaming with the upgrade. "Thanks! I'll really be able to fuck some shit up with this."

"Yes, indeed, the shit will be properly fucked. All right, O Fearless Leader, bring it on in."

Suzuki removed his HUD, walked over to Chip, and handed it to her. He was curious to know what she was going to give him. It was Chip initially who had installed his Smell Altering SD. When he first received the upgrade from Beth in the mail, he had thought it was going to be completely useless despite the fact that he had initially been rejected from the army for his English blood. Giants had a particular hatred of British blood, and they could smell it through skin. After Chip had taken a look at the SD card, she had made a few alterations that had given him a versatile tool. He was more than a little excited to see what Chip was going to give him now.

The HUD sat in Chip's hands for a few moments as she turned it over, looking through her goggles with a puzzled look on her face.

"Hmm..." she murmured. "This should about do it."

Chip popped open the SD slot and took out the Clairvoyance card. She crushed the card in between her fingers.

Suzuki instinctively reached out to stop Chip. "What the hell are you doing?" he shouted.

"My job, no, please and thank you, shut your word hole."

Chip took the pieces of the card and rolled them in her hand, crushing them up further. Suzuki hadn't noticed, but it had to take a tremendous amount of strength to break one of those cards with only two fingers, and Chip hadn't stopped there. She was pounding the pieces of the card with her index fingers, reducing it to a fine powder. Once the card was thoroughly pulverized, she poured the glittering dust back into the SD slot. Then she welded the slot closed. She handed the HUD back to Suzuki.

"Let's take it for a spin."

Chip pulled out a USB cord, plugged it into her HUD, and linked her HUD to Suzuki's. "Cast Clairvoyance," Chip commanded as she shut her eyes tight.

The familiar portal opened in front of her and Suzuki. Chip reached out and grabbed the edges of the portal. She pulled fast and hard and the portal extended, consuming the entire cave. It happened so quickly that Suzuki couldn't at first make sense of what had happened.

Suzuki was standing outside with Chip. They were no longer in the cave, they were in a forest. The trees were nearly the width of a skyscraper, and they stretched all the way to the night sky, where billions of stars twinkled infinitely. Purple knee-high grass covered the ground, and a gentle wind blew through the forest.

Houses were built into the canopy of trees. Elaborate bridges were built between each of the trees and Suzuki could make out folk walking back and forth.

Chip walked around, staring up at the stars for a bit

before they sat down in the grass. Suzuki took a seat next to her and felt the grass against his palms. "What's happening?" he asked.

"It's my home. I accessed the backend of your HUD and cards. Pumped up the strength a gigaton. Crystal clear, eh?"

"Are we actually here?"

"Nope. Kinda like a VR room. You can pick a spot on your map, hit the coordinates, and bingo, high definition spy tools. You can't go far. Say you cast it on them orcs pounding outside? You'd be able to walk a little forward and a little back, but it'll start to break up after that. Still give you a good look at what's around, though."

"You grew up here?" Suzuki asked.

"Yeppers."

"What exactly are you? I mean, you're not a mage, but you use magic. You're not a fighter or a tank or a warrior. Chipmaster isn't even really a name, it's more of a title."

"Technically, a rogue. More specifically, an experiment. Back when the military jack-shits were interested in magic-technology combos, that's when ol' Chipmaster happened. But Chip's good enough for a name. Come on, we should get going. The spell also casts a time dilation spell. Things outside are going a lot slower so you can take your time. Sounds good, right?"

"Yeah. It's fucking amazing."

Chip nodded in satisfaction. "All in a day's work."

The illusion disappeared with a loud pop and Suzuki was back in the cave. No one seemed to have noticed that he and Chip had disappeared. It was like the whole experience had taken less than a second. Chip stood up, brushed off her pants, and went to join the rest of her party.

Suzuki followed as both parties converged. *Government technology experiments,* Suzuki thought. He remembered the orb that he had used to speak with the viceroy. The orb had not been magical in nature. He knew that the moment he had touched it. Magic was still something that Suzuki didn't quite grasp, but technology was another story. He grew up with technology. Beyond a shadow of a doubt, he knew that the orb wasn't magical. He wondered what specifically the military had been testing with Chip. What more would she be willing to tell him?

A loud roar and shouting voices could be heard in the cave. It was coming from the direction the Mundanes and Horsemen had just traveled. José jumped on his axbeak and pointed farther into the cave.

"If we're still following your plan," he suggested, "we should go farther into the cave. Find something more suitable. If we try to have a straight-up fight in here, they're going to kill us."

Suzuki mounted his axbeak as well and nodded in agreement as he rode up to José's side. "Which way do you think we should go?" he asked.

José pointed at a stream of trickling water that ran between their feet. "We'll follow the water source. The pathways should narrow due to the erosion. If we hit a wall, the six of us can bust through it and then we'll have our kill tunnel."

"Lead the way."

They took off, the axbeaks moving slowly across the stones as if they were worried about their frail feet. Suzuki fell in with the Mundanes toward the back of the group, gladly allowing José to step up and take the lead. He let his axbeak slow until he was next to Stew. "Shit's pretty wild, huh?" he asked.

Stew clapped his hand on Suzuki's shoulder as he beamed. "Wild ain't the word, dude," he replied. "I still remember how hard you were fanboying when you met José. Thought you were going to cream your jeans."

"Fuck off."

"But for real, it is wild," Stew said. "I know José said that the MERCs had been watching us for a while but, honestly, I thought we were still just some dumb freshmen to these guys. I was definitely surprised when you told me that José and all the Horsemen were going to help us find Beth."

"One step closer."

"Yeah, dude. One step closer."

Beth hadn't been mentioned between the Mundanes for some time. It was not that she was a sore subject. Rather, Suzuki suspected it was because the three of them were so focused on getting Beth back safely that it didn't need to be mentioned anymore. Why bother talking about something that you're always thinking about.

José led the riders down the cavern pathway following the trickling water. They made their way down the shimmering stone path until the walls started to tighten around them. They forced the axbeaks to keep moving even as they whined uncomfortably. It did not take long until they were all walking single file in a very cramped space – exactly what Suzuki had been hoping for. After a few more minutes of shimmying through the narrow path, they came to a small opening. José cracked the wall with his sword and the stone fell away, leaving just enough space for two people to fit through at once.

It was a genius move.

If the hole had been only wide enough for one, that would have given the orcs enough time to retreat. They wouldn't crowd the entrance properly. There was also a chance that they could see it was a trap. An opening for two made it seem more natural. The horde would probably try to force their way through before even thinking it through.

Suzuki was glad to see that José was a solid strategist as well as an amazing warrior. He was the kind of leader Suzuki silently wished to be. Getting to see José working from this close up was a dream. It was like watching a player who had figured out all the tricks to break a game. Suzuki quietly wondered whether or not the stories that people told about José were actually true. He seemed to have the wisdom of an immortal.

The new section of the cave didn't seem that much different from the cavern they just came from. The only significant difference was that there was no underground pool, and there was a large hill toward the back of the cavern. There didn't appear to be any other openings in the cavern, save a large hole in the ceiling. Suzuki wondered what could have happened to cause one large hole rather than the numerous small holes in the last cavern. He didn't worry too much about it, though. Geology was never a subject he had pretended to know anything about.

While Suzuki mused to himself, the rest of the adventurers were preparing themselves for the battle to come. Diana was showing Sandy how to attach different runes to the rocks and ground to turn the entrance into a massive trap. It was like lacing the floor with dynamite, but rather than an explosion, it would guarantee a massive fire trap, causing a lot of damage without draining a substantial amount of mana.

The more melee-inclined José and Stew were going over shield and sword techniques. José was trying to convince Stew to invest in a shield by showing Stew the different ways that you could force back an enemy with one.

Stew looked disinterested until José changed tactics and

showed Stew a technique for beheading someone with the edge of your shield.

"Defense might not be as pussy as I thought," Stew said as José handed him his shield to try.

Much like Diana and Sandy, Chip was wandering through the cave. She wasn't setting traps, though. Every so often, she would look up at the enormous hill against the back of the cavern. When she finally turned around and met Suzuki's eyes, she forced a smile. Suzuki couldn't get over how weird she looked outside of the Red Lion.

When José was satisfied with their preparations, he sat down on a rock near the entrance of the cavern. The rest of the adventurers sat down around him and they stared at the entrance, waiting. Suzuki knew what to expect, but his heart was still pounding. This all seemed like a good plan, but if something went wrong, they could easily end up dead. The Horsemen were strong, he knew that for a fact, but strong wasn't invincible. He had seen how reticent José had been to have a straight-on fight.

Even José had a fear of death and could tell that the battle was not theirs to win.

The silence in the cave was almost unbearable. It was so quiet that Suzuki imagined that he could hear something breathing behind him. Something heavy and large. He looked over his shoulder.

Nothing.

It's got to be in my head, Suzuki thought. *Just getting nervous. That's all. Just getting nervous.*

José looked at Suzuki and smiled, his smile handsome and hearty from underneath his beard. As if he were reading Suzuki's mind, he said, "This is the worst part. The waiting. No matter how many times I've been backed into a wall, waiting to be overrun is always shit. It never fucking gets less stressful. But who gives a shit when you got your mates with you, am I right? If anyone is gonna keep me safe, it's going to be these fuckers."

Suzuki could relate. The quest that had finally garnered José's attention had been a turning point for the Mundanes. It was the first time that they truly thought they were going to die. It had been at that moment Suzuki realized that Sandy and Stew were something so much bigger than friends. They were who he could die next to. No doubts. No regrets. They were his party.

The walls of the cavern shook and dust and rocks dropped from the ceiling. The orcs were coming. They must have discarded their wargs to travel on foot. The ground was slightly shaking with their rhythmic march.

Clairvoyance would give Suzuki a better idea of how far they were. He concentrated on where he wanted to cast: farther down the entrance, near the other opening. The portal opened up in front of him, and he put his fingers on its edges and then flicked it wider until he stood in the center of the tunnel.

He could see the orcs approaching.

Fast.

They'd be upon them in a few moments.

Fear and excitement pounded through Suzuki's veins. There was a time when he had only been afraid, feeling as if he were floundering through each fight. Not this time. He felt a little of what he believed Stew and Sandy felt at the beginning of a fight—pure adrenaline.

Suzuki turned to José as he drew his hand ax. "They're gonna be here any minute."

José whipped down the visor of his helm and unsheathed his sword. "Then let's make sure we send a message to the Dark One. It's gonna take more than a couple of orcs and goblins to get rid of MERC."

As Stew walked up to take his place in the battle line, he chuckled to himself. "You can fucking say that again," he shouted as he puffed his chest out. "It'll take an army of dragons to fuck us up."

A chorus erupted of "Hell fucking yeah." The MERC bravado was on in full force. Suzuki had seen it a few times but never been a part of it. This time he felt invincible. Whatever was coming through that tunnel was dead.

The sound of the orcs approaching increased. Their grunts and guttural shouts could be heard reverberating through the tunnel. The ground shook from their marching.

Suzuki raised his sword as he saw the first orc's gnarled, snarling face pass into the light as it exited the tunnel. "This ends here," Suzuki shouted. "Let's fuck these motherfuckers up!"

Suddenly, the cavern became very hot. Suzuki felt like a match had just been lit underneath him. The air grew thick and heavy. Sulfur, the familiar smell of Fred crawling out of his pocket dimension and into physical reality, filled Suzuki's nostrils, but Fred was nowhere to be seen. It was getting hotter and hotter still.

Then there was a gust of wind, stronger than Suzuki had ever felt, and the Mundanes and Horsemen were thrown through the air as winds as strong as a hurricane's flung them against the wall.

A stream of fire spurted forth, a funnel of flames the deepest red and black. The flames shot forward and into the tunnel. The screams of the orcs and goblins were unceremoniously cut off as they were burned to ash.

Suzuki scrambled to his feet. Sweat poured down the side of his face, and he flung off his helm, afraid that he was going to pass out from the heat. His vision was blurry, but he could see something near the back of the cave, something enormous and hulking in size. It spread its leathery wings and shot fire up toward the ceiling.

As Suzuki's vision cleared, he could see what had killed the horde.

A red dragon. It nearly dominated the entire back of the cavern. Its body was covered in red scales that rose and fell like a wave running along its back. It had a lizard-like head with horns that sprouted from its forehead and swept back like elongated ram's horns. Its legs and arms were long and muscular. From across the room, its eyes glowed menacingly red.

The dragon turned to face the adventurers. Its serpentine face reflected wisdom and intolerance as it slunk toward the humans, each step causing them to jump as the ground shook.

A fear unlike anything Suzuki had ever felt flooded his bones. The dragon continued to advance, its gnarled, ancient body almost slithering, smoke pluming from its nostrils as they flared. There was something old about the dragon that sent a primordial dread through Suzuki.

It must have been the way that a swimmer in the ocean feels when beholding a shark.

This was a creature evolved to perfection and adept at one thing: death.

The dragon's voice boomed, and Suzuki felt it thundering beneath his skin, in his heart, and in his head. It was an ancient tongue that he could not understand, yet made total sense. Hissing with the notes of a song washed over him as the dragon crouched and continued its approach.

"Who dares trespass within my home?" the dragon

roared. "Who dares step onto the hallowed hoard? Do ye know not my name?"

No one answered.

Suzuki was too afraid to look at José, and he assumed José was just as terrified. The Horsemen and the other MERCs always exchanged stories of the monsters they had killed.

No one had told any stories of dragons.

"Will ye remain silent, creatures of flesh and dust? Let me speak my name so that you know that purest power which you have offended. I am many named. I am the Scourge of the Eastern Wilds, the Flame Which Hath No End. I have been called the Pillar of the Realm, the Snake Which the World Rests Upon, The Red Flame of Eternity. Bow before me in fear and trembling, for I am Ashegoreth, the Eldest Red Dragon of the East, the Bringer of Despair and Ash. I am the Red Death."

Ashegoreth reared up and breathed fire that rolled up to the ceiling in a black cloud. Suzuki thought it looked like hell inverted. The dragon fell back to all fours and roared, her jaw stretching wide enough to swallow everyone in the room, flames brewing in her belly, lighting her throat and mouth with an unearthly glow.

No one moved, for they were in the presence of the Bringer of Despair and Ash.

There was only silence and stillness as the Red Death stood before them.

3

———

The cavern was filled with the noxious fumes from Ashegoreth, so heavy with smoke that the Mundanes and Horsemen could hardly breathe. The dragon and the humans continued to stare at each other. It was as if time was frozen, each waiting for who was going to make the first move.

Suzuki had never seen a dragon, and the sheer enormity of the creature was still unsettling his mind. It looked as if the dragon took up all the space in the room. But if Suzuki paid close attention and set aside his fear for a moment, he could see that the dragon was in fact sitting on a mound of treasure, mostly gold and silver, that gave her the appearance of being much larger than she truly was.

The dragon could have scorched them at any moment. She had not hesitated to kill the orcs that had been trespassing into her nest. What was taking so long for her to attack?

At Suzuki's side, José still held his sword. Suzuki cast a glance at him, hoping to glean an insight into what José was thinking, to see what the plan of action might be. Speaking was obviously too dangerous. The dragon understood English. Maybe Suzuki could reach out to José using the communication of their familiars. There weren't many options.

None that Suzuki could see at least.

There was no warning for the stream of fire that jetted out at them. Suzuki threw himself to the ground, as did the rest of the Mundanes and Horsemen. The fire passed directly over them and maintained itself for some time. Finally, Ashegoreth relented. The air above Suzuki was still hot.

Stew was lying face down, not too far from Suzuki. His back was covered in soot, but he was physically okay. He looked at Suzuki with a look of serene panic. "That's a big ass fucking dragon," he whispered under his breath.

"You don't fucking say!"

Across from Stew and Suzuki, Sandy and the Horsemen had taken shelter behind a massive boulder. Suzuki checked around for a similar setup. He tugged Stew to follow him as he stood, ran, and ducked behind a formation of rocks. As he and Stew sat with their back against the rocks, another jet of fire came shooting out in their direction.

That was two attacks that Ashegoreth had fired off that had missed. Suzuki found it hard to believe that the dragon had been so ill-prepared for their arrival that she would have missed twice. It had only taken one attack to decimate the orc horde. And she had done that without warning. The dragon had taken the time to introduce herself to him and the rest of the parties.

There had to have been a reason for that.

The jet of fire disappeared, and all that was left was hot air. Stew turned to Suzuki and drew his swords. "We can take it," Stew said. "We can nail that fucking thing."

Suzuki checked his HUD. It read 7%. Higher than he expected. "Odds are too low." He sighed. "We can't kill that thing."

"We killed that elder god-thing that was being resurrected. How much harder can a dragon be than a god?"

That was a good point.

The elder god had been different, though. Suzuki had gotten lucky with a plan and some ingredients that had been laying around like eggs and flour for a cake. This was not the same scenario. Suzuki didn't have much idea of the layout of the cavern. Nor did he know what the dragon was up to. If Ashegoreth had really wanted them dead, wouldn't she have advanced by now? The cavern seemed huge to him but, to a dragon, it was only a handful of steps away from stomping on their frail, human bodies.

Suzuki met José's eyes from across the space between their hiding places. *Fuck it,* Suzuki thought. "What the hell are we going to do?" Suzuki shouted to José.

José peeked out from behind the rock before answering Suzuki. "We don't have an exit," he explained. "If we try to get out the way we came in, we're just in a fucking kill zone."

"That's not really an answer."

"I'm trying to think up a fucking answer. You got anything?"

Stew interrupted the conversation. "I say we rush the bastard," Stew shouted. "If we can't run, we might as well fight."

"You're saying that we should at least die on our feet?" José asked.

"Hell no, I'm not saying anything about dying. I say we take the dragon."

José pursed his lips. "Have you ever fought a dragon?"

"No, have you?"

"Once."

"And?"

"Surprisingly, they're even tougher than they look."

"Sandy, what do you think?" Stew asked.

Sandy was staring down at her trembling hands. When she looked up, it was fear that had taken over her face. Fear and determination. "I say we go for it."

Suzuki knew it was a terrible idea.

He had never seen a dragon, but he knew the stories. Fantasy novels and video games had dulled the viciousness and power of dragons. Suzuki had never been a fan of dragons in those genres. They were usually nothing more than vindictive creatures sleeping on a pile of gold. And if there was anything that Suzuki had figured out by now, it was that popular culture only held a fraction of what was really out there, only a kernel of truth. From the moment that Suzuki had seen Ashegoreth, he had known that the dragon was something vaster than what people read about in books.

In myths, dragons were nearly godlike forces of destruction. That wasn't all they were, though. Intelligence and wisdom were just as much a part of the stories. And Suzuki had seen intelligence on the dragon's face, he had heard it in her voice.

Without a word, Suzuki stepped out from behind the rock, straight into the path of the dragon.

Stew reached out for Suzuki, but Suzuki slapped his hand away, turning for just a second, to say, "You guys wait here. If she torches me, make sure you raise some hell."

"Wait."

Suzuki paused.

He felt oddly serene. Out from behind the rock, he could

have easily been burned alive. Yet he felt deeply that the dragon would not attack him if he wasn't facing her.

It was José who had asked for Suzuki's attention. "Do you know what you're doing?" he asked.

Suzuki shrugged. He really didn't. "I've never fought a dragon before," he admitted.

"And you want to go in there alone?"

"You old MERCs like respect. Maybe that holds up for ancients as well."

Suzuki walked toward Ashegoreth as billows of black smoke floated out of the dragon's nostrils. The dragon leaned forward, baring fangs as large as Suzuki, heat radiating at an almost nuclear level from its mouth. Suzuki raised his ax as if he were going to throw it from afar. Then he tossed it to the ground. He stripped off his chest armor and let it fall beside the ax. He continued to approach Ashegoreth.

A laugh deep as thunder rolled through the cavern. Ashegoreth had leaned back and was chuckling. Although looking more relaxed, she was dangerous still, but not ready to leap forward and take off Suzuki's head.

"Who approaches my throne, child of dust?" Ashegoreth asked.

Suzuki racked his brain for an answer. Somehow, Suzuki didn't sound nearly regal enough. Not that he thought he had any reason to lay claim to royalty, but he knew this was probably going to be the most important introduction of his life.

"I am called...er...the Most Mundane of the Mundane, uh...the Creeping Unexpected, the Tired Tactician, the Bane of Krampus, and Freer of Fae Children. Uh...the Forlorn Lover, the Rising Sun to Vampires. I am Suzuki, the Guillotine of Old Gods."

A twinkle of interest danced in Ashegoreth eyes. It was almost a human glint. Suzuki recognized it.

Curiosity.

"Those are many titles, child of dust," Ashegoreth growled. "How has one so young to this life managed to acquire such titles of luster and pomp?"

"I am no child of dust. I am Suzuki, the Guillotine of Old Gods."

"And what, may I ask, Old God has felt the sting of your blade?"

Suzuki continued to slowly walk toward Ashegoreth. He felt like he was walking into an open fire. "Less than a week ago, I descended into the depths of a village of death. Vampires were trying to bring an elder god to life to serve the Dark One. My fellow warriors and I—"

"The same warriors who huddle behind rocks, trembling with fear?"

"The same warriors who trust me to speak with you. Who are fearless. Who will rise up to smite you in vengeance if you so much as singe a hair on my head."

"Hmm...continue your tale, Bane of Krampus."

Suzuki almost wanted to scream with joy. The dragon had used one of the titles. That had to be some kind of trust or respect.

Then again, it could just be a dragon playing with her food.

Suzuki knew he had to make this stick. He had to own his own accomplishments. "We descended into the bowels of the church," he shouted, letting his voice echo through the cavern. "I stood before the viceroy of the Dark One, and I let it be known that I would wring her master's throat. We broke the ceiling of the church and let light spill through, and as the elder god birthed himself, I lay siege to his body with an army of gremouloons."

The dragon leaned forward. Suzuki was now so close that he could reach out and touch the dragon's curled smile. A chuckle bubbled up from Ashegoreth, and it rolled through Suzuki like an earthquake. "Gremouloons? Those little things? You killed a god with a vermin infestation."

"I am the Most Mundane of Mundanes. The Creeping Unexpected."

"There were many tales on the sky of a god killed by gremouloons in a house of vampires. And you think that this will make you any less appetizing to me?"

"I bear no ill will. None. We found ourselves accidentally in your nest. From one warrior to another, I offer you a gift of good tidings. A treasure to add to your hoard."

Ashegoreth's eyes widened and then quickly narrowed. It reminded Suzuki of a snake he used to have. It was the look of a hunter recognizing prey. "What is this treasure?"

Suzuki reached under his chainmail and pulled out a ring that hung from his neck by a silver chain. "A gift from my beloved. She wears the same ring. She has been captured by the Dark One, and I am on a quest to rescue her."

"Your beloved? Not your lover?"

"Er...uh...well, you see...um...not yet...or... I mean, I think that she likes me, but we've never... It's kind of complicated, I guess. So not my lover. My beloved."

Ashegoreth reached down and plucked the tiny ring from Suzuki's hand. "It is small. Lacking gold or silver. Yet it is sad and strong. There is love in this ring...it is acceptable. You may dine with me this evening. You and your friends."

Suzuki blinked. Twice. "And...uh, you're not going to kill us?"

"An enemy of the Dark One is a friend to me and my kind. Come. Join me on my gold."

Suzuki turned his back to the dragon and breathed a huge sigh of relief. He hadn't realized it, but he had been holding his breath through nearly the entire conversation. His lungs flooded with well-needed air. He walked back to the Mundanes and the Horsemen.

José smiled widely at Suzuki as he walked by and clapped him on the shoulder.

"That's something I've never seen," José exclaimed. "A new recruit sweet-talking a dragon. That's going to make for quite the story."

The rest of the adventurers came out from hiding. Everyone looked very pleased with Suzuki. Everyone except for Stew, who came up to his side, shaking his head. "So... you did just tell a dragon that you and Beth are just friends, right?" he asked.

"Seriously, dude? Is that all you got from that?"

"Nope. Had GB record your little speech for Beth too."

Suzuki blushed. "You are such a shit."

Sandy came up behind Stew and shoved him playfully. "Yeah, seriously, fuck off, Stew," Sandy interrupted. "That was fucking awesome, Suzuki. Remember what I said about trash-talking? I take it all back. Where the fuck did you learn to talk like that? You sounded like you walked out of a movie or something."

"Norse myths. I always liked the naming of gods."

"Well, you sounded godlike. The Most Mundane of Mundanes...the Creeping Unexpected...that was pretty sick. I'm gonna remember that. Kinda makes me want to name myself."

"Honestly, it felt great."

The adventurers tentatively approached the dragon's

gold hoard. All but Suzuki. He walked with a confidence that he did not know was possible. Less than a year ago, he had been grinding level after level just to fight VR dragon babies. Today, he'd introduced himself to an ancient dragon and commanded her respect. Beth wasn't going to recognize him when they finally saw each other again.

4

———

It was a dinner that Suzuki could have never imagined himself having. The Mundanes and the Horsemen were nestled comfortably in the nearly hill-sized mound of the dragon's gold.

The dragon Ashegoreth had rustled up gold plates and cups for the adventurers to drink out of. At the moment, Ashegoreth was out hunting. She had promised that she would return before sunset with enough food for them all. No one was in a position to offer help.

Suzuki knew better than to do so anyway. The hospitality and pride of dragons were written all throughout myths and fantasy stories.

No one knew quite what to do until Ashegoreth returned. The cavern was lacking in what could have been considered entertainment. There was only rock and treasure. Ashegoreth had told them before leaving to make themselves at home. That meant exploring the treasure mound to their heart's content.

"It is what any dragon would offer to another," Ashegoreth had said. "Obviously, if I find anything missing, I will burn you to a crisp." She had laughed heartily at what could only be interpreted as dragon humor. With that laughter, she had spread her wings and taken off into the afternoon skies.

So now the adventurers sat on the enormous treasure, trying to figure out just how one sits on a pile of gold. Curiosity eventually got the best of Stew. After the first ten minutes of waiting had passed, Stew stood up, sloshing around in gold coins, and dove into the pile. He pretended to swim through the gold until he yelped loudly. A golden sword had poked him in the stomach. "What the fuck else is in here," Stew asked as he stood and kicked at the sword.

They spent the better part of half an hour looking to see if they could find out just what else actually was in the pile. The dragon's treasures covered the basics such as coins, swords, and cups. Nearly all of it was gold, and whatever wasn't was made of silver. Not a piece of copper in sight. But the treasure didn't stop with those three things. With a little bit of searching, Suzuki was able to find a map that twinkled in the light shining in through the break in the roof. The map was of Middang3ard. Each region was written in exquisite purple ink that shimmered as you moved the map.

If you looked closely at the map, you could see a small figure of yourself, staring back up at you. Suzuki dropped the map in surprise and it disappeared into the hoard.

Across the pile, Sandy held up a long spear. The end of it was bejeweled with diamonds and rubies. The hilt was engraved with a language that Suzuki had never seen before. "Hey, Diana," Sandy shouted, "Check it out. I think it's elvish."

Diana came up to Sandy's side and took the spear out of her hand. "No, darling," Sandy explained, "this is actually old elvish. This was before humans came to Middang3ard.

Maybe before the races were even communicating with each other. To think, this spear could be older than any of our family lineages—and it serves as a bed to a dragon."

Suzuki sat back down and picked up a handful of gold coins. "When you put it like that, it sounds almost trivial," he said.

"Depends on how you're looking at it."

"How else is there to look at it?"

"The elves think of dragons as historians. Well, even that isn't quite right. There isn't a close human word for the idea. The elves would explain it like this, though. History is always moving forward. The past is a constant but the present may never see it and, when it does, rarely understands. A dragon is a chronicler of history. This hoard stores more tales than elvish wine could ever dream of telling. And no doubt Ashegoreth knows where each coin has come from. That is what a dragon is to a realm. They are the oldest keepers of stories and knowledge. They are ancient in the truest sense of the word."

Suzuki had never thought of dragons in that way before. Whenever he had encountered them in pop media, dragons were usually a source of antagonism. A dragon was most often a creature outside the morality of mortals, a force of nature to be reckoned with because of its destructive nature. He had never thought of a dragon as a serpentine historian.

"We are more than keepers of stories and knowledge."

Ashegoreth's voice boomed through the cavern as she descended upon her hoard. Suzuki had no idea how he had not heard or felt her flying above. Perhaps all the noise and heat that he had felt earlier was just for show. Maybe Ashegoreth had the ability to be as stealthy as she wanted to be.

Each of Ashegoreth's front claws held a dead lamb. She tossed them onto the cavern floor.

"We are history," she said. "When worlds are formed, dragons are born in their stomach. We grow and mature along with the molten lava and rocks. Flames are our wet nurses, and we are birthed before the first mortals. We watch the world take its form and wait for life to squeeze itself out. We are stewards of our realms."

Suzuki could feel Fred bristling at Ashegoreth's words. *Dragon hubris*, Fred sneered. *They claim to be the first of the first, but that isn't true. They are not eldritch dragons. There are those who are even older.*

Even though it felt foolish, Suzuki raised his hand as if he were in school. "Excuse me, but what about eldritch dragons?"

Ashegoreth turned a curious eye on Suzuki. "Ah, a student of my race," Ashegoreth said kindly. "Yes, there are those who are eldritch, a few of my kind. They were the first dragons, creatures of gray at a time before there was time. They watched a cosmos devoid of change. They are relics of a time gone past, although a few of them have woken in some time. Now, how do dustlings enjoy their lamb? Also, feel free to invite your familiars to dine with us."

Suzuki turned his thoughts inward so that they were directed at Fred. *You want to come out for a bite?* he asked.

I would prefer not. I do not like the way dragons smell.

Suit yourself.

José stood in front of one of the freshly-killed lambs as Sandy and Stew walked up behind him, holding hands. "Usually butchered," José offered. "Our stomachs are not as...apt at swallowing bones. We'll take care of it. Mundanes, I assume you're just as useful carving up animals as orcs."

Stew pulled out his sword. He was looking at José the way that someone looks at a Rockstar. Even though he had been giving Suzuki shit about fanboying, Suzuki could see that Stew was just as blown away by José as he was.

"We'll take care of it," Stew offered. "Two lambs a party sound fair enough?"

"When is life ever fair?"

"Right now. Eat what you kill, right? Or are ol' man José's bones too decrepit to bend over?"

José lifted one of the lambs over his shoulder and headed back to where Diana and Chip were sitting. "Fuck off, newbie." He chuckled. "These bones ain't that old."

The Mundanes set to the task. They stripped the lamb of its coat, Stew and Suzuki working together on the larger of the lambs, cutting the wool from the skin, tossing it into a small fire that Ashegoreth had made. Sandy worked on the other lamb, waving her wand to levitate the lamb and remove its skin. Then came the butchering, removing the entrails, and quartering the innocent creature into manageable chunks.

Ashegoreth suppled the adventurers with golden spits to roast the lamb on. A few feet away, the Horsemen were just finishing butchering their lambs by the time the Mundanes had already started roasting theirs. "Been a little while since you got your hands dirty," Stew joked.

Neither José nor Diana said anything. Chip tossed a lamb heart at Stew, who managed to duck out of the way so that the heart hit Sandy in the face. She didn't say anything as she wiped the blood off her cheek and took a bite from the heart. "It's full of nutrients," she exclaimed when she saw Stew and Suzuki's horrified faces.

Once both lambs were roasting on the spits, the two parties gathered together as a few of the familiars separated from their hosts. Stew's familiar, GB, a bizarre amalgamation of a creature with an ass's head and a gargoyle's body joined first. Then came Niv, Sandy's familiar, a large rabbit with a unicorn horn and a nose that never stopped sniffing. José's familiar also joined, a dainty lamb named Nines, who eyed the roasting lambs with fear.

Ashegoreth blew fire onto the roasting lambs and the flames danced. Then she leaned back and scratched her scaly belly as she dangled a raw lamb over her jaws, sensuously licking its head.

Suzuki cleared his throat to break the awkward silence of watching a dragon tongue its dinner. "So...how long have you been in these caves?" Suzuki asked.

Ashegoreth dropped the lamb into her mouth and swallowed it whole as Nines watched in horror and trembled behind José. "Months," Ashegoreth stated. "At least four moons, but I am not completely certain. I stopped counting once this began to feel like a prison."

Chip looked up from the lamb she was tending. "Wait, these aren't your caves?" she asked.

"No. I only came here recently. I originally lived in the East with a small group of dragons and an even smaller circle of acolytes. There was a raid of sorts among the dragons. The Dark One, naturally. No one else would be so bold to approach us. And as I have found out, no one else would have such power. A few of the dragons were captured and the acolytes were killed."

"Fuck. I'm so sorry."

"It is as it is. We had grown complacent in our home. We had all heard the stories of the Dark One, of what was planned in the shadows. It was hubris to assume that his forces would not come to our doorsteps. What he did to us was a surprise, but it was not too unexpected."

"How did he capture them?"

"I do not know. It was difficult to understand. At first, we thought that the orcs that invaded only meant to kill us. There were enough of them. They blackened nearly the entire valley. The only deaths were those of the acolytes. My brothers and sisters were captured alive. Taken someplace I know nothing of."

"And how did you get away?"

"Is it not obvious by now? I ran. I turned my back on my brothers and sisters and burned as many as I could on my way out. It was not nearly enough, though. The Dark One's forces are ever-growing. From what I have been able to gather from my spies, the Dark One is capturing dragons of all colors, ages, and breeds. I do not know how he is managing this. It has not stopped with dragons, though. His minions are capturing all manner of creatures. Even mortals. Dwarves, elves, and the like. The killing raids have stopped. Now, something else is taking place."

Ashegoreth fell into silence. Suzuki watched as Ashegoreth's face crumpled. A few tears rolled down her cheeks, only to be instantly evaporated. "I despise him," she finally said. "I will find a way to kill him and set my brothers and sisters free."

Suzuki raised his hunk of lamb meat in solidarity. He knew the feeling even if he hadn't admitted it to himself. His journey to find Beth was also fueled by an unnamable hatred. Even though he had not grown up in Middang3ard, he had seen the death and destruction the Dark One had caused.

And he hated whatever creature could do such a thing.

"The Dark One sleeps not too far from here," the dragon continued. "These caves lead to the outskirts of his domain. As I abandoned my brothers and sisters to their fate and fled to these mountains, I took a survey of the surrounding land. The caves we reside in stretch all the way to the Dark One's tower, a looming terror that seems to peer out and watch whatever comes near."

Suzuki stretched out on the gold beneath him. Dinner and the dragon's booming voice had made him tired. He felt as if he could slip into a deep sleep at any moment. "So, you're saying we could take these caves out to the Dark One's camp?" he dreamily murmured.

"Yes. Tomorrow, I can show you the way. Tonight, be content as my guests and share my bed."

Suzuki felt Stew nudging him in the side. He didn't need to look at Stew to know that he was wearing a childish grin. "Be a little respectful, Stew," Suzuki said under his breath.

"I'm just saying, I've never shared a bed with a dragon before."

Sandy grabbed Stew by the cheek and forced his attention to her. "So now you wanna fuck a dragon?" she growled.

"No, no, babe, I was just kidding around. Like a pun or something."

Sandy pointed at her eyes and then to Stew to let him know that she was watching.

Ashegoreth leaned back on the massive pile of gold and stretched out. "It is more comfortable than it looks," she assured the adventurers. "Please, feel free to retire when you see fit. I am going to bed."

In a couple of seconds, the dragon was snoring loudly.

Suzuki watched the snoring dragon as the rest of the adventurers were talking among each other quietly.

If Suzuki concentrated, he could make out their words. They all seemed so far away, though. That was all right. They were close enough. It was those voices that blanketed him and kept him warm throughout the night as he slipped further and further into sleep.

In his dreams, there was a dragon and a mountain. The

dragon stood on top of the mountain, speaking in its old tongue, a regal sound that swelled with poetry. Suzuki was only a boy in his dream, no more than five. He stared up at the dragon as it danced and spat fire at the sun. The boy Suzuki watched until the sun set and the moon rose and set too, and there was only blackness. Still, the dragon danced in fire.

5
____

Suzuki woke before anyone else.

The sun was on his face, reflecting off the gold which was his bed. He sat up and scratched at the back of his head. His hair was getting long. Some of the more mundane aspects of personal grooming had been lost on him over the last few weeks. He'd grown accustomed to smelling like sweat and blood, something he never thought he would have gotten used to. Needless to say, he rarely thought about how long his hair was getting.

In a dreamy, post-sleep haze, Suzuki dug his hand into the treasure hoard until he felt something smooth. He pulled it out.

A mirror.

Exactly what he was looking for. He turned it around so that he could see himself. His face was tanner than he remembered, and his eyes looked as if they had aged a few years. It was a weird feeling, to see himself like this, after such a short time of forgetting he had a reflection. An image of him looked back, and it was almost as if a stranger held his gaze.

The dragon was no longer on the hoard. Only humans slept among the gold and treasure. It was an odd image. These frail bodies lying on a huge pile of gold, sleeping on a pile of what many people spent their entire lives chasing.

"There is something poetic about it, isn't there?"

Suzuki turned around to see Ashegoreth sitting in the corner of the cave, her eyes half-closed in a dreamy sort of haze. "Come sit with me, Suzuki, Guillotine of Old Gods."

Suzuki did as he was told, making his way down the mountain of gold. He crossed the cavern and took a seat on a rock across from Ashegoreth. "How did you sleep, dustling?" Ashegoreth asked.

"Surprisingly well. I didn't think gold would be so comfortable."

"It isn't by nature. Our treasures form to us, which is the opposite that most creatures experience. It is usually you who forms to your treasure. But we dragons are a few of the magical creatures who do not hold to that creed. I believe the older leprechauns are the same way."

"How long have you been alive?"

"I am a young one: two thousand years. I slept through half of it. There wasn't much happening." Ashegoreth laughed.

The sound of Ashegoreth's laughter was warm and inviting. Suzuki felt he could have sat and listened to her talk all day and night. *Must be a kind of magic*, Suzuki thought.

"Hardly," Ashegoreth interrupted.

"Wait, what?"

"It isn't magic, simply the benefits of a very long life. We all know that wisdom comes with age. Comfort does as well: comfort in the kind of person that you are. And with that comfort comes sincerity. We dragons are capable of such a level of sincerity. It drips from every word. That is all that the fire burning within us is. When I breathe flames, it is merely me speaking. It is the sincerity of my words which ignites a spark. If I wish one dead, it is the earnestness of my wishes which scorches the earth. Likewise, if I wish for one to be comforted, it is my wish which warms the cave with the fires of my heart."

"How did you know what I was thinking?"

"We dragons tend to hear many of the same conversations, an irritating benefit of living for so long."

"Then why talk to anyone?"

"Occasionally, it is interesting. Such as this."

"I'm not fishing for a compliment or anything, but why? You must have talked to some pretty amazing people in your time."

"And you are not, Guillotine of Old Gods?"

"I mean...I...not really. I'm just some kid. You've probably spoken with kings and shit like that. I mean, really fucking amazing people."

"You are only in the infancy of your life. Yesterday, you proved to me you were worth speaking to instead of burning. I believe that counts for something more than you realize."

Suzuki listened to the dragon's words. Something about them rang true in his heart. He let that sink in. There wasn't much time to dwell on the advice, though. Over in the hoard, Stew was already stretching loudly enough to wake everyone up in the cavern. The rest of the adventurers were sitting up and starting to talk to each other.

Ashegoreth rose as well. "We should get back to your friends," she said softly as she stood and lumbered back to the treasure hoard.

José was already getting breakfast ready. He had snagged some of the leftover lamb hanging from the firepit last night and was tearing hunks of lamb off while Nines sat in a corner and watched, horrified. Stew was eating alongside him while Sandy leaned up against Stew's back, reading a book. "Morning, Suzy," she called as Suzuki took a spot next to his friends. "You're up early."

Suzuki snatched a hunk of lamb out of Stew's hand, to Stew's incredulity, and took a bite. "Just got a good night's rest, is all," Suzuki said. "How'd you two manage?"

Stew shrugged and straightened up, causing Sandy to lose her balance and go sliding down the mountain of gold. "Could have used more privacy." He groaned. "You know. For the boning."

"Yeah. I kinda figured you were going to say something like that."

They ate their breakfast while the dragon watched over them. While they ate, they discussed the game plan. Suzuki suggested that they take the cave tunnels all the way up to the Dark One's first main camp. The dragon aided with detailed explanations of how the Dark One's encampment was set up.

The encampment was built in a series of rings. In the center of the rings was the Dark One's tower. Each ring extending from the tower was a camp of some sort. The strongest camps, those which had the most defense, were the closest to the tower. Suzuki figured by that logic, it would be easiest to sneak into the first camp.

Ashegoreth sat up once the meal was finished, shaking her head. "You will not be able to take the caves directly into the camp. They stop a few miles outside of where the Dark One has concentrated his forces. You will be able to avoid all of the raiding parties outside the camp, though. I can direct you to which tunnels to use."

José stood and grabbed his equipment. "Sounds like a plan to me. We should get moving. Travel during the day, and we should be able to set up our own camp by night without too much trouble."

Suzuki nodded in agreement. It sounded like a solid plan. It would be much easier to work their way through the Dark One's camp if they could have a solid day and night without an encounter. The party's mana would have been recharged by now, and everyone seemed to be in a fairly good mood. Traveling would be easy, and they'd be better prepared for whatever they were going to come across.

Ashegoreth rose, a towering monster, casting a shadow over the humans standing beneath her. "Before I show you the way," she started, "I have parting gifts for you. It has been some time since I have met anyone with the resolve to stand against the Dark One. I would like to extend my thanks and appreciation for those who seek to destroy the same enemies as myself."

Stew pumped his hand in the air and nearly jumped with joy. "Fuck, yeah," he shouted. "Dragon swag! What you got for us?"

The dragon reached into her hoard. "Specifically, for you three," she explained. "Your friends are well-equipped for the challenges ahead. You three, though, your armor and weapons leave a bit to be desired. These should help you considerably."

From the hoard, the dragon drew a golden bracelet. She leaned over Stew and handed it to him.

Stew took the bracelet and stared at it, trying not to look confused or unappreciative. "Uh...thanks," he stammered. "It looks...really pretty."

"Do not lie to me," the dragon said. "It is not pretty and is hardly a piece of jewelry. But it is perfect for you. I have noticed your affinity for sharp weapons. You have a certain kind of bloodlust in your eyes, the eyes of a warrior who enjoys a good fight. This bracelet will make your weapons obsolete. While you wear it, you will have access to all of the weapons in my hoard. You can summon them at will. The bracelet will find the weapon that your heart desires and pull it from the ether, into your hand."

"Anything my heart desires? Are you fucking shitting me?"

"If it exists. You will not know what it is capable of until it arrives. I believe this will keep you interested. Please, try it."

Stew jumped off of the treasure hoard and stepped a few feet away from everyone. He slipped on the bracelet and whipped his hand back and forth. A throwing ax appeared in his hand. Perfectly weighted, sharp as a razor, and crackling with electricity. "Are you fucking kidding me?" Stew shouted. He turned and threw the ax into a rock. He held out his hand again and another ax instantly appeared in it. "I could throw axes forever!"

Ashegoreth smiled, obviously pleased with her gift. Then she turned to Sandy. "I noticed that you hold the Mask of Elroz the Storm Breaker," she said.

Sandy stared up at the dragon. She obviously had no idea what the dragon was speaking of. "Uh...I mean, I have a mask," she finally said.

"Show it to me."

Sandy wiped her hand across her face. A beautiful wooden mask appeared. Intricate runes and spellcraft had been etched into its stark features, its eyes black and empty, its mouth open in a mournful wail.

Ashegoreth nodded her approval. "Yes, that is indeed Elroz' lost mask," she explained. "He lived and died during the end of my childhood. He was a mage famed beyond renown. Legends do not do justice to his power. It was said that he could wrestle lightning from the sky and coat himself in its energy. Legends, as I said. I have noticed that your HUD already has a significant number of magical upgrades. You are also an apprentice to one of the finest mages that I have ever heard of and had the pleasure of meeting, Diana the Tempest of Ol' Regoaral."

Sandy removed her mask and looked at Diana, who blushed humbly. "Wait, I'm an apprentice to *you*?" she asked.

Diana walked over to Sandy and placed her hand on the woman's shoulder. "I guess that's a technical term," she said. "All three of you. Usually we just say mentor and leave it at that, but *technically* speaking, yes, you are apprentices. You're mine. Stew is José's. Suzuki is Chip's."

Suzuki didn't believe what he was hearing. José was Stew's mentor and Chip was his? He had hardly even spoken to Chip, and she had nothing in common with him or what he perceived as his skills. It made more sense for José to be teaching him. But he had noticed that José had been spending a lot of time with Stew, showing him different fighting techniques, coaching him on his form.

Initially, Suzuki had been jealous of how much time José had been spending with Stew, but had just assumed that they were hitting it off. Now that jealousy rose up with a vengeance. Suzuki felt like he'd been shorted. Chip didn't even seem like she belonged out on the battlefield.

Ashegoreth spoke again, speaking to Sandy, breaking Suzuki's obsessive train of thought. "Much like your companion Stewart, you are filled with lust. But I have felt how it is different. You seek power and knowledge, and you look to be the sort of person who will work for that knowledge. To you, I gift the full armor of Elroz."

The dragon dipped her claw into the treasure hoard again and removed a golden necklace with an oddly shaped ruby pendant hanging from it. She placed the necklace in Sandy's hand.

"As you know," Ashegoreth warned, "true magic always comes at a cost. I do not know what this will cost you. But the cost will only remain as long as you wear the necklace. I do know what you will gain. You will receive a bonus to all of your defenses. And you will no longer need to continuously reference your books for spells. Once you read a spell, you will remember it completely in all of its details."

Sandy stared at the necklace in her hand. "Thank you so much," she whispered. "Can I try it on?"

"You have been warned."

Sandy turned to Diana, who looked more worried than Suzuki had ever seen her. "What do you think?"

Diana bit her lower lip and folded her arms. "Elroz was a beast when it came to magic," she lectured. "His spellcraft was immaculate, but...he was very intense. The tradeoff might be detrimental. That said, it might not be comfortable."

Sandy slipped the necklace over her head. "Gimme the juice," she shouted.

Nothing happened. Everyone stood silently waiting. "Well, that was anticlimactic." Sandy sighed.

Suddenly a bright flash of light emanated from Sandy's chest. The amulet grew red-hot and seared her skin, and she screamed as she fell to the ground. Black tendrils shot from the center of the amulet, whipping around Sandy, piercing her skin, and driving themselves into her body.

Sandy screamed as she rolled on the floor. Diana reached out for her, and an energy ripple burst from Sandy and sent Diana skidding across the floor.

The skin around the amulet started to crisp and burn away. Sandy screamed in pain as her skin turned to ash, floating away until she was only bone. The ash swirled around her bones until it formed a black cloak that covered her body as the mask of Elroz appeared over her grinning skull.

When Sandy rose, it was as a wraith of some sort. Her body was immaterial, and she appeared to be composed of fine sand. She held her hand out to look at, and it wavered as if wind were passing through each molecule. "Holy shit," she whispered. Even her voice had changed. It sounded as if it were the air itself. "This is so fucking sick."

Sandy glided forward, through Diana, her body breaking apart for a second and then reforming past Diana. "I remember so much. This is amazing. Thank you."

Stew came up to Sandy's side. He tried to hold her hand, and his fingers slipped through the dust and firmly grasped bone. "Uh...babe, you're kind of a ghost. How are we going to...you know..."

Sandy laughed. It sounded like Death. "Can we marvel at how fucking badass I just became?" She chuckled. "Can you imagine seeing this coming at you, throwing lightning and shit? And this...spell, I guess? It only lasts as long as I'm wearing the amulet, which I can take off at any time. Don't get me wrong; I'm going to be wearing it all the fucking time." Then she leaned and whispered in Stew's ear, "Maybe even during sexy time." She slapped Stew's butt as she floated past him.

Stew stood in mild bewilderment before turning to face

Suzuki. He had that familiar grin on his face. "Boning the bones," he quipped.

Suzuki could only hang his head. Sometimes, his party was like hanging out with a bunch of high schoolers. The upgrade Sandy had gotten was very impressive, though, as Stew's had been. Suzuki couldn't wait to see what Ashegoreth was going to give him.

The dragon reached into the treasure hoard one last time. She withdrew her paw and opened it in front of Suzuki. A long, hawk feather rested in her hand. "This is my gift to you, Suzuki," she whispered.

Suzuki took the feather and tried to hide his initial disappointment. It didn't look as if it were useful for anything. It was just a feather. "Uh...thank you," he said.

"You do not have to try and obscure your disappointment. No, this feather will not bestow you with new powers or armor. What I have given you is so much more important. I have given you my heart. I was once in love as well. Married, actually. A hawk held my heart. We spent hundreds of years together. There was a time that I could not imagine existence without him by my side. The Dark One took him from me—before we knew what the Dark One was. He robbed me of my love, of my happiness. This is all that I have of my love. This is what I give to you. My heart, my grief, my rage and guilt. Do you accept it?"

Suzuki reached down and plucked a thin gold chain from the treasure pile. He tied it around the end of the feather and hung it on his neck as a necklace. "I gladly accept your heart," Suzuki said.

"It is not a light thing to have a dragon's heart. Take care of it."

Ashegoreth spread her wings and looked at the sky shown through the hole in the top of the cavern. "Come. Let me show you the way to the camps." The dragon stepped over the humans and headed toward the right side of the cavern.

A large rock lay against the cavern wall, far too large to be moved by anything other than a giant. The dragon leaned against the rock and effortlessly rolled it out of the way.

A deep tunnel stretched out into the heart of the cave.

"Take this until it ends. You will find yourself at the edge of a forest near the first circle of the orcs' camps. I wish you a speedy and safe journey. Beth is lucky to be able to call you friends."

Suzuki and the rest of the Mundanes thanked Ashe-goreth for her gifts. They packed up the last of the supplies and mounted their axbeaks. Once everyone was ready, they entered the tunnel, which was wide enough for a dragon to easily worm through. Even though there was no light from above or within, the tunnel wasn't dark. Suzuki could easily see ahead of himself.

As was now usual, Stew and José had paired off, as well as Sandy and Diana: apprentices with their masters. Suzuki tried to push down the wave of jealousy that rolled through him. It was difficult. If anyone should have been his mentor, it should have been José. Leadership was something that could be taught. Suzuki knew that he would have benefited from having José giving him pointers. Even Diana would have made more sense. At least Diana could have helped him with his battle magic.

Chip took up the rear of the pack. She looked at the sides of the tunnels as they walked. Suzuki cast a glance back toward her. He knew he should talk to her, try to find out what he was supposed to be learning from her. At the moment, though, talking to Chip sounded more like a hassle than anything else. He could hardly understand half of what she said, and he felt something close to disgust with her. He knew it was unfair to have those feelings about Chip.

It was childish even, but his heart had been set on José, even before he had realized he would be mentored at all.

The dragon had failed to mention how long the tunnels went on. They could be walking for days for all Suzuki knew. He really didn't want to spend it walking in silence while everyone else was getting chummy. Suzuki forced his judgment about Chip down deep in himself. He wasn't going to be a child about this.

Suzuki slowed his axbeak until he fell in at Chip's side. "So, I'm supposed to be your apprentice, right?" Suzuki asked.

Chip turned away from the rocks and beamed up at Suzuki, who, when he saw Chip smile, couldn't understand how he had been so angry before. When Chip smiled, it was like her whole face changed. You could see curiosity and wonder in her eyes, a certain playfulness that was infectious. "Oh, yeah," she cooed. "You're my one and only. The kid I'm going to be looking out for while we find something cool, big, and evil to get murderous with. How you feeling about this intimate endeavor that you and I are about to embark on?"

"Intimate?"

"Oh, intimate as all hell, young squire. But professional. Don't get your hopes up, you're not exactly the type that gets the geyser going."

Suzuki chuckled at Chip's frankness. "What exactly is your type?"

"Skinny, ratty, and covered in grease of a sort. Any kind of natural lubrication is an acceptable stand-in as well."

"Sounds gross."

"The grosser, the better."

"So, what exactly am I supposed to learn from you?"

"Oh, the pressure is on, ain't it? You're just dying to learn what I got up my sleeves, aren't ya? Well, full disclosure, I ain't got nothing hidden. Everything that I got to show you is in plain sight. Just don't be a dingus and miss it, all right?"

"Sounds easy enough."

"So this damsel in distress...she was the one who used to play with you and your pals in the old world, right?"

"The old world?"

"Earth. That's what it feels like to me. It's been a long time since we have seen it. Feels ancient to me, a crisp memory fighting the tides of time to stay pretty. That's where you knew her from, right?"

"Yeah, we used to play *Middang3ard* together. That's how we met. If it weren't for Beth, I don't know if I would be a MERC at all. She's the one who pulled some strings for me to get in."

"Oh, no, she hardly had a finger on a string."

"Wait, what do you mean? Beth was the one who sent the recruiter over to me."

"Yes, yes, that she did. But why she did it never crossed your mind, eh? That was all us. We passed the information on to Beth to get to you. Figured it would go over better hearing it from a friend. We saw a good time of murder when we watched you guys."

"Shit, I didn't know you guys had been watching for so long."

"Oh yeah, fresh talent is important. We got a lot of killing to take care of."

Chip put her arm around Suzuki's shoulder and ruffled his hair, causing him to instantly stiffen up. "So, like I said, stick close to ol' Chip, and you'll find yourself in interesting situations, to say the least."

It took the Mundanes and the Horsemen the better part of the day to get to a point where they believed they could stop comfortably. The tunnel had only widened the farther they had gone. It must have stretched for miles.

The two parties decided to take a break once they came to another underground cavern. Suzuki and José walked the length of the cavern to see if there were any other pathways. There was only one, and José suggested that the cavern would be an ideal place to stop and set up camp for the night. It made more sense to rest for the evening in case there was still a considerable way to go. He didn't want to end up hitting the orc camp after an exhausting day.

Diana and Sandy set up magical traps throughout the cavern just in case something snuck up on them. It didn't seem likely with how certain Ashegoreth had been about safely using the tunnel, but it made sense to prep for the worst scenario. This was something Suzuki realized the Horsemen were constantly doing. It was probably why they had survived in Middang3ard for so long: constant preparation.

After the traps were set, the group set about making a fire and pitching their tents. Diana supplied everyone with food again, rich cakes and salted meats that transported Suzuki to memories he had never had. By the time she had poured ales, Suzuki felt like he had lived an entirely separate, content life. He made a mental note that he wanted to find the store Diana purchased her food from.

There was no way to tell what time it was outside, but it

seemed like everyone was starting to get tired. Sandy and Stew had cuddled up to each other, Stew leaning against a rock, playing with his new bracelet by conjuring throwing knives and tossing them at a rock, while Sandy, who had yet to remove her amulet, was resting her masked head on Stew's lap while she read through a massive tome floating in front of her. Chip and Diana had retired to their tents. José was sitting on a boulder, reading from a small notebook.

Since Suzuki had heard about José mentoring Stew, he had wanted to catch a moment with José. Even if José wasn't his mentor, there wasn't some unspoken rule about not talking to him.

Suzuki walked up and took a seat next to José.

José had been drawing in his notebook. There was a detailed drawing of Ashegoreth in elaborate pen strokes. José nibbled on the end of his pen as he closed his notebook. "What's up, kid?" he asked.

"I didn't know you could draw like that."

"Well, seeing as how we don't really know each other, there's probably a lot that you don't know."

Suzuki had forgotten how prickly José could be. Sometimes it seemed like he was an open book, and the next moment, he was reminding Suzuki that a newb was a newb. "You said you've seen a dragon before," Suzuki tentatively said. "Was it like her?"

José shook his head as he opened his notebook and flipped through the pages. When he was finished searching, he handed the notebook to Suzuki. The page was filled with drawings of a dragon graveyard. There, bones stretched to the sky. In the middle was one dead dragon, partially decomposing.

Suzuki handed the notebook back to José. "It was one of my first quests," José said. "Pretty simple. Just a simple drop-off for some guy who thought he was a lord or some shit. We found this along the way. I didn't think dragons were real. You know, you hear dwarves talking about them a lot, but you know how dwarves are, always exaggerating the ancient shit that they've seen. You'd think that every dwarf was raised in a king's hall or some shit when they start telling stories."

"Milos didn't seem like that."

"That's because you've never gotten drunk with the asshole." José laughed. "Trust me, you'd get stories. Anyways, the dragon graveyard was something. I never thought that they were really that big. And I never thought I'd actually see one in the flesh. You did good, kid. That whole thing could have been a fucking bloodbath."

"You don't think we could have taken it?"

"You? Probably not. I think the Horsemen and I would have probably gotten through it, but we wouldn't have been in any shape to sneak into the Dark One's territory. We probably would have had to turn back for a bit. However, you handled the situation well. I thought that I was going to have to watch you like a hawk. Glad that's not the case."

"What do you mean?"

"Tactical thinking isn't restricted to the battlefield. Don't get me wrong, for a lot of people, that's where it ends. I've lost track of how many MERCs I know who can lead a small army, but put them in a situation where you can't stab your problems, well, they're fucked. That doesn't seem like you. I've never heard of a human wooing a dragon before but, hell, you get to see something new every day."

"What do you mean, wooing?" Suzuki asked.

José gave him a coy smile. "Ashegoreth gave you her heart."

"Yeah. I mean, she gave me a hawk feather."

"Dragons are elegant creatures. They speak in metaphor and riddles, although, granted, sincere riddles. If a dragon says she gave you her heart, that means that she gave you her heart."

Suzuki was shocked. "Are you saying she's in love with me?"

"Love is different for every species. Every person. Your two friends, they're in love. Is it anything like you and Beth?"

"I'm not—"

"Don't even try it, kid. I'm not stupid. I get the whole damsel-in-distress thing, but this seems a little more intense. But you see what I'm getting at. They don't look the same at all. You won that dragon's heart. Pretty impressive."

"Hmm. Uh...have you, you know, ever been in love before?"

"Kid, I think this is a conversation you should be having with your dad."

Suzuki blushed. "Fuck off. I'm just curious."

"Of course. I'm in love now."

"Really? Are you seeing someone or something?"

José put a hand over his heart. "Are you trying to ask me out?"

"No, I just... I don't know. The only people I know who I could talk to are Stew and Sandy. And you've seen them."

Suzuki gestured at his friends. Sandy had returned to her natural state, and she was currently ramming her tongue down Stew's throat as Stew grabbed anything he could get his hands on.

José grimaced and shook his head. "Yeah, I can see what you mean," he agreed. "They're pretty gross. All right, kid, I'll bite. Yeah. I'm in love. She's sitting over there."

José jerked his hand at Chipmaster, whose head was

poking out of her tent, her HUD splayed out in front of her as she soldered it.

"Are you serious? You haven't spoken to her since we left."

"We're working right now," José said. "And like I said, love's different for every person. Stew and Sandy might want to flirt and mess around every chance they get. Me and Chip, we know the difference between being dead or alive is paying attention. Sometimes you learn that the hard way."

"Like your fourth?"

José's face hardened and he leaned forward, his eyes boring into Suzuki's.

"What the fuck are you trying to get at?" José growled.

"I'm sorry. I wasn't trying to—"

José raised his hand and cut Suzuki off. "No, it's okay. I'm sorry." He sighed. "You couldn't have known."

"I just figured the Horsemen was a play on the whole 'four horsemen of the apocalypse' thing. You know, another Christ joke. And you know, there's four of them. I just assumed there were originally four."

"Yeah, there were four of us."

"Sorry, I shouldn't have brought it up. I'm—"

"If you apologize one more time, I'm going to knock your fucking teeth out. Own it, kid. You don't have to back down every time you upset someone. That's something that you're gonna have to learn. You can't make everyone happy. Don't bother trying. If you say something, piss someone off for trying to figure shit out, stick to your guns. We don't need MERCs who piss over themselves the first time someone actually pushes back."

"What are you talking about?" Suzuki asked. "Every monster I've killed has pushed back. I haven't backed down once."

"It's like with the leading. There are different kinds. Standing up to your friends or people you look up to, that's an entirely different skill worth investing in."

"Did they die?" Suzuki asked.

"Yeah. He died."

The two warriors sat in silence for a long time. Suzuki had already thought about what it would be like to die in battle with his friends. He'd never really thought about what it would be like to lose one of them. Even the Mundanes' decision to find Beth was motivated by their belief that she was still alive. The idea of losing any of the Mundanes was almost too heartbreaking to think about.

But it could happen.

Suzuki could see that on José's face.

José rose and finished the beer he had been sipping. "You should get some sleep, kid."

Suzuki didn't get up for a while. He sat there thinking about what José had said. It had been a lot to take in: leadership, love, and loss. Sometimes Suzuki felt like he was growing up way too fast. Other times, he felt he should have thought about all of this before he had even set foot in Middang3ard. Yet here he was. This was his life now.

Across the cavern, Stew screamed. Suzuki jumped to his feet, running in Stew and Sandy's direction as fast as he could.

Stew was fanning his legs. His leg hair was on fire and Sandy was giggling insanely. "That's not funny, babe," Stew shouted as he put out the small fire.

Sandy held her hand over her mouth, trying not to laugh too loudly. "Shit, Stew, I'm sorry." She giggled again. "I was just trying to kill that spider. I'm sorry."

Suzuki breathed a sigh of relief.

It was just his best friends acting like idiots: something

that he never wanted to stop seeing. Nothing was going to take either of them away from him. It didn't make sense to worry about either of them dying in battle. Suzuki wasn't going to let that happen. Just like he wasn't going to let anything happen to Beth.

They were all going to walk out of this alive.

Then they were going to stop the Dark One.

It was that simple, and Suzuki knew it.

6

─────

Suzuki woke to the sound of screaming. It was how he regularly woke up now. At first, he hadn't been able to tell if it was his own scream or someone else's. Now he knew where the scream came from. In all honesty, he was relieved to know he was a quiet screamer. He couldn't think of many more uncomfortable conversation topics than his night terrors.

Even when Suzuki felt that there wasn't anything to actively be afraid of, the tension from missions and quests assaulted him in his sleep. He envied Sandy and Stew. He knew that they cared as much about Beth as he did. He knew that they were also very aware of the precariousness of their lives. Yet neither one of them seemed too distraught by the situation. Sandy had even talked Suzuki down from being too stressed out a handful of times. Suzuki wished that he was handling everything as well as they were.

Suzuki exited his tent and yawned as he stretched. It felt good to have his body up and moving again. He'd gotten used to the constant walking or riding that being a MERC entailed. Sometimes camping out for the night made him restless. If he didn't have to worry about being so exhausted, he never would stop to camp. He'd just keep pushing on through the night.

The cavern was dark.

Very little light was making it through the few cracks in the rock. Suzuki wondered what time it was. Probably sometime around sunrise. Even without an alarm, his body woke him up like clockwork when the sun rose. He had hated it at first, but now he saw it as an ideal time to enjoy his solitude.

Suzuki pulled out his hand ax. It was a very modest creation, the sort of thing you would use to cut wood. Yet it had been lovingly crafted. Suzuki had only recently started to carry an ax instead of a sword. It was a welcome change, having one hand free for magic. He still hadn't quite gotten the hang of casting magic with his off-hand, but he figured he'd eventually catch on.

Sleep continued to drain from Suzuki's mind, and he felt like he was stepping through a room covered in cobwebs. Mornings like this, he was very glad that he didn't have to talk to anyone.

Suzuki leaned back against a rock and flipped his ax into the air, catching it, looking at the runes carved into the ax hilt, wondering if they were Nordic or if they had another origin.

No one was around, which meant there was no chance for embarrassment. There were a handful of spells Suzuki had seen Sandy trying that he wanted to give a shot. He always felt awkward casting around Sandy, though. It wasn't that she ever said anything, but had more to do with the fact that they both had been practicing magic for the same amount of time. Sandy had improved exponentially. Suzuki was proud of her.

Really.

Everyone who met Sandy picked up on how proficient she was at magic, and it only made sense that Diana would have chosen her for a protégé.

Suzuki was another story.

His magic casting skills were so bad that people often assumed that he was a lazy warrior, running around with a hand ax like some crazed lumberjack. The entirety of his magic casting wasn't too bad. It just didn't happen to be as flashy as a true mage's. He had actually gotten quite good at weapon enhancements. One of the reasons he was fighting with such an underwhelming weapon was as an experiment.

Since Suzuki had found the ax in a pile of rubbish at the Red Lion, he'd been drawn to it.

The ax was unassuming. Nothing had really stood out to him and that was perfect. When he took it back to his room, he had gotten started working. The first night, Suzuki had tried a sharpness enhancing spell. The blade hadn't changed physically, but when Suzuki ran it down the side of a bedpost, the ax had cut a thin strip of wood from the post as if it were fruit.

Anytime Suzuki came across a new enhancement, he added it to the ax. The ax continued to look just as mundane as any other household hand ax. Suzuki really enjoyed the poetic nature. The ax made him really feel like the most Mundane of the Mundanes.

Over the last few days, Suzuki had been thinking about something he had heard Diana say. "The only limit to human magic is the imagination of the caster."

Suzuki had been wondering if that was the case for enchantments as well. There was one that he had been hoping to work on for a while, but he hadn't been able to manage getting away from everyone to give it a shot.

Suzuki had brought the supplies with him before leaving the Red Lion. They entailed three feathers, a rope, and a lock. Suzuki placed them on the ground next to the ax. Then he sat there. Waiting for something to come to him.

Nothing.

He felt stupid, sitting there in the dark of the cave, trying to write his own spells.

Usually, enchantments came along with a list of supplies, a way to orient them, and an incantation to activate the enchantment. Suzuki hadn't thought it would be too big a deal to plan his own spell, but now, staring at the incongruity of his ideas, he realized he had been naïve.

"What you got going on at these wee hours of the early morn?" a voice playfully called from the shadows.

Suzuki looked over his shoulder. José and Chipmaster were sitting together on a boulder not too far from him. They weren't sitting particularly close, probably the same distance that he would have sat from Beth.

"Fun times?" Chip asked.

José rose and bowed slightly to Chip before jumping off the boulder and walking toward where the tents were set up. Chip also jumped off the boulder but toward Suzuki, landing in front of him with uncustomary grace.

"What's with all the random party favors?" she asked.

Suzuki scooped up the feathers and other items and tried to place them back in his inventory. He was suddenly very embarrassed. It was the kind of embarrassment that a child feels the first time it tries to walk and all of the adults laugh.

"Nothing," Suzuki muttered as he picked up his enchantment pieces.

"Wait, wait. Hold on, young'un. Are you up to what I think you are? Some good ol' magic craft?"

Suzuki sighed as he realized that he had been found out. He placed the feathers and the rest of the items back down on the ground. "Enchanting," Suzuki finally admitted.

Chip's eyes went wide with interest, becoming shining pearls of curiosity. She had a hungry, determined look on her face. "You don't say, now do you? How you going about it?"

Suzuki really didn't want to explain what he had been thinking. Saying it out loud felt like it would condemn him, that it would show his lack of preparation and forethought. Chip would see him for exactly what he felt he was, an amateur.

Chip broke into his train of thought, briefly distracting him from the swelling insecurity. "What are you trying to get set up here for yourself?" she asked.

Suzuki sighed and bit the bullet. He had seen Chip get curious enough times to know that there was no way around it. "I was trying to make a returning ax," Suzuki explained. "Like Thor's hammer, you know? Throw it and be able to bring it back."

"So you got feathers, a rope, and a lock? Hmm, not bad thinking. Feathers to make it fly, rope to tie it to the lock, which you're planning on hooking up to yourself, am I right?"

"That's what I was thinking."

Chip nodded like she was considering something. "So what's keeping you from getting all magical?"

"Uh...usually, like in the books, there's a description of how to place or arrange things and then...an incantation. But, I'm kind of freeballing this one...so, I don't really know what to do for the last part."

"Your ears been partial to Diana's words, ain't they?" Chip asked. "All that, humanity and creativity jimmer-jammer?"

"More or less."

"Well, she ain't wrong, I'll start by telling you that. Want for a hand or two?"

"You mean help? From you?" Suzuki asked.

"Exacto."

Chip pulled back the hair covering her ears, and he saw that they were slightly pointed. Not as sharp as an elf's, but definitely not human.

Suzuki tried not to stare. He hadn't really spoken with any elves since he had gotten to Middang3ard, only chatted in passing. "Are you an elf?" Suzuki asked.

"Only half, not a thing most people know. Ain't something you 'xactly brag about out in the bar."

"Why not?" Suzuki asked. "There's elves and everything else there. I didn't think it would be such a big deal."

"You'd think so, wouldn't you? But the races don't mix much, if your peepers happen to be lean on that fact. And they most definitely didn't thirty years ago. Nope, I am a rarity that I find is just as beautiful and hated as it is sparse. Kinda sad, once you start thinking about it. The Dark One's got forces of all sorts of grisly creatures, and they seem to work together just fine. José asks one half-elf to be in his party, and the whole MERC squad nearly loses whatever shits they got. But that's history. Ancient, almost. What we got in front of us are the present and the future. Humans might have the luck of being ingenious, but us elves got us our own little tricks. Namely, the trick of tradition."

"What exactly is that supposed to mean?"

Chip leaned over to get a better look at the ritual pieces that Suzuki had laid out on the ground. "Tech and magic ain't that much different," she explained. "Old man Clarke once said that to the reader, it's all the same whether or not someone dies from getting zappy with a laser or from a magic wand. Little truth in that being everything has systems it works with. Just gotta find the way a system works and whamo. You get techy-tech or magic. So you know the gist of enchantments, righto?"

"Uh...yeah, you need your ingredients, what you want to enchant, and what you want to enchant it with."

"Bingo. So you got that. Then what?" Chip asked.

"A ritual for setting the enchantment and then an incantation for activating."

Chip nodded. "So there you go. You know how to enchant."

"Yeah, but I don't know the ritual. Or an incantation."

"Well, that means you gotta write one. Let that human creativity do its job now."

"What do you mean?"

Suzuki felt like he was missing a vital step, but he couldn't put his finger on what it was. He stared at Chip for a few seconds, waiting for her to explain the rest to him. After a few moments, Chip sighed and pointed to the pile of ritual ingredients on the ground. "You already got everything all right and ready," she said. "Now you just need to get the ball rolling. So go on and get it rolling."

"How?"

"I'd start by ordering your playthings in a stack of importance."

Suzuki hadn't thought about which components to the enchantment would be the most important. It was vital that the ax levitated, but maybe not as important as it coming back.

Technically, it didn't matter if the ax levitated if it was

going to return. It could roll on the ground or maybe even reappear. The most important components were the rope and the lock. Suzuki picked up the rope, folded it, and placed it on top of the lock. Then he placed the three feathers on top of the rope.

"There," he said.

Chip looked it over. "Looks right to me. Next step, incantation. Think of words that spell out your intention or whatever. Spit 'em out while concentrating. Your familiar will handle the rest. But be specific. Might help to jot 'em down first. Get all manual. Otherwise, you'll get an ax that comes back with a vengeance. Might be forgetting which pointy part should come first, if you catch my meaning."

"Yeah, I got it. You have anything to write on?" Suzuki asked.

Chip pulled out a pen and notebook. She passed it to Suzuki as she crouched down and looked at the pile of enchantment particulars, rocking back and forth on the soles of her feet. "Been a little bit of time since I seen anyone take an interest in enchanting their weapons," she mused. "Most folks dump on the blacksmith and hope for something shiny and righteous. Nice to see a youth with a keen interest in taking care of his own shite."

Suzuki looked away from what he was writing to smile weakly. He felt like he was back in school and a teacher was looking over his shoulder. It didn't really matter how uncomfortable he was, so he turned his attention back to trying to figure out how he wanted to exactly word the incantation.

"Does it matter how I say it?" he asked.

"You mean, does it have to be all high and mighty like the dragon tongue? Nope. Plain ol' English works fine. Even shorthand. Long as you're simple and specific."

Suzuki jotted down a couple of examples of what he wanted the enchantment to do. His first few were far from specific. He could see how they might result in his ax accidentally maiming him. But after a couple more quick drafts, he found something that he thought might be specific enough.

"Tethered to the hand that you will always return home to when desired."

Suzuki handed the notebook back to Chip, who took the paper and nodded with a satisfied smile.

"That'll work just perfectly," she encouraged as she handed the paper back. "Rip that bit off just to drive the point home. Get all magical feeling, whatever you gotta do, and then bingo. You got yourself a spiffy new shine. I'll avert my eyes for the sake of your privacy."

Chip turned around and plugged her ears with her fingers as she whistled softly to herself.

A small amount of nervousness settled over Suzuki. He had already done a few enchantments before, a couple of times as he'd been prepping for his current quest while everyone else slept. This was the first time anyone was near him, let alone aware of what he was doing. He tried to swallow his nerves and continue on.

Suzuki placed his ax at the foot of the small pile that he'd built. He closed his eyes and wished that he had something to hold in his hand. He usually used the ring that he had given Beth as a sort of talisman to calm his nerves. That was gone now.

Remembering the feather that Ashegoreth had given him, he reached under his shirt and gripped it in his palm. Then he repeated his incantation as he imagined the magic binding his words, the ax, and his ingredients.

The familiar tugging of mana being released from his body shocked him at first.

Then the ax and the ingredients began to glow.

There was a bright flash of light and when Suzuki could see again, only the ax remained. A few indecipherable runes had been added to the ax. Suzuki picked it up, feeling the weight of the thing in his hand.

Chip nodded her head in approval as she stood up next to Suzuki. "So you gonna give it a try?" she asked.

Suzuki turned and threw the ax through the air. It sank into a rock across the cavern. He mentally imagined the ax returning. Across the room, he heard a soft hum.

The ax flew back at Suzuki.

It was coming so fast that Suzuki instinctually lifted his hand to protect his face. The ax slowed and then stopped, hovering directly in front of his open palm. Suzuki grasped the hilt of the ax. He held it in his hand, impressed with what he had just done.

"Shit, it actually worked," Suzuki exclaimed. "I can't believe that worked."

Chip turned to walk away, still whistling softly, before stopping to turn and look back at Suzuki. "Looks like you worked a charm." She whistled. "Might have another natural talent, if you stick with it."

Suzuki gave her a smirk. "You know, you aren't half bad as a teacher."

"Oh, you don't need to get my ears all pointy, I already know. Glad you figured it out eventually."

Suzuki felt his cheeks flush red from embarrassment. He didn't realize that his feelings about being mentored by Chip were so apparent. Guilt rushed over him and he tried to shake it off, but there wasn't anything to feel guilty about. He had just assumed what anyone else probably would have assumed about how the mentorships had been divvied up.

Whatever. Fuck it, he finally said to himself. *Just because you were being a dick doesn't mean you have to keep being one.*

The rest of the camp was starting to wake up as Suzuki walked back to his tent. Sandy stepped out of her tent, stretching as she dangled her amulet in front of her. She took a seat by the fire and magicked a tome into existence.

"How'd you sleep last night?" Suzuki asked.

Sandy pointed to Stew, who was stumbling out of the tent, his eyes bright red and bloodshot. "Hardly at all," she lazily stated as she flipped through the books.

Stew crashed down next to Sandy and yawned loudly. "Fuck, do we have any coffee?" he asked as he found a stick and picked at the fire.

"I think Diana has some of those zip beetles."

Stew tossed a rock at Suzuki to get his attention. "Hey, I meant to ask you yesterday," Stew started. "You know how Ashegoreth said that she was married."

Suzuki flipped his ax up and down as he listened to Stew. He placed the tip of his ax on his finger and tried to balance it. "Yeah," Suzuki murmured.

"I meant to ask you, do you think they ever...you know?" Stew asked.

Suzuki shrugged. "No, Stew, I do not know."

"Made the four-winged creature?"

"You are so unbelievably immature."

"Like was it a giant-ass hawk or something?" Stew asked. "There's no way it was a regular size one. Like, did she just slip it up in her—"

"Stew!"

Sandy waved away her tome as Diana came over to the fire and conjured a few breakfast supplies. "I don't think egg-laying creatures fuck like that, Stew," she explained. "You know, the whole laying eggs thing."

"Psh, dude, I know dragons fuck. Ashegoreth looks like she *hella* fucks."

Diana handed Stew and Sandy a cup of coffee without bothering to meet either of their eyes. She yawned loudly and rubbed the sleep out of her eyes before conjuring a pair of glasses onto her face. "I noticed you two made good use of that Lightfoot spell I showed you," Diana chided.

Stew's face turned as red as a tomato, and he awkwardly looked around as he fumbled with his words. Finally, after listening to everyone laugh, Sandy stepped in and saved him. "Yes, and thank you for helping us be polite with our neighbors." She giggled. "Suzuki probably really appreciated it."

A pot of porridge was boiling over the fire as some bacon sizzled. Suzuki took a bowl, ladled some porridge into it, and covered it with a couple of bacon slices. "Honestly, I didn't think that listening to you two assholes fucking would be the single worst part of going on death-defying quests." He laughed.

José was the last person to join the breakfast bonfire. His eyes were bright and awake, and he carried a small bowl of water and soap. He washed his face by the fire, and delicately trimmed his beard.

"We ready to get moving anytime soon?" he asked.

There were no disagreements. It took about ten minutes to break down the camp. Then they were off down the tunnels where light faded away. As often happened during long periods of walking, Suzuki lost himself in the dark. One foot in front of the other.

Over.

And.

Over.

It was almost meditative. He found himself drifting through memory after memory, running through his life, his decisions, letting his thoughts bounce around until they congealed into some half-formed image that he could not quite wrap his head around. He was surprised when he found that he was exiting the tunnels and staring at a relaxed, afternoon sun.

The tunnels had exited out of the side of the mountain. Beneath were hills that descended into what looked to be an open valley. In the distance, far in the distance, Suzuki could see a large tower piercing the sky. It was obscured by black clouds that were crackling with red lightning.

The black clouds hung over most of the valley, and Suzuki could see the concentric circles that made up the divisions of the Dark One's camps. It reminded Suzuki of Dante's Inferno and the rings of hell with each ring composing a different punishment.

José looked off the edge of the mountain, staring down into the Dark One's forces. "Now that is a fuck ton of orcs." He sighed as he scratched his head. "Can't say that I was expecting to see that many."

Suzuki joined the line of MERCs staring over the side of the mountain. "How many were you expecting?" Suzuki asked. "We're literally breaking into the Dark One's domain."

"I didn't think that his domain was going to be in Jersey."

"What? We're not in Jersey."

"Technically, we aren't in Jersey. But, kinda. You know, all the realms are interlaced over each other. This is the part of Earth that Jersey is in. It figures the Dark One would be operating out of this shithole. Nothing good has ever come from New Jersey."

Diana shrugged and squatted down as she peered out at the unspeakable volume of the Dark One's forces. "Not true," Diana countered. "The Jersey Devil came from Jersey. And I'm pretty sure Chip did as well."

Suzuki looked at Chip, who was staring out at nothing as if she wasn't interested in conversation or recon. "Not a stellar talking piece but, yeah, born and raised," Chip admitted.

José stumbled over the next thing he said.

"Regardless who or what is from New Jersey, we gotta figure out what we're up against," he said. "I mean, I can see the defense rings, but I have no idea what's in them. We're too far out to possibly get a read on what we're up against. They could be completely empty. Or they could be teeming with every fucking beast that the Dark One's been able to wrangle."

A light went off in Suzuki's head. "Hey, I think I got something," he exclaimed. "I have a friend who gave me a hack for the military satellites. We were thinking about using it to exploit a hole in the system so that we could sneak around the HUD babysitting protocols keeping us out of over-leveled areas. We could use it to see what the satellite feed looks like."

Chip walked up behind Suzuki and rested her hand on his shoulder. "Glad to be around someone who doesn't take a royal shit on using technology to get a job done," she said. "How 'bout you go on and pull the feed up?"

Suzuki accessed the hacking program that Real_Deal had sent him a few weeks ago.

When Beth had disappeared, Suzuki had run through dozens of different plans to find a way to get her back. One of the plans had included reaching out to his old friend Real_Deal, a gamer who had initially informed him of the rumors concerning the MERCs existence and their desire to pick up qualified recruits who didn't make the military's cut.

Originally, the program had been designed to help the Mundanes work around the level cap that the MERC HUDs had in place to keep new recruits from wandering into areas that could get them killed. The HUDs would instantly transport new recruits out of areas where they were grossly under-leveled. As it turned out, the hack didn't work nearly as well as Real_Deal implied. This was a common issue with his intelligence. He usually got the general idea, but the finer points tended to fall by the wayside.

Thus, the hack was useless for sneaking into enemy territories but had been instrumental in pinpointing Beth's whereabouts.

Suzuki's HUD displayed the satellite network floating above. He selected one of the satellites and attempted to patch into its video surveillance.

The video was garbled and nonsensical, images that shifted in and out of focus as static cut through them.

"I can't make anything out," Suzuki complained. "It's... there are no clear images. I can't tell which satellites are which."

Chip reached out to take Suzuki's HUD. "You don't mind if a take a looky-loo, do ya?" she asked.

Suzuki removed his HUD and handed it to Chip. "Nah, go for it," he said.

Chip put on Suzuki's HUD and thumbed through a few menus. She waved her hand, and a floating, holographic keyboard phased into existence in front of her. As she typed, her face went sour into a frown. She took off Suzuki's HUD and handed it back to him.

"Something's blocking the feed," she explained. "And it's not magic."

José checked over the edge of the hill again. He looked worried, his stern face betraying the slightest hint of emotion, the first tiny crack in a stone sculpture. "What about that spell you used before, Suzuki...the one you got upgraded?" José asked.

"It's too big of a space to look through. I could pick a spot, but I'd only be able to see a few feet ahead. And I wouldn't know where to start with this huge ass place."

"True, true. What would I do in this kind of situation?"

"Uh...I don't know. Pray about it?"

"That's the last thing that I would do, kid. Ideas, anyone? I don't like the idea of walking blindly into this situation."

Stew joined the growing queue of MERCs looking over the side of the hill. "I don't know," he thought aloud. "We still got a lot of area to cover before we even get close to the first ring. Maybe we should wait until we're in a better vantage point to assess the situation."

Everyone turned to face Stew, each MERC wearing a similar look of surprise.

Suzuki had to admit to himself that he was a little impressed with Stew's sudden foray into rationality. "Are you saying that you don't want to run in, headfirst, and risk getting yourself and your teammates killed?" Suzuki asked.

Sandy eyed Stew suspiciously as she walked around him and prodded his chest with her finger. "Where is my boyfriend, and what have you done to him?"

Stew shrugged and walked away from the edge. He puffed his chest out a little as he straightened his shoulders.

"Nowhere," he said. "I still want to show those asshats what the Jenkins is but, like José's been telling me, we gotta find the best vantage point to unload a bunch of whup-ass on these fools."

"It's so sexy when you use your head, preferably to crush

someone's skull, but this whole thinking thing is pretty cute too."

"Babe, I'm always thinking. My brain is my most important muscle."

Suzuki broke in, "Actually, the brain isn't a muscle. It's an organ and only has a faint amount of muscle tissue to support—"

"Dude, I was just saying a thing. You know, like an idiot."

"You mean idiom."

"Could you just cut the nerd shit for a bit? Let's find a better place to scope out what we're up against."

Evening was fast approaching, and the MERCs were making their way down the edge of the mountain as it sloped into the green hills. José and Suzuki led the way, followed by Sandy and Stew, and the veteran MERCs watched the rear. The hills were covered in dense trees, and it was difficult to make out anything more than a few feet ahead. Needless to say, it was taking some time for the MERCs to orient themselves.

Suzuki had never been one for tracking, but José seemed to think that he was a natural. There were only a few times that José redirected Suzuki's path. For the most part, he let Suzuki figure out which way they were going to be heading. It was still a little weird to Suzuki that José wasn't taking more of a hands-on approach to the whole quest. They were about to descend right into the heart of the Dark One's camp. Or maybe this was one of many camps. If the Dark One was actually busy trying to conquer all of the different realms, it didn't make sense that he'd be holed up in Middang3ard.

Maybe the whole quest wasn't nearly as dangerous as Suzuki had thought. José definitely wasn't acting like he was on a suicide mission.

After an hour of walking, the MERCs descended into a valley. The trees grew thicker, and the little bit of sunlight faded as the valley collapsed into darkness. Diana and Sandy moved to the outer part of the MERC formation, each of them casting an illumination spell. Four small blue orbs floated above the MERCs, casting enough light to see, but not nearly enough to draw attention.

José held up his hand and stopped the formation as he put his finger over his mouth and pointed ahead.

Suzuki strained his ears. He could hear something rustling up ahead and nothing else. He moved closer to the trees and looked through the branches and leaves.

A group of orcs was sitting around a fire, cooking a meal. They were chatting with each other in low voices. A troll sat near them, its head bent down low, drool dripping from its slack jaw. It was nearly seven feet, extremely muscular, gray, and beset with a look of confusion resting heavy on its brow.

José held up seven fingers and showed them to everyone and then pointed to his right and motioned that they should follow him. Sandy raised her hand, attaching the red amulet to her chest.

Her skin turned to ash and cloaked her as her face went chalky, and the mask of Elroz covered her face. She then raised her wand and a silver light slipped from its tip and formed a bubble around the MERCs, its side dripping as it conflated into itself and soaked into their feet.

Then she touched the wand to each of their lips and then her own.

When Sandy spoke, it was as clear as if she had been raising her voice, but still, it sounded muffled somehow.

"This way we can still talk," she whispered. "And our movements will be quieter."

Diana flashed Sandy a thumbs-up and a proud smile as José motioned for the MERCs to follow him. They made their way through a thicket of bushes and José held his hand up again to signal for the MERCs to stop.

Past the bushes, there was another camp. This one was filled with eight goblins and three sleeping wargs. The goblins bickered with each other as they roasted meat on sticks.

The wargs snored comfortably, one of them stirring as a goblin dropped a piece of meat. The warg leapt forward and snapped up the meat before the goblin could do anything.

Once he was satisfied, José led the MERCs back to the original clearing they had been watching the orcs from and shook his head as he paced.

Suzuki didn't understand why José seemed so perturbed by the orcs and goblins. The camps were far enough away that they could probably manage to sneak in between the two. And if it came down to a fight, Suzuki knew that everyone was capable of handling a few orcs and goblins.

"What's got you all bothered?" Suzuki asked. "They're just orcs. We've killed scores of them."

José looked back at the campfire burning a little way away. "That's not the cut of orc you've seen before," he explained. "You know about the whole level system, don't you? For MERCs or the military, levels are basically just a fancy way to talk about how much damage your gear can put up with. Orcs and goblins, though, that's an entirely different story. Their tribes are split up by strength, and some tribes are stronger than others. It's not exactly a direct correlation, but it's close enough. You guys have been fighting mostly rookies with occasionally something a little tough, and you all saw that war chief riding after us. But that's nothing compared to these guys. We're outnumbered. And these guys are probably just the tip of the iceberg. I'm guessing these shit heads aren't even a part of the first ring. They're sentries. If we slip up here, we're fucking dead. So what are we gonna do, Suzy?"

"What? I'm planning this one?" Suzuki asked.

"You're our tactician. Of course, you're planning it. Try not to get anyone killed."

Where to start? Suzuki felt the pressure. Oddly enough, he knew that it wasn't coming from anyone other than him. José had never put Suzuki in a situation that he hadn't been prepared for and the Mundanes trusted him with their life. He still felt the pressure, though. It was a block in his mind, weighing down his thoughts. What if it really was as dire as causing the death of all of his friends?

Suzuki knelt down and ran his fingers through the dirt. José crouched beside him and rested his hand on Suzuki's shoulder. "This is what separates real leaders from the assholes who just want to be the shit," José whispered. "Those assholes, they don't give a shit about anyone. They just want the credit and the parade. You see 'em in the military. You see 'em in the MERCs. Not as much, but you still do. It's a fucking shame, but it is what it is. They're not real leaders. A real leader knows what's being sacrificed and what's at risk. They know that if anything happens to one of their own, it's on them and no one else. That's what it takes to be a leader. You think you got that?"

Suzuki didn't need to be asked twice. He knew what he had to do. The whole reason they were all out tramping through the Dark One's miniature version of hell was that Suzuki was very aware of the risk to any of his friends. He knew that Beth could end up dead. If it had been either

Sandy or Stew, he would have mounted a rescue party just as quickly.

"Can you do this?" José asked again.

Suzuki drew two circles in the sand. Then he stood up, looked around at the other MERCs, and nodded. "Of course," he said. "We don't want to alert anyone that we're here. I don't know how many sentries are posted, and I don't know how far we are from the first ring of camps. So we're going to take it slow. Nothing noisy. Take advantage of Sandy and Diana's ability to keep us quiet."

Sandy stepped forward to catch Suzuki's attention. "It won't do anything to silence them, though," she countered. "If a fight breaks out, it doesn't matter how quiet we're going to be."

"Which is why we aren't going to fight. Chip, how are you at sneaking?"

Chip cracked her knuckles as she pulled down her goggles. "Been a while since I been asked that," she said. As Chip spoke, she shimmered in and out of sight until her body was invisible. "Some things magic tends to have a blind eye about. Refracting light? Best leave that to the gears and whistles."

"Perfect. Here's the plan. We do this, and we should be golden."

7

The MERCs waited until the moon hung pregnant and swollen in the night sky over the orc and goblin camps. The wind blew through the crowded trees and branches, creating almost the sound of windchimes.

It would have been beautiful if not for the loud shouts and cheers of the orcs as they downed ale after ale. They sang songs of their kind, songs which made no sense to any of the MERCs, but sounded as if they were dripping with a pathos that Suzuki had not known orcs to be capable of.

It didn't matter, though. They were the enemy.

If Suzuki had wandered into the camp unarmed, the orcs would have cut him down within seconds. That was the thing to remember.

At first, the MERCs were going to wait until the orcs drank themselves to sleep. That wasn't happening, so Suzuki rolled with the punches. They split into two different parties, no longer the Mundanes or the Horsemen. Suzuki went with Chip and Diana. José separated with Stew and Sandy.

Suzuki's party crept toward the goblin camp on the

eastern side of the clearing. Diana and Suzuki crawled across the grass as Chip used her grappling hook to swing herself to the treetops. What they were attempting was going to require a nearly perfectly synchronized attack. If any of the goblins fell separately, they could alert whatever else was in the forest.

From the high vantage point, Chip looked down at the goblins while Suzuki and Diana moved closer to the camp.

The goblins spoke softly, passing their drinks back and forth. They seemed much more excitable than the orcs had. Whatever they were speaking of must have been interesting. Even though Suzuki didn't understand their language, he could tell that they were speaking rapidly with each other.

Suddenly, one of the goblins stood up and drew his sword.

Suzuki took a huge breath and held it in. At his side, Diana tensed as well. He hoped that Chip was just as conscious of what was going on in the camp.

The goblin which had drawn its sword spit on the ground and another goblin jumped from its seat, smashing its ale gourd to the ground before whipping out its thin sword. The two goblins circled each other while the rest jumped to their feet and started chanting. When they attacked, it was with the quick viciousness that Suzuki had assumed was reserved for enemies.

This was the perfect chance. Suzuki motioned for Diana to move forward and they rushed through the last stretch of trees until they were practically inside the goblin camp. Suzuki pressed himself against a tree and cast a glance at Diana, who was doing the same.

Across the clearing, Stew, Sandy, and José were also moving into their positions. The orcs were still drinking and talking loudly. None of them noticed as the three MERCs moved through the trees and surrounded them.

Suzuki watched the MERC group. José met his eyes, smiled, and nodded. Then he pointed ahead, signaling to Suzuki to pay attention to what was in front of him. Suzuki turned his attention back to the goblin party.

The two goblins were still fighting each other, their steel clashing loudly in the night. Even if Sandy hadn't cast a sound-dampening spell, the goblins probably wouldn't have heard them. Suzuki motioned for Diana to move around to the back of the camp and flank the goblins.

He wished that he had gotten a better idea of what Chip was planning on doing, but she had slipped away too quickly once she had rendered herself invisible. *She'll figure it out,* he thought to himself. *There's an obvious reason she's one of the Horsemen.*

Once Diana was in position, Suzuki signaled to her that it was time. Diana waved her wand through the air and a clear, golden light shot out from it and spread over the camp, creating a bubble. None of the goblins seemed to notice.

Suzuki knelt down to see where the edge of the bubble touched the ground. It looked solid enough. This would give him and Chip a bit more time.

Activating his Scent SD, he changed his scent from "Cedar Branch" to "Raw Human," and even though the scent was extremely specific and not in the SD card's database, Fred helped bridge the gap between intent and practicality.

Then Suzuki readied his ax and waited. He checked his HUD, but it didn't give him a percentage chance of success, instead displaying "???." *"Huh?"* he muttered to himself. *"What the fuck?"*

Too many variables, Fred said. *Your plan isn't fully formulated in your mind. That is why the HUD displays what it displays.*

I see.

Plus, you have the Horsemen with you. And their HUDs are not integrated with yours. Normally HUDs will communicate with each other, take in as many variables as possible. But the Horsemen's HUD's are blocking communication, so any attack that involves them will always come out muddled.

Suzuki blinked his eyes. *Blocked? Why?*

Because the Horsemen don't use their HUDs to calculate their chances of success.

What? Suzuki said. *They don't use their HUDs?*

"*I didn't say that. SD cards, maps, inventory, yes. But calculating success? That is a crutch they rarely use.*

Humph, Suzuki muttered to himself. *No percentage success calculations. That's why these guys are legends.* He turned his attention back to the camp.

The goblins were still fighting, their caustic shouts muffled under the golden umbrella of Diana's spell. None of them seemed to notice that they were slightly less audible than before. As the goblins circled each other, the wargs sleeping by the fire woke up, their noses twitching.

Before any of the goblins noticed what was going on, the wargs stood and bolted toward Suzuki. Only one of the goblins lost interest in the disappearance of the wargs. There was a fight going on.

The first warg leapt over the few bushes separating Suzuki from the goblins, its red eyes searching as its nose twitched with anticipation, its jaws foaming with hunger. Suzuki knew that he only had a few seconds to act.

He whistled while laying low to the ground. The pack of three wargs turned their attention to the source of the noise.

They bounded toward Suzuki. A warg pounced, sailing through the air and connecting with Suzuki, who lifted up his flaming ax and caught the warg in the mouth. The beast refused to die and continued snapping at Suzuki as the two other wargs began to circle, ready to come in for the kill.

Up in the trees, there was a clicking sound accompanied by the quiet whir of gears. The two wargs dropped dead, two circular saws in their backs.

Suzuki grabbed the warg's mouth and pried it off his ax as he scrambled away. He held his hand out, and the ax returned to him instantly. He raised it high and brought it down on the warg's head. In the distance, he could still hear the goblins dueling with each other. Suzuki motioned toward the goblin camp as he moved forward. In his peripheral vision, he could see Diana advancing as well, her wand pointed out directly in front of her.

When Suzuki was satisfied with his vantage point, he raised his open palm in the air. The goblins were still fighting each other, one scrambling on the ground, the other standing over his former peer, sneering and spitting, his black teeth gnashing wildly.

Suzuki closed his hand into a fist.

Diana waved her wand toward the goblins and there was a bright flash of light. Suzuki tossed his ax through the air and it sailed clear over the hedges, landing square in the largest goblin's chest.

The goblin went flying as it screamed.

Suzuki thought of his ax, and it pulled itself from the goblin and returned to his hand. He threw the ax again, this time taking off the head of another goblin before he recalled it back to his hand.

A shimmering shadow fell into the center of the camp. The light refractured and bent and Chip sizzled into existence. She pulled a thin metallic slab from her back. As she turned to face the goblins, the slab extended and took the form of a bow. She ran her fingers down the top of the bow to the bottom, and a thin, silk string appeared as she nocked an arrow and let it fly, impaling a goblin through the eye.

Suzuki had never seen anyone move so fast. It was as if Chip's body were made of water. He didn't even see Chip drop her bow, but she was now holding two small daggers.

She rushed forward between the three remaining goblins. There was the sound of tearing flesh, and blood splattered across the ground.

The goblins fell, and the camp was silent.

The three MERCs checked through the camp for any other bodies. They gathered up the corpses and shoved them into one of the tents, closing the opening. Then they took the warg bodies and tossed them into another tent. When they had finished taking care of the bodies, they slunk in the direction of the orc camp.

Suzuki saw only the tail end of the destruction that had been unleashed on the orcs. Sandy was floating back down to the ground, her body nothing more than ash and skeleton, crackling with energy as she peered down at the scorched orc bodies beneath her. Stew, crouched down next to an orc nearly twice his size, pulled his sword out of the orc's neck, while José, who held an orc over each of his shoulders, walked through the fire to toss the bodies in the cover of a tent.

The six MERCs looted the camp, grabbing what gold they could and looking for anything of value.

One of the orcs had a keyring which Suzuki tossed to José, who gave it back to him. Suzuki looked through the keys and then hooked them to the side of his armor. "Can you track where the orcs came from?" Suzuki asked Chip.

Chip shrugged. "Can and will, but I'd have to say, José has the nose of a truffle pig if you're looking to hunt down anything," she confessed.

"All right. You scout ahead. Stay up in the trees. If you see anything, let us know via the familiars. We'll be behind you on foot."

"Got the sound of a leader croaking through your voice, eh?"

José nodded and slightly touched Chip's shoulder with a small, almost unnoticeable gesture before leaping into the trees. Chip followed closely behind him and they were soon lost in the greenery.

The rest of the MERCs made their way slowly through the forest, stopping every few feet to survey the area around them or to check above and see how far Chip and José had gotten. Suzuki didn't think that there would be too many sentry parties located around the Dark One's defensive rings. They already seemed like overkill. It didn't hurt to be safe, though.

The forest was thinning, and Suzuki assumed that meant that they were getting closer to the first outer defense ring. Suzuki thought about using the clairvoyance spell to survey the area but remembered that he would need a specific spot. If he wanted to look for Beth with the spell, he would need to know specifically where she was.

Otherwise, he would just be choosing places at random. There was no certainty that he'd be able to see Beth at all or work out a strategy based on what he could see. Making their way through the forest until they could come to a better vantage point made more sense.

Suzuki was surprised that the attack on the goblin and orc camps had gone so well. It wasn't that he didn't have faith in Sandy or Stew but, rather, they had never tried to do anything like that before.

Usually, the Mundanes were thrust into situations that they didn't quite understand and had to make sense of on the fly. This was the first time that Suzuki could remember them taking their time to formulate a solid plan and implement it since their old days of playing *Middang3ard* together. And they had pulled it off effortlessly. That was probably one of the perks of working with the vets. It was almost like being around the Horsemen was serving as a reminder to slow down, to take everything in and reduce needless mistakes.

The sound of chanting broke Suzuki's concentration, but he couldn't tell where it came from. Briefly, he thought he'd imagined it, but then he noticed the other MERCs stopped too and he realized that it must be real. He cradled his ears and tried to listen.

The chanting was coming from within. It felt as if someone had inserted a chant into his head in words he had never heard before, in a nonsensical language.

Suzuki didn't need to raise a hand to signal that the party should stop. Stew was looking around, trying to find the source of the chanting. Sandy was harder to read. She only floated by Suzuki as he wracked his brain, looking for answers. Diana was the only MERC who seemed to have a handle on the situation. She pointed to the right, near an alcove embedded in the trees.

"It's coming from there," she whispered. "Magic."

Sandy floated over to Diana so she could get a better look. "What kind?" she asked.

"Necromancy, I think. We're going to have to be extremely careful. Numbers don't mean anything to a necromancer. They don't need to move fast. They don't need to hit hard. So we need to instead."

Sandy couldn't hide her surprise. "Orcs can use magic?"

"They have the ability. As with humans, most have lost touch with what they were capable of. Most magic users are necromancers, basic necromancers as well."

A voice broke through Suzuki's head, much like when Fred would speak to him. It was José's voice, and it sounded distant and fuzzy. *Hey, kid*, he said. *We got eyes on the orc. He's got a small camp. Couple of undead, but nothing serious. What are you thinking?*

You and Chip hit him from above. Take care of the undead, and we'll neutralize the necromancer.

Neutralize? I like the sound of that. On your mark?

No, we'll move when you're ready.

All right. Gimme a moment to get into position. Shit, Chip, will you stop fucking around and pay attention. We're on the necromancer. Yeah, we're gonna drop in. Sorry about that, kid. We're all ready. Moving on the bastard right now.

Suzuki leapt over the last of the trees blocking him from the necromancer. He landed, skidding slightly as he raised his ax and assessed the situation. He heard the other MERCs landing behind him.

The orc necromancer standing before them was a diminutive creature. It was the same height as the usual orc, but it looked to be atrophied, its skin hanging loosely, its eyes gaunt and sallow.

Its skin was a filthy gray, and it stared dumbly at the MERCs in the small, circular clearing. The undead orcs that surrounded the necromancer looked much livelier, even though they were corpses. They hadn't started to rot yet, and their eyes glowed a sickly red. The clearing smelled of decomposition.

An arrow struck one of the undead and it fell forward, its eyes staring lazily ahead. The rest of the undead formed a tight ring around the necromancer as it started to wave a bone wand.

A volley of arrows rained down from the trees as José jumped into the clearing, bringing down his sword as he screamed.

One of the undead stepped forward and took the brunt of José's attack. It fell lifeless on top of José as the rest of the MERCs sprang forward and tore through the circle of death protecting the necromancer. Suzuki hacked off the head of one of the undead creatures and tossed it to the side as he stepped closer to end the necromancer.

The necromancer was gone; the only trace remaining was a singed section of grass where his body once stood. Only the bodies of the undead remained.

Suzuki and José knelt down to inspect the grass, then looked at each other, both very confused and suspicious. "Did you kill him?" Suzuki asked.

José shook his head as he stood up and looked around the clearing. "Nope," he finally said. "Hands up, who killed the weird, witchy guy?"

None of the MERCs raised their hands.

Sandy drifted over to where the necromancer was, the trail of her ashen cloak casting small ash particles that drifted up to the full moon above. "Wish it had been me." She sighed. "I was really hoping to pick up a relic or something. Get my undead on."

"He's got to be around here someplace. But we're getting too close to the outer ring to be chasing any noisy orcs around. What's the game plan, kid?"

Suzuki ran his fingers over the singed earth. It was warm as if the necromancer had spontaneously combusted.

But there had been no explosion. There was no way that the necromancer had just croaked. This was Middang3ard, and nothing was that easy.

"Uh...honestly, I wouldn't mind a little help on this one," Suzuki finally said.

"That's a good trait to have. Being able to ask for help is one of the defining characteristics of a good leader."

"All right, Dad. Thanks for the lecture."

José laughed as he paced across the small clearing. "All right, I'll lay off the lectures." He chuckled. "I say we make camp here for the night. Have Chip and Diana scout ahead so that we can get a clear idea of what we're going to be up against in the morning."

"What about the necromancer?"

"That's why we're camping here for the night. He's an orc. He's not going to want to leave a kill. If we stay here, odds are it'll draw him back and we won't have to worry about him alerting anyone. In the rare occasion that he's an orc with half a brain and does go to alert someone, we'll already have a defendable position that we're comfortable in. We'll sleep in shifts tonight since we're so close to the outer camps. We'll keep the clearing defendable, catch a little sleep, and slip on in tomorrow. Sound good?"

"Sounds good to me," Suzuki said as he turned to Sandy and Stew. "What do you guys think?"

Stew shrugged as he sheathed his sword. "I don't know, dude. Sleeping in the middle of enemy territory doesn't sound like the greatest idea.".

"What about you, Sandy?"

"I want to get my hands on that necromancer. See what his entrails tell me."

"Uh, so that means you're in favor of the plan?"

"Yeah, why not? We all saw how huge the Dark One's

camp is. It might take us a week to make our way through the whole thing."

"Looks like you're outnumbered, Stew."

Stew walked over to a rock and squatted as he yawned. "Works for me, dude," he said. "Just think it's a little weird taking a nap at the enemy's doorstep. I really don't want to call any attention to us with all the sounds of satisfying love that are gonna be coming from my tent."

"Or you could use that sound-dampening spell."

"Sometimes the sounds of ecstasy cannot be silenced."

José stepped between Stew and Suzuki. "All right, then, if you two are done flirting with each other—"

"Uh, bro, I was talking about fucking my girlfriend. Not Suzy."

"Whatever helps you sleep at night. As I was saying, let's get started building camp while the rest of the Horsemen do some recon. Then we can get some sleep and start over in the morning."

There weren't any complaints from the MERCs. Chip and Diana leapt into the trees and disappeared. Those who remained got started building the camp for the night. The work went quickly enough, and it wasn't long before José, Sandy, and Stew were sitting around a small fire, roasting some meat and talking quietly.

Suzuki sat in his tent, staring out at the flames of the fire. He couldn't put his finger on it, but something felt off to him. As he lay back in his tent, he chalked it up to exhaustion. The day had been long. Hell, the last few weeks had been long. He was surprised every morning that he was able to make it out of bed.

It was nearly an hour before Chip and Diana returned to camp with news. As it turned out, the MERCs were fairly close to the first ring of the Dark One's defenses. Luckily, they were still out far enough that they wouldn't be noticed. Neither Chip nor Diana had been able to find any other sentries.

The necromancer must have been the last line of defense before the Dark One's camps were exposed.

Even though Suzuki knew the Dark One was the scourge of Middang3ard, he hadn't expected there to be so much resistance. Why would Beth be held at such a central location? Suzuki didn't doubt Beth's abilities as a fighter or those of her compatriots, but it seemed like such an extreme prison for what, at best, were a couple of grunts.

There were so many things that didn't feel like they added up. Suzuki could have thought about them all night, except José broke his concentration to figure out the guard shifts.

"Groups of two sound like they'll work best," José said. "I say we do a veteran and a rookie. Any of you used to taking night watches?"

Stew shook his head and leaned against Sandy's back. "No, we usually just clock out for the night." He yawned.

Sandy leaned over and kissed Stew's cheek before tucking her amulet beneath her shirt. "We've never been this close to anyone before, though. I mean, I guess we could have been ambushed. I never really thought too much about it."

José stoked the flames of the fire, the yellow light brightening his eyes. "That's something you might want to get in the habit of thinking about. That's how people end up dead. First shift will be Diana and Sandy. Second, Chip and Stew. Suzuki and I will close it out. How does that sound?"

There were no disagreements.

Suzuki thought to thank José for giving him two shifts to sleep but decided not to. He didn't want it to seem like he thought José was playing favorites. although he was excited that José had picked him for the overnight shift. The inner fanboy within Suzuki hadn't died. He was still going to get to spend the night talking with someone he respected and looked up to.

Suzuki retired to his tent and watched Diana and Sandy set themselves up for the night. He wanted to sit and talk with them for a bit, but he was overwhelmed with how tired he had gotten all of a sudden. Instead, he nestled into his sleeping bag and pulled out a book that he had bought in an elvish shop on an errand to persuade José to help out with their current mission. At the time, he had thought the idea was stupid, but here he was with José and the rest of the Horsemen, curling up to read an enchanted book.

Despite his pessimism, even Suzuki had to admit that some things were working out well.

The pages of the book were empty. Suzuki heard a voice, warm and inviting, bubble up from the pages and spread through his mind. *What kind of story do you want to hear tonight?* the voice asked.

Something light. Maybe a bedtime story. Something like that, Suzuki thought.

The pages of the book started to fill with images, slowly tracing themselves over the worn and yellowed pages. Suzuki saw the outlines of a massive dragon and an eagle, both intertwined with each other as the pages filled up with color. Suzuki heard the tale of the dragon wooed by the eagle and how they had met riding the summer winds over the Floating Palaces of the Pure Elves. How time had stood still when they were next to each other and how they could think of nothing else than each other when they were falling from the sky, their wings held close to their bodies, death rushing toward them, yet so quickly averted.

Suzuki tried to pay close attention, but something about the voice of the storybook was lulling him to sleep. He drifted off before he realized he was sleeping.

Suzuki's dreams were black.

If he had been awake, he would have said they were nightmarish. He found himself in a hole, and he didn't know how he had gotten there. Someone was screaming for help. He wanted to go to help, but he couldn't find the way out. His fingers scratched at the soft dirt of his prison.

After a while, he realized that he was the one screaming.

Above, there was a large light that was not the sun.

It had the texture of a lightbulb, something large and glassy. Suzuki reached for it, and he felt himself floating upward. If only he could touch the light...

He felt its warmth and knew that he wanted to be within it, to become one with the light.

The light was just out of his grasp. Suzuki could feel his arms straining to get to its glow. If only he could get a little closer. Then he heard the voice. Someone was calling to him. He wanted to look and see who it was, but he felt that if he looked away from the light, it would disappear. He would never get close enough to it. Maybe it was worth ignoring the voice calling to him if he could just get his hands on that light.

Then it was all gone.

Suzuki could feel himself being shaken awake, the dream fading as he tried to grasp it. The light was gone. He had been so close, but now it was gone. Anger bubbled up in Suzuki's chest, and his throat tightened. Whoever pulled him away from that light was going to pay. He was going to drive his ax through the interferer and go back to sleep.

Suzuki grabbed his ax and raised it as he stood, not caring who it was. He was going to bring the ax down as hard as he could and then go back to sleep. Nothing sounded as good as sleeping right now. It felt like he hadn't slept a day in his life.

He'd just kill the intruder and go back to sleep.

A hand touched Suzuki's shoulder.

Suzuki batted his eyes, trying to make sense of the world around him. Everything was out of focus. He couldn't make sense of where he was. The world was a collection of blurs and shapes that held no meaning. Then he heard a voice, soft and confused. "It's me, Suzy...what are you doing?"

Reality snapped back into focus.

Suzuki was standing over Sandy and Stew. He was in their tent. His ax was raised above his head and Sandy was staring at him. "I...I don't know," he muttered.

Sandy grasped her amulet and her body exploded in a flash of ash. Suzuki felt a strong gust of wind as he was blown out of the tent, Sandy's body swarming around his as he hit the ground with a heavy thud.

Sandy's spectral body reformed and she was holding her wand, pointing it at Suzuki's head.

Suzuki threw down his ax and stood up, his hands raised. "Wait, hold on," he said. "Hold on! I don't know what I was doing in there."

"Were you dreaming?" Sandy asked.

Suzuki shook his head. "I mean, I was asleep. The last thing I remember is falling asleep."

Sandy lowered her wand and looked around the camp. "I was having fucked-up dreams, and I woke up," she whispered. "I dreamed I killed you and everyone else in the camp. When I woke up, I was on top of Stew." Sandy stopped when she saw Suzuki's eyebrows raised. "Not like that," she said. "I had his sword in my hand."

"What the fuck is going on?"

Sandy pursed her lips as she considered his question. "It's got to be the necromancer. He's fucking with our dreams. A curse, maybe. Sleeping is pretty close to being dead. Anyway, he's still around here somewhere."

Suzuki looked around. The campfire had gone out. No one was on watch.

"Who's supposed to be out here right now?" he asked.

"Should be Chip and Stew, but Stew's in there, so you and José?"

"Check the tents. Be quiet."

Suzuki and Sandy went to Diana's and Chip's tents. They were both sleeping soundly. Then they walked over to José's and peeled back the opening. José was inside. He was sweating as he twisted and turned in his sleeping bag. His hand was wrapped tightly around his sword.

Sandy closed the opening of the tent as she said, "That's not a normal way to be sleeping. We should wake him up."

Suzuki shook his head. "I don't think that's a good idea. Remember what happened when you were awakened? And we know each other pretty well. What if he flips out when we wake him up? You've seen that guy in a fight. He could probably kill both of us before we even touched him."

"So what the hell are we going to do? Are we on guard duty now?" Sandy asked.

Suzuki considered this. "Guard duty isn't enough. Even if we're out here, that necromancer is probably in their dreams, fucking things up. We gotta find him and take care of this shit."

"How are we going to find him? He fucking vanished. What about Clairvoyance?" Sandy asked.

"I don't know where he's at. I can't just pick a place randomly and hope it's him."

"We can spell-split," Sandy said.

"What the hell are you talking about?"

"The upgrade I got. I can cast two spells together, interweaving them so they work like one. You can cast Find Your Target and Clairvoyance through me, then we can rip out the fucker's heart and get a good night's sleep."

"I can cast spells through you?" Suzuki asked.

Sandy nodded. "Sort of. It's still our familiars doing all the heavy lifting, but it'll work. I've been practicing it with Stew."

Suzuki gave her a wry smile. "So *that's* what you two have been up to all night."

Ignoring this, she said, "All right, give me your hands."

Suzuki took Sandy's skeletal hands. They were cold. "What does it feel like?" he asked.

"At first, it was like I was coming apart at the seams, until I got used to it. Now I feel okay. Still a little...unsure at times, but there's so much magic. I can feel it all around me. I guess this is why humans forgot how to use it. The whole experience has been...eye-opening. I don't know how the other races deal with it, feeling this much magic in the world."

"Maybe humans would be different if they did too. Maybe Earth would be different."

"Yeah. Maybe. Come on, let's finish up this spell."

Suzuki shut his eyes and focused on the two spells. He was surprised at how difficult it was to concentrate on two different spells at once. It was like trying to sing two songs at the same time. He felt them jumbling together and almost spilling out of his mouth. Then the world around him went dark.

Once everything came back into focus, Suzuki saw that he was crouched in a tree. Sandy was still beside him, holding one of his hands. Straight ahead was the necromancer, crouched in another tree. His eyes were dull and glazed over, and a red aura was permeating the air around him. He was chanting softly in his sleep.

"Can you see us?" Sandy asked.

"What do you mean?"

"Where the camp is? Can you make anything out from here?"

Suzuki scanned beneath the trees. He could see a faint light, that of a campfire. "Yeah, I got it," he whispered.

"Cool. Point me in the right direction when we get back. Unless you think you can hit him."

"I could try to ax him. But if you can, like for sure, go for it."

"I can. Let's do it."

Suzuki broke the illusion and they were both back in the clearing. He quickly got his bearings and pointed in the direction that he believed the necromancer to be. Sandy raised her wand and whipped it forward and then back as if she were casting a fishing line. A rush of wind went through the trees. It was powerful enough to knock Suzuki a little off-balance.

A body came flying out of the tree. It was the necromancer. He landed face-down in front of Sandy and Suzuki. Before Suzuki could say anything, Sandy waved her wand with vicious efficiency.

The necromancer's neck burst open, spraying blood over Sandy's mask. His head fell to the ground, and Sandy scooped it up. She stared into his eyes.

"Sweet," she murmured. "Diana will know what to do with this."

"Other than put it in the ground?"

"Nah, Suzy. Knowledge is in the brain. Gotta get the brains to get the knowledge."

Sandy conjured a piece of string and wrapped it around the necromancer's hair. She hung the head from her waist and pulled her amulet out of her chest. Muscle, tendon, and then flesh sprouted over her bone. Finally, hair forced itself out of her scalp. The sight was gruesome, to say the least. "I don't think I'm ever going to get used to that." Suzuki winced.

"Same here." Sandy laughed. "The hair growing feels really weird. We should probably burn the body. Waking up to a dead orc in the middle of the camp is a little morbid even for me."

Sandy rolled the necromancer's body over. "What the fuck is that?" she asked as she knelt.

Something large and silver had been implanted into the orc's neck. At first glance, it looked like a metal plate, but when Suzuki took a closer look, he could see that it was electronic in nature. It looked almost like a small CPU chip. The chip had been severed by the cut that Sandy had made.

Suzuki ran his finger over the chip. It was definitely technology. Nothing magical about it. "I don't know," Suzuki admitted. "A microchip."

"What the hell would an orc be doing with a microchip?"

"I don't know. Chip was telling me that the military used to do experiments with magic and technology. Maybe the Dark One is up to the same thing. Using tech to make the troops stronger. Something like that."

"Maybe. Whatever it is, we'll have to figure it out eventually. Come on, let's get some sleep. We're going to have to be up in a bit."

"Actually, technically, I'm supposed to be up right now. You know, guard duty and shit?" Suzuki said.

"Suit yourself. I'm going to get some more sleep. And Suzy, thanks for not killing me in my sleep."

Suzuki shrugged. "I can't wait until we never have to say anything like that again."

"Really? I think it's keeping life spicy. I'll make sure to leave the part about us holding hands out of the story when I tell Stew."

"Why, would he get jealous about something that stupid?"

"Maybe jealous isn't quite the word," Sandy said with a wink. "Also, maybe let's just keep the whole thing between us. No one really needs to know that they almost got killed in their sleep. 'Sides, it's nice to have our own adventures every once in a while. Guess it's a good reminder that the Mundanes are able to take care of themselves. We can just tell 'em we found the asshole and took care of it."

Suzuki groaned as he sat down near the fire. The orc's body was still next to the flames. Suzuki absentmindedly picked at the microchip implanted in the orc's neck. *Things just keep getting weirder and weirder,* he thought.

8

———

Suzuki was still awake when the rest of the MERCs got out of bed. They washed the sleep from their eyes, had a brief breakfast, and started planning what was to come next. Chip and Diana reiterated what they had found from scouting the night before – the first ridge of the Dark One's forces was not too far off, that it would be less than a two hours ride, and there were no other sentries along the way.

Suzuki and Sandy didn't bother mentioning anything that had happened the night before even though the necromancer's head hung from Sandy's waist.

José stood and cleared his throat as he looked past the clearing. "So, we know how far we are," he began. "We know where we're going. But the how is obviously missing. There are way too many of these fuckers to be able to sneak past. It might have been possible with the sentries, but we're gonna need a better plan than sneaking through trees and taking out whoever is in front of us. Fuck, I'm pretty sure there aren't even trees around. So we're fucked on that end of things."

No one offered any ideas.

They all sat in silence, trying to figure out what the next course of action would be. Suzuki was blank on ideas. Just the two sets of sentries that they had had to deal with the night before had slowed them down considerably. That was the case with everything that had happened since they left the Shire. The Dark One's forces didn't seem to be particularly intelligent, but they were adept at slowing them down. That being said, the Dark One's forces had no idea what Suzuki and the rest of the MERCs were up to. The obstacles had been merely circumstantial at this point. What the hell were they going to be in for when the Dark One had an idea of what was going on? It seemed like too much to think about at the moment.

Suzuki felt the familiar unwrapping of Fred from his consciousness. He was surprised to see Fred taking an interest in the conversation. For the most part, the other Mundanes' familiars were fairly chatty, and most of them had built some kind of relationship.

Not Fred and Suzuki, though.

There were moments that it seemed like they were at least tolerant of each other's existence, but that was the most that Suzuki seemed to be able to get out of him. Answering questions. Helping with magic. That was the extent of their relationship. That was why it was disorienting for Fred to suddenly speak up in the back of Suzuki's mind.

Eyes closed, Suzuki reached out to Fred, trying to meet him halfway, to at least extend an olive branch. *What's up, Fred?* Suzuki asked.

In Suzuki's mind's eye, he could see Fred uncurling his long, forked tongue, leaning over, his lizard-like eyes narrowing. *"I believe I have a solution to your infiltration problem, human,"* Fred hissed.

You were actually paying attention to what we were talking about?

I am always paying attention. Usually, you're having a conversation that is not worth my time. This, on the other hand, is different. You are in a particularly unfortunate situation that I believe I have an answer for.

So what are you thinking? Suzuki asked.

The Dark One's forces are going to be on the lookout for humans. There are none currently enrolled in his army. If any of you were to be caught, you could not pretend to be anything other than transgressors. I, on the other hand, could pass between the Dark One's defenses unnoticed. He has already amassed a collection of eldritch creatures performing his will. I could go unnoticed.

So you're just going to waltz in there while we wait on the sidelines?

Fred uncurled further, taking up more room in Suzuki's mind. *Not exactly. You would accompany me.*

How? You just said that humans would be caught if they were just walking around.

By possessing me, much the same way that I am in you. The role is reversible. If you wish, we could switch positions. You would exist within a pocket dimension of my body. I could listen to the inane things you will no doubt have to say. And together, we can find your friend.

How come you've never told me before that we can do this?" Suzuki asked.

Because the idea of you existing within me is disgusting. It's already bad enough that I have to slink around behind your unconscious mind. I'd prefer it if you weren't privy to all that makes me what I am, but this is a desperate situation.

What is so desperate for you about us getting Beth back? You've hardly given a shit before.

Do you want a solution, or would you prefer to keep asking questions? Fred asked.

All right, all right. Let me talk to them about it.

Suzuki pulled himself out of his head and reengaged with the conversation around him. Diana and José were debating something fiercely while the rest of the MERCs watched, slightly bored. Suzuki cleared his throat and, when all eyes were on him, scratched his head as he began to speak.

"I think I got something," he muttered.

José clapped his hands as he smiled, his shining teeth beaming out from behind his grisly beard. "Fuck, yeah," he exclaimed. "That's what I'm talking about. What do you have for us, kid?"

"Uh...I'll possess my familiar and pass through the Dark One's defenses as one of their own."

José's smile instantly faded. "You want to switch places with your familiar?" he asked.

"Yeah. Fred's an eldritch demon. He'd easily be able to pass for one of the Dark One's lackeys."

José shook his head. "Exactly. He's an eldritch demon, and you want to give up control of your body and get in his head."

"Uh, if it gets Beth back, yeah. I don't see what the big deal is. We just switch places for a while."

Diana stepped forward, waving her hand. Her face looked as if she were contemplating life and death. "Hold on, it is a big deal," she interrupted. "The only reason that Fred exists as he does within you is because of a shit ton of magical defenses and safeguards. He can't completely possess your body without risking severing his tie to you. Fred is dependent on you to maintain his own existence outside of the Garden of Familiars. If you step into Fred's mind, you're going to sever those safeguards. You won't have any control over him. He'll have free reign. If he wanted, he could lock you in his mind for the rest of eternity, and you wouldn't be anything other than an afterthought, a ghost of a feeling that he could repress. He could erase you from existence. That's what you're giving him the power to do."

"What do you mean, erase me from existence?"

Diana took a deep breath and pushed her glasses back. "We had a MERC try something similar years and years ago with an eldritch creature. At first, it seemed like a good idea. They were almost chummy. Once the mission was over, though, the eldritch creature pushed the MERC back to the furthest recesses of his unconscious mind. He, in essence, wiped the MERC from the face of the earth. No body. The little bit of his mind buried under a fucking demon. And that was that. There was nothing we could do about it. He literally ceased to exist. That's what you're talking about risking."

This was all information that Fred had managed to leave out of his casual suggestion. Suzuki searched for Fred through their connection but felt nothing. Either the imp had no feelings about what was being said, or he was doing everything in his power to conceal it from Suzuki.

"The god that the vampires were trying to resurrect, that god was an eldritch creature. Do you know exactly what an eldritch being is? Or did you get suckered into picking one up as your familiar without having the possibilities explained to you?"

Suzuki flushed with embarrassment. He had never thought to ask. He'd heard the term from reading different books and playing different campaigns, but he'd just assumed that Fred couldn't be as bad as any of those fictional depictions. He had been a familiar in a garden, just like all the rest. But maybe someone had mentioned something...

"An eldritch creature is an ancient," Diana said, breaking into Suzuki's train of thought. "They used to be gods. They existed before dragons, before worlds. They floated on the outskirts of reality, fighting their petty wars in delusions of grandeur. They believed themselves to be something great. But just like anything else, they eventually fell. The only difference is that they have a chip on their shoulder about it. And they're all waiting for a chance to make themselves glorious again. Eldritch creatures were the first to give themselves over to the Dark One. They practically lined up to serve him. That's the kind of creature that you're suggesting that you give your body over to. Is that what you want to do?"

Suzuki didn't know what to say. He'd wondered why Fred always spoke to him with such disdain. He'd assumed that it was due to a superiority complex. Nothing had prepared him to find out his body was host to an ancient creature that might betray him as easily as one would sit down for breakfast. "Is there another option?" Suzuki finally asked.

No one answered.

"I'm getting Beth back," Suzuki said. "I don't care what I have to do. I'm getting her back."

Suzuki felt José's eyes digging into him. He couldn't meet them. He looked at the ground and balled his fingers into a fist so tight that it drew blood in his palm. "She's...important," Suzuki whimpered. "The most important. I don't care what I have to do."

José nodded. "Guess that solves that. Suzuki will let Fred out, and the demon will pose as part of the Dark One's forces. We'll all do recon on the outskirts until Suzuki finds out where Beth is. Once he lets us know, we move in hard and fast. We get Beth and her friends out and then we get out. Sound good?"

The silence of the MERCs was almost deafening. "So how do I do this?" Suzuki asked.

Diana shrugged her shoulders as she turned to regard the trees behind her. "That is between your imp and you," she spat.

Suzuki turned his thoughts inward and directed them at Fred. *You heard all of that, right?* he asked.

Fred slithered out to meet him. They connected through time and space as if they were staring each other in the eye. *Yes,* Fred hissed. *I heard their doubts.*

So how do we make this happen?

Just allow me.

Suzuki wasn't sure about that. *That's it?*

Fred nodded. *Yes. That's it. Submit.*

Suzuki imagined himself sitting in a tree, his hands wrapped tightly around a branch. Beneath him was a darkness that he had never seen. He stared down into it. A sickly, warm air floated up from the darkness. It felt as if there were something foul and evil slinking about in the dark, wrapping itself around anything and everything it could get its body near.

One finger relaxed, then the next. Suzuki let go. He imagined himself falling into the dark chasm that was Fred.

Suzuki did not know how long he fell. He lost track of everything. He felt his body dissolving, each and every atom individually exploding and disappearing. There was a song, somewhere in the distance. He thought it might be Beth singing, or it could have been him screaming. Whatever it was, he felt himself fading away.

As Suzuki's body drifted away, the air in the clearing

changed. It fumed with the scent of sulfur and a gray cloud of smoke floated above Suzuki's body as it broke into a billion pieces and drifted away. A scaled leg stretched out of the black smoke. An arm quickly followed, then there was a pop and a gelatinous mass of pus and cracked lizard skin fell from the cloud onto the clearing's grass. It shook and gyrated until it hardened.

Then it shattered, Fred's whole body spilling out onto the ground.

The imp stood.

He was about five feet tall, with ram's horns that curled around the back of his head. His whole body was an unnatural red. Each scale on his body moved individually, as if a wave rocked through his skin. His eyes were deep and menacing, older than the dragon's and more devious. A snarling smile rested on his face as he stood to his full height and let out a small plume of fire from his writhing lips.

"Ah." He sighed. "The realm of flesh and blood. How long it has been since I have smelled the sweet scent of life?"

Fred took a step forward. His eyes widened as he lost his balance and fell flat on his face. He tried to lift himself, but his arms were too weak. Instead, he lay there, shifting his head to his side, coughing a small spit of flame. "It humbles me, but...could someone help me up?"

The MERCs stared for a moment in surprise. Finally, Sandy leaned forward and helped prop Fred up. It was hard to tell whether Fred was grateful.

"This...this is new to me. It has been some time since I've had a true body. I don't remember being so wobbly."

Diana knelt next to Fred. She whipped out her wand and pointed it at him. "Where is he?" she asked.

"The boy?"

"He has a fucking name, imp," Diana snarled.

"As do I."

"What is his?" Diana demanded.

"Suzuki."

"All right, Fred. Where is he?"

"Orienting himself. I will not let him get lost. Please, give me a moment, and I will retrieve him. Then we will find his precious Beth."

———

It was dark. There was nothing ahead or behind. No top or bottom. Suzuki could not see his body. Nor could he feel it. He stared ahead, only remotely aware that he needed to see to stare. He wasn't certain where he was. If such a place could even be called "being." The closest thing that he could remember was floating, like maybe down a stream.

A river, perhaps. He tried to bring the memory forward.

There was a river. It had been cold when he first entered, but after a few seconds, his body got used to the feeling. He wondered how he could ever have thought it was cold before. There were people all around him. The river wasn't too wide. When he looked ahead, he knew he could swim to the other side of the riverbed. To his left, past the large group, there was a steel tower that people had climbed on. They were taking turns jumping off while the ones in the river cheered and laughed.

A man was floating beside him. He recognized the man, but he did not know why. There was some meaning that this man held in his gaze as he stroked his beard and sipped his beer, smoking a cigarette and lazily watching the sunrise.

Suzuki could taste the water on his lips and smell the barbeque from a few feet away. There were dogs everywhere, barking and playing. Suzuki looked down at his hands.

They were smaller.

Unarmored.

If someone were to attack him right now, he'd be defenseless, but he felt like that was okay. No one would pull such a stunt in a place like this. There was too much relaxing to be done.

The man sitting across from Suzuki threw a rope from his rubber innertube to the shore. It slipped over a tree branch, and the man used the rope to pull himself closer to the shore as he grabbed Suzuki's innertube and brought the boy along with him. And that was what Suzuki was; he could tell now. He was a child, much like the other children running and playing in the bed of the river or near the volleyball courts. Why wasn't he playing with the other kids? The children seemed to having so much fun.

Once they had gotten to the shore, the man rose and tossed his beer can into the trash. He came back to Suzuki, wading through the knee-deep water. "You should go play with them," the man encouraged. "They're having a lot of fun, aren't they?"

Suzuki looked at the kids near the volleyball court. They didn't look real. The more he stared at them, the more they quivered and waved like a heat illusion. One of the children looked at him with bright red eyes. The child's lips were curled in a snarl. "I don't like those kids," Suzuki whimpered.

"You gotta start getting out there, Suzuki. You can't just hide back here with me all the time."

"I'm not hiding. I don't like them."

"Why not?"

The children at the volleyball court were screeching at

each other. They had sprouted wings and they were flapping them violently, tossing up dirt while they hissed and snapped at each other.

"They don't look nice."

"Not everyone looks nice all the time."

"But what if they aren't? What if they really aren't nice?"

"Well, you won't know until you go and talk to them, will you?"

Suzuki thought he had an answer for the man, but his mouth wasn't working. He reached up and touched his teeth. They were still in his mouth. As well as his tongue, though no matter how hard he tried, he couldn't get words to come out.

"Just go say hi. It's not like they're ogres or something."

The man pushed Suzuki forward and he stumbled toward the children on the volleyball court. As he walked, the ground beneath him trembled. Bits of rock broke apart from the rest of the earth. A massive chasm opened up like some gaping jaw of a creature freshly woken and starving. The children at the volleyball court fell into the chasm. Suzuki whirled around to see where the man was. All he was able to see was the faintest glimpse of the man's hands as he sank into the earth's gash, the water of the river flowing behind him, drowning whatever may have been— and the earth kept shaking. Suzuki looked down. The earth beneath him was opening, and his mouth mimed a scream as his feet lost their footing and he fell into the darkness.

The boy sat alone in a space which was neither full nor empty. He stared at the cosmos around him, unaware of his place, of time, or of existence itself. There was light, yet it was not light.

It was almost like a noise, something loud and exploding in the distance.

This light cast no heat. Instead, a rush of cold poured from wherever the light stemmed from. The boy looked down at his feet, at his hands. They did not seem to be attached to any one place specifically. He called out to the dark void, but there was no answer.

He was uncertain of how long he had been sitting.

The cold light in the distance grew larger and brighter. The boy covered his eyes as his body was awash with white light that made his skin feel as if it were peeling back. He found himself curled in a ball, staring at the light through narrow, winking eyes. Once the waves of light passed, the boy was sitting alone. There was darkness, but it was different somehow. It was a darkness that has known light. The boy watched where the light came from, hoping for answers.

He did not know how long he sat there, but by the time he felt his eyes become sleepy, he could see that change was afoot. The light had grown large and bold. It was beginning to take shape—an elegant process. It blossomed stars which grew and fell apart until they were sucked into the light as it carved its body out of the black stardust that swirled in that void of life. And life came from this void. The boy did not know what grew within the void, but he could not avert his eyes.

Days passed. Months. Eons. Time itself was created anew, and worlds died around the bright light as it took its own form. The boy recognized something about the light and its growing body. He did not know what. He assumed that he would understand in more time. There seemed to be enough time, no need to rush. The boy stayed silent and watched while time stretched ahead of him, and one of the first lives was born to the universe. One of the first eldritch ones.

The boy felt something on his rock. A presence. He turned back to see what it was that could have pulled his attention away from the growing, breathing light ahead of him.

It was an imp. Small and red with delicate scales and wings as if it had been hatched only hours ago. The imp's fiery eyes watched the boy. "I am surprised to have found you here," the imp hissed as it slunk forward.

The boy did not understand. "Why would it be odd that I am here?"

"Most humans are only concerned with their own memories in this place. They dive into themselves and forget everything else around them. Yet, here you are. Watching my memories as I have watched yours, without nearly the amount of work, though. You just stumbled into them."

"These are your memories? What are you remembering?"

"Being born."

The boy looked at the light. He felt the cold burn from the billions of stars pouring fuel into the eldritch soul birthing itself. "Who am I?" the boy asked.

"A human. A very determined human. Perhaps the dumbest, most stubborn, determined human I have ever met."

"What am I doing here?"

"You are floating within my subconscious. We are rescuing your friend Beth. Simple enough?"

"Beth?" the boy asked, the corners of his memory sparking.

"Yes, you've been yammering on about her for the last month. Have you already forgotten?"

The boy was quiet for a moment. He closed his eyes and thought hard. Beth. He didn't have much of an idea of what the word meant. Yet still, the stars warmed around him as if they were calling her name. "Beth," Suzuki said. "I love her, don't I?"

"Deeply."

"And I'm looking for her?" he asked.

"You've found her. Now we are rescuing her."

"Good. What do I have to do?"

"Remember and be present. I understand that it is confusing within me. But remember who you are, Suzuki. If you do that, we will both come out of this alive."

The boy nodded. There were things that he had forgotten. He knew that now. Somewhere beneath all of the stars, he could see himself, staring back up at himself, two eyes perfectly mirroring each other. He was Suzuki. This was his familiar's confusing mind. Beth was close by. The plan was going to work.

Fred opened his eyes. He slowly forced himself to sit up. He was laying in the middle of the MERC camp, all of their eyes on him. He moved slowly, the way that one moves when they've forgotten the language of their own body. As he tried to use his arms to prop himself up, his wings flapped manically.

Sandy knelt down in front of Fred and reached out to push him over with a dainty finger.

Fred collapsed onto the ground, hissing fire as he tried to climb back to his feet, his tail whisking back and forth spasmodically. "Human, what the hell do you think you're doing?" he shouted.

Sandy shrugged as she stood up. "He can hardly walk." She sighed. "This isn't going to work. No one is going to believe that an imp that can hardly even move is part of the Dark One's army. He's going to get us caught."

"MERCs don't even believe that I'm capable of not serving the Dark One. Why would any of the Dark One's forces think otherwise."

José nodded as he stroked his beard. "That's true," he said. "Honestly, he might not even be questioned. He is an imp. An eldritch imp at that."

"Exactly. I don't have to act evil. I am one of the oldest evils in the history of the cosmos. Now where am I going?"

"We still don't know where Suzuki is. You could have just traded places with him. How the hell do we know you aren't conning us?"

Fred hissed loudly as he rolled onto his ass. He scooted back against a rock so he could support himself. "How can I assure you that your friend is not lost in the vast complexities of my subconscious?" Fred asked.

Stew drew his sword and pressed it to Fred's throat. "Don't fucking play dumb," Stew growled. "We know you get how these things work. Show us Suzuki is still alive or I'm going to take your head off. Got it?"

Fred smiled, a sick, vindictive show of teeth dripping with aggression. "And just how is that going to help your situation?" Fred asked. "If you take my head off, Suzuki goes along with me."

"It helps our situation because I'm not a naïve idiot who came on a rescue mission without being aware of what we are *actually* trying to do. We're here to get Beth. Suzuki knew that before he took a gamble on you. That means if you try to keep that from happening in any way, you're expendable."

"You would sacrifice one friend for another?"

Sandy crouched next to Stew, resting her wand against Fred's temple. "Suzuki would want us to get Beth," she said. "And he'd want us to kill anything or anyone who tried to keep that from happening."

Fred nodded as his tongue flickered out from behind his snout. "Noted," he finally said. He closed his eyes as if he were concentrating.

The voice that came out of Fred's mouth was not his own. It was softer, more confused, and slightly frightened. "Uh, guys? What's going on?" the voice asked.

Sandy pressed her wand deeper into Fred's temple. "Okay, you can mimic voices. How the fuck do I know this is Suzuki?" Sandy asked.

Fred's voice changed back to his own. "You could ask him a question. One that is specific to him and no one else."

Stew clapped his hands together as his face grew serious. "All right. I got one," he exclaimed. "What's the first thing you masturbated to?"

Sandy raised her eyebrow. "Are you kidding me?" she shouted. "This isn't the time to be fucking around. We need to—"

Fred's voice jumped back up a couple of registers. His eyes went a little soft and he sighed. "Are you fucking serious, Stew?" he asked. "You could've picked anything to ask me, and this is the one you went with?"

"Dude, I got to know. Is this you? Tell me now! What did you rub your first one out to?"

"An encyclopedia."

"Be more specific."

"Fuck, are you serious?"

"What?"

"A diagram of the female reproductive system."

"What encyclopedia?"

"Seriously, dude?"

"I'm not joking."

"Ugh. I told you, the blue ones that used to come in the mail. With the gold tree on the cover. I jerked off to one of the pictures of reproductive systems. And I guess it wasn't really the reproductive system. I was mostly jerking off to the description of how bodies respond to different kinds of arousal, and what's happening—"

"Yeah, that's Suzy."

José didn't look convinced. He leaned forward and looked at the imp, who squirmed uncomfortably. "He told you what he used to jerk off to?" José asked.

Stew shrugged as he stood up and walked away from Fred. "Yeah, dude," he said. "We're best friends. Of course, I know about the first time he jerked off."

"You're kidding me. Aren't you all supposed to be best friends? You all know the first time each of you jerked off?"

Sandy helped Fred to his feet and brushed off his shoulders as the imp looked around cautiously. "Of course we do," she said. "Stew jerked off to She-Ra. I came while I was watching some time-lapse decomposition videos. I guess you'd have to talk to Beth. It's not really cool to be telling you. Party privacy, you know."

The Horsemen grouped together as if trying to show *their* solidarity. It could have been confused for insecurity if they hadn't been smiling so widely.

Fred sat in the middle of them, his eyes darting awkwardly, trying to see where he stood in the situation.

Suzuki saw all of this happening.

It was as if he were behind a waterfall, watching the world from behind a pillar of water. He could hear and he could see, yet all the images and words were distorted. If he focused, shut his eyes tight (what were his eyes in this black place of nothing?), he could make sense of what was happening. He had been speaking to Sandy and Stew only a few moments ago, yet if felt like it had been hours and hours. This wasn't going to work.

He needed to be present.

Fred was in the process of standing up when his body started convulsing. He fell to the ground and started kicking as he coughed up little balls of fire. Words came flowing out of his mouth, a language that was unidentifiable; it was deep and old, mixed with a childish form of English.

The MERCs swarmed around the imp. Diana was the first to reach his side, trying to prop him up as if she could help. Slowly, the imp's convulsions stopped. Diana stared into the imp's eyes. "Suzuki?" she asked.

Fred twitched to the side, his jaw going slack. "You guys can't tell anyone what I told you, all right?" Suzuki's voice said, speaking through Fred's mouth.

"Whoa," Stew said. "This is getting weird."

Fred's face went stony and he picked himself off of the ground, obviously in more control of his body than he had been before. "Silent, human," Fred spat. "This is my body for now. You cannot—"

Fred's voice trailed off as he tripped over his feet, his left eye twitching manically. "No, no, no," Suzuki interrupted, speaking through Fred's body. "I'm coming along for the entire ride."

"This is no different than me being in your body!"

"Huge difference! I'm not used to this kind of shit."

"Then I expect you to at least, how do you humans say

it? Chill out? If you continue interrupting me and trying to take control of my body, I will not be able to pass as one of the Dark One's servants."

"All right, you got me there. But I don't want to be in the dark, Fred. That shit is weird. I feel like I'm losing myself."

"Then keep yourself awake. Do not let yourself fade. If you maintain your focus, you will not disappear. It'll be like riding in the front seat of a car."

"What the hell do you know about cars?"

"Enough to make an analogy. Now, are we going to do this?"

"Yeah. We're doing this."

Fred made his way through the last of the thicket of the forest. The Mundanes and the Horsemen had allowed him to go forward with the plan. They were going to be sticking to the shadows and the trees to watch. No one had mentioned that they didn't think that Fred was going to be able to pull this off. Suzuki felt the doubt, though. As Fred had walked through the forest, slowly regaining control and comfort in his own body, Suzuki had been concentrating on keeping himself anchored and aware of what was going on.

It was easier said than done. Suzuki would see the world through Fred's eyes and then within seconds be thrust into an onslaught of both his and Fred's memories. They washed over him, and there were times he wasn't certain whose memories were whose. He didn't understand how Fred had existed within him for so long, tossed to and fro with the memories of a person he'd never really met. Suzuki was starting to get the hang of the process, though. When he felt himself slipping away, it only took a little bit of concentration to reel himself back in.

The trees thinned out, and Fred approached the outer section of the first ring. From where he was, Suzuki couldn't tell whether or not the defenses were actually rings. He also couldn't tell where his perceptions ended and Fred's began. Was he feeling apprehensive, or was it Fred? Either way, it didn't matter who was feeling what. This was the situation he was in, and he had to keep his wits together. He guessed Fred had to as well.

Most of the outskirts of the camp were tents, hundreds of them for as far as Fred and Suzuki could see. If this was in fact a ring, neither of them wanted to consider just how many of the Dark One's forces were stationed here. The camp that lay before them already easily outnumbered the MERC encampment only a few days' ride away. If this was the sheer volume of forces the Dark One had at his disposal, then an all-out war was impossible. Fear washed over Suzuki, so thick and sticky that it drenched him and he felt as if he were drowning. He realized this was Fred's fear.

What the hell did Fred have to be so afraid of? What was his stake in all this? These were questions that Suzuki couldn't answer at the moment, but he made a mental note to come back to them. He needed to know why Fred harbored these fears.

The camp Fred was wandering into was a mix of different races. Orcs and goblins intermingled, talking briefly or helping each other with various tasks. There wasn't anything particularly interesting about this to Suzuki. He'd seen orcs and goblins working together since he'd come to Middang3ard. Fred had told him that it was uncommon for the two races to be able to tolerate each other, but it was all that Suzuki had seen so far. It seemed as normal as dwarves working alongside Elves.

The surprise came when Suzuki saw centaurs walking among the goblins and orcs. It seemed as if they were doing business with each other. Most of the camp was separated into smaller camps. In the middle of these, a group of centaurs was sitting with a small group of goblins. Fred couldn't make out what they were saying to each other; he had never been any good at reading lips. But Suzuki knew that centaur should not be in the Dark One's camp. At most, centaurs were morally neutral, from everything Suzuki knew about them.

That being said, all he knew was from books. Suzuki could tell that, even from afar, centaurs might be completely different from what he had imagined.

There were at least fifteen centaurs grouped together near the outskirts of the camp, speaking with what appeared to be an orc leader. The centaurs were wild-looking creatures. From the waist down, they had the legs of brawny stallions, made of pure muscle, twitching as they stamped their legs in what looked like impatience. The rest of their body was human and almost equally as muscular. Their hair was long and tangled; their faces scrunched a little bit as if some of their equine nature had tried to move North.

The orc was covered in tattoos and rested on a large cleaver. He would occasionally walk away from the pack of centaurs to some of the goblins, who were fiddling with a grinding stone. One of the orc's eyes had been gouged out, and he was missing multiple teeth. This made it difficult for Suzuki to tell that the orc was actually smiling while it conversed.

Fred stepped out of the forest and walked slowly on all

fours up to the camp of the Dark One's forces. At first, no one paid any attention to the imp, but once the first orc turned his attention to Fred, all eyes trained on him.

One of the smaller centaurs stepped away from his pack and stamped his feet loudly in the dirt. "Who goes there?" the centaur asked.

Fred spat a little ball of fire on the ground and hissed slightly under his breath. "Who are you to question me?" Fred countered.

Suzuki had managed to keep himself present enough to see how bad of an idea this was. There was nothing stealthy about Fred's tactics. If anything, it seemed like Fred was gearing up to start a fight. Even though Fred and Suzuki had been sharing a body for the last few weeks, he hadn't assumed that Fred had anything but a calm temperament.

Maybe eldritch creatures were just bullies, and for a second, Suzuki didn't know whose side he was on.

The centaur reared up on its hind legs and smacked its chest with a heavy thud. "Alzor the Swift," the centaur boasted. "Regional scout of the Hinterlands. I am to convey recon information to the Dark One. Now, who the fuck are you?"

Suzuki could feel Fred scrambling for an answer, and it was like Fred's mind was momentarily exposed in all of its fear. He obviously hadn't thought this far ahead. Why had he been so eager to volunteer himself without having anything remotely resembling a plan? It seemed odd that Fred would have been so overcome with a desire to help the Mundanes that he would have placed himself in danger. The imp had a different stake in the game, and Suzuki just wished he could figure it out.

Fred reared up on his hind legs as well. "I do not answer to you, Alzor," Fred spat. "I lived a thousand lives while your people were still trying to figure out if they wanted to fuck horses or people."

It was obvious that Fred had hit a nerve because all of the centaurs started shouting. They looked as if they were ready to stampede and trample Fred beneath their hooves.

The scales on Fred's back bristled. "Oh, did I upset you?" Fred sneered. "Do you have the temperament of an idiot animal or an idiot human? Do your legends recall whether it was your horse god who had the balls to jump a human bitch, or was it some sad old man who could only get it up for his mares?"

Alzor lost it.

He pulled off the bow resting on his shoulders and nocked the arrow before Suzuki fully registered what was happening. The arrow went flying toward Fred, who leapt toward the arrow, spitting a short stream of fire, instantly reducing the arrow to ashes. Then he whipped his tail at the centaur, the end splitting into three sharp edges that shredded the earth directly in front of the creature.

The two creatures circled each other, the centaur towering over Fred as it stamped its feet and continued to fire arrows, Fred spitting thin streams of flame that nullified the centaur's arrows.

Suzuki could feel wave after wave of Fred's emotions rocking him. The imp was annoyed and invigorated. Suzuki felt the dance of a fight, and it had woken something up within him; he could see why Fred had wanted to bond with someone who was actually going to do some fighting.

It felt like Suzuki was out there getting his hands dirty. There was almost no distinction between what Fred felt and he felt at that moment.

Fred's anger, his bloodlust, and his insecurities blended with Suzuki's, and they were inseparable.

Alzor shouted as he tossed his bow to the side and pulled out a broadsword. Two more centaurs stepped out with their swords as well. The orcs, goblins, and remaining centaurs made a ring around the three centaurs and the eldritch imp.

"Are you so weak that you must team up on a shrimpy imp?" a goblin shouted from the outskirts of the ring.

Alzor swung his sword at Fred, who dodged the attack and scampered up the centaur's arm, spitting fire as he ran. He sank his teeth into the centaur's throat, finding the large, pulsing artery and tearing it out in a smooth, clean jerk, then gobbling it down before spewing a jet of flame that incinerated Alzor's body.

Alzor's charred skeleton hit the ground. The other two centaurs backed off but didn't leave the circle as Fred turned to face them. The imp hissed again and sent out a cautionary spurt of fire as he flicked his tongue. "This is the part where you leave," Fred gloated. "Unless you don't value your life. Please remain if you have no fear of death. I will gladly remind your friends why the eldritch ones are not to be mocked."

The centaurs both galloped toward Fred. Suzuki could feel the demon's heart jumping. He'd never seen Fred this excited before, and something about Fred clicked.

He wasn't just an ornery imp with delusions of grandeur; he was something that enjoyed fighting and killing, and not out of any sense of malice.

Suzuki could feel the excitement of being challenged, of testing yourself against odds that could possibly blow up in your face.

Fred was loving it.

So was Suzuki.

Fred dodged the first centaur's blade, skidding across the

dirt. He hardly lost any speed before he jumped, flapped his wings a couple of times, and sailed through the air, landing on the first centaur's face. He opened his mouth, his small jaws stretching to an unnatural size, and poured a slow, seeping slush of magma onto the centaur's face.

The centaur fell to the ground, screaming, clutching at its face, which had been reduced to a gel of skin on top of a bone-white skull. He lay there, convulsing and whimpering in pain as Fred jumped off of his body and walked toward the last opposing centaur, who threw his sword on the ground and retreated from the circle. "Fuck this," the centaur shouted. "You win, you win. All right?"

Fred reared up on his hind legs and looked down at the two centaurs he had killed. "Are you certain? You don't think you can end me?"

"I'm done. You win, all right?"

The orcs and goblins booed as they broke up the circle and returned to their business. Fred stood near the bodies of the dead centaurs, collecting himself, and Suzuki could feel him planning his next move. A rush of Fred's thoughts washed over Suzuki. He understood what Fred had been doing.

Orcs and goblins loved a good fight, and something about it caused their brains to lose interest in everything else. By starting a fight, Fred had caused the goblins and orcs to lose interest in him, while ensuring that the centaurs were too intimidated to question him any further.

It had been a good idea.

Fred walked past the main outer orc camp and ventured farther into the first defense ring. There were small camps set up sporadically. Most of the camps were of one race, but Suzuki could see different races speaking and talking together, just as he had seen earlier. Most of the races were speaking amicably with each other or were working on projects together.

Fred and Suzuki passed a group of goblins building a tower. Orcs helped move some of the larger pieces of lumber.

One of the orcs bumped into a goblin. The orc dropped the large piece of wood it had been lugging around and snapped at the goblin, and they both drew their swords. They circled each other for a moment before the orc cut the goblin down. None of the goblins seemed to notice, other than picking up the goblin's body and dragging it away from the construction zone afterward.

Suzuki reached out to Fred, trying to bridge the small gap between their minds. *Fred, that's not normal, is it?* Suzuki asked.

Fred walked through the construction zone, listening to the orcs and goblins chatter to each other.

No, Suzuki, Fred answered. *It is not. As I've said before, it is extremely uncommon to find goblins and orcs working together. It is even more so for a fight to break out like that and the goblins do nothing to avenge their fallen brother. It is disconcerting. Even more bothersome are the centaurs. Centaurs are not dark creatures. They are neutral. As long as I have been alive, I have never seen centaurs tolerate goblins or orcs. Centaurs make eldritch creatures such as me look humble. They have intense pride in their blood, in their pure stock. They believe creatures such as goblins are beneath them, inferior forms of evolution. To see them trading with goblins and orcs is troublesome. It is no doubt the Dark One's influence. What do you think?*

You're asking me for my opinion?

Fred pursed his lips. *We do not have time for your coyness, human. We are working together. Let's work together efficiently. It is only a matter of time before someone else tries to figure out what I am doing here. I highly doubt there are many eldritch creatures enrolled in the Dark One's schemes. I will be noticed eventually.*

The Dark One was resurrecting that eldritch god.

That is true, Fred agreed. *Perhaps I would rather believe that whatever the Dark One has been doing hasn't touched the eldritch, but you are right. They did rebirth an elder god. Perhaps no one is off-limits.*

Across the camp, Suzuki and Fred heard an ear-splitting scream. A few of the goblins looked up and chuckled. *We should see what that is,* Suzuki suggested. *I know we're here to get Beth, but we gotta figure out what's going on before we can find her. You need to do a better job blending in.*

And how do you suggest I do that?

If anyone asks what you're doing, tell them that you're here to relay information to the viceroy. Tell them that you have information about some elder god or shit. Something that a grunt wouldn't know anything about. If you're going to act all uppity around everyone, you need to put it to good use.

That isn't a bad plan, human, Fred said.

Exactly. You can still be an asshole. This way, you being an asshole won't get us killed. Now let's go check out where that scream was coming from.

Fred made his way toward the scream. It was not difficult to trace. More screams were coming from that way, deep, guttural wailing that sounded as frightened as pained. Fred and Suzuki continued to make their way through the camp, Fred sticking to the side of the crowds of goblins and orcs who walked by, talking as if they were long comrades.

Suzuki felt unnerved by the scene.

He wondered if he was still picking up on Fred's emotions or if being so deep in enemy territory was starting to get to him.

They finally found the source of the screams. This section of the camp was built mostly of tents. There was a corral in the middle of the tents, and it was sectioned off with heavy steel beams that made Suzuki think of a giant cage. The steel beams had huge flickering lights posted on them. The lights flashed brightly every couple of seconds and emitted an odd, high-pitched sound.

Orcs and goblins were rushing back and forth, shouting at each other in garbled voices. They were excited. One of the larger orcs walked through, swinging a large stick and knocking over anyone small or dumb enough not to get out of the way. Goblins walked behind him, rolling over anyone unlucky enough to get hit by the stick. Once a pathway had been cleared, six huge orcs came walking down the pathway. They held chains that were tied to a giant. The giant's head was bowed, pulled down by the chains around its neck.

There were more giants being led by large orcs. Five in total. The orcs prodded the giants with magical staffs causing sparks of lightning to shock the giants anytime they slowed down. Suzuki was reminded of a video he had seen as a child of poachers forcing elephants into cages with cattle prods. The elephants had looked defeated, their deep black eyes pits of despair.

Suzuki saw the same look in the faces of the giants. *That's not right,* Suzuki said.

No, Fred agreed. *It is not. Giants are noble creatures, and some of the oldest. The first giants were carved from the stones of their homes. They are creatures wise beyond the years of mortals. They should not be treated like this.*

Suzuki was surprised to hear Fred speak with reverence about any creature other than himself. A little bit of Fred's mind opened up to Suzuki. He could see Fred's various opinions about the different races in Middang3ard. It was surprising. Suzuki had assumed that the tone Fred took when talking of any of the different races had been that of a snob.

Seeing through Fred's eyes, it was the voice of a tired parent, one who knew his children yet still didn't understand them. Nonetheless, he loved them for their differences, even if he couldn't grasp them.

Fred quickened his pace, flapped his wings, and flew to the top of one of the steel beams. He perched next to one of the flashing lights and leaned forward to watch what was transpiring in the corral.

The orcs had brought in the first giant.

It took a while, but the orcs managed to get the giant into the center and surrounded it. Suddenly, the giant leapt forward, grabbing one of the orcs and slamming it into the ground repeatedly. It turned around and, using the dead orc as a club, smashed another orc into the ground.

Outside the corral, a few of the orcs holding the other imprisoned giants handed their chains to the orc reinforcements running toward them. The giant wranglers stepped into the corral, each of them armed with an electric staff. They circled the giant, who had gone to full berserk mode, mindlessly stomping on anything that moved. His feet fell with enough force to shake the beam that Fred was perched on.

The giant's feet reduced two orcs to mush as it leaned forward and somersaulted through the corral. One of the larger orcs managed to get out of the way and run to the side of the giant pen. "Bring in the ogres!" the orc shouted.

Toward the back of the corral was a long steel shed that stretched a couple of dozen feet. A heavy sliding door cut it off from the corral, and a handful of goblins stood beside it.

When the orc shouted, the goblins climbed up the door and undid its locks.

Two ogres burst out of the opening. Their eyes were bright with bloodlust, their hairy bodies nothing more than corded muscle intent on killing. They were smaller than the giants but faster, more vicious. Their matted hair was soaked with the blood of past battles.

The ogres let out a blood-curdling shriek as they bounded into the corral.

The giant turned its nose up and sniffed the air. It was at this moment, seeing this simple gesture, that Suzuki realized he had never seen a normal giant before. Maybe it was having his memories spliced with Fred's, but Suzuki suddenly realized how off every giant he had ever seen had looked.

Their eyes were always devoid of intelligence. They had a hollowed-out look, as if whatever was once inside them had been gutted and tossed to the side. That was not the case with the giant who was staring down the ogres. His eyes looked sad, as if they understood the monumental challenge that lay before them. Suzuki realized that the giant *did* understand.

Whatever the Dark One was doing to these creatures was beyond simple control.

Fred pierced through Suzuki's mind, bombarding him with images of giants throughout the ages, so many that Suzuki couldn't wrap his mind around all of them. He just let them sink in, allowing them to inform his current perspective.

Yes, yes, Fred said, interrupting Suzuki's train of thought. *But how is he doing it? Why is not nearly as important as how?*

Outside the newly-formed echo chamber in Suzuki and Fred's intertwined minds, the ogres launched their attack on the giant. They surrounded the giant and started raining blows down upon its head. The giant whirled, trying to smack at least one of the ogres, but it was too slow. One of the ogres jumped and drop-kicked the giant in the chest, sending him flying into the steel barricades of the corral.

The giant hit the ground and stayed down. He looked up, his eyes wet with tears, his jaw broken. While the giant lay there in defeat, the three ogres pinned it down. An orc jumped over the side of the corral, holding a massive brand. He was hardly able to hold it up by himself. He leaned against it and scanned the corral for an extra hand. The only other orcs in the corral had been flattened to mush.

Those standing outside the corral didn't look particularly willing to jump back in with the giant.

The orc looked up at the beam Fred was perched on and cleared his throat as he waved Fred down. "Get your ass down here," the orc shouted. "Could use some of that eldritch strength for this."

Fred thought about ignoring the orc for a second but realized that there was no way out of the altercation. He had to pass for one of the Dark One's foot soldiers, so Fred spread his wings and took off, gliding down to the orc.

The giant had stopped struggling.

He lay there, staring blankly ahead, his eyes heavy with defeat as an ogre pressed its knee into the back of his neck. Fred landed by the giant's side as the orc was struggling with the brand. The steel brand was nearly five feet long and thick, shooting off sparks of energy every few seconds. Suzuki couldn't tell what the design on the brand was. It didn't look like any magical runes that he had seen so far. He dipped into Fred's memories and couldn't find anything that remotely resembled the symbol.

After Fred landed, the orc thrust the brand at Fred, who

barely managed to keep from dropping it. Suzuki and Fred could tell the moment that they touched it that the energy coming off of the brand was not magical.

The orc picked up the other side of the brand, and with Fred's help, hoisted it high enough to approach the giant. "All right, you know what to do," the orc grumbled. "Let's just take care of this."

Fred tried to keep his face neutral and betray nothing. "I haven't branded many of these creatures," he said. "Where do the brands for giants go?"

"We just changed them to the neck. Helps pick up the frequency better. Right above the shoulders."

Fred nodded, and the orc guided the brand to the giant's neck. Skin sizzled, and the giant flailed as it screamed in pain. The air filled with the smell of burning flesh. After a little bit, the giant's body went still.

Suzuki heard a light ringing in his head.

It was similar to the ringing his mother had told him signified losing a frequency of hearing. He didn't know if that was true or if it was just some old wife's tale, but he knew the ringing when he heard it. The lights on the steel beams of the corridor flashed brightly in time to the frequency. When the orc removed the brand from the giant, there was a large microchip planted firmly in the giant's neck. The flashing blue light on the chip pulsed in rhythm with the ringing tone and the lights on top of the corral.

The ogres released the giant and backed away. Suzuki noticed that the ogres also had similar chips on the back of their necks.

That was when it clicked for Suzuki.

This was how the Dark One was controlling so many different races. He wasn't uniting them through diplomacy or anything so benevolent. This was mind control, and for some reason, he was using technology instead of magic. Perhaps it was a combination of them both. Either way, Suzuki knew what was being used to control so many races.

It took a bit of time, but the giant stood up. It looked around shakily. There was nothing left of the soft kindness that Suzuki had seen in the giant's eyes as it lay there, waiting to be branded. Instead, the giant looked ahead with hollowed-out, glazed eyes as if he were waiting for an order and had no purpose until then.

Outside the corral, the two other giants shouted. Their words were in their own language. It was a sad, slow, guttural language, and Suzuki realized that he had never heard any of the giants he'd seen speak. He had just assumed that they were too stupid to have a language, that they were just mindless, rampaging, killing monsters. Now he could see how wrong he had been. There was so much more to these giants than he could have assumed. Was that true of the orcs and goblins as well? Had the Dark One stripped each of these races of who they were in the pursuit of control?

The orc with the brand shooed Fred away as he passed the brand to the giant. "Thanks for the help," the orc muttered. "Now get the fuck out of here. We got to get these giants finished up so we can start with the dwarves."

Fred looked around the corral, trying to locate where the dwarves might be kept. "When did the dwarves arrive?" he asked.

"A few days ago. We've been working on new collars and chips for them. They need special chips. So do the elves. And the humans."

"How many dwarves do you have?"

"Just a handful. Our chips burnt on the last batch we had, but these new ones should last."

"And the humans?"

"First round of tests. Captured a group a few weeks back that we're planning on implanting. Soon as we finish up with these assholes," he said, motioning toward the giant who stared dumbly ahead, transfixed by nothing.

"Where are the humans?" Fred asked, trying to sound more curious than prying.

"You sure as hell got a lot of questions..."

"The viceroy sent me to brand the humans," Fred quickly offered. "I was unable to find them due to the sloppy organization of this camp, something the viceroy also expressed a desire to know about."

The orc's face went white and he stumbled over his words. "I didn't know the viceroy had taken an interest in our camps," he mumbled. "They usually aren't this disorganized. You weren't planning on including that in your report?"

"If you prefer, I could include how an orc kept me from being able to fulfill my duties to the viceroy. If you would prefer that report."

The orc threw his hands in the air as he shook his head. "No, no, I'll let you know where the humans are. I wouldn't want to disappoint the viceroy." Then the orc leaned close to Fred. "Are the camps that bad?"

"It should not be nearly this difficult to find the humans."

"We gotta keep them separate from everyone else. They're crafty, and keep finding ways to escape. Between you and me, they're pretty disgusting. But crafty. We found one of them with...uh...their parts in another one's mouth. We went in there to break it up and were ambushed. They almost escaped."

"Yes, humans are known to use their mouths for...unsavory things."

"That's the least of it. Anyway, you can find them over near the eastern section of the second ring. If anyone gives you any trouble, just tell them Mal-der gave you clearance. Hope that goes over with the viceroy well enough."

Fred nodded. "Your cooperation is greatly appreciated. I will inform the viceroy of your diligence and hard work."

"Thank you, thank you. That means a lot, coming from you. It isn't often that we receive an eldritch lieutenant in our camp."

Fred lost his focus for a moment. "A what?" he asked.

"Eldritch lieutenant. You know, eldritch creatures who've been chipped for the Dark One." Mal-der's eyes narrowed suspiciously. "Why wouldn't you have heard of the rank you've received?" he asked.

"Because unlike you pathetic sacks of shit, I did not need to be microchipped to perceive the greatness of the Dark Lord. I willingly joined his ranks."

Mal-der backed off and raised his hands as he bowed his head apologetically. "I'm sorry, my lord," he mumbled. "I did not realize that you were one of the Foresworn. My apologies."

Fred casually bowed his head to acknowledge Mal-der. "Don't worry about it. Continue with your branding, and I will let the viceroy know how hard you are working. That is all."

Fred turned and flew out of the corral, out in the direction that Mal-der had pointed to for the human pens. He landed just in time to see a line of dwarven and elvish prisoners being marched through the camp. They were being driven by orcs who whipped them every few seconds. Their shouts and cries rang throughout the camp. Suzuki tried to see if any of them were MERCs, but their clothes were too tattered.

A vicious roar broke through the camp. The elves and dwarves being herded jumped. Their faces looked broken. Whatever fight they had had was gone. They were cowed, and were being herded like cattle.

Another roar, this one closer. It was loud enough to make Fred jump at the sound. He whipped around, looking for the source of the noise. As he looked upward, three dragons flew by. They were so large that they nearly blocked out the sun.

The dragon in the middle of the flying formation had a heavy chain around his neck. The other two dragons flew down to land, pulling the third dragon by the chain. When they landed, the earth shook.

The chained dragon blew a column of fire across the camp as it tried to pull away. Before the chained dragon could move any farther, the two gray dragons attacked it. Their claws tore into the red dragon's skin, and they blasted it with fire until it roared one last time and lay still, smoke still floating from its skin. Then the two dragons, along with the orcs and goblins standing around, dragged the dragon toward the branding corral. Suzuki noticed the dim, distant look in the gray dragons' eyes. It was similar to that of the giant.

All around the camp, orcs, goblins, centaurs, and gnomes busied themselves. They were moving so quickly that Suzuki and Fred could hardly tell what they were doing.

There was a feeling of urgency, but Suzuki couldn't figure out just what they were doing. Other than the orcs and goblins taking care of the branding, it seemed that the rest of the camp was moving just for the sake of moving. It reminded Suzuki of a bee colony he had seen as a child.

He had been walking with his father through the gardens near his house. His father had wanted to show him something important. In the corner of their backyard was a beehive. They had never touched it. It was understood that if you didn't bother the bees, they wouldn't bother you. That didn't stop their neighbor from setting out pesticides. The poison had gotten to the bees, his father explained as he pointed to the beehive. The bees had all migrated out of the hive and were walking in circles, extremely organized yet driven mad from the pesticides —exactly like the races being controlled by the Dark One.

Fred tried to make his way through what had become a maze of bodies moving back and forth between tents, some of which were empty and others that were filled with dead bodies covered in microchips. The smell of rot and burning computer processors made it almost too much for even Fred to breathe. *Where did the orc say the humans were being held?* Fred managed to utter.

Suzuki concentrated as much as he could to pull himself out of the feelings and thoughts that Fred's mind had descended into. *Over there,* Suzuki said, mentally pointing to a section of the camp outside of the camp. It must have been past the first ridge of defenses.

The second defense ring was not composed of tents. Instead, there were well-made wooden structures and barracks that stretched out into a somewhat mountainous region. There were fewer orcs and goblins. Instead, it looked like the area was patrolled mostly by ogres. Suzuki figured that was because there was no branding going on. This was just for prisoners. The prisoners were probably kept away from the branding area until they were so broken down they couldn't resist.

As Suzuki and Fred tried to get their bearings, they could see a line of humans being herded toward a large, stone building. The humans had the same look as the elves and dwarves they had seen before. Dirty and broken, unable to raise their eyes. Completely broken. "Follow them," Suzuki whispered. "That's where we're going to find Beth."

Fred scampered off to hide in the shadows as ogres patrolled about. Even if there was less going on in this section of the camp, the security was much more intense. If the ogres were only guarding humans, the Dark One must have thought humanity was pretty important.

She's close, Suzuki thought. He could feel it in Fred's gut. The imp and he were barely separate from each other at this moment. They both knew what they were here to do, and nothing was going to stop them. They had seen a glimpse of the perversity of the Dark One's methods. The mission had silently become so much more than rescuing Beth. Once Beth was free, they were going to shut this place down. This was going to be the first step in bringing down the Dark One.

9

———

Suzuki was trying to come up with a plan, but nothing was clicking. Too many ways to fuck this up...and Beth was only a couple hundred feet away.

A couple hundred feet away!

This was what the last few weeks of his life had been leading up to. He needed a plan, a way to get her out of there.

But nothing was coming to him.

Beth was being kept in a prison that was built directly into a stone mountain. It looked like a stony iceberg had been dropped into the Dark One's camp specifically for the purpose of detaining prisoners. The few guards that Suzuki could see were mostly orcs and ogres. Ogres were the muscle. Orcs were providing the smarts, Suzuki expected.

None of the guards seemed to be too focused on what was going on around them. Suzuki thought that he and Fred could sneak in if a distraction was provided. But the rest of the MERCs were outside the camp. If Fred and Suzuki started the distraction themselves, there was no way that they could avoid getting caught.

It seemed like the only option was to try and infiltrate the orc ranks. So far, Fred pulling his rank as an eldritch creature had worked well enough. Maybe that was something they could continue to use to their advantage.

Fred bristled his scales as he prepared to speak with the orcs standing guard at the foot of the mountain. Suzuki was still getting used to what it felt like to share a body with Fred. He would have preferred to be completely focused on his mission, but the flux of Fred's emotions and the way that Fred was responding to his thoughts was still unnerving.

He felt it intertwined in a way that he didn't think was possible with his familiar.

Suzuki reached out to Fred. *So, what do you think we should do?* he asked.

Your thoughts are correct, human, Fred replied. *If we try to distract any of the orcs ourselves, we will get caught. The best option is to try and pass undetected as one of the Dark One's Lieutenants. We will continue to pose as one of the viceroy's officers.*

Are you ready?

As ready as I believe I can be in this situation. Let's go.

Fred took a deep breath, a very human sign of anxiety, and approached the guards. Suzuki felt Fred trying to make himself as physically imposing as possible. It was an odd thing to watch, the imp's internal insecurities manifesting in how he held himself, being aware of his small stature while also aware that he could kill whoever accosted him. However, given the sheer number of the Dark forces, fighting wasn't an option, and Fred had to rely on other means of intimidation.

The orc guards standing outside of the foot of the mountain were flanked by two ogres, who glared at Fred as he approached. The orcs lazily looked up as if they couldn't be troubled to give Fred any of their attention. "The fuck you want?" one of the orcs growled.

Fred hissed and his eyes narrowed as if he had located prey. "This is the holding area for the humans and elves, am I correct?" he asked.

"Who the fuck is asking?"

"The eldritch lieutenant to the viceroy."

The slovenly gaze of the orcs sharpened. They stared at Fred with what could have been construed as an intelligent curiosity. "What here has caught the attention of the viceroy?" the other orc asked.

"A routine security check. The viceroy has heard that security has gotten lax in the first, second, and third rings. I am here to assess the situation and report back to the viceroy."

"Security is good. You can tell that to the viceroy," the first orc replied.

"If you had been given the specific task to check how secure and safe the defenses were, would you so easily be deterred?"

"Like I said, security is good," he repeated.

Fred sighed and shook his head. He folded his arms as he laid his wings against his back. "Listen, I'm not going to bullshit you. I know how you must feel. I'm not here to tell you how to do your job. I get it, guard detail isn't the most appreciated job. How long have you been on-shift?"

The orcs looked at each other. Suzuki noticed they both looked extremely tired. "'Bout five days," one of the orcs said.

Suzuki could feel Fred's mind running, putting together the pieces, grabbing from Suzuki's own observations in real-time. The orcs would have been microchipped like the rest of the races in the camp, but it seemed that the microchips worked differently for each race. Unlike the giants, the orcs didn't seem to have their intelligence or personality destroyed. They were conscious of themselves, more or less. This was probably why they were responsible for a complicated task like guard duty.

Larger creatures such as giants and ogres must have been chipped so that they could provide brute force. The camp couldn't run with only that, though. There had to be some kind of middle ground. That was where creatures such as the orcs and goblins came in. Their microchips must have been specially designed so that they were still capable of being controlled without sacrificing their cognitive abilities.

That also meant that they could be conned.

Fred shook his head, doing the best to mimic what he felt solidarity must look like. "Everyone needs to rest." Fred sighed. "Even orcs. I've heard from some of the other tribes that the majority of the orcs in this camp feel as if their work is not being appreciated."

One of the orcs nodded in agreement. He leaned against the club he held in a posture that Suzuki had often seen overworked construction workers take. "You can say that again," the orc said.

"Listen, I'm not here to bust your ass. I'm not here to look at what isn't working. All I want to do is take a look at how the prison is running and be able to give the viceroy a good report—and put in a good word for the orcs who are working their asses off."

"All right. What do you need us to do?"

"I need to check all of the cells. See the condition of the prisoners. Also, to see the condition of the guards."

"Well, I'll tell you right now, we're all pretty burned out. Fights keep happening. Especially with some of the new recruits."

"Who is in charge here?"

The orc pointed to the mouth of the cave. "Come on, follow me," he said. "I'll introduce you to the boss."

The orc stepped into the mountain and Fred followed him. The tunnel into the mountain was smooth as if it had been carved into the mountain for the express purpose it was being used for. Electric lights were strung along the sides of the wall so that the passageway had the odd look of a black and white Christmas. The hallway continued on until it opened to a cavern with multiple branching passages. There were at least a dozen. "This way," the orc said as he took the path farthest to the left.

The orc continued to guide Fred down the long, stone hallway. There were multiple small rooms on the side of the hall, blocked by gates. Suzuki wondered if these were holding cells. No sound came from them, though. If there were prisoners in the cells, then they were extremely quiet.

As Suzuki walked with Fred down the path, he couldn't help but be reminded of ants. It was almost as if the orcs had burrowed into the mountain with some unconscious need to express their hivemind. This was different than any hive mind that Suzuki had ever read about, however. There was still so much individuality. It made sense, though. For an army as large as the Dark One had created, mindless drones wouldn't ever get the job done.

Finally, they came to the end of the hall. A large wooden door with a slide for viewing separated the tunnel from the room. The orc knocked on the door twice before the slide opened and a pair of beady eyes looked through the slit. "Who is it?" the voice asked.

The orc cleared his throat, perhaps trying to seem more official than he was. He said, "I have a lieutenant from the viceroy to see the captain."

The slide closed, and after a few seconds, the door opened. The orc motioned for Fred to enter, which he did. The door shut firmly behind him.

The captain's office was far from what Suzuki had expected. The walls had been polished even smoother than those of the rest of the cave. There was a large wooden desk in the middle, the sort of desk that you would find in an office. On top of the desk was a massive computer, complete with a holographic screen. The walls were covered with small television screens which piped in feeds of each individual prison cell.

A large orc sat at the desk. He was covered in ceremonial tattoos and was at least a head taller than the orc that had brought them in. His face was covered in scars, one of his eyes dead and white. He stared at Fred from behind the nearly-transparent holo-screen.

In the corner sat a dwarf. He wore a simple black tunic, and he had a healthy, brown beard. He had a clipboard, and he was furiously taking notes on the prisoners shown on the computer screen.

The orc captain rose from his chair and approached Fred. He raised his right hand and pressed it over the middle of his chest as he slightly bowed his head. "It is a pleasure to meet a Lieutenant of our esteemed Viceroy," the captain said. "I am Ogareth, the captain of this re-integration camp. How can I serve the viceroy?"

Fred spoke before either he or Suzuki thought their response. "Reintegration camp?" Fred asked.

Ogareth raised his eyebrow as his lips turned to a snarl, exposing his large bottom fangs. "Yes, reintegration. Is there—"

"My apologies," Fred countered. "The viceroy rarely uses

technical terms. It's usually just theatrical whispers and gestures. You'll forgive my ignorance."

Ogareth chuckled lightly as he relaxed and returned to his seat. He motioned for Fred to take a seat across from his desk. "No, no, that is understandable. I know how the higher-ups can be. Specifically, the viceroy. I'm glad that we don't have to have direct contact with her like those unlucky bastards out in the field."

Fred laughed as well, internally relaxing. He was growing more comfortable with the role that he was playing. Suzuki relaxed as well as he marveled at what the microchips must have been doing to the orcs. The microchips had most definitely turned the orcs into drones... bureaucratic drones.

Listening to the captain talk was like watching a manager at the DMV.

Ogareth cleared his throat, spit out some yellow phlegm on the ground and leaned forward as he folded his hands together in an uncanny middle management position. "So how can I help you?" he asked.

Fred mined Suzuki's memories for a similar position to take, and he thought back to the first time that he had gotten in trouble with his manager at work. He had remembered what his father had told him.

Don't look too submissive.

Cross your legs.

Present yourself as professional as possible.

Fred did just that. "I'm not here to cause any trouble," Fred started. "The viceroy has some general concerns about the security of some of these facilities. How prisoners are treated, whether or not there are any...glaring safety issues. That sort of thing."

"Why would the viceroy be concerned with how the prisoners were treated?" the orc asked.

"Reintegration," Fred said, feigning boredom. "We've been finding that the mental state of prisoners is vital to how well reintegration works."

"Can't say that I really understand that. We're just here to stomp the shit out of them until they get taken away for the reintegration branding."

"Think of it like this, the more shit you stomp out of them, the more space there is for the programming," Fred said.

Ogareth laughed and smacked his knee with his hand. "If that's the case, then there's going to be a lot of space with this new batch. Come on, I'll give you a tour." The orc stood and walked over to the television screens that the dwarf sat by. "What you wanna check out first?"

Fred looked over the screens, hoping that Suzuki would be able to find Beth in the dizzying array of pixels. There were too many screens, though. The orc didn't make it any easier when he swiped to the right, showing even more screens. He continued to swipe, occasionally stopping for a moment, but eventually continuing on. "There's a lot to choose from," Ogareth said. "And this is one of the smaller facilities too. I can't imagine what those assholes up North have to deal with. So what's your poison."

"Humans. I've always had a particular hatred for humans. Particularly military."

"Why not the MERCs?" he asked. "I feel like they're the bigger pain in the ass. The military is easy to track down. Very showy. Picking them off is almost like drowning a baby, if you get my drift. The MERCs are a royal pain in my ass. Just earlier today, I got reports that a handful of those dipshits were trying to make their way down here."

Suzuki's figurative ears perked up. He was glad it was Fred's job to maintain composure right now. "Oh, really?" Fred asked. "How arrogant. What did you do to them?"

"Sent my best chieftain with a raiding party to take care of them. They should be rotting in the fields by now. Ulrag hasn't ever lost a battle. He's a good orc. Glad he came along so willingly."

Fred nodded with approval. "Good riddance. The only good MERC is a dead MERC."

"Never truer words. We don't have any MERCs here, but we got a lot of military. Care to take a look?"

"I'll take the full tour. It would delight me greatly to see the despair on their faces."

"Great. I'll have Ansalm take you. Unfortunately, I'm on paperwork today," Ogareth said.

"Understandable. I'll make sure to mention to the viceroy how hard you've been working."

"Appreciated. We're all doing our best to serve the Dark One."

Ogareth took a seat at his desk and turned back to his work. Meanwhile, Ansalm had gathered up his notebook and a small knapsack. He strode toward the door and waited there politely until Fred picked up on the hint and followed him.

Ansalm didn't speak as he led Fred down the hallway to the main convergence of tunnels. He looked down at his clipboard and twirled his beard as he sighed heavily. "So human military?" he asked. "That's what you're after?"

Fred nodded as he tried to commit the various branches to memory. Suzuki was doing the same. He didn't want to think about what sneaking back into this place was going to look like, but he knew that if they were going to make it work, they couldn't be working blind.

Each turn taken was going to need to be memorized.

The dwarf lowered his clipboard and stared at Fred with his small, brown beetle eyes. "Why the interest in military?" he asked. "We have a ton of humans. Civilians. Villagers. Why are you so keen on military prisoners?"

"Because indoctrinating the ignorant masses is not something that I or the viceroy is concerned with. Sheer numbers may be intimidating, but I am much more interested in the captives who show combat potential."

The dwarf smiled with a crooked, sinister display of teeth. "Good enough for me," he said. "Let me show you the way."

Ansalm walked to the right of the cavern and choose one of the pathways. He briskly walked past Fred, and Fred had to run to catch up with the dwarf. Despite his short legs, Ansalm could move. His walk was practically a jog. Fred opted to fly down the cramped tunnel instead of trying to keep up with the dwarf.

Suzuki was still attempting to keep track of each turn the dwarf took. It gave him time to try to understand what he had witnessed in the captain's quarters. Whatever the microchips were doing to the orcs, it wasn't only making them bureaucratic, but also extremely efficient. His earlier thought of them being something like the DMV had been completely off. The orcs were operating with the seamless fluidity of the Gestapo, and somehow the efficiency was more horrifying than if the Dark One had just been manipulating the orcs through mind control. The casual tone the captain had taken about torture and breaking prisoners was frightening.

Was that what they were doing to Beth? Suzuki didn't want to think about it, but he already knew the answer.

Beth was military.

She was strong.

If there was anyone who the orcs were going to try and break, it was going to be Beth. Suzuki knew it didn't matter, though. He knew that Beth could take it.

Whatever the Dark One's forces were trying to throw at her, she could take it.

Ansalm continued to guide Fred down the winding tunnels, taking turns right and left almost at random. Suzuki could feel himself getting lost. It didn't matter how much he tried to pay attention to what was going on. Right. Left. It didn't matter. He could vaguely tell that they were descending deeper into the mountain, but he had no way of orienting himself.

Farther and farther into the mountain they went. Suzuki could feel Fred's anxiety. It was something more than losing his place. Suzuki could feel Fred's fear of enclosed spaces, a form of claustrophobia, a feeling born from the freedom of the sky. Fred was trying to keep it together, but he was counting the seconds until he could run screaming out of the mountain.

Suzuki tried to unfold himself onto Fred. He imagined himself as a warm blanket and hoped that the sentiment could be understood. *Come on, Fred*, he said. *"We gotta keep it together. We're almost there.*

How do you know, human? Fred snapped. *All of this looks the same. I have no idea how you and the other humans can stand places like this. There's no air. I feel like I'm suffocating.*

It's just in your head, Fred. We'll be out of here soon enough.

The sooner, the better. It's taking everything out of me not to kill this dwarf and be done with this entire plan.

Ansalm looked back as if he could read Fred's mind. "We're almost to our first batch of prisoners," Ansalm gleefully cooed. "I believe that you'll be quite impressed with our work so far. Please, do tell the viceroy what we've been up to." The dwarf stopped walking. He turned to his left and pointed at a cell. "Would you like to see what's inside?"

Fred did his best to force a grin. "Please, I'd like nothing else," he hissed.

Ansalm took a light from the side of the wall and waved it in front of the cell's bars. The light cast dimly. Fred strained his eyes to see. Even with his heightened sense, he could barely make out what was inside the cell. "Would you like to step inside with me?" Ansalm asked.

Fred nodded. "If it would help me to see your work, yes."

Ansalm pulled out what looked like a remote from his pocket. He waved it over the cell and Fred heard the cell unlock. The door swung open with a faint creak.

Even with the light, it was difficult to see. By the time Fred and Suzuki's eyes adjusted, they both wished that they had not.

The cell was filled with bodies. It was difficult to tell if they were still alive. The smell did not help. Something was rotting.

Ansalm shined a light on the cell's contents. A man sat in the corner of the cell, holding his arms close to his chest as he shivered. His body was covered in sores, his chest completely bare and split down the middle, where his heart could be seen pumping from inside his ribs.

Suzuki fought the urge to vomit.

Fred fought the urge to run from the room.

Ansalm continued to shine the light on the contents of the room as Fred tried to avert his eyes. When the light shone upon his face, he grinned grimly, flashing his teeth so they caught the light from the lantern.

The inhabitants of the room realized there were other people in the room with him. That was when the lamentations began. The cell flooded with the cries of the damned, the begging, the hope of an ending to suffering. The cell was a bedlam of pain.

"Do you believe this will please the Dark One?" the dwarf asked.

Fred stifled the urge to purge himself. Suzuki wondered absentmindedly as he retreated to a part of Fred's mind where he could cope whether Fred was reacting to his feelings of disgust or if they were genuine. "The Dark One will be pleased," Fred managed.

"Wonderful. Would you like to see what we have in store for the...how should I say...more ardent prisoners?"

"Please."

Ansalm and Fred exited the cell and the doors clanked loudly as they closed. Then they turned to the tunnels, which grew ever darker as they progressed. Suzuki could no longer focus on the direction they were turning.

He did not see any more cells or any more turns. All he could see were the faces of the military officers hanging from walls, screaming, asking, and pleading for an end to their suffering.

The walls grew closer as they trod through the dark tunnels of despair and pain. Neither Fred nor Suzuki were aware of how long they walked, the demon's wings flapping monotonously as Ansalm's quick feet continued on their path.

Finally, Ansalm stopped. He pointed to a cell and nodded, grinning gleefully. Fred opened the cell and stepped in. Ansalm followed and closed the door behind him.

The cell was empty save for a few chains. Ansalm shone his light on the bareness of the cell. His voice cracked when he spoke. "This is the cell we reserve for traitors," Ansalm whispered, his voice low and ominous. "It is a privilege to see this cell...unless you have transgressed."

Suzuki felt Fred muster all of his courage. "Then why have you brought me here?" Fred asked.

Ansalm looked at Fred. His expression was pure and simple. "You are a traitor, are you not?"

A thousand responses flashed through Suzuki's head. None of them would have helped; he understood that they were outed.

This was going to be the end.

They would have to kill Ansalm and hope to find some way out of this labyrinth. Then they could find Beth.

"I am no traitor," Fred said.

Ansalm smiled sweetly. "Oh, you aren't? I saw how you looked at those prisoners. There was sympathy in your eyes. Even such a creature as you could feel sympathy for their pain. It was so obvious, as if you had lost your eldritch power. As if humans had tainted you."

Ansalm reached behind his back. He withdrew a small remote and pointed it at the wall. There was a bright flash of light. He was still smiling when Suzuki and Fred could again see his face. "You're a MERC, aren't you?" Ansalm asked.

Fred said nothing.

Ansalm rushed to the door and closed it behind himself. He was still smiling, but the sickly sweetness had evaporated. "Thank the gods." He sighed. "You have no idea how long I've been waiting for you."

10

———

Ansalm's eyes looked hollow and he breathed very slowly as he crossed the room.

There was hardly any space in the small cell. If they attacked, that would work to their advantage. Fred knew that he was faster than the dwarf.

Stronger, too.

He'd be able to eliminate the dwarf before there were any witnesses. Burn the body, take the clipboard, and make their way through the maze of cells.

The dwarf raised his hands in a sign of submission. "Wait, wait," he whispered. "I know what you must be thinking. Hear me out. I'm on your side." He pulled out a small badge and presented it to Fred and Suzuki.

The badge had the MERC insignia on it.

Fred's scales bristled as he eyed the dwarf. "What the hell is going on here?" Fred asked.

"You think that all that MERC has up its sleeve is brute force? We needed to see what the Dark One was doing on the inside. I'm part of the Espionage Department."

"I didn't realize that MERC had spies."

"What good is having spies if everyone knows that you have spies? We try to keep that information to ourselves. I've been waiting for someone to try and infiltrate this camp. Couldn't have asked for a better person, myself."

"Better person?"

"You're Suzuki's familiar, right? Isn't José with you?"

Fred shook his head. "No, José did not accompany us."

"But he's on the mission, right?"

"He is, but we entered the camp ourselves. We thought it would be wiser if we separated."

"It wasn't a bad idea," the dwarf said. "Security here is tough. I'm surprised that you made it this far. Changing places with your host was a smart idea. Pretty sure you'd be dead otherwise."

"What have you been doing here? Have you learned anything about—"

"Let me just stop you there. Almost nothing. I've been posing as one of the dwarves that defected to the Dark One's side. There's a shit ton who joined up with him. They figured that it was better than being dead. Can't blame them. They aren't warriors. But I don't have a microchip, so the orcs tend to keep me at a bit of a distance, even with the fabricated paperwork. This place is like a goddamn office. Most of the communication isn't done person to person. It's done through the microchips, direct data transfer. Everything is on a need to know basis. I've been scraping by what I can get so that I can make this work, but I'm going to get found out eventually."

"And what is your plan to get around this?" Fred asked.

"There's one. I'm going down with the ship. Unless this camp gets taken out, I'm dead. The least that I can do before I get found out is spring some of our guys. Our military guys, I should say. There are no captured MERCs here."

Ansalm smiled with a little bit of pride. "Take no prisoners, leave no prisoners. But you're looking for military folks?"

Suzuki couldn't hide his excitement and forced Fred to say, "A young woman named Beth."

"I don't know any names. The Dark One doesn't care about any of that shit. All I know is cells with humans, elves, and dwarves and whether they're civilians or not. It's military that you're after? Let's see what I got..."

Ansalm looked through his clipboard. He flipped through pages, chewing on a pen. Suzuki couldn't get over the mundaneness of the situation. The MERC spy was just a pencil pusher. Who would have thought that it would be such a vital and important position to have infiltrated? Ansalm probably didn't think it was too glamorous. Especially with his impending death hanging over him.

Suzuki could feel Fred approaching him mentally. *Do you think that we can trust him?* Fred asked.

Suzuki nodded, not that Fred saw it. *He did show us the badge.*

That could have been provided by the Dark One, Fred said.

I think he's good. If he's full of shit, we can just come back and kill him later.

Sounds good to me.

Ansalm looked up from his notebook and turned it around for Fred to see. "So, we got multiple levels of cells. They're all mixed up. There isn't really any order to any of it. We just have some tagged, and others we don't bother with. The military ones are what we tagged. New and old arrivals too. How long has your guy been here?"

"They were captured roughly two weeks ago."

"They're probably dead."

Fred watched Ansalm's matter-of-fact face. It was as if working in a bureaucratic office of the Dark One had rubbed off on the dwarf's bedside manner. "What do you mean, she's probably dead?" Fred asked.

The dwarven MERC pursed his lips. "Most of the military is processed for reintegration within a week. If they can't break them by then, they kill them."

"Beth is still alive."

The MERC turned his head, confused. "How do you know? Have you been in contact?"

"No," Fred admitted. "But I know. She's still alive."

"If you say so. Come on, we'll take a look at the feeds. There should be another control room that we can check out that has a bit more privacy."

Ansalm turned to the door, opened it, and stepped outside. He turned to Fred and motioned for Fred to follow.

Fred ducked his head low as he walked forward. He still had misgivings about the situation. Anyone could come up with a fake badge and a sob story. Neither of those meant anything alone. This could easily be a trap.

Suzuki picked up on Fred's thoughts and reached out to present his own. It could be a trap. There was no way around that possibility. If they were realistic, though, it would take a lot of foresight to assume that the Dark One's camp had prepared for the specific situation of a MERC switching bodies with a familiar by providing a dwarf who didn't have microchips to pose as a MERC spy.

Possible, but highly unlikely.

It still feels too convenient, Fred thought. *We could be walking into a deathtrap.*

Well, this is a time for you to show off just how strong an eldritch creature you are, Suzuki countered.

My powers...ugh, I hate having this conversation with you, human. But my powers are not what they used to be. They have been dormant for too long. I am still recovering from the skirmish we got into earlier.

Are you serious?

If we find ourselves in trouble, I will have to revert back to your body. And you will most likely be killed.

Yeah, I kind of figured the killed part. I didn't need you to spell it out. We... Fuck it, we might as well see how this pans out.

Fred and Suzuki followed Ansalm down the winding paths of the prison caverns. Distance had ceased to have any meaning some time ago. They walked in near darkness, the only light occasionally coming from lanterns flickering on the side of the polished stone walls. They moved silently as if they were ghosts. They were prisoners themselves, perhaps.

After some time, Ansalm turned a corner and opened a door. Inside was a room covered in television screens. There were an orc and a goblin sitting in front of the screen, snacking on large pieces of roasted meat. They looked up at Ansalm and Fred as the dwarf and the imp walked into the room.

Fred's body tensed.

This was the fight that he was worried about, and Suzuki prepared himself to take back control of his body. One orc and goblin? Plus a middle age, slightly overweight dwarf?

Suzuki could probably tear through them before either one of them realized what was happening.

Ansalm stepped across the room and placed his hand on the orc's shoulder. "Take a hike, you guys," he ordered.

The orc and goblin grumbled as they got out of their chairs. "No one's up to anything," the orc complained. "You'll be lucky if you even see a tit."

The two foot soldiers shuffled out of the room and closed the door behind them. Ansalm sat at the chair and waved a control scheme into existence in front of the holo-screens.

Fred stood beside the dwarf. "What were they talking about?" he asked.

"There's a couple of peeping tom viewing rooms. Sometimes the prisoners get desperate and try to make the last moments of their lives a little less grim. There's a general understanding between the guards that you'd like some privacy to...alleviate your frustrations at the prisoners' plight. I've found that these rooms are the easiest to check in on prisoners without being disturbed. Even orcs don't want to walk in on each other with their dicks in their hands."

"Interesting way to do your job, but you must enjoy—"

"It's nothing I enjoy," the dwarf said. "I enjoy not being tortured and reintegrated. So, if you please, look through these screens and find your friend. Maybe we can get her out of here if it isn't already too late."

Fred turned his attention to the screen. There were too many to count. Each of the cells was filmed from a corner of the ceiling. It was difficult to make out anyone's face. Suzuki tried to push himself closer to the forefront of Fred's mind. He knew he would recognize Beth the moment that he saw her.

All he needed was a glimpse.

They flipped through screen after screen. Soldiers lay or sat on the ground, some of them propped against the wall. The few faces they did see looked drained of all life. It was looking at a corpse in a mocking parody of the living.

There!

Fred stopped scrolling through the screens. In the bottom corner screen, there was a group of soldiers standing, some of them pacing. One of them had short hair, and she kept throwing glares at the security camera. Out of nowhere, she threw a rock at the camera and flipped it off. Then she went and sat in a corner as she crossed her legs and stared up at the device.

Fred pointed to the screen. "That's Beth," Fred said. "That's who we're looking for."

Ansalm nodded and enlarged the screen. "She is still alive... Oh, it's her," Ansalm muttered.

"What do you mean, 'it's her?'"

"She's been a massive pain in the ass to the captain. I personally respect her. A few days ago, she talked her fellow soldiers into having a—what do humans call it?—circle jerk? When the guards came in to break up the flagrant breach of conduct, she slipped out of the cell. She killed five guards singlehandedly in the dark before the captain was able to bring her in. Then she got thrown in solitary, which was an even worse idea. She managed to convince a guard who was bringing her food to get close enough to the door so that she impaled his toe with a poison dart. She killed ten more guards when they attempted to silence her."

"Why isn't she dead yet if she's causing so much trouble?"

Suzuki had wondered the same thing, but he was overjoyed to know that Beth was still alive, although he didn't understand why the captain would deal with her causing so much trouble when he could just have had her killed.

Ansalm sighed and shook his head. "Reintegration," he explained. "If you haven't noticed, most of the orcs and goblins working here aren't just mindless drones. They have personality. Honestly, if I didn't know how the whole operation worked, I would have assumed that they were happy volunteers. But it's the reintegration. The stronger the personality prior to being chipped, the more cognitive function that remains afterward.

"That's how the Dark One has managed to not only build such a massive army, but also have generals who are competent. The captain is grooming her for reintegration, slowly breaking her down with her time here. And when she's ready to kill herself, he was planning on swooping in and giving her an option—or taking her by force. She's actually been scheduled to be taken to another holding facility today."

"We need to get to her as soon as possible."

"What's with the sense of urgency? This seems like more than just MERC business."

"This isn't MERC business," Suzuki forced Fred to shout. "This is *my* business. MERC didn't send anyone to break her out. I came here for that."

Ansalm sighed and took his clipboard back. "That is a shame," he said. "I was hoping my reports were being seen. Still, it's better that you're here than no one at all."

"So how do I get to her?" Fred asked.

"It won't be easy. I'll have to guide you there from the control room."

"I would prefer to be told. I have an exceptional sense of direction."

The dwarf shrugged. "Not in a place like this. It isn't just designed to get you lost, it's designed to ensure you end up alone, insane, and ready to serve the Dark One until your dying days."

Ansalm held out a MERC earpiece for Fred to take. Fred slid it into his ear and felt it instantly connect to Suzuki's neural HUD network. "Like I said," Ansalm repeated, "I'll guide you. Just listen to me, and you'll get to your friend. And...will you do me a favor?"

"It depends how much it puts my life at danger."

"Open any cell that you can. No one will notice, not even

the prisoners. They've been here so long, they won't even know what's going on. I know you weren't sent to take this camp down, but you have no idea what we could do by starting a riot. That's the one thing the Dark One didn't think of when he commissioned this place to be built. It never crossed his mind that anyone would escape, let alone lead a riot."

"Fine. Let me know where to go, and I'll free anyone along the way."

Fred stepped closer to Ansalm. He bared his fangs, and the fire burning within his stomach poured smoke out of his nostrils. "And if this is a trick," Fred growled. "I will return, and I will reduce you to ash. Then I will find your loved ones. I will make your entire lineage pay."

Ansalm took a step back and straightened his tunic. He didn't seem fazed by Fred's threats. "I know that was meant to be horrifying, but after working here a few months, well, let's just say you're going to have to try harder to be scarier than the Dark One. But trust me, I am not tricking you. I want to see those soldiers out just as much as you do."

"Then let's get going."

Ansalm kicked the door open for Fred. When Fred closed the door, he heard Ansalm's voice in his ear. "Go right."

Fred listened and started to make his way down the hall. He and Suzuki had spent so much time beneath the earth that they were unable to tell one hall from the other. The only frame of reference they had was the occasional direction from Ansalm. As they walked down the tunnels, orcs and goblins led prisoners back and forth. Most of the prisoners could hardly walk, their faces covered in bloody bruises. Occasionally, they were supported by the orcs who guarded them and berated them as they were dragged through the dark, hellish tunnels.

Suzuki felt as if he were locked in the body of a giant monster. He was a blood cell speeding through a vein along with thousands of other blood cells in sections of the body that he didn't even know existed. Above was the brain. Only something horrible could be deeper in the mountain.

Suzuki wondered how much longer Beth was going to last. He wasn't sure how long any of the prisoners that he had passed by had been in the dark, but they all looked ready to crack. Beth was stronger. A few months ago, he would have said that she was the strongest one in the party. That was not an opinion he would stick to anymore. Sandy and Stew were completely different people than the kids who had first stepped into Middang3ard. He hoped that he was as well.

Fred turned another corner, and Suzuki pulled himself out of his thoughts. He noticed a cell full of humans and elves that was unguarded. Fred went to the cell and peered in.

One of the prisoner's flinched at the sight of Fred's glowing eyes. Fred's fingers found the latch for the lock, which he undid silently and quickly before disappearing back into the dark of the tunnel. Suzuki half expected the prisoners to come running out of their cell.

No one left.

It might take them some time to get the strength to risk escaping, Suzuki thought.

Ansalm was still relaying directions to Fred. "How much longer are we going to be doing this?" Fred asked, obviously annoyed. "The prison cannot be this large."

"It isn't," Ansalm replied. "There are small teleportation devices throughout the tunnels. Think of it this way: for every step you take, that's two backward as well. It takes a considerable amount of time to navigate. Did you have any idea about how you and your military friends are going to get out of here?"

"We hadn't thought that far ahead. I am trying to, how do you say, play it by ear."

"Well, you're doing a great job so far. I'll let you know if I think of anything."

The longer they traveled the tunnels, the more lost Suzuki felt. He was tired of sitting by and not doing anything. He knew there wasn't much he could do, but all the same, he would have preferred if he were at least in his own body. This was just irritating. It was like being stuck in the backseat while on a road trip. You might be seeing the same thing as the driver and passenger, but somehow, it was tedious and lonely.

Fred passed by another cell of soldiers. He didn't bother looking inside. He just unlatched the door and continued on. Neither Suzuki nor Fred was paying attention to how many cells had been opened after a time. They had no idea where they were or how long they had been walking. There was only Ansalm's voice, the only guarantee that they were not stuck in some nightmare, occasionally bringing them back to reality.

"Wait, stop here."

Fred halted.

"These are high-priority prisoners. They need to be released."

Fred turned to the cell on his right and reached out to unlock it. A hand came out from behind the cell and grabbed Fred's wrist. Fred instantly tensed, preparing to bite the fingers off whoever had touched him. Suzuki asserted his personality over Fred's for a moment, giving the imp a second to think before acting too rashly.

The prisoner held onto Fred's hand. "What are you doing here?" the soldier asked weakly.

Fred said nothing and tried to remove his hand from the imprisoned soldier's grasp.

"I asked you a question, imp."

"You are not in a position to be asking questions," Fred said.

"So why not answer then? You don't have anything to lose, do you?"

Fred ripped his hand from the soldier's. Then he unlatched the cell door and swung it open.

The soldiers within the cell stared blankly at the imp as the cell door creaked. "What are you doing?" the soldier asked.

"Freeing you," Fred answered.

A soldier in the back of the cell tried to get to his feet. He fell over, and another soldier helped him get upright. "Don't trust him," the infirm soldier said. "It's a trick."

Fred raised his hands as if it would put the soldiers at ease. "No trick," Fred assured them. "You're free to go."

The soldier nearest the cell scoffed loudly. "Oh, yeah." He laughed. "Like the Dark One is just going to let us go."

"The eldritch do not serve the Dark One."

"Tell that to my buddies who got smoked by one."

"An eldritch who serves the Dark One loses the right to call himself eldritch. You are free to leave. I suggest you free as many of your friends as you can on your way out."

The soldiers watched Fred from inside the cell. Even when Fred had turned and left, they were slow to leave. When they did decide to leave the cell, they had pried bars off of the cell. Their eyes were full of fire and fight.

Suzuki flared up in Fred's mind. *That was stupid*, he shouted. *They're going to tell someone the moment that they get caught.*

Fred chuckled as he turned a corner via Ansalm's instructions. *Suzuki, I fear that you may have less faith in your compatriots than I do*, he replied.

I'm just saying it was a stupid idea. You could have just left. What was that? Trying to help the eldritch reputation or something?

If the Dark One's forces are indeed as vast as they are beginning to seem, it would be in our best interest if the military and MERCs knew that just because they perceive us to be evil, that does not mean that we are all lining up to sell our souls to a megalomaniac with delusions of grandeur. When the fight is brought to the Dark One, I hope to be fighting as an equal, rather than a suspect.

Hmm. Suzuki didn't know what to say. He hadn't heard Fred imply anything other than disgust for anything that wasn't eldritch or ancient, and he had yet to hear Fred take such a strong stance on the Dark One. Mostly Fred had only mentioned how uncomfortable seeing multiple races working together was. Now Suzuki was seeing that that discomfort may have been deeper than a sense of pride.

They traveled for what seemed like another hour.

The sheer boredom was causing Suzuki to slip back into Fred's subconscious. It was not a place he wanted to go. Every time he felt himself sliding into the dark, it was as if he were losing himself. It was growing increasingly difficult to keep himself afloat among the waves of unconscious memory when all he could see through Fred's eyes was the infinite stone walkways and flickers of light. He wondered if it was the same way for Fred as well.

When Fred was living in Suzuki's pocket dimension,

Suzuki could hardly tell that Fred was there. Is it because he was drowning in Suzuki's subconscious? Maybe the imp was just better at keeping himself grounded. Regardless, Suzuki was sinking. He only faintly remembered what they were in these tunnels for. Maybe that had been part of Ansalm's plan. To drive them so far into the tunnels that they forgot themselves. It could be a part of the reintegration.

Suzuki felt Fred pierce his thoughts. When Fred spoke, it sounded far away, too far away to be real. *Yes, I was having the same doubts*, Fred said.

What? What are you talking about?

Ansalm. If he did mean to reintegrate us, driving us insane in the bowels of a mountain would make us quite susceptible to the reintegration.

Fred shook his head. *But we've been releasing prisoners...*

It could be a ploy to gain our trust. If we could be this lost, think of the prisoners. We probably just released them to be driven mad.

Fred sat down and leaned against the wall. *This does not bode well.*

They sat there, panic seeping in. The walls were closing in around them. The tunnels were smaller, hotter than before. Guards would be patrolling through the area soon. Fred and Suzuki were suddenly filled with the desire to end the mission, to find their way out as soon as possible.

It was the walls. They were tightening. Suzuki could feel them choking him. This was where they were going to wander until their dying days. They were lost. Ansalm had played them. This was going to be where they went mad.

We're not going to go mad. Fred sighed.

I didn't think we were going to, Suzuki retorted.

I could feel what you were thinking. You were panicking.

I wasn't. I felt that coming from you.

Fred was silent for a little bit. *This is why it generally is frowned upon for humans to switch places with their familiar. It becomes...difficult to keep yourselves separate.*

It doesn't feel like you've been having a hard time so far.

If I had not been so preoccupied with keeping you out of my mind, Fred said, *I might have seen that this was obviously a trap. And if you weren't so consumed with me, you would have as well.*

That almost sounds like a compliment.

What part of that sounds like a compliment? Fred asked.

The part where you think I would have done the same thing as you.

It is not. Merely an acknowledgment.

You do think that this is a trap? Suzuki asked.

At this point, I cannot tell. All that I can say for certain is that we are lost. Do you have any backup plans?

I think our best plan is to kill our way out.

Fred laughed. It was stressed but had a hint of something Suzuki had yet to hear in Fred's voice: comradery. *We continue to follow the dwarf's instructions?*

Do we have any other choice right now?

Fred rose and started to walk again. *No, I suppose not. Let's get back to it.*

Suzuki's legs felt heavy. They might give out at any moment. It wasn't the physical strain. Something about the mountains had been sapping strength from both of them since they'd first entered. It must have been some form of defense from the Dark One. Fred probably would have picked up on it if the defense had been magical in nature. Suzuki assumed that it was tech, though. What he wouldn't have given to have brought the Chipmaster along for the ride. She would have been able to help with the situation.

Ansalm's voice broke Suzuki's thoughts. "Turn left up here," Ansalm said. "This should be your friend's cell."

Fred pressed himself against the side of the wall. *What are the odds that we're walking into an ambush?* he asked.

Eight out of ten.

We could split up. That way, you could take a few out, and I could, as well. We could go out in a blaze of glory, as you humans call it.

Eh, I say we hold on it. You never know.

Fred sighed and nodded in agreement. Then he turned the corner.

The hallway was empty. It dead-ended at a single cell. Fred went to the cell and unlocked it. He slowly swung the door open.

Beth sat in the corner, and she looked up as the door creaked open. Her eyes were bright and fiery. It didn't look like the hellish living conditions had gotten to her. Other than Beth, the cell was empty.

"You're who they sent to get fucked up today?" Beth asked as she stood up. "Let's get started."

Here she was. Alive. In the flesh. Still strong, still defiant. Still everything Suzuki loved and admired. He needed to be closer to her, to let her know that he'd come to get her out of this shithole. Suzuki surged forward, and Fred lost the reins of his body. For a moment, it was Suzuki's. He was running toward Beth, his arms outstretched, ready to pick her up in an embrace.

Suzuki got one of his arms around Beth. He was over-flowing with things to say. He felt her arms around his shoulders, returning the embrace. Then he felt them tighten. He looked in her face, and there was murder in her eyes. "You're going to have to try harder than that," Beth shouted as she picked Fred up and body-slammed him to the ground. Then she rolled over on top of him and commenced to strangle the life out of his body.

Fred gasped for breath as he tried to figure out what to do to let Beth know that he was on her side. Suzuki could hardly keep himself from laughing, even though he could feel the life slowly choking in him. He should have known better than to surprise Beth with anything.

Beth clenched her fingers tighter around Fred's throat. "Fuck you," Beth growled. "Fuck your Dark One. Fuck your parents. I'm taking you out."

Fred cackled softly as Suzuki's personality bubbled to the forefront. "You taking me out, douchenozzle?" he asked.

Beth let go of Fred and jumped back. "What the fuck did you just say?"

"Douchenozzle. I was referring to you, just so you know."

"Suzy?"

"In the red, scaly flesh."

"Oh, my God."

Beth threw her arms around Fred. Her body trembled with tears as she cried. "I knew you were coming," she whimpered. "I told them you were going to get me out of here."

Fred held Beth in his arms, pulling himself back so that Suzuki could be more present. They stood there for a while, Suzuki in Fred's body, holding her tightly as Beth cried the last few weeks into his shoulder. Then they were silent for some time.

Beth pulled away from Suzuki and Fred. "How the fuck did you get here?" Beth asked.

"Not important," Suzuki answered. "We have to figure out how we're getting out."

Beth walked to the threshold of the cell. She peeked her head outside it. "You have no idea how long I've been waiting to look past this fucking cell. I swear to God, I would have ripped these bars out and beat every fucking orc to death if I could have."

"We're going to get out of here," Suzuki said. "Then we'll figure out what to do."

"I'm not leaving without my squad."

"Well, where the fuck are they?" Suzuki asked.

"No idea."

"Hey, Ansalm. You down for springing more kids?"

There was a crackle over the earpiece. "You fucking bet I am," Ansalm whooped.

Fred placed his hand on Beth's shoulder. "All right, we're getting your guys out. Let's get at it."

Beth clapped her hands and gave Fred a hug. "Fuck," she whispered as she pulled away. "This is really fucking weird."

Fred raised his hand in a sign of deference. "Please hold on," Fred said.

Suzuki felt something pulling on his stomach. Then his skin felt like it was inside out and he was coughing, trying to pick himself off of the ground. He looked down at his hands. Fred had reversed their possession. Suzuki stood and looked into Beth's eyes with his eyes, for the first time in months.

Beth touched Suzuki's cheek. "It's really you," she whispered. "Holy fucking shit, it's really you."

Suzuki felt Beth's rough hands across his face. He had never felt her hands across his face. His heart was in his throat, beating faster than it had ever beaten before. "Yeah, I'm here," Suzuki murmured. "I'm here."

Beth embraced Suzuki, her heart was racing against his. She was trembling, and still crying. "I didn't think it was going to be like this," she said finally after breaking the embrace. She was still holding onto him, her arms around his waist. "But I'm glad it's you getting me out of this shithole."

"Glad you waited around for me."

"Fuck off. Fuckin' douchenozzle."

"I'm assuming every dude in the military was lining up to save you."

"Well, at least you showed up. Honestly, I don't even know if anyone noticed we were captured. There hasn't been—"

"No one knows. No one ever knows. Apparently, a load of MERCs got captured, and no one knew about it. The Dark One is picking MERC and military off, and no one is even noticing."

Beth nodded and looked around the cell as if she were trying to piece something together. "It makes sense. There's too many of them. We're losing people and can't even keep track of them. That's what happens when you fight an infinite army."

"Fuck it. We need to get out of here. We'll figure out what to do about that later."

"What do you mean we'll figure out what to do about that later?"

Suzuki turned to Beth. "The Dark One," Suzuki said. "We'll figure out what to do about the Dark One once we get out of here."

Beth laughed. There was a tad bit of mania in her voice. "What are you talking about? Taking on the Dark One?"

"You're fucking right I'm talking about taking on the Dark One."

"Suzuki, we're outgunned. Have you seen this place? This is only a fraction of what he's capable of. How the fuck do you think we're going to take him on?"

"That's what we're here for. Did you forget that?"

Beth looked down at her feet. After a few seconds, she looked up at Suzuki and smiled weakly. "Wasn't expecting to hear that from you," she said. "You've changed, Suzy. In a good way."

"All I've thought about for the last few weeks is getting you back. But I haven't forgotten why we're here to begin with. Someone needs to stop the Dark One. And that's going to be the Mundanes."

11

———

The plan was simple enough. Suzuki, Fred, and Beth were going to sneak out of prison and return to spring the rest of Beth's platoon. On paper, it sounded like a great idea, and as long as Suzuki didn't think too much about the technicalities, it seemed like something that could easily be done. Ansalm had been able to lead Fred and Suzuki to Beth, why wouldn't he be able to lead them to the other soldiers?

Fred and Suzuki switched their bodies back. Beth looked a little unnerved by standing alone in her cell with the imp. Hearing Suzuki's voice coming from the imp had been a little disconcerting.

"So, we found a mole in the Dark One's fortress," Suzuki said.

Beth nervously checked outside of her cell. "Convenient," she murmured. "And it's not a trap?"

"That's what we thought too, but it's been working out so far."

Ansalm's voice crackled over Fred's earpiece. "You know I can hear you guys, right?"

"Oh, yeah. Guess I kind of forgot about that. You *aren't* setting up an elaborate trap, are you?"

"Honestly, if I had that kind of planning and foresight, I wouldn't be working a bullshit spy gig in the heart of the Dark One's prison camp. I wish I had that level of cunning."

"So where to?" Beth asked.

"All right, first you're going to head left. Then—"

Suzuki could hear the sound of a door opening over the earpiece. Then there was some scuffling and a couple of loud voices. It sounded like someone was shouting, then silence.

"Ansalm?"

No reply.

"Ansalm!"

Still nothing.

Suzuki tossed his arms up in defeat. He knew that everything had seemed way too easy. When did anything ever really go according to plan?

Beth crossed the room and clapped her hand on Suzuki's shoulder, and Suzuki's heart raced. He knew she was trying to comfort him. He must have looked extremely stressed out. Even when they had been playing on VR, Beth always seemed to be able to tell when Suzuki was getting ready to lose his cool. "Your mole get dug up?" Beth asked.

Suzuki nodded as he tried to keep himself from pacing, a bad habit that he knew always annoyed Beth a little. It annoyed him a great deal more. "Yeah, that's what it sounds like," Suzuki said. "Fuck. That was supposed to be our way out of here."

"What's the back-up plan?"

"Honestly, I don't have one," Suzuki admitted. "I've kind of been making this one up as I've been going."

"Oh, free-balling, eh? Didn't know that you had it in you. Isn't that more Stew's role?"

Suzuki chucked. "Eh, yeah... gotta try new things, right? Don't want to be the same emotionally stagnant and timid jack-off that you've always known, right?"

"Uh...that seems a little self-deprecating but all right."

Suzuki laughed nervously. He almost felt like he was on a first date or something, which was ridiculous given where they were.

It must have just been jitters from the mission.

In his mind, Suzuki had imagined that he was going to swoop in and save the day. He was going to be cool and calm.

Beth was going to be extremely impressed.

Maybe even swoon.

So much for that, and Suzuki mentally kicked himself for having such childish expectations. Then he kicked himself again for thinking about that teenage shit when he knew that he could be in a life or death situation within a few seconds. This was game time. He had to get his head back in the mission. There would be time to fawn over Beth later.

Beth crouched down and touched the dirt floor of the cell. She looked up at Suzuki and smiled.

Suzuki's heart skipped a beat. It started pounding so hard that he could hardly think. His heart had never beat this fast in a fight. All he could think about was leaning over and kissing Beth. So much for fawning later.

Beth took a handful of dirt from the floor and watched it fall in between her fingers. "What we got, Suzy?" she asked.

Suzuki knelt down beside Beth so that their knees were almost touching. Beth shifted her weight a little so that she wobbled backward and smiled at Suzuki as she laughed lightly. Her eyes were dancing the way that Suzuki always loved dancing as if they were little fireflies.

"Nothing," Suzuki finally said.

"You know, if I have to die in an orc shithole, I'm glad that you're here to die with me," Beth said.

"I have lost track of how often I've shared that sentiment."

"We just going to wait here until the orcs come get us?" Beth asked.

"We could get information from them. Like maybe how to get the hell out of here."

"Oh, not these fuckers, especially the ones who come for me. It's usually at least four. And they are some tough sons of bitches."

"How tough?"

"Not as tough as me. They have been trying to break me since I got here. Hasn't happened yet, and it ain't gonna."

Beth stared at Suzuki, and he could see the pain in her eyes. She wasn't broken, but she was hurt, and whatever had happened to her in the tunnels of the prison would stay with her.

Suzuki wanted to find the orcs responsible, to rip their arms off and beat them to death, to watch blood drip from their heads as they begged for help. Everyone who had hurt Beth was going to pay.

Anyone who had laid a hand on her was going to die.

Beth wiped a tear from her eye as she stood up and cleared her throat. "Fuck it," she said. "We could dig our way out."

"We'd need a shit ton of spoons."

"I think shovels would be more useful."

"They'd lack the classic prison break feel."

"Fuck, I've missed you."

Beth threw her arms around Suzuki and held him tight. He could feel her face nestled up against his neck. She was warm and crying. They sat there for a little bit, the door of the cell still open as if, for these moments, they didn't need to care about being found, about living. They were together. Suzuki had always wondered how Beth had felt about him. Now he felt he knew.

Finally, Beth pulled away from Suzuki and dried her eyes. Suzuki kicked at the dirt floor, trying to figure out what to say. He knew that there had to be something, but nothing was coming to him. There was too much. Then it clicked. "Close the door," he said.

Beth didn't ask any questions and shut the cell door.

"This whole place is a fucking ant colony. That's why it's dug into the mountain like this. We need to think like ants."

Beth chuckled and shook her head, every movement she made reminding Suzuki why he loved her so much. "Dude, you've been here for a couple of hours, and you're already starting to lose it," Beth joked. "You would be prime for reintegration."

"Fuck off, just hear me out. When ants are building their colonies, they don't have a clear idea of what they're doing. It still works out. But sometimes, a few ants get separated while they're tunneling. They just start a new tunnel. That tunnel becomes part of the colony's framework. None of the other ants even notice it because they're all in different tunnels. If we dig our way out, no one is gonna catch us. We'll just be adding one more aimless tunnel to the list of other tunnels."

"What about my squad?"

"We get out first, then come back for your squad."

"And you think you and me can dig our way out of this? Dig ourselves out of a whole goddamn mountain?"

"Not just you and me. The Mundanes."

Suzuki opened his HUD and scrolled through the various menus and options. He set his location to broadcast to his party members, then he started typing a message.

The rest of the Mundanes and Horsemen were sitting around a campfire, talking quietly. They had made camp on the outskirts of the second defense ring. After Fred and Suzuki left, they had spent most of the last day performing reconnaissance. They had split into two groups, Sandy and Diana had taken the Northern part of the rings. Stew, Chip, and José had explored the Southern and Western section of the rings.

One they had finished, they had gathered to exchange their information. The two sections of the defense rings were nearly polar opposites. The North was predominately thick forests, not unlike what the two parties had seen when they had first left the dragon's lair. There were a few sentries sporadically throughout the forest, but nothing to have raised any alarm. Sandy and Diana had been able to easily avoid being detected. They had taken a detailed survey of the area, jotting it down on a magical scroll that allowed them to be able to see a photorealistic depiction of any spot on the map that they were interested in.

The Southern and Western sections of the ring were nothing like the North. Instead of forests, there were black deserts that looked as if they had been lifted from the Sahara. There was a sudden temperature change and, if José hadn't mocked Stew so thoroughly, it would have been easy to assume that they had walked onto another continent.

Now the Mundanes and the Horsemen warmed themselves by the flames, the night air crisp and even as their noses filled with the smell of roasting meat. The mood of the camp was tense. No one could say why exactly. It could have been boredom. Fred and Suzuki had been gone for a long time. There was only so much recon that they were capable of. More likely, though, it was a rising feeling of dread. It had been unspoken, but everyone had assumed that Fred and Suzuki would have been able to roll into the prison camp like the wind. Yet they were still gone. And no one had heard from either of them as well.

Stew pulled a piece of meat from the fire and offered it to Sandy, who was sipping a cup of tea, staring out at the trees that surrounded them. "They should be back by now," Sandy whispered to no one in particular.

Stew took a seat beside her and wrapped his arm around her shoulder as he picked at the meat on the plate. "It makes sense that it's taking them so long," Stew consoled. "You've seen how big these fucking rings are. I wouldn't be surprised if they were still trying to figure their way around the damn place."

Sandy wasn't so sure. "It's been a whole day. Something might have happened."

"Knowing Suzuki, something probably did happen. But he'll get himself out of it."

"We should have gone with him."

José yawned as he stood and walked over to his tent. He laid down so that his head was poking out of the tent, resting on his hands. "You two worry too much," José said. "They've been gone for a day. That's nothing. Chip, you tell them about the time that you were shipwrecked for a week on that one hydra quest that we were on."

Chip looked up from the HUD that she was tinkering with. She killed her soldering iron and placed it in her lap as her lips curled into a smile, her eyes taking on the dreamy look of reminiscence. "Nay," Chip squeaked. "I have yet to entertain them with my various misfortunes."

"You should tell them. Put their stressed little hearts to sleep. Maybe we'll get some sleep if they decide to stop acting like a bunch of pansies."

Sandy snapped at José as lightning crackled around the edges of her eyes. "We're not pansies," she growled. "Our friend could be dead, trying to help our other friend, who could also be dead. Sorry for not being a detached asshole."

"It's a joke, kid. Get those panties out of their bunch and nut up, all right? We've all been here before. It ain't easy. It ain't comfortable. But sitting around and feeling shitty ain't going to help anyone."

"What the hell do you think we should be doing?"

José disappeared into his tent for a moment and returned with a smile and a bottle of ale. He tossed tankards to Stew and Sandy before crouching before them and pouring the tankards full. "No," he said. "It's time to trust your teammate and prepare for the worst. Not obsess about the worst and try and outthink fate. It's time you listen." He cupped his ear as he said those last words.

The wind blew through the camp, and the flames from the fire flickered slightly before reasserting themselves. There was a bit of a chill. Stew inched closer to Sandy and held her tightly. "What are we listening to?" Stew asked, his voice betraying his irritation.

"Just wanted to shut you up for a few seconds." José laughed as he poured himself another drink. Chip and Diana watched from the fringes of the campfire. "Didn't realize that you both were going to become blubbering crybabies once Suzuki was out of here," José chided. "Would have thought—"

A short sword flew past José and landed firmly into the tree behind the MERC. It was a narrow miss. José looked at Stew, who hadn't bothered to lower his arm, allowing José to soak up how serious Stew was. "We care about our friend," Stew said. "Fuck off if we're worried."

José pulled the sword out of the tree and tossed it at Stew's feet. "No one is saying that you shouldn't be worried," José explained. "I'm saying you two shouldn't be acting like he's already dead. For someone whom you both love so much, you both seem to have pretty low expectations for him."

"What the hell is that supposed to mean?"

"A few years back, we were contracted to take care of a hydra infestation on the coast. Generally, that's a pretty boring gig, nothing much to pay attention to. This was back when we still didn't know what the Dark One was doing. There were all these explosions of monster activity, and we couldn't figure out what it was. Hindsight is a bitch. Anyways, we didn't think anything of it at the time. I told Chip that she can take care of the hydra. I didn't really think much of it at the time. The last time that I'd seen a hydra infestation, it was a little thing, hardly bigger than a dog, running around a village and scaring the goats. I figured it was something like that. I should have thought better, though. But I didn't. Chip went to go take care of the problem."

José downed the last of his ale and poured another. He watched out from behind the fire. Both Diana and Chip had faded into the darkness of the forest as the last bit of sunlight disappeared behind the horizon.

"Chip had to catch a boat from the MERC encampment. That should have been my other clue. Why the fuck would they need to sail to who the fuck knows where just to take care of a poodle-sized hydra. But I was young. I didn't ask the right questions. And that's really what the difference boils down to most of the time. Whether or not you're asking the right questions. Most people aren't. That's something that I had to teach myself. Anyway, Chip ended up on the coast of where Mexico would be on Earth. I didn't think twice about it. Neither did Diana. Then we started hearing these reports. Apparently, this wasn't a poodle with five heads. Half the coast had been torn up. The military was out there as well. The number of casualties was easily more than the MERC or the military had seen up to that point. And we had sent our Chip out there to take care of that hydra all by herself. None of us there to watch her back. How the fuck do you think we felt?"

Sandy and Stew were silent, waiting for José to finish whatever it was that he had to say. Instead, José turned to Chip and tossed a rock at her shadowed silhouette. "What the fuck did you do?" José asked.

Chip sighed and leaned out of the shadows so that only her face was visible, bright and fiery as the flames tap-danced across her irises. "I done already told you, I ain't got much to add to the story," Chip stated. "If you're going to embarrass me, might as well finish up the job, ya wanker."

José lifted his hands in a mock-defensive manner. "All right, all right. Like I was saying. Chip was out there in a kill zone off the coast of Mexico. After the first day, we started seeing reports about the coast. Everything is shut down. The hydra has apparently gone nuclear. As far as I knew, Chip was dead. Every other MERC who went out that way was. But that was before I trusted Chip. I should have back then, but we all have shit to learn. I guess my lesson was learning to trust my guy's skills."

Stew was completely into the story. His eyes were wide

as he waited for the tale's resolution. "What happened? What happened to Chip?"

"Well, as you can see, she's still alive."

"I mean, how'd she get out?"

Diana stood up from the fire and went over to Chip, who was lounging lazily near the trees. "Come on, Chip," Diana coaxed. "You have to see how much suspense is in the air."

"Nope. How about you tell them about the time your wee lil ass got stranded in the seven deserts? How's that one for a tell?"

Diana chucked. "Hell, no, that shit was embarrassing."

"I'd say more gross than embarrassing, but aye, your desert trek was embarrassing. As was my hydra incident. So, that said, you show 'em yours, and I'll show off mine."

Diana smiled devilishly, the way that teenagers grin at each other when they've been egging themselves on for too long. "Fine," Diana said, causing Chip's jaw to drop. "I'll show them." Diana walked back to the campfire as Chip jumped out of the trees and followed. She sat down and pulled a small crystal ball from her HUD and tossed it over the flames. The ball exploded into a thousand shards that floated above the flames and spread out as if they were stars. Then lights started to bounce in between the lights until they connected, little silver threads tying them all together, stitching together a screen that seemed to stretch out over the entire night sky.

The screen showed Diana in a desert. There was nothing but sand in the sort of desert that looks like an extension of the infinite. Each grain of sand reinforces the unstoppable heat and vastness of the geography without the least concern for the plight of humanity.

Diana was hunched over, kneeling. Her hands rested on her kneecaps. Her robes were drenched in sweat, huge dark spots underneath her armpits. She looked like she was barely able to stay conscious, swaying side to side as she struggled to breathe. After a couple of minutes of resting, she took a deep breath and forced herself to her feet. She started forward, wandering the desert like a lost wraith, a dead thing already defeated by the heat and starvation.

Stew leaned back on the ground, and Sandy lay next to him as they stared up at the screen. The fire crackled around them. "What the hell were you doing out there?" Stew asked.

"I was supposed to be securing an ancient artifact. We were ambushed and a spell that I cast teleported me to the middle of nowhere. José and Chip didn't even know where I was. Neither did I. I had to figure out how to get back or at least let them know where I was."

Sandy sat up and grabbed one of the Jive Bugs Diana had set out for a snack. They were little insects, coated in a magical glaze that made them taste like a cross between a pretzel and sour candy. They also had a nice little punch of energy. "How'd you get out of this one?" Sandy asked.

Diana leaned back and motioned for Sandy to pass her the Jive Bugs. "Just check it out," she said.

The desert-bound Diana struggled to make any headway. She had been walking for some time. There was nothing around her whatsoever. But beneath her feet, there was something moving. The sand was disturbed, and then the tip of a fin appeared out of the sand. Diana saw it and her eyes went wide. She stopped walking, held herself perfectly still as she muttered the words of a protection spell, a thin blue aura extending over her body. Her wand was in her hand instantly.

Another fin appeared. Then another. There were at least three of them, circling around her. Diana didn't have a lot of time to plan. It was all reaction. She aimed her wand at her feet and created an explosion that sent her flying through the air. She landed about twenty feet away, rolling across the sand as she jumped to her feet. She was near a small collection of rocks that shot out of the sand. It didn't take long for her to scamper to them. She pulled the hem of her robes up and watched the fins coming near her.

Fear is an interesting thing.

It is experienced by all.

Yet there are times when you can see it plainer than you have ever seen anything. This was what Diana's face looked like. Her eyes were open as only terror can open them. Shivers racked her body, and she was crying as the fins multiplied around her. Three. Five. Ten. Circling the pile of rocks like sharks. Diana sat there, crying for some time. The sand creatures waited for her to slip up, no doubt starving and ready to eat. Then, out of nowhere and for what seemed like no reason, Diana's face hardened. She didn't stop crying, but she didn't bother to wipe the tears from her face. She stood up and raised her wand to the sky and then brought it down with a quick slashing movement. Then she sat down and waited.

After some time, Diana was pulled forward a bit. She grinned as she gripped her wand, stood up, and pulled hard. She tore one of the creatures out of the sand and tossed it onto the rocks next to her. The thing looked more like a stingray than a shark. Its mouth was wide and it looked to be smiling with razor-sharp teeth that occasionally snapped at Diana.

The body ridges like serrated paper and it thrashed. Diana pointed her wand at the beast, there was a flash of light, and the creature lay dead. Next Diana split it open with an energy attack from her wand. She looked through its entrails for a few moments before sitting down again.

Diana waved her wand around the dead body of the sand ray. The ray's blood floated up into the air as Diana continued to weave her magic. The iron from the blood separated and Diana tossed it to the side as she magicked the remains over to her.

Clean, distilled water hung in a bubble, floating through the air. She took a sip and sighed in relief.

The screen went black and Diana waved it away with her wand. "And *that's* how you survive being stranded in the desert," she said.

Stew sat bolt upright, blinking disbelievingly. "That's how you survived? You became a sand vampire?" Stew asked.

"It's not a vampire if you don't drink their blood."

"I don't know, dude...that's a very thin line you're walking there."

Diana laughed as she sat back down across from the rest of the party members at the fire. "I know, I know. I didn't stop hearing about it for years. Everyone was convinced I was going to sneak into their room and drink their blood. Up until we came across real vampires. Then everyone stopped joking."

Sandy was staring up at Diana with a look of near worship. "That's so fucking sick... how'd you get José and Chip to figure out where you were?"

"I didn't. I lived off those sand rays for almost a week as I trekked the desert. That's just not as interesting to watch. There's a lot more crying, though. You know, the usual 'how am I going to survive this' kind of stuff."

Stew grabbed another piece of meat and held out his

tankard for José to fill up. "Uh… don't get me wrong, but this was supposed to be encouraging, right?"

José poured Stew some more ale before pouring himself a tankard as well. "If you got the point, it would be." José sighed. "If Diana could live off of sand sharks—"

"Sand rays."

"Whatever. If Diana could figure out how to live in a desert with no food or water, I'm pretty sure Suzuki will be able to get back to us. He's resourceful. He'll figure it out."

"Did you have any close calls like that?"

José shrugged. "I've never had a close call my entire life."

"What the hell is that supposed to mean?" Stew asked.

"It means I've never had a close call."

"Bullshit," Stew said as he turned to the other members of the Horsemen. "What's the worst situation José's ever been in?"

Chip shrugged as she walked back to her tree and climbed into the branches. "He don't like to talk about it," she called back. "Might have an easier time sucking off a giant."

Stew, Sandy, and Diana laughed loudly while José did something neither of the Mundanes had seen him do so far —blushed uncontrollably. "If you guys are finished," he muttered as he retreated to his tent, "I'm going to get some sleep."

"Wait, wait," Stew called. "I wanna hear this. You gotta tell us."

"It's not a funny story."

"Fine. We won't be dicks."

José sighed heavily as he lay back down in his tent. Even if he was serious, he was giving off the air of a kid at his first sleepover, trying desperately not to look uncool. "All right. It's a pretty straightforward story. There used to be Four Horse-men. We were contracted to look into a village that had been overrun by a recent infestation of banshees. Now at the surface, no big problem. Banshees are a left-over problem. They just don't come into town because they want to stir up trouble. Banshees only come out when people are going to die. And when it's that many people, it means that you're going to have a lot of dead bodies on your hand. We figured that we just had to find the source of the banshees, find out what's going to kill these people. It sounded like we actually lucked out on something, like we got a heads-up for something fucked up that the Dark One was going to be responsible for. You don't get a lot of chances like that. Lucky us, right?"

José was silent for a moment, his face heavy with his memories. It was as if he had aged a century. The lines in his face settled in deeply. Listening to his talk, you could see the stress etching itself into his face.

He cleared his throat and started up again. "The banshees were the problem. Plain and simple. They weren't there to warn anyone about death: they *were* the death. We had shown up in the village a few days earlier, did some scouting around. There were goblins not too far away, but hardly enough to give any of us a problem. We got to drink-ing, having a good time. We were still keeping our eyes open but didn't think there was anything to worry about. We even saw the banshees. They weren't too far off, but there were hardly any of them. If they came through the town, it was enough that we could herd them out. So, like I said, no problem. The banshees came through around one in the morning. Quiet as death. No shrieking. No screaming. Noth-ing. There were hundreds of them. We didn't know where they came from. We didn't know how they multiplied so fast. There were more banshees than I'd ever seen my entire life. They rolled through that village like a fucking plague. Do you know banshees kill?"

Sandy and Stew said nothing, only shook their heads.

"No one did. You know, before that night, there had never been one recorded case of a banshee hurting anyone. At most, they were just a nuisance. A loud, creepy-as-fuck nuisance, but that was all. I woke up, and there were people in the street. The banshees hadn't made a sound. They just came into the village and started dragging everyone out of their homes. No one made a sound, not one fucking person. The banshees were pulling families out. Moms, dads, kids… everyone, and slitting their throats in the streets. Everyone was silent. I was surprised when I woke up—and I was too late. They had already taken the Horsemen. I came outside…I came outside…well, everyone in the village was dead. Most of the MERCs were dead. Nathan was dead. I saw his face staring at me, his head nearly cut clean off, as soon as I opened the door. Chip and Diana were gone, and I had no idea where they were. It was just me and a village full of pissed-off banshees."

"What the fuck did you do?" Stew whispered.

"I hid. I shut the door, and I hid until the crack of dawn. I could hear the banshees making their rounds through the village, opening every door, hunting us down. I hid until they opened my door. I cleaved those in half and waited a little longer before going out. Most of them were preoccupied with the sun coming up. Banshees hate the sun. Not vampire level, but it still makes them uncomfortable. I was trying to figure out why the fuck they were standing around. I didn't have too much time to do that, though. I got started with the killing—as many as I could. I lost myself for a bit but came to just before I axed the last one. I made her take me to where the rest of the Horsemen were. There were other prisoners too. I killed every last banshee and goblin in that camp. The end."

José finished his beer, turned around, and closed his tent.

Diana looked at José's tent. She moved like she was going to rise and go to him, but leaned back in her seat. From the darkness of the trees, Chip chuckled and said, "Good story, right?"

Stew scratched his face, trying to find something to do with the uncomfortable silence. "I didn't think that it was going to be...so fucked up," Stew murmured.

Diana conjured a cup as she went to the fire and put on a pot of water to boil. "You don't stay alive in this job as long as José without seeing a lot of fucked up shit," Diana said.

"Yeah, I guess...I was expecting something a little more...inspirational."

"As far as José is concerned, that is inspirational."

"But one of your guys died. Nathan? Was that his name?"

"Yeah, Nathan did die. But only Nathan. So that's the inspirational part. José swore that he was never going to lose anyone else. Ever. And he's gone through some crazy shit to keep that from happening. That's why he never helps out any of the rookies. He hardly ever even helps out any of the vets. He feels like their lives are on him. It weighs him down a lot, but it's better than Chip's story at least."

"How could Chip's be any worse than that?"

"Trust me, you don't wanna hear Chip's. No one does, right, Chip?"

Chip could be heard moving in the branches. "Aye. Ain't no happy moral at the end of that yarn."

"So?" Stew stood up. "You got to tell us. After all that, you got to tell us—"

There was a loud ping. It sounded like a firecracker

going off. Sandy jumped and yelped. She pulled her HUD off and looked down at it. The sound had come from the HUD. There was a blinking icon on the screen. Chip moved through in the darkness to get closer to the campfire.

Sandy looked down at the HUD. It was also beeping on the side, a blinking green light that was just barely noticeable. "What the fuck is that?" Sandy asked.

Chip reached out for the HUD and Sandy handed it to her. "'Tis a distress signal from your fearless leader, complete with geographical location. I'd wager he's either found your missing mate or he's in need of a little rescue."

"Where is he?"

Chip plugged her HUD into Sandy's to download the coordinates. When she was done, she handed Sandy back her HUD. "Looks like he's plum in the middle of a fucking mountain." She laughed. "Honestly, you little shites seem to have a thing for mountains. Ain't never spent so much time underground as with you three."

Sandy checked the coordinates on her HUD, then brought up a digital image of the location. Just as Chip had said, Suzuki was smack in the middle of a mountain range that started in the second defense ring. "How the fuck did he get in there?"

Diana shrugged her shoulders and crouched down to look into the flames. "Not nearly as important as how we're going to get him out of there. It's in a less than ideal place."

"What do you mean?"

"Suzuki's been gone for a long-ass time. Whatever he did to get in there, it took a bit. It's time that he probably doesn't have to be wasted. We need to get in and out quick. Unfortunately, mountains aren't something that you can easily sneak into."

Chip laughed as she nudged Diana. "No, not like that time we snuck into that plantation to rile up those orc—"

"Not the time, Chip. We need to figure out how we're going to solve this. Did he send a message at all?"

Sandy checked her HUD for messages. There was one from Suzuki. All it said was, **Found Beth. Low signal. Evac immediately.**

"Not a useful one." Sandy groaned. "At least we know Beth is all right. Thank fuck the suspense of that is finally over. You got any cool magic tricks to pull out of your bag for a climactic save?"

Diana shook her head as she scratched her chin, her brow furrowed in concentration. "Nope, I got nothing. A teleportation spell from that far away, into a structure, could end up with us fusing. Think the Montauk project, but a lot less sexy."

Chip laughed loudly as she doubled over and held her sides. "Only your lady bits would be remotely aroused by that horror show. And I'm shite out of luck too, lads. Any teleportation I could rig up would give us away. And would also have a possibility to splice us up nice and pretty. It could make Diana's ideal orgy, at least."

"It's not my ideal, but close enough."

Sandy sighed in exasperation. "Okay, I get that all this is just par for the course for you guys, but I am not comfortable cracking jokes while my best friends are waiting to get captured."

"Nobody is waiting to get captured. What makes you think Suzuki and Beth are just sitting around, waiting to be picked up?"

"Why the hell else would have they have messaged us?"

"Because they know you're smart enough to figure something out. Just like they're smart enough to figure something out. You guys are supposed to be a party, right? How long have you been running together? You don't have the slightest inkling of what Suzuki and Beth might be thinking?"

"Honestly, those asshats are probably sitting around making dumb-ass prison jokes about digging their way out with a spoon. Fucking nerds."

There was a loud pop that sounded almost like a cow breaking wind. "Did someone say digging?"

The Horsemen and Mundanes turned around. Standing behind them was a small gargoyle with the head of an oversized donkey. Its mouth hung open, giving it the impression of being a slack-jawed yokel from a cartoon. The rest of his body was the stony texture you would find on a carving at a church. His eyes were wide and bright blue, the same color as Stew's. He kicked bashfully at a rock next to his feet. "Y'all did say digging, right?" GB asked.

Stew knelt across from GB so he could look his familiar in the eye. "What are you getting at, GB?"

"I just heard y'all talking about digging, and I thought I'd like to talk about digging too. Cause you know, I like to dig. But who doesn't like digging? And you guys never talk about digging. Niv never wants to talk about digging. Fred never wants to talk about digging. Oh, well, once he wanted to talk about digging graves, but he wanted to talk about digging my grave. And you know, I just want to have a good chat about digging."

"Do you…like digging?"

"Oh, gods, yes. I used to dig all the time with my last partner. We were always looking for new places to dig. The smell of good dirt. He'd wake me up in the middle of the night and say, 'GB, we're going out and digging tonight.' Just all night, sitting around digging. Really getting into that good dirt."

GB sighed affectionately. "I loved that guy. Always the first one to get a shovel."

"How good are you at digging, dude?"

"Oh, I'm the best. I been the best for years. If you want a hole, all you gotta do is tell me. I'll get there. Straight down. Side to side. Upside-down. I'll dig it."

Stew motioned for Sandy to hand GB her HUD. "What about this?" Stew asked. "How long will it take you to dig to there?"

GB looked at the coordinates and his ass-face turned up in a huge, goofy smile. "This? Shucks, I can dig this in a couple of hours. With a little help." GB leaned over and winked at Stew. "Don't worry, I'll take care of most of it."

"Sounds like we got a plan. A couple of hours isn't too bad, and he'll do most of the heavy lifting."

Sandy leaned closer to Stew and whispered in his ear, "Are you sure this is a good idea and not GB doing that weird thing?"

Stew shrugged as he rested his hands on his hips. "What kind of weird thing?"

"You know, how I make things really weird?"

"Honestly, I feel like him being into digging *is* the really weird part."

Both Stew and Sandy were distracted by the sound of another pop. They turned around, and GB was already ankle-deep in a hole about ten feet wide. Diana and Chip were watching the familiar work, both of them looking on with a fair amount of admiration. Sandy walked up to the hole, shaking her head. "Unbelievable," she murmured.

The bowels of the mountain were silent. Suzuki, in Fred's body, was making his way through a series of winding tunnels, looking for something they could dig with while also keeping their eyes open for any cells that had prisoners who could be released. So far, they had not found anyone or anything. To keep other guards from noticing Beth and becoming suspicious, Suzuki and Fred had rigged a fake neck chain from the broken chains that had been found in Beth's cell. Beth dwarfed the imp, and it took everything in Suzuki's power not to start cracking jokes as he led Beth around. "I know you're fucking getting off on this," Beth muttered under her breath.

Even though Suzuki had been thinking (and trying very hard to pretend he had not been) about the obvious kink factor, he still felt himself figuratively blushing at Beth's words. He opted to let Fred reply. "My human is preoccupied at the moment," Fred said.

"Preoccupied with what? We're both looking for the same shit. I just happen to be the one who looks like I'm in a bad kink snuff film."

"He is planning... Where is your familiar? I don't sense him anywhere near you."

"Wait, you guys can do that?"

"Yes, we have ways to communicate with each other. Old magic. Where is yours?"

"They took him. That's one of the reasons I didn't want to just bounce the fuck out of here. It was as soon as I got captured. Someone had mentioned back in boot camp that the Dark One had a way to separate humans from their familiars, but no one took it seriously. It seemed like it'd be too hard."

"It would be a good plan. But how are you still here? Humans require their familiars to tie them to magic. If you are out of touch with magic, you should have been transported back to Earth. Explain yourself."

"Okay, buddy, just because you have a chain around my neck doesn't mean I'm not going to kick your ass, so watch your fucking tone. That's what I thought too, about the familiar. We had it drilled in our heads pretty thoroughly that we were to do everything that we could to keep from being separated from our familiars. Boot camp also really stressed that it's extremely fucking hard to separate us, so hard that it can be traumatic enough to kill both the host and the familiar. Trust me, I was surprised when they ripped Ros'ten from me and I didn't get sucked back into a magical vortex."

Fred considered this. "The Dark One must have designed a way to keep you two connected. That has to be it. There is absolutely no way your familiar can be separated from you without causing you to return to Earth. The connection must just be different than it was before."

"So how does all that work? I mean, is Suzuki inside of you?" Beth asked.

"To an extent. When we bond with our hosts, a pocket dimension within the host's subconscious mind is created. Since we are of magical nature, our physical existence is already tied to the vast unknown of the mind. It is hardly a hassle to revert to pure energy to exist within that domain. As our powers are combined with our human's, it also gives their bodies more elasticity. That is why humans are able to perform feats of magic without burning themselves alive."

"Are you saying that you change the ways our bodies work?"

"It is... irritatingly difficult to explain to humans. You have been so long without magic that you can't even wrap your head around the basics. It will suffice to say that looking at the world simply as physical atoms and nuts and bolts only distances you from the truth. When I was bound to Suzuki, I occupied a place within him that is not bound to space or time. I exist within him. All of him, everything that he has ever been, is, and will be. That is what Suzuki is doing with me right now."

"Sounds pretty intimate. Not something that I would expect a demon imp to be willing to do."

"It...was uncomfortable at first, but it has grown on me. He is surprisingly good company. It has been...interesting to experience what he feels me experience, and interesting to be so connected with a human."

Fred and Beth turned a corner. There were two orcs standing and chatting. They jumped to attention immediately. "You're stuck with that one today," one of the orcs joked. "Don't let her get close to you with her mouth."

"Clear tore off another guy's ear a few days ago," the other orc said.

Beth grinned widely to show off her teeth and then chomped down hard. "You fucks are lucky that's the only thing I could get my mouth on," she shouted as Fred led her forward.

Fred yanked the chain hard enough to pull Beth off her feet. She hit the ground with a dull thud, grimaced in pain, and glared up at Fred, who snickered evilly. "Silence, human," Fred said. "I don't have time for your theatrics. Yours either." Fred turned his attention to the orcs. "I am transporting this...trash. They are going to require a series of humiliating tasks to break down her psyche. Where can I find a shovel and a large pot?"

One of the orcs raised its eyebrows and leaned in to get a better look at Fred. "Who exactly are you?" the orc growled.

"Lieutenant and emissary to the viceroy," Fred hissed back.

"We didn't hear about the viceroy sending anyone to—"

"Does the viceroy regularly convey her orders to you?" Fred growled. "I failed to realize that the two orcs guarding the shit room would be personally notified of her direct intentions. I apologize if you're offended. Next time I will make sure the viceroy notifies any and every sack of shit I come across. Should I also relay that I was obstructed by the guards of the shit room? Your names, please."

"Hold on, hold on," the larger orc said. "We don't need to take it that far. I know where you can get some shovels. We can just keep this talk...between us."

"Good. Now, where can I find a shovel and a pot?"

"Just follow this tunnel down the hallway and turn left at the second entrance. It's a maintenance room. There might actually be a sign there. Fuck if I know why it's the only room for miles that's got a sign. Guess people are looking for shovels a lot."

"There are a lot of bodies to bury." The second orc chuckled.

"Good." Fred yanked on Beth's chain again, forcing her to get to her feet to follow him. "Come on, human. We have torturing to do."

Beth stumbled to her feet and followed Fred, tripping over the chain and her feet every couple of steps. She cast a hateful glance at the orcs, who chuckled at her as she walked by. When the orcs were out of earshot, Beth whispered, "You can loosen the chain a little bit, asshole."

Fred did as he was asked. "Sorry," he said. "There was... I had to pull from Suzuki's memories for...inspiration. Lying is not something I am used to."

"What the fuck memory did you get from Suzy where that made sense?"

"Something called BDSM. I believe humiliation is a subcategory of sadism. He has significant memories—"

Suzuki forced his words out of Fred's mouth. "We are NOT talking about those memories," Suzuki growled. "We *are* paying attention to our fucking mission, right?"

Beth tried to stifle a laugh. "Wait, are you telling me that Suzuki has BDSM porn locked up in his memories?" she asked.

"You don't need to know what I have locked up in my memories."

Beth jogged to catch up with Fred, leaned forward, and whispered in his ear, "We are going to have *so* much to talk about once we kill our way out of here. You have not heard the last of this."

Fred and Suzuki pointed ahead at the left turn that the orcs had told them about. "I believe we are here," Fred said, regaining control of his voice. "We should continue the charade in case we are questioned again."

Beth slowed down and resumed her posturing as a captured, beaten prisoner. There was no one in the hall, only the door they had been informed about. Fred approached the door hesitantly and knocked twice. When no one answered, he pushed it open with his clawed foot and casually stepped inside.

The room was barely lit, but it was full of tools. Hoes, shovels, and all manner of gardening tools were shoved against the walls. There were also quantities of binding materials, and some huge machines whose purpose eluded Suzuki. He thought they might have something to do with moving earth. They were large enough to have been used to dig the massive tunnels that composed the majority of the prison. "Map this room to my HUD," Suzuki told Fred. "We might be able to use those...whatever the fuck they are."

Fred sighed in irritation but listened to Suzuki. "Why would we mark something for potential use?" he asked.

"Come on, dude, just trust me. You're trying to get used to this whole roll-with-the-punches thing. So am I, and I have a good feeling something that big could be used to cause some serious damage. Trust me, it's a *real* good feeling."

Beth grabbed one of the shovels and propped it on her shoulder. She turned to face Suzuki and, even from behind Fred's eyes, his heart dropped at how gorgeous she was with a shovel in one hand, her other resting lightly on her hip. Suzuki was always surprised by how graceful Beth looked performing the most mundane actions. The chain around her neck might have been helping, but it was probably best to think about that later. "Let's hurry up and get out of here," Beth said, interrupting Suzuki's thoughts. "I don't know a comfortable way to walk out of here without looking suspicious. And don't you even look at those handcuffs over there, or I swear to God I will rip you both apart."

Stew and Sandy were five feet underground. Completely underground. GB had outlined his game plan for the dig. Initially, he had been too excited to talk to any of them; he had just gotten to digging. His claws and hooves had removed enough dirt to build a small mound, and the whole time he had muttered a few words under his breath over and over as a mantra: *gotta dig, gotta dig.* And digging he was! Eventually, after peeking his head over the rim of the hole he'd dug and seeing the looks of bewilderment on the faces of the Mundanes and the Horsemen, he pulled himself out of his soil paradise and explained his methodology.

"We're going to dig down for a few miles like I'm doing now. Dig it, gotta dig it up *good*." His emphasis was almost uncomfortably sexual. "But we're also digging at a slant. Diagonal. Until we come to the first rest stop. Then we dig out. We make ourselves a little bit of room. Then we start digging up. Then make another rest stop. We keep digging on this zig-zag until we come up in their room."

Sandy raised her hand and instantly felt embarrassed. For a moment, she'd betrayed a nerdish habit leftover from years of intense schooling. "Um..." she murmured. "How are we going to deal with the tunnels when we leave? Aren't we just leaving a trail to be followed?"

"Nope, nope! I'll let you guys go ahead, and I'll come up behind you and knock the tunnels down. I don't have to worry about them collapsing on me. As long as Stew's good, I'm good. Isn't that right, buddy?"

GB jumped and gave Stew a high five. They laughed together like a couple of jocks who had had too much to drink too often and still weren't tired of it. "Dude, we are going to dig the fuck out of that mountain," Stew shouted.

"Dig the fuck out of it and fuck it," GB shouted.

Stew's smile disappeared. "No, dude. No. We are not going to do that."

GB hid his cartoonish ass of a face behind his hands. "Oh, I know. We're just digging. Well, got to get back to it!" The familiar whipped around, flapped his wings, and dove back into the hole.

Diana walked up between Sandy and Stew and watched the donkey gargoyle dig into his pit. "You guys know that familiar is a little off in the head, right?" she asked.

Sandy nodded. She was beyond being surprised by GB.

This was the least odd thing she had seen him do. "Yeah, we know he's fucked," she agreed.

"Like, really weird."

Chip leaned into the conversation with a wide, beaming smile, the face of someone trying to stir up trouble and start shit. "She wants to know if you two love-birds been porking with the ass," Chip butted in. "Me too, to be frank. He's a little...horny, to say it in the politest way."

"Nah, not really our thing," Sandy said as Stew went beet-red. "Although he does work some pretty good magic on a cock when we want to spice things up."

Chip's eyes nearly popped out of her head. "Oh, this is a need-to-know tale. Why have you been holding out on all the gushy details?"

Stew stepped in front of Sandy, Chip, and Diana, still blushing bright enough that he should have passed out from too much blood pumping to his head. "All right, ladies," he said as he cleared his throat. "Shouldn't we be getting to the digging? We've got a lot of miles to cover, and friends who are depending on us."

Diana pulled out her wand and went to stand over the steadily deepening hole that GB was digging. "Stew's right," she said as she waved her wand and conjured each party member a shovel. "We can talk while we work. I've always been interested in the role that familiars play when using magic to enhance or augment sexual performance or plea-sure. I've been thinking about writing a paper on the subject. I know it happens, but I rarely meet anyone willing to talk about it."

"I am not willing to—"

Sandy pushed Stew out of the way and blew him a kiss as she jumped into the hole. "Of course." She giggled. "I have been wondering the same thing. Like, I know that some people have to be using magic to get their fuck on."

Stew stood in the clearing with Chip, his face burning brighter and brighter. He was holding his breath, and his acne looked ready to pop out of his skin. Chip walked up behind him, smiling and shaking her head. "Ooooh, boyo, you are in for an uncomfortable next few hours." Chip whistled as she walked past Stew. "You ever had your sex life dissected by a group of eggheads with a thirst for unknown, profane knowledge?"

"No. I talked to my doctor once about a lump on my balls."

"Was it a profane lump?"

"It felt pretty profane."

"Boyo, you in for a long night. If you need a shoulder to weep on, let me know. Unless your gal is a jealous gal and thinks you're trying to get slobbery on my neck places… unless she's into that. Either way, this'll be a teeny bit interesting."

"I fucking hate you, GB."

Fred, Suzuki, and Beth made their way back to the cell that Beth had been found in. They didn't come across any other guards along the way. They closed the door and locked it with the chain that Beth had worn around her neck. Beth looked down at the dirt floor and sighed as she sank the shovel into the ground and removed the first clump of dirt. "This is such a shitty idea." She groaned as she dug up another clump. "How long do you think this is going to take?"

Fred tossed his shovel on the ground. "Much too long for

two people. We should at least use all of our bodies. Are you certain that you locked the door?"

"As certain as I am that both of you were getting off on me being chained up like a bunch of little pervs."

Suzuki cringed. He knew that Beth was joking—or at least he hoped that she was joking. It was hard to tell. It was even harder to tell because it'd been so long since he had seen Beth. She had always had a wicked sense of humor. Her jokes made Sandy and Stew look tame. One of the first things that he had fallen for with Beth was how sharply she could cut anyone down. In the VR realm, her tongue was as notorious as her sword.

"We should separate," Fred said, breaking Suzuki's train of thought. "It will make the work go by faster."

"All right," Suzuki agreed. It'll be nice to have my own hands for a little while."

"Yes, human, that's the body part that I assumed you would be most happy about."

Suzuki wished that he could crawl under a rock. Now he wasn't just getting it from Beth, but Fred was ganging up on him as well. At least Stew and Sandy were nowhere to be seen. It would have been unbearable to have four people working on him. Especially if one of those individuals had been living in the vast subconscious of his memories for the last few weeks. There was too much ammunition. *Why the hell couldn't I have been stuck with serious party members?* Suzuki thought.

There was a feeling like being ripped away from sticky gum, as if his entire body had somehow been cocooned against a wall by a spider. It was not really a painful sensation, but it was uncomfortable all the same. Suzuki saw his body melting before him, bones pulled out of thin air, his muscle and skin growing out over his skeleton. The oddest feeling was his hair sprouting from his scalp. He imagined this was what the earth must feel like during spring. It was far from pleasant. But by the end of it, he was standing in the middle of the cell, heaving, trying to catch his breath, wiping the obscene amount of sweat pouring from his forehead. "Feels good to be back," he muttered. "All the way back at least."

Fred walked away from Suzuki and stretched out his wings. "I would have to agree with that." Fred groaned. "I am glad to have my mind to myself for some time." Fred closed his eyes and stretched his hands out in front of him. The cell filled with the smell of sulfur as a demonic shovel appeared in Fred's hand. The spade was wicked and curved, the handle ending in a frighteningly realistic depiction of a demon with its mouth gaping. "We should begin."

Fred, Suzuki, and Beth started to dig. It was difficult to get the first layer of crust broken up, but once they got down to the soft earth beneath, digging became much easier. That is not to say that the work went by easily. Suzuki was sweating within a few minutes. He pulled up his HUD and selected his leather armor. It was still going to be hot, but at least he wouldn't be completely unarmed if someone were to break into the cell. He thanked whoever was in charge that his body worked overtime without any issues in Middang3ard. It was an aspect of the realm that he had taken for granted recently. Back on earth, this much digging would have winded him enough to have an asthma attack.

At Suzuki's side, Beth dug with the routine of someone who had years and years of practice. She had perfect form. Every time she bent forward to remove some dirt and tossed it over her shoulder, Suzuki thought she looked like the ideal of someone digging. It was the definition of beauty. As Beth leaned forward, she looked up at Suzuki, her face drenched with sweat. "What the hell are you looking at?" she asked.

Suzuki coughed loudly and went back to his digging. "Nothing," he murmured. Rather than talk to Beth about how he'd been staring at the way that her neck tensed when she gritted her teeth, he gave himself to the work. He paid attention to the rise and fall of his shovel, to the earthy grunting coming from Beth and Fred as they toiled into the ground. Suzuki didn't know exactly how they were digging out of the mountain. He didn't know how tunneling worked. He wasn't even sure where exactly they were in the mountainous prison. For all he knew, they could just be digging straight into another cell. Still, it was better than waiting on their asses. He hoped that the Mundanes and the Horsemen had come to a similar agreement.

GB had stopped the digging to set up their first rest stop. There was hardly enough room to stand. The two parties had been digging extremely claustrophobic tunnels at the command of GB, who was always ahead of the rest of them, digging with ferocity. The rest of them were left to widen the tunnel enough for them to move through, but not enough to affect structural integrity. Luckily, no one suffered from a fear of enclosed spaces. There ended up being more room once they finally did stop to rest. GB paced around the small bubble underneath the mountain and continued to carve away the stone and rock until there was enough room to sit comfortably.

Sandy stared at the sides of the rest stop. GB hadn't been joking about how much he loved to dig, and he had under-sold his talent. With GB leading the way, they had been able to cut straight into the hard rock that would lead them to Suzuki and Beth. As a result, Sandy was able to see the shimmering geodes underground. Her face sparkled in their reflection. She had never seen raw geodes shine like this before. "Stew, you have to see this," Sandy said as she tugged on Stew's belt.

Stew looked up and almost didn't notice the underground beauty that his attention was being called to. He instantly turned back to sharpening his shovel before it clicked. Once he looked back at the geodes, it was almost impossible for him to look away. "You don't see that every day," Stew murmured.

"Fuck, I don't think I've ever seen anything like this."

Chip and Diana were sitting in the middle of the rest stop, talking with each other quietly. They looked at the two Mundanes, still speaking under their breath. GB sat at the far end of the rest stop, near where he was going to begin digging again. "Beautiful down here, isn't it?" GB asked.

Stew lightly touched the geodes. They were unnaturally cold, and it felt like he was running his fingers across an ice cube. "Dude, how did you get so good at digging?" Stew asked. "Don't you fly or something? I always saw the wings and just assumed you were like an imp or something."

Gb shook his head, still looking at the eventual tunnel. "No, I was born underground," GB said. "I spent most of my life underground. That was until the grimpons forced us out."

Diana's ears perked up at hearing new information. "Did you say 'us?'" she asked. "I wasn't aware there were other gargoyles like you."

"We aren't really gargoyles. Not like regular ones, at least. We've got enough similarities for humans and elves to think we're the same, but the dwarves know. They've seen us for years."

"How come the dwarves have never said anything?" Stew asked.

"When does a dwarf ever tell you anything about the underground places if you don't ask?"

Diana nodded thoughtfully as she walked over to study the geodes with the Mundanes. "True, true. They are extremely tight-lipped about what they've experienced underground. Some of the military think that the war would be going differently if the dwarves were more forthright about their underground experiences."

GB stood up and lumbered over to the rest of the group. He sat down next to Chip and hung his head. The boyish joy that had been in his eyes before was gone. His face sank, and he looked at his feet with a misery that seemed acutely out of place. "Nope," he said. "The only things down in the dirt are more dirt and what the dwarves made. They've shared all of that, even us."

"What do you mean, 'even us?'"

"The dwarves made us. They made us out of stone and dirt to help them build."

Diana rushed over to GB and knelt beside him. She grabbed his hands as GB's eyes turned back to their usual goofiness. "Are you saying the dwarves created you?" Diana asked.

GB shook his head sadly, his goofy eyes making him look all the more miserable and melancholic. "Yep. They made us to dig, and the grimpons forced them to leave us behind. Then the grimpons ate almost all of us. The military took the rest of us. The dwarves don't need us for magic, so we always go to humans and humans never dig. They never have a reason to. That's how we live."

Stew and Sandy went over to GB and took a seat next to him. The gargoyle was crying, shimmering tears that rolled down his face like small diamond pebbles. Stew put his hand on GB's shoulder to try to comfort him. "Dude, how come you never told me about this?" Stew asked. "We're buddies, you know you can talk to me about anything. I mean, you pretty much talk to me about anything even when I don't want to hear it. How come you didn't tell me this?"

"It's not funny. It's just sad."

"GB, you don't have to always be funny."

The gargoyle-like creature looked at Stew. "I thought humans liked funny. They're always saying I'm funny."

"I mean, you are, but you don't have to only be funny. Take me, for example. I'm hilarious. But I'm also strong. Sexy. And extremely smart. You know?"

GB smiled a little bit. It did little to mask the sadness on his face. He sighed heavily. It sounded like he would never stop sighing. "I don't like to talk about it. That's why. I don't like to think about it. It's more fun to talk about that time that we made your dick turn fuzzy."

Stew coughed loudly and covered his face as he blushed brighter than he had the whole day. "Dude, I told you that you need to stop saying that shit out loud!" Stew shouted. "Boundaries, remember? You need to remember our boundaries."

"Sorry, Stew."

"Like we talked about, with boundaries. If you don't want to talk about this, you don't have to. Just say something."

"I can talk," GB said, nodding his head. "It's okay."

Diana didn't waste a beat and turned GB to face her as she pulled her glasses down. "Good. Now I have some questions for you," she rattled on. "When did the dwarves make you? Were you slaves? What kind of work other than digging did they have you do? Are you organic? Do you have organs? And what the hell were the grimpons?"

"I don't know when we were made. And we weren't slaves. We didn't have to dig if we didn't want to, but that's pretty much all we did. Dig, dig, dig, dig. And I don't think I have organs. There's nothing squishy in me. And grimpons are dirt worms. They eat everything that digs."

"What do you mean?"

"They feel you digging in the earth. Then they come gobble you up."

"On the dwarven planets."

"Everywhere."

The ground in the rest stop started to shake as the walls trembled. There was a terrible rumbling that rolled and rolled until it was a near-deafening thunder. GB jumped to his feet, that huge goofy grin back on his face. "That's a grimpon!" he exclaimed. "Now you can see how they like to eat all the good diggers!"

Stew reached out and shook GB like a rag doll. "Are you fucking telling me we're digging a hole in a planet filled with giant worms that eat anyone who is digging underground?!" he shouted.

"Oh, no, Stewart. They don't eat anyone. They just eat the best diggers!"

"Why didn't you tell us this before we started digging?!?"

"Because grimpons are half the fun of digging!" GB shouted as the walls around him shook. Then the rumbling became too much to bear, as did the shaking of their structure. The walls of the rest stop started to come down. Stew raised his arm to shield Sandy, who had pulled out her wand and pointed it at the quickly-descending ceiling. Then everything went dark.

Across the mountain, in a tunnel of their own, Fred was napping quietly as Suzuki and Beth dug their tunnel. Apparently having a physical form had worn Fred out, and he had passed out quickly after they began digging. Suzuki had strapped Fred to his back as Fred explained the situation. Fred said that it could take as little as ten minutes to three hours. Suzuki hadn't had a chance to tease Fred at all before the imp fell asleep. It wasn't difficult to move the imp. He hardly weighed anything. Most of the time that Fred had been sleeping, Suzuki had had him strapped to his back.

Suzuki and Beth worked in silence. The only sound in the tunnel was that of their shovels. After the first hour of digging, they had stopped dealing with soft dirt. Now it was bedrock and stone. Suzuki had gotten around the issue by enchanting Beth's shovel so that it was as hard as a diamond. He even managed to transmute it so that it was shaped more like a pickaxe. Instead of bothering with his shovel, Suzuki found it easier to use his ax. The ax was much sharper. He was also hoping Beth would notice how sick it was. Unfortunately, she seemed very obsessed with their current task.

In a lot of ways, Suzuki was glad that they weren't talking. There had been so much building up in him that he wouldn't even know where to start. Suzuki tried to trace the genesis of his feelings. He had been doing this for a while now, ever since Beth had left to join the military. At first, he thought that the feelings he had were motivated by the fear of missing out on an adventure. The longer he sat around at home, the more he realized that was not the case. He had been in love with Beth for a long time.

Love. It wasn't how Suzuki would have phrased it that long ago. Even a couple of weeks ago, he still wouldn't have attached the word to how he felt. He didn't know what had changed to make him comfortable with saying it to himself. He just knew it. That was why he was here. He loved Beth with all of his heart. She had been the sole motivating factor in his life for longer than he remembered. It was Beth who had dragged him out of his shell when they were playing VR, and it was Beth who had encouraged him to step up to the plate and start leading the Mundanes with his tactics. If it weren't for her, he never would have made it to Middang3ard. He never would have had the guts to fight.

Beth looked at Suzuki and clicked her tongue at him. "Hey, Douchy Suzy, you're falling behind. Pick up the pace."

"Fuck off, you're not the one with an imp strapped to his back."

"If you're gonna be a little bitch about it, we can switch off. I mean, if you think that you need help from a malnourished prisoner, be my guest. I would have thought that the MERCs were keeping you well-fed and strong. Guess I joined up with the right outfit."

"Trust me, I'm well-fed and strong. Strong at least, but the food hasn't been all that good for a while."

"Okay, I was joking, but that definitely hit a nerve. The food that we get at the barracks is shit. They aren't trying to shower us with a lavish life, even if we are the last defense against the Dark One."

"Did you mean what you said back there? About not being able to defeat him?"

Beth stopped digging and let her shovel fall to the side. She turned to face Suzuki, shaking her head. "No, that was the torture talking," she said softly. "It was rough in there. Daily beatings. There are only so many times you can let someone kick your teeth out."

"Looks like you still got a couple."

"They used shit to heal me. Weird shit. It wasn't magic."

"It's because the Dark One isn't using magic. I don't think he's using it at all. You know he's microchipping the different races to control them."

"I had an inkling. I've been hearing things between the walls."

"All of their communication is tech, and I wouldn't be surprised if some of the weapons are too."

"I haven't seen any tech weapons."

Silence fell between them, only it wasn't heavy. It felt natural, a breath of life in their conversation, into this odd time, the two of them alone, beneath the earth.

Suzuki spoke first. "I'm sorry about what happened in there. Shit sounds fucked."

"It was. And I didn't even get the worst of it. Some of my platoon couldn't take the torture. Some of them didn't come back."

"I'm sorry."

"Thanks. I appreciate it."

Beth wiped tears from her eyes. She turned as if she were getting ready to get back to digging, but instead, she fell to her knees. Her body shook as she sobbed and pulled at her hair. She screamed, and it was the sound of pain, pure and unadulterated.

Suzuki knelt next to Beth. He reached out to put his arm around her.

Beth slapped Suzuki's hand away. "Don't touch me," she shouted, stumbling over her words, barely able to get them out. "Don't fucking touch me. Where were you? Where the fuck were you, Suzuki? I needed you. I fucking needed you! I told them you were coming for us. I promised them we were going to make it out, all of us. Every fucking one of us. And I let them die. I couldn't do anything. I let them die, and I couldn't stop any of it."

Beth curled into a ball, hugging her knees between her arms, and fell against Suzuki. She cried until there were no more tears. Her body continued to shiver as she sobbed breathless gasps as if all of the life were being forced out of her lungs. She held Suzuki's hand hard enough that he could feel the bones in his hand squeezing against each other. After some time, Beth was quiet, her back heaving heavily, up and down, in a slow rhythm.

"I tried to get here faster, Beth. I'm sorry. I tried as hard as I—"

"Don't apologize. I know. That's why you're here now. I just... I was close to cracking. I'm glad you came. I knew you would."

"What else would I do?"

"Some people wouldn't come. I know they wouldn't. We're expendable. We're just grunts. Hundreds disappear every day, and they never send search parties. We're pawns in a game, Suz. At least us military are."

"I would never leave you."

"Never split the party, you know," Beth said with a weak laugh.

Suzuki took Beth's chin in his hand so that she could see him; so that she could look him in the eyes. "No, Beth. I mean, I will never leave you."

Beth smiled weakly. She looked like she was made of glass. "I know, Suz. I know." She rested her head against Suzuki's shoulder. They both stared out at the geodes sparkling underground. "Could we just stay here for a little while. God, I wish I was anywhere but this hell hole, but I'm too tired. I just need to sit for a little bit."

"Where do you want to be?" Suzuki asked.

"I don't know. At your place. I never got to see where you lived, like your room or anything."

"It's nothing special. It's kind of shitty, like the kind of nerd cavern you don't want to show anyone."

Beth shrugged. "I still want to see it. I'd much rather be there than here. I'd rather be there than anywhere."

Suzuki knew Fred was asleep. He didn't know how this was going to work out, but he was going to try anyway. He focused, shut his eyes, and tried to clear everything from his mind except for one thought. Everything but one image. He whispered under his breath, "Clairvoyance."

Everything changed instantly. Beth and Suzuki were sitting on Suzuki's bed. The room was modest-sized. The walls were covered in posters from different anime series and D&D campaigns. A large bookcase took up most of one of the walls, and books were spilling from its shelves. The *Middang3ard* VR lay next to a computer, with far too many crumpled napkins sitting next to a bottle of lotion. Suzuki sighed loudly and hoped Beth wouldn't notice.

Beth looked around the room and then sleepily looked at Suzuki. "How did you do that?" she murmured.

"Magic. Getting to you required a lot of upgrades."

"This is exactly what I imagined, cum rags and all."

"We could...uh...go someplace else. If I've been there—"

"No, this is good. This is perfect. This is where I want to be."

Sandy opened her eyes. She couldn't see anything around

her. Her hands reached out in the dark until she found her wand, and she picked it up and cast an illumination spell. The cool, pale light revealed the collapsed tunnel.

Stew was sitting up against the wall. There was a massive gash across his forehead and he was bleeding profusely. "Stew!" Sandy shouted.

Stew's eyes fluttered open. "What's up, babe?" he whispered as he touched his forehead. He looked at his bloody fingers with glazed eyes. "Oh, babe, 'tis just a flesh wound." He chuckled as he slumped forward.

Sandy waved her wand, casting a healing spell as fast as she could. She rolled Stew over on his back. The wound was already nearly done stitching itself up. She tried to waken Stew, but he didn't move. Then she remembered one of the first lessons that Diana had given her on advanced magical healing. Magic can and will always heal physical wounds. It doesn't always heal the ramifications of those wounds. Specifically, head trauma. That's why most MERCs wore helmets, but there wasn't time to think about that. She had to figure out the situation. Sandy pushed Stew back up against the wall and flipped her HUD down. She scanned his body for injuries using the nice feature Chip had added to their HUDs when the Mundanes and the Horsemen had left the Red Lion.

The HUD displayed Stew's body. He had a minor concussion. Sandy sighed with relief. At least it was only minor. Stew would probably wake up in a little bit. That, however, didn't help her with the situation she was in right now. Sandy prodded Stew with her wand a few times before she got up to check the extent of the damage. She checked to see how bad the collapse in the tunnel was. After going over every inch, she thought it was safe to say that the tunnel was airtight. No air was getting out, and none was getting in.

Sandy pulled out her amulet from Ashegoreth. She pressed it to her chest, and her skin dissolved into ash and cloaked her in a miasma of decay. After she had adjusted to being formless, she plunged her hand into her chest.

No organs.

No lungs.

No need for air.

Perfect. This would at least buy some time. Sandy sighed as she leaned back against the other side of the wall so she could keep an eye on Stew. Just blowing her way through the rock wasn't going to help. The grimpons could pick up on whatever she was doing. There was also a chance that more of the tunnel could collapse. The whole point was to use the tunnels to get to Suzuki. If there was anything she had learned from that nerd, it was that you don't sacrifice a plan because it didn't work. You improve it if you can. Using tunnels to get Suzuki and Beth out was the best idea, and Sandy wasn't going to sacrifice the work they'd already done.

"Fuck."

Sandy conjured a tome. She flipped through a few pages and nodded her head, then she cast the book aside. She didn't have time to read through anything. If the Amulet of Elroz was worth anything, she was going to find out soon enough.

Suzuki thought that Beth was sleeping. He was surprised when she spoke, her voice soft, almost as if she didn't want to hear what she had to say. "Suzy..." she murmured.

"Yeah."

"Does anyone else call you that?"

"Uh, Sandy sometimes. why?"

"You remember how you got that nickname, right?" Beth asked.

"I don't know. You were making fun of me or something."

"You know why Sandy calls you that?"

Suzuki shook his head. "'Cause she's teasing me. Same reason you're always calling us douchenozzles."

"Sandy calls you Suzy because I asked her to."

"Why?"

She pursed her lips as if she wasn't sure she wanted to tell him. Then she shook her head, and with a determined look on her face, she said, "So you wouldn't forget about me. You know, because you'd keep hearing it. Like, so I'd be kind of like an afterthought."

"You didn't have to do that."

"You remember why I called you that?"

"Yeah, you were saying that I was soft. You were saying I was really soft, like a Susan or something. You settled on Suzy."

Beth chuckled. "Right. That's not what I meant, though. I didn't say what I wanted to. I was scared. I was really fucking scared, so I was joking. I'm tired of being scared, Suzy."

"So why'd you call me that? I thought you were just saying I was a bitch."

Beth leaned in close. "It's 'cause you're pretty. I think you're really pretty. And I was afraid you'd get butt hurt because I didn't say handsome or some shit and I was scared that you would think it was weird. I guess I was mostly afraid of admitting that I thought you were."

"You think I'm pretty?"

"Yeah. I think you're really pretty."

They were quiet. Suzuki didn't think there was anything worth saying. He was still enjoying the feeling of stillness that had settled over the illusion of his room. It was quiet enough that Suzuki could hear Beth crying softly.

"I'm so tired of being afraid," she choked through soft sniffles. "I have been so scared for so long."

Suzuki reached out to her and pulled her in close. "There's nothing to be afraid of."

"There is always something to be afraid of," Beth said, leaning into him.

Beth's sobs faded and were replaced with quiet snores. She'd drifted to sleep, leaving him with his thoughts. There were far too many to figure out. All he knew was that this was right. Whatever was happening right now was right. It went beyond words and had no need to be spoken. At least right now. He also believed Beth. There was always something to be afraid of. But that didn't change anything for him. He'd been living with fear since he'd come to Middang3ard, some fears larger than others.

And the next thought Suzuki felt clearly, unclouded and distilled into a pure rage that twisted his stomach and set his entire being on fire, was simple: The Dark One was going to be afraid.

The Dark One was going to fear Suzuki. He would fear his face. He would fear his war cry. He would fear his ax as it descended on his neck, cleaving his head from his body.

The Dark One would know fear.

12

Diana woke up covered in dust. She tried to stand, but her body refused to listen. She could not tell where she was.

All of the world was dark.

When she inhaled, it was only the scent of dirt, of soil broken apart and suffocating. "Chip! Sandy!"

There were no answers.

Diana reached out into the dark and fumbled around until she found her wand. She grabbed it and held it tightly as she tried to prop herself up.

The air was thin. There was hardly enough to breathe. The darkness was swimming, and Diana rested her head against the wall. She felt as if the world were caving in around her—but it already had.

Sandy was somewhere.

So was Stew.

Chip wasn't a concern, she could take care of herself. Diana had no worry about that. Both she and Chip had been through worse situations than this one, if not worse, at least comparable.

There was still a tunnel. It would have been impossible for the grimpons to have collapsed the rest pit that they'd built and separate all four of the MERCs. They had to have gone somewhere. It wasn't like they could have just been transported into the dirt unless the grimpons had some kind of magic that Diana had not sensed at first. More likely was that everyone was split up through the tunnel that had been built. All that Diana had to do was figure out how to reconnect with the other tunnels. It'd be easy enough. She sat for a few moments, thinking of the different possibilities, of various outcomes and variables. In the back of her mind, she wished that she could have been trapped with one of the newbs.

This would have been a good time to observe how they reacted under pressure.

Air was the first thing to take care of. When she had been connected to the other tunnel, air had still been funneling through their initial hole. Now that she was cut off from that hole, she had to make sure she didn't suffocate. First things first. Diana cast a protection bubble around her head. It was a trick that she had picked up for underwater missions. Then she pressed the wand to the clear, soapy bubble. The wand passed through the bubble and Diana cast a small whirlwind spell.

Typically, it was an offensive spell, but if the caster was skilled enough, the expansiveness of the spell could be reduced and the wind focused for other purposes. In Diana's case, that meant a constantly circulating cycle of fresh air. Scratch suffocation off of the list.

"Find target," Diana murmured as she sat up, her body still aching from whatever the grimpons had caused to happen.

A golden spear of light flew out of Diana's chest as she

absentmindedly checked her inventory for her mana supply. She had enough to ease her mind. She'd easily get out of this without dipping into her magic reserves.

The golden spear ended at the wall of the enclosed tunnel. "Perfect," Diana muttered to herself as she pointed her wand when the spear had disappeared. A small blue light shot out the tip of her wand, burrowing itself into a sigil which she drew, covering the section of the wall in ancient, magical chicken scratch. When she was done, she tapped her wand against the rock and dirt.

It was neither an explosion nor an implosion. The rock merely collapsed in on itself. There was now a bit more walking room. Diana repeated the sigil work and carved out another bit of the stone and dirt, making a fresh tunnel to connect to wherever else the rest of the MERCs were.

At this rate, this was going to take forever. Diana hoped that whatever was going on with the rest of her friends, that they had figured out a similar plan. In her earlier panic, Diana had forgotten that she could at least try to communicate with the rest of the MERCs. She flipped down her HUD and jotted a message quickly, pinging her location. She sat in the dimly lit tunnel, waiting for a response.

After a few minutes, Diana's HUD pinged. Chip had apparently had the same thought. Diana patched her HUD into Chip's so they could talk. "You still alive?" Diana asked.

Chip's voice came garbled over the HUD's comm. "Barely, and hardly happy about it," Chip complained. "Just once, I'd like one of these shenanigans to go right for a change. My assbone is off-kilter, and I've noticed that there is a surprising lack of ale in these here tunnels."

"Have you heard from José?"

"Aye, he already gave me the scoop on what I figured would be the plan. Converge on the little newbs, righto?"

"Exactly. Might want to link up first, though. You know those grimpon things are—"

Diana's tunnel started to rumble. Something was chewing through the earth surrounding her. "Speak of the fucking devil and he, she, or it will appear. Hold on, Chip."

Diana backed up and placed her ear against the wall. She strained her ear to listen to which direction the rumbling was coming from. Then something dawned on her. If the grimpons were digging through the dirt looking for something to eat, that meant they were leaving tunnels as well. That meant more traveling space, and the potential for less digging.

All Diana had to do was lure the grimpon toward her. Now that she knew what she was up against, whatever the fuck those things were, they weren't going to get the drop on her again.

The rumbling increased. Whatever was coming for Diana was coming fast. Diana's tunnel shook violently and Diana raised her wand, the tip bristling with energy. Then one of the walls of the tunnel collapsed, sending dirt and dust flying everywhere. Diana held her breath and patiently waited for the dust to settle before she fired a blast. Her heart was racing, but she kept her cool. If there was one thing Diana knew she was capable of, it was waiting for the precise moment to be as deadly as possible.

Diana could see a silhouette through the dust. This was her chance. She raised her wand and sent forth a lightning whip, the energy tethered to the tip of her wand.

"Holy shit!" a familiar voice shouted.

Diana withdrew the whip and cast the same whirlwind spell she had used before. The dust shot backward in the direction that whatever stood before her had come from. As the last of the dust cleared away, Diana could see who her assailant was.

José was doubled over, coughing loudly as he tried to fan away the last bit of dust. "Are you trying to fucking kill me?" he shouted.

Diana laughed, and she walked over to José and helped him to his feet. "I figured I'd give a warning just in case it was you. Besides, I knew it was going to take more than a little bit of lightning to kill you," Diana joked.

José dusted himself off and walked farther into the small enclosure. He held an ax in each of his hands, and his face was dripping with sweat. His armor had been removed and his scar-covered chest was heaving with exhaustion. "You seen the gargoyle?" he asked.

"No, I've hardly moved from this spot. How'd you find me so quickly?"

"Not my first time being stuck underground. Honestly, it's happened much more than I'd like to think is normal. You pick up a few tricks. Besides, with all the upgrades Chip's dumped into these HUDs, I honestly don't think I'm ever going to lose track of you two."

"I don't know if that's a good or a bad thing."

"It's definitely an irritating thing."

"And Chip?"

Diana nodded. "She messaged me that she's trying to zero in on the newbs. Figure if I linked up with you, we could get through this faster. I had a feeling you'd be taking your time."

"I don't want to burn through all my mana and risk bringing the tunnel down on myself. And, if I'm going to be honest, I don't work well in enclosed spaces."

"Could have had me fooled."

"So we're digging?"

"Yep."

"And the grimpons?"

"I didn't get a good look at them, but they were fast. Let's try to be faster next time."

Suzuki jerked awake violently. He wasn't sure where he was. The last thing he could remember was falling asleep with Beth at his side. They had been... back home? That didn't make any sense. Slowly, Suzuki started to come out of the haze of sleep.

Too slow, Suzuki thought. *It never takes me this long to wake up. Something's keeping me down. It's almost like a drug.* He tried to push through the fog obscuring his mind. *Where the hell is Beth?* he suddenly thought.

When Suzuki tried to look around in the dark, he found that his neck was stuck. The muscles were working, but there was something restraining him.

That was when he first felt the warm, sticky substance on his neck. That was all he could feel, though.

His whole body was numb.

The fluid covering his neck up to his chin was probably all over his body. That was probably what was keeping him drowsy and incapable of moving.

"Beth?" Suzuki whispered. "Beth, are you there?"

Suzuki heard a soft groan from not too far away. A couple of feet, if that. "Suzy..." Beth murmured. "Is that you?"

"Yeah, yeah. It's me."

Suzuki could hear Beth struggling. Whatever had wrapped him up had taken care of Beth as well. "Ugh." Beth groaned again as she tried to fight the oppressively sticky, slimy substance covering her body. "What the fuck is this shit?"

"No idea."

"Fucking great. I get sprung from a jail cell just so some subterranean perv can cover me in its love funk. This day just keeps getting better."

"Do you know anything about what kind of creatures are in the mountain?"

"Not really. There were rumors about different magical creatures being brought into the camps, but I don't think I ever heard anyone talking about anything actually in the mountains."

They were both quiet for a few minutes, Suzuki trying to figure out how the hell he was going to get out of a seminal cocoon if he couldn't use his hands and Beth silently fighting the fluids that held her down. "Actually," she said after a while, "I did hear something about the mountain. The tunnels that were being used for the prisons, they weren't dug by the Dark One. There was already something here, and the Dark One's forces just moved in and made use of what was already here. Every so often, some guards would turn down the wrong tunnel and end up disappearing. It happens when they move prisoners sometimes. Whatever dug those tunnels is probably still using the ones that weren't taken over by the Dark One."

"All right, so we know there's definitely something else in this tunnel. Obviously, whatever it is uses the tunnels to hunt, but it can't be too starved for food."

"What makes you think that?"

"Well, it didn't eat us right away. Either this thing is pretty well-fed, or it's got other plans for us."

"Dude, we're probably lunch for some queen or something. The whole mountain feels like a giant anthill."

"Let's hope we're just lunch."

Something moved in the darkness. The chamber Suzuki and Beth were in was larger than Suzuki had first assumed. It was nothing like the small tunnel they had dug earlier, or any of the other tunnels they had walked through in the prison. This room was large enough to have an echo. Whatever was moving around in the dark was close, but not close enough to reach out and touch. Not that Suzuki could have if he wanted. It didn't matter. The thing moving in the darkness was getting closer.

It was the clicking Suzuki noticed first. It reminded him of a toy he had owned as a child, an electronic dolphin. When you pressed a button on the back, the dolphin would do an electronic impersonation of a real dolphin's echolocation. The sound was a little bit off on the toy. It sounded as if it were drowning as it clicked away. The creature moving in the darkness sounded very similar. The second sound Suzuki picked up was something dragging itself across the ground. Maybe the creature searching for its way in the dark was gimpy or carried a large club. Whatever Suzuki imagined, it didn't seem good, but he was going to find out soon enough. Too bad he couldn't do anything to defend himself.

There was a sudden brief flash of light. It looked like when a firefly's butt illuminates, but much larger. For a second, Suzuki could make something out in the darkness. He could see the emaciated body, bones sticking out so that the ribs were pronounced, the large, white eyes sunk deep in the creature's skull like those of a dead fish caught up in reverential prayer. It had long arms and legs, feet with grossly disfigured toes that jutted out like a bundle of straw. Its arms hung so the creature's massive knuckles dragged across the ground as it walked, its dull-gray head swaying from side to side as it drooled, its tongue vibrating at a fever pitch against the roof of its mouth while it wheezed heavily, the bones of its spine moving up and down as if they were rearticulating themselves with every labored movement.

The disgusting grimpon moved by stretching its arms forward, then pressing its palms against the ground in an almost apelike fashion. The grimpon clicked its tongue and lumbered its way toward Suzuki and Beth.

The light went out, and Suzuki realized that the brief flash had come from the grimpon. Its skin must have been bioluminescent. Maybe it was a defense mechanism, but with the current situation, it was more likely a way to secure its prey.

Suzuki struggled against the hardened fluid holding him in place. It felt like the more he moved, the tougher the gelatinous goop covering his body became. Or it could have been reacting to the presence of the grimpon, which was now close enough that Suzuki could smell its breath, a rancid, foul scent that reeked of rotting flesh, decay, and something frighteningly sweet. The grimpon took Suzuki's head in its oversized hand, its cold, wet flesh sticking to Suzuki's face. Its fingertips had large suction cups that clung to Suzuki's face as he tried to turn it away. The creature was stronger, though. It forced Suzuki's face forward as its skin lit up again, casting a sickly yellow glow across the vast underground room. The grimpon stared into Suzuki's eyes as it ran its fingers over his face, each suction cup sucking Suzuki's face. He felt the suction cup puncture his skin as the grimpon pried Suzuki's mouth open with its other finger.

The grimpon forced its searching fingertip into Suzuki's mouth as Suzuki gagged. Suzuki bit down as hard as could, but the grimpon didn't seem to mind. The only sign that it acknowledged Suzuki's teeth was a quiet moan that escaped its mouth and the increasing brightness of its glowing skin as it clicked its tongue. The grimpon opened Suzuki's mouth with its other hand and tried to force both of its hands down Suzuki's throat while he tried to keep from vomiting, the sickly-sweet smell from the grimpon wafting into his nose, making him feel dizzy but surprisingly awake and alert. He was getting used to the grimpon's hands in his mouth, propping his tongue, gently piercing the sides of his mouth.

Beth screamed, and Suzuki felt the grimpon withdraw its fingers from his mouth. The light of the room dulled as the grimpon slowly retreated into the darkness. The sweet scent stayed in the air. Suzuki could taste it on his tongue. He realized his mouth was full of something mucus-y and sweet. The realization made him gag, and he spit it up so that it trickled down his chin.

"Jesus fucking Christ, Suzy, that fucking thing just fist-fucked your face," she whispered, her voice tense with desperation. "That was so fucking disturbing."

Suzuki shook his head, confused. "What the hell happened?"

"Are you serious? Did you not see any of that?"

"I guess I did. I don't know. My brain feels fuzzy. It's hard to think straight. I'm actually really tired."

"Don't you fucking go to sleep on me."

"There was something...something in my mouth, right?"

Suzuki felt the world around him slipping for a second.

He really wanted to go to sleep.

His body was exhausted, and he was extremely thirsty. Whatever he had spit up on his neck was getting warmer.

He wished he could wipe it off or rub it into his skin.

That was what he wanted to do.

Rubbing it into his skin would be best.

That was the last thought he had as sleep rose up and

crashed upon him, sending him spiraling into the darkness of his nightmares.

———————

Sandy sat in her collapsed tunnel, meditating. Stew was mumbling in his sleep at her side. He hadn't shown any signs of waking up, but he also hadn't shown any signs of brain damage. This wasn't reassuring Sandy at all. She still hadn't figured out a way to start moving any of the dirt out of the way. Most of the magic that she knew was extremely explosive. Even her sigil and rune work tended to focus around trap magic that could cause massive elemental damage. There didn't seem to be a way for her to start digging herself and Stew out of this mess without killing them both.

As Sandy meditated, she let her mind wander. Each spell she had ever read stretched out before her like a tapestry, an endless number of possibilities, yet nothing was clicking. It seemed there were too many options. This was the problem that Sandy had had when she first started playing *Middang3ard* with the Mundanes. The magic system that the game had been programmed with had always been extremely flexible. Newbs who were magic users had as difficult a time deciding what they could cast as what was available to be cast. In retrospect, Sandy could see that it was good training for getting to real Middang3ard. There were almost no mana restrictions because of her close bond with her familiar. The most she really had to worry about was making sure she didn't burn herself out. She'd noticed that since receiving so many magic upgrades, her casting seemed much less to deal with her mana and more to do with her physical stamina and creativity.

Creativity, however, was what she lacked at the moment. It was just like when she first started playing *Middang3ard*.

Sandy shook her head in frustration. She looked down at her wraithlike hands, the dust floating between her skeleton fingers gripping her wand. What good was all this magical power if she didn't know how to use it? Her head was full of spells, and so far, it hadn't been enough to get her and Stew out of this mess. She would have cried out of pure irritation if she currently had tear ducts. Here she was, wearing the enchanted armor of a renowned mage and it was going to end up rotting underground because she couldn't figure out a reasonable way to use magic to do anything other than electrify or burn things.

Come on, Sandy, she thought to herself. The tunnel was starting to feel smaller, the walls constricting around her. She was glad she didn't need to breathe in this form. Otherwise she would have been hyperventilating. That was just one more thing that wasn't going to help the situation. How the fuck did Suzuki deal with these kinds of situations? Granted, he did have three people to back him up, but Sandy had always been impressed with how quickly he seemed to come up with solutions. And here she was, incapable of even finding a useful spell.

Sandy's mind continued to wander over her insecurities and anxieties, her meditation causing flashes of random or tangential memories to cross between her closed eyes. Then there was something more than just a flash. She felt wind on her skin. When she opened her eyes, she looked down at her hands. They were covered in skin. She looked around, trying to place where she was. It was a garden, one not too different from the garden that her father used to take her to to meditate. There was a cherry blossom tree in the middle of its spring bloom sitting beside a sand garden. Monks walked back and forth through the garden, tending the flowers or meditating quietly by themselves.

"This is what suffocating feels like."

Sandy turned to the source of the voice. Suzuki was sitting at her right. He was dressed as a monk and smiling softly, his eyes closed tightly. "Or I imagine it's what suffocating feels like," he mused. "I've never done it before. But I imagine this is the closest you've ever been as well."

"What the fuck is going on, Suzuki?"

"I believe you are having a near-death experience. This is what you've conjured to make sense of your impending death."

"You're saying that I imagine you as a guru?"

"I don't make the rules, Sandy. I am only a manifestation of your subconscious. You need to take your visions up with yourself."

Sandy sighed and ran her hands through her hair, pulling it so that she could feel her scalp stretching. "I don't have any fucking answers." She sighed, exasperated. "And I can't believe that my last moments alive are going to be stuck getting lectured by you. This fucking sucks."

"Technically, you're lecturing yourself."

"Fucking great."

"Why do you think that you would see Suzuki as your guide to death?"

"I don't fucking know why I'm seeing Suzuki."

"Does Suzuki know why you are seeing him?"

"What the hell is that supposed to mean?"

"What does that mean, indeed?"

"What are you trying to tell me? What the hell are you trying to say?"

Suzuki opened his eyes and continued to smile. He slightly tilted his head as he pointed to the cherry blossom tree. "Trees bloom," he said. "That is what they do. Painters paint. Writers write. The earth grows and it dies. What is it that you do?"

Sandy was close to tears. She didn't realize that they were gathering against the back of her eyelids until she had to choke them back. "I don't fucking know what I do!" she shouted. "I don't fucking know what I'm supposed to do! Stew is going to die. He's going to die and it's my fault, and all you can fucking do is give me riddles about what I'm supposed to do? What the fuck do you do?"

Suzuki shrugged, and he closed his eyes again. He inhaled deeply and exhaled slowly. "Button mashing is for newbs. Do you remember when I told you that?"

"Yeah, I remember. And?"

"You don't have any buttons, yet you are still behaving as if you do. Why do you want to have buttons?"

Sandy gasped and her eyes snapped open. She was back in the tunnel. Stew was still sitting against the wall, snoring softly. "Fucking button-mashing," Sandy muttered to herself. Then it clicked. She didn't know why she hadn't figured this out before. The answer was in front of her the entire time.

It didn't matter how many spells she knew. It didn't matter how quickly she could whip them out and mash them together. That was just insecurity. Anxiety. Fear. If she was going to get through this, she was going to have to act like what she knew she was.

A mage. A badass mage.

Sandy stood and raised her hand. Her wand disappeared and was replaced with a gnarled wooden staff. She didn't know why, but she felt that it was a better choice. Then she grabbed Stew and dragged him away from the wall, into the center of the tunnel, by her side. When she felt she was ready, she took a deep breath. Then she focused her mind on one thing. Expanding. The whole world around her growing farther and farther away. The walls being pushed back. And at the same time, she felt the outer tunnels, the ones that she was cut off from getting closer and closer. The tunnel that she was in rippled with energy. Sandy did not stop focusing. Her body suddenly felt very faint and light. But she did not stop focusing. And reality pulsed around her.

Diana and José were digging as fast as they could. They had created a system. Diana would cover the walls with runes and sigils, breaking down the earth so that it was easy to move, expanding their tunnel outward for structural integrity, and José would shovel.

José had stripped off his armor and was double axing in a straight pathway toward where they both had assumed Sandy and Stew were.

The MERC leader worked with a grim determination, his face almost as rough-hewn as the stone he cut through. His axes rose and fell with the constant beat of a metronome. One ax rose as the other fell, chipping the stone away, sending sparks flying up into the air as José's labored breathing mixed with the sound of cracking rock. The man worked with an urgency that had not been present over the last few days. It was as if he were possessed. His eyes hardly turned from the burgeoning tunnel in front of him. He only occasionally turned to ask Diana to recast Find Target so that he could be assured that he was moving in the right direction. Once the golden light of Diana's arrow faded, José would return to his mad cutting away of their potential death.

It had been a long time since Diana had seen this side of José. Between his flippant attitude, brash arrogance, and gambling, she had forgotten that beneath all of that bullshit, there was a man who was a MERC. A MERC who took his job and their party seriously. It was a pleasant change. It was also unfortunate that it had taken a near-death experience to bring this out of him.

That being said, José was a beast. He was moving faster than a mechanical mining machine. There was no magic either. It was all muscle and sheer will, breaking straight through the heart of the mountain. It was no wonder that José was seen as God by many of the MERCs, not just the newbs, the vets too.

Diana coated the walls with another round of sigils. They were making headway. She knew that one of the reasons that José was cutting through the rock so easily was because her sigils were softening up the earth. They were a team working as it was meant to. They had slid into their roles so effortlessly.

Somewhere out there was Chip, playing the hardest role of all. Diana knew she was going to come through, though.

José slammed his ax into the rock and sighed heavily as he leaned over and tried to catch his breath. "How much longer do you think we're gonna be at this?" José asked.

Diana pushed past José and covered his wall with sigils with a wave of her wand. "Don't know," she finally admitted. "They can't be too far unless they're digging in the opposite way. I hardly doubt that Sandy's forgotten how to use Find Your Target. We should be coming up on them in a little bit."

"She could be panicking. Something fucked could have happened to Stew. They could—"

"You need to calm down. You're not helping anyone if you go into 'worried dad mode.' Keep it together, all right?"

"I'm not—"

"You are. This isn't the same thing as... It's not the same. Do you understand me?"

Diana placed her hand on José's shoulder and he looked up at her. His eyes were heavy and full, little brown pools that seemed to stretch down infinitely into his soul. "I understand." José sighed. "Let's go find these kids."

José turned back to the earth, his axes hanging heavy, as if they were a responsibility. A weighty, sharpened guilt.

Suzuki awakened.

His eyes were stuck together, his eyelids plastered with some kind of mucus. The feeling had completely gone out of his feet and his hands. It was as if he were a suspended head, cut off from the rest of his body. The only feeling that remained was in his mouth, which was held open by what seemed to be a web. Whatever it was, it was strong. A sense of horror slowly crept up Suzuki's spine. He forced his head to move and his eyes to open a crack. The room was no longer as dark as it had been. The dim, glowing, yellow-green light had returned, and it had multiplied.

Twenty grimpons encircled Suzuki. Suzuki checked his HUD. Seventeen percent chance of surviving a head-on fight. Shit.

The monsters were crouched down, their legs up against their chest, their arms wrapped around the perversely long appendages. Their sickly white eyes eerily mirrored the luminescence from their skin. They were clicking their tongues in some odd percussive symphony that sent Suzuki's head reeling. He tried to look away, but he could hardly move. His eyes kept working, though, and he tried to take in as much as he could. Out of the corner of his eye, he could see Beth, who was also cocooned. Her eyes were closed. Whatever the grimpons had given Suzuki to put him to sleep, they also must have slipped to Beth as well.

The space Suzuki was in was larger than he had initially thought. Now that there were so many grimpons lighting the area, he could see that they were actually in some kind of cavern, although a very different one than the dragon's. This did not appear to have occurred naturally. The walls were covered in bizarre etchings and drawings.

If Suzuki could find a way out of the cocoon, he thought he'd be able to take the grimpons. They looked frail enough. Generations of living under the mountain and scavenging food probably hadn't caused them to evolve into particularly good fighters. That must have been why they had captured him and Beth while they were sleeping. They were opportunists at best.

The grimpons continued to click their tongues. It sounded as if they were praying or singing. And somewhere, in the darkened, cavernous tunnels, something large moved. Suzuki could hear it scraping against the sides of the tunnels. The scraping mixed with the clicking and Suzuki suddenly felt he was going to need a change of plans.

The thing moving in the dark screeched. It was the sound of a thousand voices, of hunger and lust mixed with anguish and despair. Suzuki tried to pull away from the sound as it bored into his brain, but he was stuck. All he could do was listen, trying to catch a glimpse of whatever approached.

He saw the thing coming in the dim yellow light as it moved with a jitter of its emaciated body, its skin hanging over its thin arms and legs like a sack of wet clothes laid over a chair to dry. Its hair hung over its shoulders in ratty clumps, its scalp bare in patches. The clicking was growing louder and louder. Its eyes were sweeping over everything in the cavern, shooting forth rays of dead yellow lights as if some sort of demented light bulb were glowing behind that pale, stretched, and yellowing skin. It was gibbering as it clicked its tongue, slobber and drool trickling down its chin as it gummed its toothless mouth together with a smacking, jabbering repetition that set Suzuki's nerves on fire.

Suzuki looked at the mucus that had covered and hardened around his hand. It was of no use. His fingers were incapable of moving. His body was useless to him.

Only his eyes still had purpose. And that purpose was to behold the grimpon king as it dragged his heavy, hairy palms across the ground like a great white ape once lost in the hills, lost long enough to have wasted away to a skeleton of its former strength, to have sat by ponds and rivers, coughing, hacking, trying to remember its name until it could only recall the sound of coughing, of clicking, of small, silver fish torn in its hands and swallowed in haste.

The grimpon king took Suzuki's head in his hand, much like the other grimpon had earlier. He moved Suzuki's head around as if he were surveying a piece of fruit. Then the grimpons surrounding Suzuki and Beth converged on him. Suzuki felt fingers pulling at his face, the small suction cups on the grimpon's fingers pulling at his skin, piercing it, letting the blood flow free. Suzuki screamed and regretted it as he felt the grimpons tugging at his lips, holding his mouth open as he gasped for air. The king grimpon's solemn face was before Suzuki, his huge sagging lips hanging nearly off the bone as he stretched his mouth open, his tongue slinking out from behind those toothless jaws. His tongue was covered in hairy bristles as if a host of small spiders had taken up residence on it. The grimpon king ran his fingers across Suzuki's skin as he pulled himself up to his full height, towering over Suzuki as if he were some ancient and grave calamity set to befall the world beneath him, holding his arms together in some old and forgotten sign of prostration. The hall was now silent; all was silence other than the clicking of the grimpon king's tongue as the skin across his face peeled back so his jaws could be seen as they split open. The gaping maw stretched all the way down his throat, lined with small bulbs that glowed with the same feeble light shooting forth from the king's eyes, which were held on a swivel now that his face had broken apart. His hairy tongue was searching for Suzuki's mouth as Suzuki tried to pull away, his eyes wide with terror, his screams filling the cavern.

The clicking stopped.

Instead, there was the sound of cracking dirt, of earth collapsing on itself, of a massive explosion and screams. The grimpons scrambled.

Suzuki tried to make out what was happening in the pandemonium but it was too dark. The grimpons' bodies had lost their light, and they had scattered into the darkness. All that Suzuki could see were sparks far too close to his head, his ears deafened by the sound of grinding.

There was a flash of light, and Suzuki's body was suddenly free. He fell to his feet and looked up.

What he saw almost made him scream. Chip was standing over him, but she was not as she ought to have been. The right side of her face was nearly obliterated, her skin barely hanging on, and underneath, a series of gears and lights were shining brightly. Her left arm had been ripped off. Pieces of cable snaked out of her shoulder blade like multicolored tendrils. Her right arm was even harder for Suzuki to comprehend. The skin had changed. Up near her shoulders was regular skin, but the farther down her arm you looked, the less like skin it seemed to be. It appeared metallic, but it was flaking. Instead of a hand, Chip's fingers converged in a smooth light canon. It looked like something pulled out of a science fiction story. It had an elegant, swooping oval design that broke apart and reconvened around a singular, glowing blue light.

Chip's hand smoked as she aimed at Suzuki's feet. She fired once, clearing away whatever had been keeping Suzuki captive. "Get off your fucking ass now!" Chip shouted as she whipped around, her left eye practically bulging out its socket, the skin around it glowing with an odd blue hue, as if there were only gears and cables beneath her epidermis.

Suzuki jumped to his feet. He didn't bother looking anymore at Chip. Whatever the fuck was going on with her, this wasn't the time or place to try and figure it out.

Chip grabbed Suzuki, her eye now popping out of the socket and hanging from a cable. "Where the fuck is everyone?" she shouted. Her voice sounded completely different. All her vocal ticks were gone, and her voice was much deeper, almost inhuman.

Suzuki ran over to Beth and tried to pull her out of the mucus cocoon. "What are you talking about?" Suzuki shouted, aware that the clicking from the grimpons was beginning again. "No one—"

"They should be on my tail. The Horsemen and your guys. I was broadcasting my signal. They should—"

Chip was cut short as something tackled her in the dark. She screamed as she rolled over and fired off two shots of blue plasma that lit the cavern for a brief moment, illuminating walls covered with grimpons, their mouths hanging open, their tongues vibrating back and forth as their bodies undulated against the smooth cavern walls. The Grimpon king was standing beneath them, his arms outstretched as his tongue lolled out of his mouth, the hairs on his tongue growing longer and waving as if a breeze had blown through the cavern.

Suzuki reached for his ax. There was nothing. He pulled down his HUD frantically to check his inventory. He had left it somewhere, or it had been taken from him. Then he remembered.

A grimpon tackled Suzuki and they both went rolling. Suzuki was barely able to get to his feet as the grimpon's legs and arms thrashed about, trying to wrap Suzuki in a deadly embrace. Instead, Suzuki punched the grimpon in the face and held it down by its neck as he raised his other hand and thought of his ax. He gritted his teeth and hoped this was going to work.

Across the cavern, there was another crashing noise. Suzuki looked over, still holding the grimpon down.

There was a hole in the cavern, one the grimpons were quickly running away from. As the dust settled, José and Diana were illuminated by the occasional bursts of yellow light coming from the scattering, scampering grimpons. José screamed as he beat his ax to his chest, his silver armor sliding over his body as it materialized, a helm cobbling itself into existence, its ram's horns swooping down nearly to José's back. At José's side, Diana stepped forward, waving her wand as she floated off the ground, three cracks of lightning flying it in an awesome display of passive magic. "Suzuki, is that you?" Diana shouted.

Suzuki pulled himself to his feet and slammed the heel

of his foot into the grimpon's face. He felt a sudden urge to lift his arm and open his hand. As he did so, he felt the weight of his ax, slamming into his palm, which he instinctively closed before he brought his ax down on the grimpon's head. "Who the fuck else would it be?" Suzuki shouted.

"Where's Sandy? Where's Stew?"

Suzuki left the grimpon's corpse and went to Beth. "No idea," he shouted to Diana as he hacked Beth out of the cocoon. "I'm honestly surprised to see you guys here."

Beth fell into Suzuki's arms. He held her up for a second before slapping her across the face, causing her to instantly snap awake. "Come on," he said. "We need you up now."

Suzuki put Beth on her feet as she tried to blink the haze out of her eyes. She slapped her HUD and her armor shimmered onto her body, a short sword and buckler conjuring themselves into her hands. "What am I killing?" Beth sleepily asked.

"Whatever the fuck isn't human."

"Good enough for me."

Beth leaned forward as if she were going to fall back asleep. Then she bounded forward into the darkness as the lights of the grimpons flashed sporadically. There was a loud screech and a grimpon's body flew across the room, landing at Suzuki's feet, its head removed from its body. "Am I killing all these motherfuckers by myself?" Beth shouted.

Suzuki threw himself into the dark, following Beth's voice. He had no idea where she was. The cavern was too dark. Other than the occasional flashes of light from the grimpons, Suzuki had nothing. He turned and felt something against his shoulders. He reached out and took hold of it. The skin was soft and slimy. Suzuki raised his ax and brought it down on the thing's skull. "Hey, could I get a little bit of light in here?" Suzuki shouted. "I don't want to ax anyone accidentally."

From the darkness, "Working on it!"

Suzuki stumbled and felt something grab him. He raised his ax, but a callused hand reached out and pushed back his palm. There was another flash of yellow light. Suzuki saw José, his helm covered in blood, his sword in one hand, a grimpon at his feet, its sickly appendages twitching in death. José's helm disappeared, and Suzuki could see his face. José was beaming. "Now this is a goddamn scrap, ain't it?" he exclaimed.

The lights went out again. Suzuki felt José move past him, then there was another body, its fingers around Suzuki's throat, casting him to the ground.

There was a flash of light, this time from a bolt of lightning landing at Suzuki's side. Diana floated past him, three grimpons grasping at her as dozens of grimpons crawled across the ceiling like roaches fleeing the light. Diana waved her wand, sending the grimpons closest to her flying through the air. Then she spoke with a deep voice, so deep that Suzuki could hear it in the core of his being. A gust of wind flew through the cavern, lifting a handful of grimpons into the air where they hung for a few seconds before their flesh burst into flames. They fell to the ground but didn't stop burning. The flames spread across the bodies of the dead so that there were bonfires all throughout the cavern.

Suzuki turned, catching a grimpon running past him and sending the creature flying, instantly bursting into flames. Then Suzuki knelt and ran his fingers over his ax so that it glowed brightly. He shone it in the cavern of madness and death as José leapt across the room, tackling the grimpon king. José drove the creature to the ground, both of them skidding across the dirt as the king struggled to its feet, its ass shaking violently as four legs burst out of its rectum, its chest swelling and cracking open at the sternum, four or five bones pushing themselves through the gap in his chest cavity. The bones protruded and snapped open, the head of an old man forcing itself out from behind the bones, his jaw dropping open nearly three feet. A slithering stinger unfolded from his mouth. The main head of the king clattered his tongue as he swiped at José with his shovel-like hands.

José dodged the grimpon king's stinger as the king fell to the ground on all its legs, breaking its back so that it stood as some scorpion abomination, its two mouths clicking and clacking, its legs scuttling forward as the horde of grimpons massed behind, their eyes beaming yellow light while the bodies of their brethren burned.

Suzuki called his ax back to him and leapt through the air at the grimpon king, passing José and slamming hard into the king's massive body. He drove his ax deep into the monster as the grimpon king slapped him off. Suzuki fell to the ground. He looked up and rolled to the side as the king tried to puncture him with his legs. Suzuki tried to get to his feet when he saw another body flying through the air onto the grimpon king.

It was Beth. She was jamming her sword into the gap in the king's chest. The king was screeching, backing up against the wall, his arms flailing as his stinger snapped against Beth's neck repeatedly. Beth screamed and raised her shield to block the attack.

Suzuki scrambled out from under the grimpon king's feet. He jumped onto the monster's back and brought his ax down on his neck. The cavern lit up from another flash of lightning. Suzuki could see Beth's face clearly, covered in black and green blood, her eyes alight with the thrill of the fight. She raised her sword in the air and brought it down with enough force to send the grimpon king stumbling backward as Suzuki chopped at the monster's main head. "This one is ours, Suzy!" Beth shouted.

The grimpon grabbed Suzuki, tossed him into the air, and slammed him against the ground. His main head slammed into Beth, who fell next to Suzuki. The grimpon king reared up on his legs and screeched.

Suzuki jumped up and helped Beth to her feet. He picked up her sword, raised his hand, and called his ax back. "This one's ours," he agreed.

Beth and Suzuki rushed the grimpon king. Beth went low, sliding under his feet, cleaving off two of his right legs, causing the monster to topple to the side. Suzuki went high, soaring through the air, landing on the king's chest, using the king's secondary head to climb higher until he was staring the grimpon king in the face. He raised his ax, and with every fiber of his body called lightning into his blade. The ax burst into a flame bright enough to light the entire cavern. Suzuki plunged it deep into the grimpon king's head, yet he didn't stop there. He pulled out his ax and then went for the neck, hacking at the king's throat as if it were a piece of lumber.

The clicking stopped. There was only the sound of the ax tearing skin, of steel piercing flesh.

The grimpon king's dead body fell to the ground. The Horsemen, Beth, and Suzuki cloistered around the body as the mass of remaining grimpons swarmed the walls and ceiling. Diana cast another bolt of lightning that lit the cavern in a bright flash of whiteness, illuminating hundreds of grimpons running over each other, pushing between the other's arms and legs just for the chance to tear any of the MERCs apart. The MERCs clustered closer together as they raised their weapons, preparing for what looked like it could be their last stand.

Suzuki held out his hand, and his ax flew from across the room into his palm. José and Diana were at one side, Chip at the other, launching blast after blast of glowing blue plasma. Beth was pressed to his back. He could feel her heart pounding in her chest as she slammed her sword against her shield, shouting at the grimpons around them.

Beth reached back for a second and touched Suzuki's cheek. It was enough to distract him. He turned to face her. She smiled, wiping blood and chunks of flesh from her face. "So, this is how we're going out? Shame the whole party—"

There was a sound like a person blowing up a balloon and then letting all of the air out of it. Everything in the cavern pulled forward for a second before being blown back. Suzuki struggled to get back to his feet as the contents of the cavern spun around, the whole world going upside down for a second, righting itself, and then flipping once more.

The cavern was no longer dark. It was bright as day.

Sandy was standing at the end of the cavern's tunnel. Her skeleton still stood out, but it was draped in vines, in blooms and blossoms, a crown of cherry blossoms resting on her brow. She held Stew in her arms. The earth around the opening in the tunnel from which she came was covered in grapevines. the grapes bright purple and ready to burst. As she stepped forward, the ground beneath where she floated burst open with life. Grass grew and flowers sprouted and opened their petals to a sun that they perhaps would never know.

The grimpons ceased moving. They turned their blind eyes toward Sandy, who was beaming light that haloed her ivory skull as she turned her skeletal grin toward them. "Never split the goddamn party," she whispered.

Tendrils exploded from Sandy's body. They wrapped up the grimpons, snaking over them with an intelligence far beyond Sandy's body or her understanding of magic. They gripped the grimpons and lifted them into the air as flowers and foliage sprouted around the cavern, a blinding light still ushering forth from Sandy, who was now covered in a blanket of grass, flower petals falling from the ceiling all around her.

The grimpons screeched, their tongues clicking uncontrollably until Diana raised her wand as Sandy raised her staff. Diana touched her wand to one of the grimpons, and a fire spread across the cavern, setting each grimpon aflame.

Silence reigned in the cavern. Only the sound of burning flesh, the soft wheezing of last breaths taken slowly with agony. Sandy walked past the burning bodies, her body aflame and bright like some saintly maiden of death long forgotten within the annals of mythology. Without warning, the flowers covering her body curled up and turned brown and dead. The ashes floating around her drew to the bone and solidified as flesh, and her skin returned. She fell to the floor in a heap of her own robes, her breathing shallow. Stew slipped out of her arms and dropped to her side.

All around the Mundanes and the Horsemen lay the bodies of dead grimpons. The only smell in the cavern was that of blood.

Suzuki ran to Sandy and sat her up. Her robes were gone. She was dressed just as she would have been back on Earth. Beth came up and knelt down beside Sandy as Stew murmured in his sleep. "Is she going to be okay?" Beth asked.

Diana knelt beside Sandy, taking Sandy's head into her

arms. She checked Sandy's pulse and then listened to Sandy's heart. Finally, she looked up and smiled. "She'll be okay. She's just tired. Give it an hour or two and she'll be back up, which is saying a lot. I've never seen a display of raw magic like that before. Ever. And she's going to bounce back from that."

José wiped the blood off his swords as he smiled and patted Suzuki on the back. "You Mundanes never fail to disappoint." He looked around at the dead bodies that littered the cavern. "Maybe we should take a breather. It looks like we might have some catching up to do."

Suzuki nodded as he surveyed the damage. Taking a breather was probably a good idea.

13

———

It took the Mundanes and the Horsemen nearly an hour to clear up all the bodies. They mostly worked in silence. It was easier than talking. Suzuki had noticed that he often needed some decompression time after a fight of that magnitude. The fear of dying and the rush of life wasn't something that he could easily put into words. Sometimes it felt good just to rest with the knowledge of his own mortality. That, and he never really felt like much of a conversationalist when he was picking up decapitated heads.

Suzuki was methodically looking through the grimpon corpses for something specific.

The king.

It took him a bit longer than he had hoped: the dead all seemed to blend together. He did eventually find the king, and he propped up the grotesque, cave-dwelling creature to take a good look in his eyes. Both sets. When Suzuki was satisfied, he chopped the head off and returned to the fire the two parties had slowly gathered around, leaving the other pyre of bodies to burn unwatched.

José and Diana were sitting together and talking quietly.

Beth was still tending to the bodies. Sandy and Stew were sleeping together, their backs leaning on each other's, both of them snoring loudly. Chip sat across from them, staring into the fire, her bad eye still hanging out of her skull, staring down at her missing arm. She sighed and kicked at the fire.

Suzuki came and sat next to Chip, placing the grimpon king's head next to her. Chip looked up from the fire, her bad eye flashing bright blue. Her other hand had returned to normal and she picked up the grimpon king's head, staring into its dead, cataract eyes. "Now that's a nice souvenir," she murmured. "You planning on keeping it? Would make a proper ashtray. Speaking of that, you don't smoke, do you?"

Suzuki shook his head.

"Damn it," Chip said as she tried to get to her feet. Suzuki could hear the gears beneath her body grinding. Something sputtered, and she sighed and sat back down. "Be a sweetheart and go get me a cig from José, would you?"

Suzuki nodded and went to José. "Chip wants to know if you have any smokes?" Suzuki asked.

José reached under his armor and pulled out a small wooden cigarette case. He handed it to Suzuki and leaned in close so that only Suzuki could hear him. "How's she doing?"

"I don't know. How the hell can you tell? I mean, what is she?"

"No fucking clue." José sighed. "We found her batshit out of her mind in the woods years ago. She's been with me ever since. Never seen her get this trashed before."

"Does she need replacement parts or something?"

"Don't know. She keeps what she does to herself. Never seen her lose an arm before."

Suzuki thought about walking away and not saying anything. It wasn't any of his business. Then he turned back to look José in the eyes. "Someone needs to reach out to her. *You* need to talk to her."

José shook his head. "We'll talk soon enough. Get your shit together soon. We gotta figure out what our next move is going to be."

Suzuki went back over to Chip and handed her the cigarette. She rested it in her lips and then leaned forward, lighting the cigarette with the campfire. As she exhaled a cloud of smoke, she sighed and smiled a little bit. "Thanks, boyo. Nothing like a little tinder after a scrap."

The flames crackled and Suzuki took a seat next to Chip, watching Sandy and Stew sleep. "Your voice sounds different," Suzuki said.

"Oh, yeah? It's about time. The ol' corpse is trying to build itself back up. Peep a gander a little closer, and you'll see something right magical."

Suzuki took Chip up on her claim. He scooted a little closer and looked at her face, which was torn to shit, her eye hanging out and her skin all chewed up as if she had been thrust face-first into a lawnmower. And there was something crawling in the folds of her cut-up, gashed face. They looked like tiny bugs, but they were too small to be bugs, and too fast. As Suzuki leaned closer to get a better look, he could see that they were millions of almost indiscernible creatures, slowly stitching Chip's face together like the most ornate of tapestries. "What the fuck are those?" Suzuki asked.

"Looks like magic, don't it? They're me, I guess. I know when I get all broken up, that's what's underneath. So, I think they might be me."

"And what are you?"

"José tell you?"

"All he said was that he found you in a forest."

"Found me, fell in love with me, fucked me, found out that all my bits are gears, bells, and whistles with no heartbeat, but enough love to drown the world."

Suzuki was taken back by that, but he held himself steady, poker-faced. "Uh...he didn't say all of that...I thought you said you were a half-elf from New Jersey."

"I remember being a half-elf from New Jersey. I remember seeing my grandfather die, and holding his hand while he slipped away. I remember my first kiss...and fuck. I remember going to college, my bootcamp with the military, deciding to shack up with MERC, my first kill, the hot blood on my face. I remember all that. But I don't think it happened 'cause I don't remember at any point getting lost in the forest, but that sure as fuck happened. Last time I checked, half-elves had a pulse. Can't say I can remember ever having one of those."

"You don't know where you came from?"

Chip shrugged. "The MERCs been trying to figure it out for years, pulling me apart and seeing if they could put me back together. If it weren't for José and Diana, I probably would still be on an operating table. But no, no one knows who built Pinocchio. It's the best-kept secret on Middangeard as far as I'm concerned."

"You'll be okay?"

"I'll be good. Go hang back with your Sleeping Beauties and make sure that nothing happens to 'em. I'll see if I can get Diana to keep me company. Stitching your body up is an exhaustingly dull task, but I'm tired of talking about me."

Suzuki shook his head and forced a smile. "Hey, no. You still owe me that embarrassing story."

Chip chuckled. "Survive this and maybe I'll tell you. Until then, what's your plan, boyo?"

"What do you mean?" Suzuki asked.

"You rescued the girl. You're the hero. What next?"

"You guys rescued us."

Chip nodded at the others. " I think that honor goes to Sandy."

"We're not done yet. Beth and I still need to find her familiar. It's still attached to her, just not in her, you know?"

"I've heard of such things before."

"Her captain, too. He's still in there. Beth said she's not going without him."

"How'd you find Beth?" Chip asked.

"We had an inside guy. He said he was a spy for MERC, but we got separated from him. He went radio-silent."

Chip raised an eyebrow. "Happen to catch his name?"

"Ansalm."

"I didn't know Ansalm was still active in these parts. Squirmy little bastard. Think he still owes me six ales and a goat. Don't ask 'bout the goat. You said he went silent on you?"

"Yeah. We didn't know what happened."

"All right. Gimme a second." Chip laid down, lifted her eye, and set it back in its empty socket. Then she closed her eyes very tightly. After a few seconds, her entire body started humming and vibrating. Suddenly it stopped. When she sat back up, her eyes were back to normal. "Kinda need these to give you a hand," she murmured as her eyes rolled back, the whites shining like small light bulbs.

"What are you doing?"

"Accessing Ansalm's MERC info. It's not something we're supposed to be doing, but once you get hooked up to the system, you're always hooked up. So, let's see... He is most definitely assigned spy duties in the defense rings, and it looks like his HUD is still active, so he's still kicking. Let me see your HUD."

Suzuki removed his HUD and handed it to Chip. She held the HUD in her good hand. Her fingers split apart, and small soldering irons came out from some white long cables, with snakelike heads coming from the others. The cables inserted themselves into Suzuki's HUD as Chip began making upgrades. When she was done, she handed the HUD back to Suzuki and he slipped it on over his head.

"There you go." Chip sighed. "That's about all the juice I got in me without passing the fuck out. You'll directly patch to Ansalm and be able to send communications through your familiar from just about damn near anywhere. Just let me know when you're done with it. I don't want a connection like that to stick around for any...uncomfortable situations."

"Then the plan is to get in touch with Ansalm and find the captain and Beth's familiar. Then get the fuck out of there."

"How you gonna do that?" Chip asked. "Last time I checked, this place is a little bit windy."

Suzuki sighed as he shook his head. He had no idea how they were going to get out quickly. He knew that they'd be able to manage if Ansalm was guiding them along the way, but their last attempt to escape from the prison hadn't exactly ended up going well.

"No fucking clue." Suzuki groaned.

"Hmm. Well, I was saving this one for a big one, but I think this might be the biggest that we're gonna get."

Chip pulled up her HUD and scrolled through her inventory. A small Bluetooth headset with a glowing blue button materialized in her palm. She handed it to Suzuki.

"That's a one-time teleportation device, keyed to me. You hit that button, and anyone holding your hand will come whooshing back to me. Make sure to close the circuit. You want more than one person, make sure you're all holding hands. Take it off as soon as you get back because it's been known to...fry the brains a little bit."

"Yeah, I can see why no one uses teleportation."

"Magic can fuse you. Tech will sizzle your gray mess. All this helpful enough?"

"Fuck yeah, it is."

"Great. Now get scampering. We ain't got a fortnight to be camping here. Best be making the best of our time."

"And you'll make sure that Sandy and Stew are okay."

Chip nodded at Sandy. "Me and Sparkle Fingers will take care of it. See what José's thinking 'bout doing too. He's probably cooking something up."

Suzuki rose, staring at the flames. "Thanks," he said. "For saving my ass. And all of this. I mean, everything—"

"Don't worry about it. MERCs stick together. Now just try not to get yourself skewered while you're out living your nerd boy dreams."

"I'll try."

Suzuki made his way over to José, watching Beth out of the corner of his eye. She was still posted up by the fire, glaring at it as if she could divine some kind of meaning from its flicker. Suzuki assumed that she was still processing what had happened and what they were going to do. He wondered if being in the military was anything like being a MERC. Even though Suzuki had formerly had his doubts, it seemed like the MERCs did more than just stick together. Never in his life would he have imagined three near-strangers risking their lives multiple times in the day for him. And on top of that, even with all of the damage and pain, they still seemed like they were having a good time. Chip was hardly even able to stand, and she didn't seem fazed at all. Diana was tending to Stew and Sandy's wounds without so much as a word of complaint or worry. They were the very definition of adventurers, of badasses. Only José seemed to be bothered. Since they'd been out, Suzuki had seen a brooding, pain-stricken man, not the same man who had brushed off jokes about being the second coming of Christ.

The Horsemen were definitely the stuff of legends.

José had moved to sit on a boulder farther away from the fire. He was smoking one of the hand-rolled cigarettes he had lifted from the cigarette case that had been given to Chip. He ashed the cigarette unceremoniously on his knee as Suzuki approached him.

Suzuki climbed up on the boulder next to José, who didn't bother to look at him. "She's gonna be okay," Suzuki assured José.

"Yeah, I know. That still doesn't keep me from worrying. So, what's your next step? We're not exactly in the position to rest. We probably should keep moving until we get out of the Dark One's territory. It only makes sense that the asshole would build a fortress in such a shithole as this."

"Beth and I are going back into the prison. We're going to get her captain out and figure out whatever the fuck they did to her familiar."

"What good is a captain without an army?"

"I don't know if I'll be able to get both. Like you said, we're still crunched for time."

"Does she know that?"

"I don't know."

"A small army would be helpful, though. I think I can take care of that."

"What do you mean?"

"Stew and Sandy will be waking up soon enough. You saw how much heat that girl is packing, and I got a good feeling about Stew. I think he's holding a lot back. I don't really think there's a weak link among you. I feel comfortable leaving them with Chip, Diana, or by themselves. I'll head back into the prison and spring whoever I can. Bring them back here."

"How are you going to find your way back? It's really fucking confusing in—"

"I always find my way back. Trust me."

Suzuki nodded as he stood. "All right. So, we'll meet back here. Go from there?"

"Yeah. And kid, just want you to know, you're doing good."

"Thanks. It means—"

"No, I mean you're doing really good. You've got the makings of a great leader. I haven't seen many guys who will put this much of themselves on the line for one person. It's impressive. So...be safe. If you need anything, let me know. You get yourself into a jam, you let me know. Promise me."

José turned to face Suzuki. His eyes were heavy and sad and he looked ancient, but only for a moment. "Don't do anything stupid. Promise me."

Suzuki stuck out his hand. José took it, and they shook. "I promise," Suzuki agreed as he walked off to join Beth at the bonfire. He sat down, unaware of how close he was sitting to Beth. She looked at him and leaned her head on his shoulder as she sighed heavily.

"It's time to go back in, isn't it?"

The flames flickered, casting sparks that floated up to the top of the cavern. "We can't leave your people, and no one knows how far you can be from your familiar."

"My people. We've been here for weeks, and no one's launched a rescue."

"You don't know that. You've been—"

"Six of you got me out, countless other prisoners and me. What the fuck—"

"Those other prisoners—we don't know what happened to them. they could have been—"

"No one came for me. The only reason I'm going back for the captain is that I'm not fucking stupid. He's got intel. He was separated from the rest of us. Whatever he has is important, but I don't even think the mil is going to try to grab him back. The motherfuckers."

"We're going to get him, and we'll get you back to Ros'ten. Don't worry."

Beth chuckled under her breath as she rose and pulled out her sword. She watched the steel glint in the firelight. "You know, I get that we're still connected," she started, "but I miss the fucking guy being so close. Even if he's annoying as fuck...reminds me of the Mundanes. You know, still connected...still missing being close." Beth smiled at Suzuki as she sheathed her sword. "And annoying like someone I know."

Suzuki smirked. "I'm not annoying. I'm fucking brilliant."

"You'd be great at that game 'Two truths and a lie.' When are we going?"

"Now. There's not enough time to spend fucking around."

"What about Sandy and Stew?" Beth asked.

"The Horsemen got them."

"Do they?"

Suzuki nodded. "Yeah. They do. Just like I got you."

"Fine. Let's go."

"Do you need anything?"

Suzuki pulled up his HUD. "To get fucking moving."

He looked through his list of contacts, which included every MERC he had come in contact with until he came across Ansalm's name. There was a phone icon next to the name and Suzuki hit it. The HUD rang like a phone from back home, and Suzuki was instantly transported to the first time he had called Stew to try and set up a day to raid. Stew hadn't answered any of his messages, so Suzuki had gotten fed up and called him. Suzuki remembered waiting for Stew to pick up the phone, dreading the first time that they were going to talk, nervous about what he was going to say even though he knew exactly why he was calling. Stew had picked up fast enough, and they had planned out the raid. It hadn't been awkward or uncomfortable at all.

The ringing stopped and a voice squeaked over Suzuki's HUD headset. "Who the fuck is this?" Ansalm rattled.

"Suzuki. You—"

"I know who you are. How'd you get this line?" the line crackled.

"We're coming back."

"You got out? Why the hell would you be coming—"

Suzuki didn't have time for this. "Beth's captain is still in the prison. So is her familiar. We need to find them. Can you help?"

There was a pause that seemed to stretch on forever. Then Ansalm cleared his throat, saying, "I know the familiar. That'll be easier. I'll need the captain's name."

Suzuki looked at Beth and said, "I need his name."

"Captain Wyatt."

Suzuki repeated the information to Ansalm, only to be greeted with a squeal that Suzuki would have never thought a dwarf capable of making. "Beautiful, just beautiful,"

Ansalm squeaked, sounding almost like a halfling. "They're being held in the same processing facility."

"What's the processing facility?"

"I don't know. I don't have clearance. It's different than the reintegration areas, but I have no idea what is there."

"Can you get us in?"

"I can guide you."

"Good enough."

Suzuki and Beth made their way back through the grimpon tunnels toward the prison cells. They were silent as they moved. The earth was already dug out for them, and there was nothing to speak about. There was no work that needed to be done. They kept their silence, and Suzuki concentrated on whatever needed to come next. Once they got to the section of the tunnels that opened up into the prison cells, Suzuki hit his HUD and called Ansalm. There was a brief ring and then the sound of a headset being picked up. "You guys ready?" Ansalm asked.

"Only if you are," Suzuki replied.

"As ready as either of us is ever going to get. Go straight forward and then turn left at the third right."

Suzuki reached out for Fred. He hoped that the imp was done resting. He hadn't bothered to communicate any part of the plan. He figured that if Fred was awake, he'd hear it. If not, then Fred would have to roll with the punches.

Fred rustled in the dark place of Suzuki's mind. "What is it, human?" he hissed.

"Doing a little bit of sneaky-sneaky, if you know what I mean..."

"Ugh. Fine. Pay more attention this time around, though. I am still...recovering."

"Are you going to be okay for this?"

"I'll be more than okay. That being said, I still would appreciate it if you paid closer attention to what is going on. It would make the strain more tolerable for me."

"I can do that. Let's go."

Suzuki felt the now growing familiar oddness of having his body pulled out from underneath him, his skin melding and shrinking into a form that was not properly his own, yet vaguely familiar, his forehead stretching, and his eyes narrowing as scales rippled over his flesh and wings sprouted from his back. When the transformation was complete, the eldritch imp Fred stood by Beth's side. "I don't have any chains this time," Fred purred.

Beth took a step behind Fred, taking the posture of a prisoner. "Thank God," she replied. "If I had to do that again, I might have had to sink a knife into your throat."

"I'd gladly see you try."

"Trust me, you wouldn't gladly see any of it."

Ansalm broke through their bickering. "If you two wouldn't mind, how about you take care of what you both are jeopardizing my mission to accomplish? Straight forward and left at the third right."

"What does that even mean? Left at the third right?"

"You'll know when you get to it."

Beth and Fred followed Ansalm's instructions, ignoring the different pathways as they continued straightforward on their path. As Ansalm had predicted, they understood what the left on the third right meant when they came to the fork in the road. Somehow the tunnel had split into two left turns and three right turns. Two of the turns were simple to understand. They could be seen with the naked eye. The other three were more complicated. They shimmered in and out of sight as if they were a mirage.

Fred pointed to the entrance on the right side toward the back. "That's the one we're going to be taking," Fred suggested.

Beth looked at the different entrances and sighed heavily. "How do you know that is the one?" she asked.

"It is an old orc riddle. They never use left or right. They rarely count anything. If the number is more than one, trust me, it's the highest one. And if they ever suggest left or right, it is always right."

"But Ansalm isn't orcish."

Fred pursed his lips, impatient. "No, but he's conveying instruction based off what orcs have told him. Am I right, Ansalm?"

The audio feed crackled slightly, but Ansalm's voice still came through strong. "More or less," he admitted. "I haven't really seen much of these tunnels before. This is mostly what I've heard talked about."

"Are you saying that you don't know where we're fucking going?" Beth shouted before realizing where she was, clasping her hand over her mouth as if she could somehow still silence her words.

"No, I do know where you are going. I just haven't described it to every MERC who wanders into the Dark One's fucking territory. Now are you going to take the turn or are you going to wait to get caught?"

Beth and Suzuki took the turn. They continued down the meandering tunnels, heeding Ansalm's instructions as they went, occasionally stopping to speak with guards who had questions as to why a human was being led unchained throughout the prisons. Fred was able to easily dissuade any of the orcs by dropping his fictional rank to the viceroy. That was until one particularly nosy orc named Thrak wouldn't leave his line of questioning alone.

Thrak had already held up Beth and Fred for nearly ten minutes, asking inane question after inane question. Suzuki couldn't figure out if the orc was extremely suspicious or just extremely stupid. Most of Thrak's questions tended to be concerning what the specific details of Fred's mission to the viceroy were. Suzuki was prepared for this, though. He had rehearsed an entire monologue on trying to better the rights of the workers in the prison. When Thrak got to questions, Suzuki took over Fred's mouth and started talking. By the time Suzuki had finished his Marxist lecture, a look of vague concern had come over Thrak's face.

Thrak leaned against the wall and touched his club to his head. "Wait a minute," Thrak thought aloud. "So, what you're telling me is that us workers aren't being treated fair?"

Fred clapped his hands together to encourage Thrak to continue using his brain. "Exactly! You aren't being treated fairly at all. These are practically slave conditions."

"Well, I mean, we are pretty much slaves."

Thrak turned and pointed to the microchip attached to the nape of his neck.

Fred waved Thrak's concerns away. "Yes, yes, I can see that you are microchipped, but have you truly lost yourself? Do you wake up in the morning and struggle to remember what Thrak needs or what Thrak wants?"

"Uh...yeah, all the time. I don't really remember ever wanting anything before wanting to serve the Dark Lord."

"And is this how you wanted to serve the Dark Lord?"

Thrak shook his head and sighed heavily. "No. I used to be a warrior, a cousin to one of the five chieftain warlords. Very distinguished. Very respectable. And now...well, even if I wanted to serve the Dark One, I didn't want to do it in this shithole. No one wants to be a fucking prison guard. It's fucking bullshit."

"Which is *why* I'm here. Just because we have to work doesn't mean that it has to be shit work. Once our voices are heard, things are going to start changing around here. These are assignments that orcs and goblins actually want. So instead of treating you guys like the grunts, like the idiots, like the—"

"Slaves."

"Exactly."

Thrak nodded as he thought, scratching his chin in a contemplative gesture that one does not often see orcs making. "You know what," Thrak exclaimed. "I got a buddy who you should talk to. He really likes this kind of talk. He's always going on about these big ideas and how things around here need to change. I think that he'd have some useful stuff to let you know about. You know, for changes."

"Uh...I'm actually on a pretty tight schedule. I don't know—"

"And we can get that human bitch a collar so she won't run off on you."

Fred's eyes darted over to Beth. Her face was still sullen, taking on the look of one already beaten and broken. If she had heard the orc, she didn't show it.

Thrak reached forward, grabbed Beth's hand, and jerked her forward.

Fred's scales rustled as he crouched low and prepared to fly at Thrak. He could rip the orc's throat out within a few seconds and be done with the whole situation. Just as Fred was preparing to do just that, a group of orcs and goblins came walking down the tunnel, talking animatedly with each other. They stopped and greeted Thrak, who beamed at them, saying, "Hey, guys, this is the viceroy's guy. He's here to try and clear up some of the bullshit."

Fred smiled and waved weakly. "Yes. Don't spread the word, though. There's no easier way to kill a union than needless talking."

The orcs and goblins muttered among themselves. Apparently, "union" was not a word that had slipped into their language.

Thrak pulled Beth forward again. "Come on, we don't have a whole lot of time to waste. We're not too far from my friend. He's going to get a fucking kick out of you."

Fred followed Thrak past the group of goblins and orcs who were watching Fred much closer than he had been comfortable with. Killing Thrak was out of the question now. His disappearance would be noted. Perhaps he'd even be missed. And if he didn't return to his post in a timely fashion, they might send someone looking for him. Ansalm had been capable of leading them this far, but Fred doubted that the dwarf could direct them on how to escape from an angry, orcish mob. Following Thrak seemed like the best bet.

Suzuki tried to reach out to Ansalm without speaking. He was going to push his HUD to find out just how big of an upgrade Chip had given him. Besides, Suzuki hardly understood the technicalities of how body-swapping and HUDs worked. Fred obviously wasn't wearing Suzuki's HUD. Now that Suzuki thought about it, he wasn't sure if he was wearing his HUD half the time. He never felt it on his face unless he needed it.

Hmm... Suzuki thought. *That is kind of odd.* Suzuki benched the thought and turned his attention to reaching out to Ansalm. He imagined himself calling Ansalm, dialing a number, and he imagined the dwarf's face in his mind's eye.

There was a click in Suzuki's mind, an audible click, and then Ansalm started talking. "What the hell are you guys doing?"

Suzuki sighed a breath of relief, and he figurately patted himself on the back. "We almost got caught," Suzuki explained. "We're being led by some orc named Thrak."

"You met Thrak? And he actually talked to you?"

"Yeah, what's the big deal?" Suzuki asked.

Ansalm narrowed his eyes. "Thrak is the single meanest, toughest orc on that tunnel grouping. Did he say where he was taking you?"

"Said he had a friend who would want to talk about orc working conditions."

Ansalm threw his arms up in exasperation. "Are you trying to start a fucking union? MERCs really changed their espionage tactics since I did training."

"I've sort of been making it up while I go."

"Well, whatever you're doing is working. Thrak's taking you straight to the captain."

"You fucking serious?" Suzuki muttered.

"Completely. I'm going to sign off. Orcs around here are starting to get suspicious. Reach out if you need anything, all right? Good luck."

"Thanks. Good luck to you too."

Thrak continued to lead Fred and Beth down the stone tunnels. Suzuki noticed that there was less stone in the walls of these tunnels, though. There were steel reinforcements that could be seen. A bright light shone at the end of the tunnel.

Suzuki felt Fred turning inward to speak to him, saying, "I can feel Ros'ten. The bee is here."

The light from the other side of the tunnel was almost blinding. As Fred's eyes adjusted to the light, he could see that Thrak had just led them into a giant circular room. The room was sleek with a futuristic look, and it stretched straight up into what must have been the summit of the mountain. Various tables and desks covered the floor. Orcs and goblins in white jackets walked back and forth between the tables, stopping and talking, sharing notes on holographic notepads. The walls were covered in cells. Instead of steel bars like Suzuki had seen in the lower levels of the prison, these cells were closed off by what looked to be pure energy. The cells stretched all the way up to the top of the mountain.

Orc and goblin scientists whizzed by on floating dollies. They zipped around from cell to cell, taking notes. The whole place had the feel of a medical facility ripped from the most recent pulp sci-fi novel. It looked extremely out of place in an orcish hell pit in Middang3ard.

Fred's eyes were bewildered. Even he was impressed. He turned to Thrak and asked, "What is this place?"

"Research and development. It's where all the eggheads go. I mean that in a good way. My friend is an egghead. Looks like an egg, at least. Sort of."

Thrak continued to guide Fred and Beth through the swarming hub of scientific advancement until they came to a large metal table. A man lay on the table. There was an apparatus over his head which connected to a computer monitor next to the table.

A quiet sigh came from Beth. Fred turned to face her, and he could see that she was breathing heavily. This was no doubt the captain.

Thrak slapped Beth across the face. "Keep your eyes to yourself, human," Thrak shouted.

Suzuki surged forward, held back only by Fred's will. *Hold yourself back, Suzuki,* Fred whispered internally. *If you give us away in here, we are dead.*

I'll fucking kill him, Suzuki growled.

No doubt. Now may not be the right time, though.

Thrak pointed to one of the descending, floating platforms. "There's my friend," he exclaimed.

The floating platform landed directly in front of the steel table. A qulippoth stood on the platform. It was a massive number of black tentacles attached to a bulbous black body that was smooth like dolphin skin. The qulippoth had one eye that took up most of its body, its red iris looking like a ring of fire floating in a sea of snow. It rubbed itself with its tentacles, flicking away a thick layer of mucous that its body was secreting. As it rolled off of the platform, its tentacles reached for the computer monitor and its body jiggled and pulsed.

Thrak stepped forward, ready to introduce the parties at hand, saying, "Zeke, this is my friend Fred. He's got some really interesting ideas that I think you'd be interested in. Seems like you two would get along."

Zeke turned his massive, cyclopean eye on Fred and Beth. If it were possible, the eye grew even wider.

All of Fred's scales rippled and stood on edge as he growled under his breath. Suzuki felt himself being forced farther away from Fred. It did not feel intentional. It happened so fast that Suzuki assumed it was an instinctual reaction. Whatever this thing was, it put Fred on edge in a way that Suzuki had never seen. Suzuki struggled not to drown in the waves of unconscious material coming from Fred. Somehow, he stayed above it all and pulled himself closer to what was going on.

Fred and Zeke were circling each other. Both were hissing, though it was difficult to discern where Zeke's voice was coming from. "What the fuck are you doing here?" Zeke shouted.

All around the sterile room, orcs and goblins stopped what they were doing to watch what was happening.

Fred reared up on his hind legs, shot out a thin blast of fire, and roared, a much louder sound than one would have assumed his small body was capable of. "What the fuck are you doing here, Ezekiel?" Fred asked. "That is the real question."

Zeke's tentacles launched forward, wrapping Fred up faster than he had time to react, snaking toward his neck. Fred countered by biting down hard on Zeke's tentacles, causing the qulippoth to screech in pain as it rolled away, slapping Fred in the face as its massive eye teared up. Zeke wiped away the tear and turned to look at the computer monitor that Beth's captain was hooked up to before looking up and snapping his tentacles at the workers in the facility. "Get your asses back to work," Zeke shouted. "There's nothing to see here."

The orcs and goblins throughout the facility turned their attention back to work, occasionally sneaking glances to see what else was going to happen.

Fred's scales continued to bristle as he approached Zeke, who looked as if he were trying to pretend that Fred had left the room. Finally, Ezekiel sighed and turned to face Fred. "I thought you were helping the other side," Zeke said. "What are you doing here with a human prisoner?"

Suzuki could feel something deep and important welling up in Fred. The imp was going to open his mouth and say something that could damn the mission. Suzuki was interested to know what it was since he still couldn't put together anything about the imp. This was not the right time, though. This was the single worst possible moment to learn anything about Fred and his relationship with other eldritch creatures. Suzuki did the only thing that he knew would help. He took control of Fred's body, only for a second, centering himself in Fred's mouth, saying, "I never defected. I was only a spy."

Zeke turned his body to face Fred as his tentacles absentmindedly stroked Captain Wyatt's cheek. "A spy. Honestly, Fred how dense do you think I am? I should have you brought in right now, history aside. You can't think you can just show up here and—"

"I'm not lying. It was my assignment. You know that those of us who aren't chipped are the only ones capable of that."

Suzuki tensed. That statement was a gamble, a very well-thought-out gamble but still, not a certainty. From what Suzuki and Fred had seen, there were eldritch creatures who served the Dark One. If they did serve the Dark One without the microchip mind control, it would make sense that they were the ones who could be trusted with the cognitive function to lead a double life.

Zeke looked up with an eye much sadder than Suzuki felt an eldritch creature had the right to have. "We thought you betrayed us," Zeke said softly.

"I am no traitor," Fred spat. "I am more loyal than most. I am loyal enough to sacrifice my stature, my reputation, to be seen as nothing more than a pawn by humans. That is the extent of my loyalty."

"Then how has your spying brought you here?"

Suzuki pushed forward to speak for Fred again. "Initially, I was sent to infiltrate the MERCs. After I lost my first human, through no fault of my own, I was able to secure another. He also was weak-willed and pathetic. After his death, I returned to the Dark One to be given a new position. I was... in disgrace. The best that I could get was this remedial position, reporting on the working situation of various facilities."

"How the mighty have fallen."

"Indeed."

Fred asserted himself back over his body, not quite flinging Suzuki out of his mind, but rather, slightly nudging him away. Still, it was done with a sense of urgency that betrayed Fred's actual intentions. "Why are *you* still working for him?" Fred asked.

Zeke looked away from Fred, which required turning his entire body away. "We are both ancient," Zeke started. "We have seen worlds and races come and go... yet we are still so young. There were so many older ones before us. Do you know what my parents wanted to do? They wanted to convert the universes to screaming madness. That was their one hope: to wake up one day and see the jabbering, mindless mouths of mortals screaming in confusion and chaos. Then they had me. All that went out the window, but I still want that. I want what they couldn't have. Does it really matter how we get there?"

"So, what do you do here?"

"The Dark One has put my talents for influence to good use. I'm responsible for designing and augmenting the different rings that link the microchips to his will."

Suzuki was instantly curious, but he knew that there was no way for him to outright ask Zeke to explain himself. This was going to take a little bit of weaseling. Fred moved aside for Suzuki to come to the forefront again. "What would need augmenting?" Suzuki asked.

Zeke laughed, an eerily robust sound. "You probably don't know anything about the rings, huh? You were before all of that, self—sworn just like me. I don't see why you would have bothered learning, especially if you were deep undercover. The microchips don't do the controlling. They're just receivers. What actually controls them is a ringtone, broadcast over millions and millions of miles. The tech in the microchips is impressive. They have nearly limitless range, something that we've worked hard to keep MERC and the military from getting. The ringtone is where the real magic lies, though. It's a digitized version of my parents' song, the same song that drove the roving tribes of El-Kador insane with rage. That's what I augment. I change the tones to accommodate different races. I'm slowly building a symphony if I want to be grandiose. You see, just like my parents had wanted, the whole universe will hear our song."

"How do you augment it?"

"Detailed note-taking." Zeke chuckled. He pointed to Captain Wyatt before turning a knob on his computer terminal.

Wyatt screamed and his body convulsed beneath his bindings, his teeth clenching hard and his eyes rolling back as foam frothed from his mouth. Each second looked unbearable, his veins nearly ripping from his skin as he thrashed.

Zeke turned off the machine and Wyatt went still, the only indication he was alive the rising and dropping of his chest.

Suzuki tried to catch Beth's face from the corner of his eye. She was emotionless. He wondered how she could stay so calm. If he had seen anything like this happen to Beth, he would have been unable to contain himself. Suzuki was glad that Beth could be so stone-faced, though. If she had lost her shit at that moment, they would have been goners.

Zeke leaned over Wyatt's body in a very matter-of-fact fashion, the way that a doctor examines a patient. The only difference was that there was no benevolence in the action. Even morticians looked more loving than Zeke did at that moment, his massive, singular eye glaring at the human who still twitched as electric spasms rocked through his body. "You see, each race has a different frequency for control," Zeke started to explain. "Some of the...lower races...have lower frequencies. It is hardly a challenge to control orcs or goblins. They already have caste systems. They are still stuck in the infancy of war. Their cultures haven't evolved enough to separate themselves too far from the organic song of the cosmos, the song that the eldritch, my fathers and mothers, sang. They respond easily and quickly to the ring that was initially designed for them. They become obedient but have no idea why. Because of this minute distinction, they are able to obey and never lose track of themselves. They retain their autonomy in some regard, and are able to serve as if they were born to do so. The rings designed for eldritch creatures are completely different. In most cases, they don't even work. Luckily, nearly all of the eldritch old ones have chosen to be here. The few who wish to have nothing to do with the Dark One have fled to parts of the universe unknown...for the time being."

"And what of giants? Trolls? Those sorts of creatures?"

"They are interesting breeds. Much of their brains is still a mystery. No one knows what giants value or what their lives are like other than giants. It's the same with most magical creatures. For them, we use a blunt force ring. Nearly all of their personality is wiped. They exist to listen. That is all. If they are not given orders, they will sit and waste away. We have to schedule them to eat, in fact. We've lost whole tribes while we tried to figure this out. But they're easier to deal with than dragons."

"Dragons? You have dragons?"

"Do we? So many of them. They were the hardest to figure out. That was until we got to humans, but we'll talk about that in a minute. Dragons are as old as the eldritch, and in some cases older. But their minds are like a cross between orcs and humans. Much of what they experience is purely instinctual: it happens on such a low level of awareness that they couldn't even articulate it. Yet they have the same level of consciousness as humans. They have distinct cultures with multiple languages and their own myths. To be honest, it was breaking dragons that gave us our first indication of how to work with humans. That, at the moment, is our real focus. Humans are the final race to be reintegrated. It hasn't been going well. They haven't responded well to any of the rings we've designed for them so far. I personally think it's because rebellion might be hardwired into their brains. It's a difficult thing to subvert. Their individuality is also unprecedented, that and how cut off they are from magic. Working with their familiars has given us a little bit more insight, but we are still not close to cracking the code."

"What about their familiars?"

"I needn't refresh your memory on familiar/ human relationships. You already know as well as I do what it's like. That being said, we think that there is a link between their lack of magical understanding, the conscious mind, and how they intermingle with their familiars. The military and MERCs also don't know how this aspect works, even though they employ it without discretion. I, however, will figure it out eventually. And the songs of chaos my family dreamed of will be spread across the universe, each ringtone a microcosm of what they had hoped would come."

"That's very beautiful. I'm glad that you can finally make them proud. Not all of us are so lucky."

Zeke looked at Fred, his freakish eye conveying more emotion than Suzuki felt was comfortable. "I...uh...I'm sorry, Fred. I wasn't thinking—"

"You don't need to apologize."

"It's one of the reasons that I felt the need to be so concerned with humans. If it weren't for their...constant intrusions, we wouldn't have lost so many. Your family—"

"Was not killed by humans. They died in this war. They died in the Dark One's war."

"Do you mean to imply—"

Fred shook his head. "I imply nothing. I know who I serve. That does not mean I am blind."

"Please, Fred. You must be careful—"

"I do not need to be careful. There was no war until the Dark One created one."

Fred looked down at Wyatt and pointed at him. "Are you done with this one? There is important intel the viceroy wishes to extract from him, as well as this human's familiar."

"I wasn't notified of any requisitions for their removal."

"Do you wish to relay this to the viceroy? Or should I?" Fred asked.

Zeke shriveled up slightly and the color of his skin changed from a deep black to a bright white, nearly as white as the rest of the sterile medical facility. "No, no, you don't have to do that. I can release the human." Zeke hit a button on the monitor and Wyatt's restraints were removed. He motioned for Thrak to help Wyatt up and bind him. Thrak did as he was told and handed the restraints to Fred.

Fred took the chains and motioned for Thrak to shackle

Beth as well. Once the humans were properly bound, Fred yanked their chains. Wyatt was hardly able to stand. He was murmuring unintelligibly. Beth stared at her feet, hardly blinking, her teeth grit behind her lips, her jaw slowly grinding over and over. "Now I will need her familiar released," Fred ordered.

Zeke floated away, gesturing for Fred to follow him. "This way, old friend," Zeke said as he led Fred, Beth, and Wyatt to a containment cell where Ros'ten flittered about nervously. The familiar was a massive bee, easily the size of a large cat. Its antennas were bent low, and it was hovering frantically as if it had been pacing for hours. Its massive compound eyes looked up and saw Beth, and the bee dropped to the ground as if in shock.

It was the first time that Suzuki had seen Beth betray even the slightest sign of emotion. She leaned forward, ever so slightly, as if a breeze had just rocked her. Her eyes widened and her mouth went a little slack, perhaps from the words she wished to pour from her throat. But she wrapped herself back up in the guise of a broken person. At her side, Wyatt registered nothing. Drool trickled down his chin.

Fred walked up to Ros'ten's cell and pressed his hand against the blue energy field. It crackled, sending a wave of pain flowing through his and Suzuki's body, but he didn't pull his hand away. He just stared at Ros as the bee fluttered its wings and returned the gaze. "Release him," Fred commanded.

Zeke floated up to Fred and rested one of his tentacles on the imp's shoulder. "And what exactly am I releasing him for?" Zeke asked.

"I require him for the viceroy."

"And what does the viceroy plan on doing with them?"

"Do you seek to question the –"

"I'm not stupid, Fred. I know you aren't a spy."

All of the blood drained from Fred. Both he and Suzuki instantly ran through a dozen different scenarios. They could torch Zeke and make a break for it. They had the instant transporter that Chip had given them. That was easily the best bet. Beth already knew how it worked, and all they had to do was grab Wyatt. But Ros'ten still wasn't free. They'd have to figure out how to open the cell first.

Ros'ten's cell whooshed open. The bee lazily fluttered over to Beth, who no longer could contain herself and threw her hands around the giant insect, fighting back tears and covering its face in sloppy kisses.

Zeke's grip on Fred's shoulder grew tighter as Fred turned to face the eldritch cyclops' eye. "None of us was looking for this kind of war," Zeke finally said. "This... dishonorable shit show. Count yourself lucky that your family did not see you become what I have. Consider this an apology from an elder one to an elder one."

"You betray yourself. If—"

"The viceroy is here. I advise you to stop using that cover. You will be found out sooner rather than later."

Fred rested his hand on Zeke's tentacle. "My father always said you were born a pure nightmare, that the cosmos did not deserve a god such as you."

"Yes, and my mother told me tales of you lighting the heavens aflame merely to see them burn."

"Thank you, Zeke."

"Now be quick. Leave this place. Let the Old Ones find their way."

Beth grabbed Fred and Wyatt's hands. Ros'ten had already been reabsorbed into Beth's body. Fred touched the headset in his right ear and the world around them melted.

Everything broke into billions of pieces and went speeding past them faster than could be seen. They were falling deep into the earth. Suzuki could feel himself being pulled away from Beth and the rest of them, but he held on as tightly as he could. Beth was screaming, and he found that he was as well.

Then he hit the ground hard.

Suzuki jumped to his feet. He was back in his body. They were in the grimpon cavern, near the bonfire, where Chip was sitting.

Chip had apparently finished her repairs. She looked as if nothing had ever happened. She smiled when she looked up and saw the Suzuki and the rest of them. "Looks like your rescue mission went off swimmingly." She chuckled.

Beth and Suzuki both fell forward and vomited. Suzuki felt as if his guts had been pulled out of his mouth and then forced back up through his ass. He wanted to sit down, but his entire body was sore.

Beth was laying on the ground next to him. Wyatt had passed out.

Diana and Sandy rushed over to help Suzuki and Beth to their feet. Diana pulled out two healing potions and handed them each one. "Go ahead and drink it up," Diana encouraged. "We have more than enough of them to go around."

After Suzuki caught his breath and started to feel normal, he turned to take stock of what was happening in the cavern.

Soldiers covered the cavern's floor, at least a hundred of them. Many of them were bandaged and laying on makeshift cots. José was tending to the wounded who could sit up, spooning out water from a huge gourd hanging down his back.

Diana and Sandy were tending the soldiers who now covered the floor of the cavern where the grimpon bodies had once been. The two mages were casting healing spells over the soldiers. The air was full of the smell of early blooms and blossoms, coupled with cinnamon and sage. They were talking as they worked.

Suzuki walked over to where the soldiers lay to get a better view of what was happening. He was not prepared for what he saw. When he had been freeing the prisoners, all of the military that he had seen appeared to be shallow parodies of humans, their bodies emaciated and frail. In the little bit of time that Sandy and Diana had spent with the soldiers, they had apparently been able to reverse nearly all of the damage that had been done, if not all of it.

Sandy strolled over to Suzuki and took his hand. "You need to go see Stew," she said. "He's worried sick about you. Then bring Beth over. Diana's going to see to her before we get a whole reunion thing going. She's probably still in shock. I don't want to send her over the edge."

"Good idea."

Stew was posted up by the campfire, which had been built to an extraordinary size. He was slaving over multiple boiling pots and simmering pans. His skin sheened with sweat as he ran with ingredients to what was cooking, back to ingredients, chopping vegetables and seasoning meat. He looked up as Suzuki approached and he smiled widely, dropped what he was doing, and ran over to Suzuki. He threw his arms around Suzuki, nearly knocking him to the ground. "Jesus Christ, dude, I thought you were a fucking goner," Stew shouted.

Suzuki pushed Stew off and turned his attention to the variety of delicious smells coming from the pots and pans.

"Oh yeah, so worried that you had to stress cook?" Suzuki teased.

"Fuck you, I wasn't stress cooking. When I woke up, Diana put me to work. I've never seen her look so mean before. I thought she was going to cut my head off. She said it was the least I could do to pay her back for keeping me from dying. Sandy says I wasn't close to dying, though. Diana's just being a dick."

"It looks like you got a lot of mouths to feed."

"Yeah, you would think that I was a chef or something. But I figure it gave me something to do while everyone was getting ready for you and Beth to get back."

"So, what the fuck happened to you?" Suzuki asked as he motioned to Stew's bandaged head.

"Oh, you know those...grimpons, that was the name, right?"

"Yeah."

"Those grimpons collapsed our tunnel. I got knocked out before any of the fighting got started, which was such bullshit because I have been *aching* for a good fight. There hasn't been a whole lot of time for the good lady and me to reacquaint each other with our nasty parts, so—"

"Stew!"

"I'm just saying. If I'm not fucking, I'd prefer to be fighting. The two big Fs. But how'd things go on your end?"

Suzuki knelt next to one of the sizzling pans of meat. He grabbed a fork lying on a plate and skewered himself a piece. The little morsel was cooked better than anything Stew had given him before. It was rich with flavor and coated his tongue with a velvety sensation. "Shit, dude, when did you get so good at cooking?" Suzuki asked.

Stew didn't bother to hide how proud of himself he was, all smiles and puffed-out pecs. "Diana and Chip have been giving me pointers and shit. Oh, fuck, dude, did you hear about Chip? The whole...cyborg thing?"

"Not even sure if she's that. Cyborg implies you were human once."

"Uh, robot?"

"No, robots are just machines. I think she's more of an android."

"I'm going to hate myself for this, but what's the difference?"

"Androids are robots that are built with the intention and capacity to pass as human. And I think half-elf falls in that category as well. Chip was definitely passing."

"Everything except for the fucked-up way she talked. It seems like it's toned down since she got all ripped apart."

"I don't know, I thought it was kinda charming."

"Yeah, you would. So, where the fuck is Beth?"

"She's in a tent with her captain. He seemed pretty fucked up when we got him back. She's been through a lot."

"I kinda figured. While we've been out adventuring and shit, she's been a fucking prisoner of war. I don't know what I'd be like after all of that. She was gone for a while."

"A couple of weeks."

"It probably felt like an eternity. Those tunnels were fucked. I felt like I was locked in there forever. That was just a couple of hours too. I can't imagine what it must have been like to have been there for weeks. It probably felt like years."

"Yeah, she does seem a little worn out."

"Sandy said that we should give her a little bit of space at first. Let her settle in so that she's not overwhelmed. Her dad was a POW, and she said when he came back, he needed a few months to adjust to everything. We don't really have that time luxury, but a couple of hours might at least give her some room to breathe. Just let her know that we'll come when she's ready."

"Sounds good."

"Dude. I'm glad you're okay. We were worried 'bout you there for a minute. Props to getting Beth back. You're practically 007."

"I don't think that 007 ever did any rescue missions."

"Dude, he had to have done at least one. I'm talking all of the 007 movies. There has to be one where he saved someone. You can't go your entire career as a secret agent and not save one person. Impossible. I'm going to call you out on that one. You were practically 007. Not nearly as suave or charming. You did get the job done, though. Probably looked shitty doing it too."

"I looked like a goddamn eldritch imp the whole time. It feels good to be back in my body."

"I can fucking imagine. Now get out of here. You're distracting me from my sauces."

Suzuki took another piece of meat and wandered away. He had never seen a camp this big before. There were almost too many people to see. It didn't really matter, though, because he knew exactly who he wanted to see. He made his way past the resting soldiers to the tent that Wyatt was recovering in. Beth was most likely there.

The tent that Wyatt lay in was modest, mostly just a cloth pitched over a few rods. Wyatt lay on a cot, his body covered in scars and open wounds. Two electric nodes were attached to his temple. Beth stood next to him, holding his hand while she looked down at him.

Suzuki's heart sank when he saw Beth holding Wyatt's hand.

Beth looked up at Suzuki. She didn't bother letting go of Wyatt's hand. Instead, she motioned for Suzuki to come closer to them both. Suzuki did and stood at Beth's side. "He was my drill sergeant at boot camp," Beth explained. "And then I was put in his platoon. He's a tough motherfucker. I didn't think that I'd ever see him this...broken. He keeps going in and out, muttering in his sleep. Someone named Diana popped in earlier and cast a couple of healing spells. She said that he should be good as new by tomorrow, at least his body will be. I'm just waiting for him to wake up."

"What for?"

"Orders."

"Are you serious? After what you just went through? You all need to take a break. Get some rest."

"There's no time. You heard what Zeke said before we left."

Suzuki nodded. He hadn't forgotten. The Dark One was getting closer and closer to creating a ring that would allow him to control humans just as easily as he controlled orcs and goblins. If that were to happen, the war would be over. Suzuki had already seen a few dwarves under the Dark One's control and a halfling as well. Humans made up a bulk of the MERCs, and the military was almost entirely human. If the Dark One succeeded in perfecting that ring, that would effectively destroy the military and disable the MERCs.

"You think he's already got a plan?"

Beth's face scrunched as she tried to fight back the tears. They came on suddenly, surprising her and Suzuki. Beth choked them back down. "I don't fucking know, Suzuki," she whispered. "All of this...it's way beyond me. I don't fucking know what to do. That's not my job. My job is to kill the Dark One's forces."

"You know what he's going to say when he wakes up?"

"I have a faint idea."

"We're going to have to go back in there."

"Yeah, I know that. I just don't know what we're going back in there to do."

Wyatt did not wake up for another hour. When he did rise, it was with screaming and shouting, his eyes flashing brightly as he tried to climb out of bed, attacking anyone who stepped close enough to him, screaming until finally he exhausted himself and lay on the cot, breathing slowly and heavily as if each breath was to be his last. When he finally opened his eyes, Suzuki could see that they had lost their shimmer. They sat in his skull like two dead frogs floating to the water's surface. When Beth placed her hand on Wyatt's shoulder, he flinched away so hard that he nearly fell out of his cot. His eyes were wide with terror.

Beth tried again. This time Wyatt let her hand stay. "Sir."

Wyatt tried to sit up and groaned in pain. "Where the fuck am I, private?"

"We got sprung from jail. Meet Suzuki. I told you he'd come for us."

Wyatt sat up straighter and looked Suzuki over. A little bit more color and life was coming into his eyes. He cracked a smile, a weak-looking thing hanging on his face like the last leaf of fall. "This stringy bag of bones?" Wyatt asked through a laugh. "This is the guy who busted us out?"

"Us and half of our military captives. Someone else took care of the other half."

Wyatt laughed and slapped his kneecap, wincing from the pain. He was starting to look livelier. "You don't look like you weigh any more than a hundred pounds soaking wet.

You fought your way through that hell hole and rescued us?" he asked.

Suzuki smiled, aware for the first time of how confident he was. He had fought his way through the Dark One's defense ring to save Beth. Weeks earlier, he had killed orcs, giants, and Christmas monsters to save Beth. He had wooed a dragon to save Beth. He'd devised a plan and snuck through the entire prison, a place where he would have been killed within minutes if he'd been caught, all of that to save Beth. "Yeah, I did," Suzuki said, pulling at his loose-fitting tunic. "I'm a lot more impressive looking in armor."

Suzuki raised his right hand. His ax came whooshing into the room, landing squarely in his palm. The ax's blade was still covered in blood. "This is the ax that all of Middang3ard is learning to fear."

"All right, all right, slow down, kid. No need to get all medieval on me. I was just busting your chops. I really appreciate the save. I know Beth does. She was practically drowning the cell with how wet she'd get every time she brought you up. Most of the boys have been waiting for weeks to meet this 'brave and fearless' Suzuki, the warrior mage who was going to kill his way to our safety."

Beth's face flushed and she turned so that she didn't have to look Suzuki in the eyes. "I just knew you were going to come for me," Beth explained.

Suzuki smiled, feeling even more proud and confident. "You weren't wrong, were you?"

"No, I wasn't."

Wyatt sat up more and rubbed his face. "No, no, she wasn't. Which, all jokes aside, is extremely impressive. What you MERCs did in a few weeks was something the military wasn't capable of accomplishing. Your team must be huge. How many of you are there? A hundred? Two hundred? I can't imagine how many of you it would have taken to storm this place."

Suzuki shrugged and smiled uncomfortably. "Uh... there's seven of us," he said.

"Are you fucking telling me you freed a hundred soldiers and us in the heart of the Dark One's defenses with seven fucking MERCs?"

"I mean, it hasn't been a walk in the park."

"Beth, you undersold your boyfriend."

"I'm not her—"

Beth put her hand over Suzuki's mouth. "I didn't want to talk him up too much. No, sir, we've uncovered intel about how the Dark One is controlling the different races."

"Oh, I know. I've been finding out firsthand. But refresh my memory. It might be helpful to hear words about what my body's been learning."

Wyatt swung his feet over the side of his cot. He took a deep breath and then jumped out of bed. He wobbled. Beth reached out to help him steady himself, but he pushed her hand away. After tottering like a poorly-built skyscraper, Wyatt stood up straight. "Let's hear what the MERCs have to tell me. We'll go from there."

14

I t was difficult to tell what time it was while nestled deep in the Dark One's reintegrated mountain, but Suzuki thought that it was close to evening. It felt like evening to him at least. This would be the time that most of the MERCs would be returning from their missions and quests. They would be singing, dancing and drinking, celebrating the fact that they were still alive, still trying to fuck up the Dark One's vile plans for Middang3ard and the other realms of elves, dwarves, halflings, and humanity. Suzuki hadn't really thought about it much, but he missed the Red Lion, the MERC hub that all the mercenaries congregated to when they had off time. The Red Lion had started to feel like home. Not a home away from home or a stand-in until he found someplace better. It was an actual home.

The feeling must have been mutual to all the MERCs.

While Suzuki had been waiting for Wyatt to come to, the Horsemen and the Mundanes had done everything in their power to make the cavern where they were all recouping as close to the Red Lion as possible. When Suzuki walked outside of Wyatt's tent, following Beth and Wyatt, he was surprised to see how much had been done to change the former grimpon cave into a drinking establishment that would have made the Red Lion's owner, Wendy, proud. The walls had been decorated with flowing red sashes that were emblazoned with the de facto MERC insignia, a roaring lion. A few rows of tables had been set out and were lit by candles. Tankards of ale sat on the tables beside plates.

Sandy had rigged a display of pure magical creativity to hang over the tables. She had gathered a bunch of sticks and strung them together, enchanting them to float and lit them on fire so that it looked to the naked eye that a bonfire had conjured itself into existence. Diana and Sandy were talking quietly about the little bit of flair.

All of the soldiers had risen and were sitting at the tables. None of them looked much the worse for wear; the most severely wounded was Wyatt, who even now, at the sight of the tables and the display of ingenuity that filled the cavern, was already starting to look less weak. He still needed help walking, though, leaning on Beth as Suzuki pushed ahead of them, to guide them to a seat with his fellow MERCs.

Beth helped Wyatt into his chair and turned to speak to Suzuki, saying, "How come I haven't seen Sandy and Stew yet?"

Suzuki pointed over to the corner of the cavern, where Stew and Sandy were now waiting. "They wanted to give you some space to, you know, get used to not being tortured in a prison," Suzuki said. "But they want to see you before we sit down, you know, to get all the mushy shit out of the way so that your friends don't have to see it."

"I don't give a fuck who sees it. Come on."

Beth took off running toward Sandy and Stew. She tackled Sandy to the ground, wrapping her arms around the tiny mage then lifting her into the air until they both fell down, screaming and giggling. Then she clambered off of Sandy and threw her arms around Stew, struggling to get them all the way around his muscular back. "Holy fucking shit," Beth shouted. "I thought I was never going to see you guys again!"

The hugs hadn't been enough. They all stood around, each aware that there was much that they wanted to say, but not certain of where to start, of what was most important. Sandy hadn't intended on beginning the outpouring of emotion, but she was the first one to start crying as she grabbed Beth and embraced her. Through her tears, she managed to choke out, "I thought you were fucking dead. I thought this was all just some fucked up circle jerk of a mission because I thought you were dead and I am so fucking glad that you aren't. I'm so fucking glad."

Sandy and Beth stopped hugging and Beth faced Stew, who was also crying softly. "Oh shit, you too," Beth said as she wiped her face.

Stew nodded somberly. "The tears of a warrior are the purest. They hide no guilt, no shame. They are only emotion, pure and unfiltered. That's from *The Art of War*."

Beth laughed as she hugged Stew again. "That is *not* from *The Art of War*, you fucking goofball."

"Oh, yeah? Then where is it from?"

"That shitty kung-fu movie you were always going on about."

"Whatever, dude. You get the idea. And now, if we're all done standing around with our cocks out like a bunch of high schoolers, how about we celebrate that the Mundanes are the fucking reigning champions of Middang3ard?"

"Reigning champions, huh?"

"Obviously. We can't be beat. Period. We're pretty goddamn unstoppable."

Stew threw his arm around Sandy and they headed toward the tables. Beth and Suzuki followed, standing closer than Suzuki ever thought he and Beth would. As they walked to the empty seats next to the Horsemen, Suzuki's hand brushed against Beth's. Or was it the other way around? Did her hand brush his? Either way, neither of them jerked away. Their fingers kept slightly touching, skin against skin, sending tingles up and down Suzuki's spine, causing all of the small hairs on his body to stand up straight as if he had just been electrified. Suzuki felt as if all of his body was contained in those two fingers that continued to brush against Beth's.

All together for the first time since their adventures in Middang3ard had commenced, the Mundanes went to the seats of honor beside the Horsemen at the head of the table. Wyatt sat beside them, staring at his empty plate, his eyes hollowed out in a hunger that would have been humorous if he had not just been sprung from jail.

José stood as the Mundanes sat down. He cleared his throat. "I won't waste your time with speeches and words. I'm starving, so I can only imagine how hungry you must be. Eat, drink, and have a good fucking time!"

Diana waved her wand over the tables. Goblets magically filled with ale, and plates were covered in sumptuous dishes, steaks cooked to rare perfection, their juices aching to be released from just the slightest pressure, vegetables steamed to a ripe stiffness, casting off their aroma, a plate of sweet desserts for each table, curious delights and bizarre meats that Suzuki (and probably anyone else other than Diana and maybe Stew) could hardly begin to guess. On the Mundanes' table, a giant insect appeared on a silver platter, its exoskeleton popped open down the middle so its gooey white meat was exposed. Even though Suzuki initially felt a wave of disgust at seeing the creature, the smell wafting from its splayed carcass discounted any hesitation he initially had. He scooped a hefty bit of bug guts onto his plate, covered it in what looked like caviar but smelled like mutton, and started eating, washing down his first few bites with a healthy mouthful of ale.

The soldiers were slow to start eating, but once they started, they tore at their food ravenously. The only military who ate with any sense of decorum were Wyatt and Beth. They both ate with an air of composure that Suzuki assumed came from being officers, although he didn't see why Beth would be acting like that. He had heard Wyatt refer to her as "Private."

The Horsemen were not attempting to look like anything other than rowdy adventurers. José was practically pouring food into his mouth while he joked and laughed with Chip, who was back to her usual lewd and bawdy self, egging José on for a game of strip poker, guaranteeing that she could get most of the soldiers down to their underwear in less than an hour. Diana was smiling, eating, and occasionally interjecting a fact into the conversation, or talking quietly with Sandy, who was too busy shoving food in her mouth to be much of a conversationalist.

Finally, the feeding frenzy stopped. Now was the time to sit back with full bellies and cups. José cleared his throat and stood. "It's been a long time since I've had the pleasure of fighting beside our distinguished military," he boomed. "I am honored to have helped you in any way. I pray that this is the first step in putting behind our past differences in methodologies. As you see tonight, we fight the same enemy. Let us not make enemies of each other."

A few of the soldiers raised their tankards and clanked them together. The cavern was filled with the shouting of "Here, here!"

Wyatt drank the last of his ale and poured himself another tankard full. Even though he was looking healthier, there was something off-putting about his face. Cynicism and skepticism had burrowed themselves deeply into the creases and wrinkles of his forehead. "How exactly do you think we should put those differences behind us?" Wyatt asked.

José shrugged and made himself another plate. "You're talking to me like I'm the one in charge," José said. "I'm not a captain. These aren't my soldiers. If you want to address us, you address all of us. We aren't an army, we're a party, in case you couldn't tell from the festivities."

"Fine. What do you all propose we do to bridge that gap?"

Stew ripped off a hunk of flesh from a giant roasted bird leg. "Sharing is caring, dude," Stew suggested. "The military has a shit-ton of intel that you keep to yourself, right? I'm guessing we probably have tons of shit that you guys have never even seen before. That's a place to start. Why the fuck weren't we sharing information before, anyways?"

"How do you know we weren't?"

"From using my fucking head. If the military had your coordinates, wouldn't they have sent someone out to get you guys by now?"

Beth shook her head. "I sent my coordinates to the military and Suzuki," she sighed. "They could have found us if they wanted."

José waved away Beth's concern as he reached over the table and poured her another drink. "No, it's never that easy. You have a bureaucracy to deal with. Us? Some, but much less. And don't forget, we have the Mundanes. They aren't easily dissuaded."

Wyatt sighed and leaned forward. His brow was troubled, and he looked over his shoulder to see if any of the other soldiers were close enough to overhear him. "You're not completely off," he whispered as the Mundanes and Horsemen leaned in. "We do have more intel, a lot of intel that most of our guys don't even know about. Take what happened in the reintegration camp, for instance. My higher-ups know exactly why we were there. We weren't picked up for a reason."

Beth's face hardened and when she spoke, her voice was seething with anger. "Wait, what the fuck are you saying?" she growled.

"We were left there because I was given a mission—a mission that I obviously failed. The military has known for some time that the Dark One has been controlling various races with microchips and race-specific ringtones. It's been classified information. My mission was classified as well. But for the sake of transparency and trying to mend the different ways things have gotten fucked up, here you go. My mission was to allow my platoon to be captured by a group of red orcs. We had it on good authority that since we were humans, we would be taken to a reintegration facility to be experimented on. While at that facility, it was my responsibility to find, procure, and destroy the human-specific ring and any others that I was able to track down."

Beth slammed her tankard on the table, nearly breaking through the wood as she stood and drew her sword, pointing it at Wyatt's throat. "Are you fucking kidding me?" she shouted. "We were just fucking bait?"

Wyatt hung his head. "That's putting it politely," he admitted.

"Fuck you! Fuck your whole fucking military!"

Beth slammed her sword into the table and stormed off, leaving her sword behind. Suzuki stood to go after her, but Sandy grabbed him by the wrist. "Let her go," Sandy said. "She probably needs the space. I know I would if I just found out how expendable I was to someone I trusted."

Wyatt filled his tankard up again. He drank slowly, eyeing the MERCs from behind the rim of his tankard. "I know I would." He belched when he was finished drinking. "Beth's one of my finest. And I couldn't tell her shit. I had to watch while she got the shit kicked out of her just so that I could get into a position where I could find something out. And I found out shit. Diddly-shit. So, yeah, trust me. I know this is fucked up. I don't need a lecture right now, not if you're thinking about giving one."

José raised both his hands as if he were surrendering. "No, not at all," he said. "I was actually going to tell you that if you need to take a minute to speak with Beth, to try and smooth things over, feel free to. It might be better sooner than later. It seems she's got a lot of respect for you. That's not something that I want to stand in the way of you fixing."

Wyatt stood and politely nodded at the Mundanes and the Horsemen before walking over to his tent. As Wyatt walked away, José leaned forward, folding his hands together, his eyes deep and thoughtful. "So, what are you guys thinking?" he asked.

Stew spoke with a mouthful of food. "Mil sounds kinda fucked."

Sandy snorted derisively as she wiped off the food that had been flung from Stew's mouth. "Please, Baby, stop talking with your mouth full. It's not hot when your mouth is full of food. And I think we gotta take advantage of this. That's what Suzy would do."

Suzuki was looking over his shoulder at Wyatt's tent. He could see Beth and Wyatt talking. They were both gesturing animatedly. Finally, Beth slapped Wyatt across the face, her finger only a couple of inches from his nose as she spat on the ground and then flipped him off. They were shouting loud enough that Suzuki could almost make out the words. Beth turned to walk away from Wyatt. Instead, he grabbed her wrist and spun her around. He pulled something small and black from his pocket and placed it in Beth's hand. Then he went back to his tent. Beth walked back to the banquet table, her head hung, her eyes dark and brooding. She took a seat next to Suzuki, downed all of her ale and poured herself another one. "What are we talking about?" she briskly asked.

José motioned toward Suzuki. "We were just taking a vote. What do you think, Suzuki?" José asked.

Suzuki leaned back and smiled as he sipped on his ale. "Sandy's right. That's exactly what I would say. We are here. We have a small army. We should fuck shit up. If the Dark One has a ring in there, I say we wreck the place and take it."

Sandy squealed and grabbed Stew's arm. "Oh, Babe, we could be like the Fellowship," she joked. "I call dibs on holding it. Stew, you can be my Sam. Because you are obviously my bitch."

Stew spat out his beer and stood up, waving his hands, his face beet red. "No fucking way," he disagreed. "I am way too badass to be Sam. All he does is run around like, 'Oh, Mr. Frodo, oh, your burden, oh, let me hold you. So not me. Besides, you're a mage. You should obviously be Gandalf."

"But you are so devoted to me. That's so badass."

"Sam is so not the badass I am. I'm ax-throwing murder-machine badass. Sam's only cool because he's got so many feelings."

Sandy stood and kissed Stew on the forehead before drawing him close to her. Stew stopped arguing and went very quiet, almost like when you throw a curtain over a bird's cage. "Babe, you have so many feelings, though," Sandy cooed. "And you would totally hold the ring for me if it was too heavy on my emotional state, right?"

"Yeah, of course. Ain't nobody fucking with my girl. Not even a magical fucking ring."

Suzuki slammed his hands on the table. "You two both know we aren't talking about a literal ring, right?" he shouted as the Horsemen erupted into laughter. "It's a ring*tone*. You can't—"

Sandy raised her hand and put a finger to Suzuki's lips. "Hush, hush," she condescendingly whispered. "Haven't you ever heard of roleplay?"

"I've told you both that I DO NOT WANT ANY PART IN YOUR WEIRD SEX GAMES!"

Beth looked at her former party members with a look of bemusement mixed with mild disgust. "Jesus Christ, have you two always been like this?" she asked.

Suzuki hung his head while he poked at his food. "Honestly, they've gotten so bad since they actually got together," he said. "It's like Middang3ard turned them into teenagers. They've sexualized things that I've never even heard of before. Every fucking thing is an innuendo. I can't even eat around them anymore."

"I can see why." Beth giggled as she pointed over Suzuki's shoulders.

Suzuki turned to see what was going on and wished he hadn't. Sandy was bumping and grinding on Stew, reciting elvish poetry as Chip pounded a drumbeat on the table, while Stew rowdily downed his beer. José and Diana were trying their best to keep their shit together, but after a few more seconds of the gross display of affections, they burst out laughing, José falling to the floor, laughing so hard that he had to hold his guts. Suzuki sighed and chuckled. "Welcome back to the Mundanes," he said to Beth. "As you can see, we've really grown up."

"It's good to be back. I've really missed you guys."

José raised his tankard and shouted loud enough for the entire hall to hear him, "Tomorrow, we take the Dark One's ring!"

The military soldiers looked around, obviously confused by what was going on. Beth laughed when she saw their faces. "The military kids know how to have a good time, but this is on a whole other level." She chuckled.

Suzuki poured Beth another glass of ale. "This is nothing," he said. "Imagine an entire bar of this shit. And this is just the first hour."

"I fucked up when I chose the military over the MERCs."

"Well, you're here now. The party's back together."

"We're never splitting it again."

"No. Never again."

"Never."

Suzuki leaned back in his chair as he started to relax. Beth was talking to a soldier at her side. José and the rest of the Horsemen were mingling with the soldiers as well. Sandy and Stew had finally remembered that they were in public and started to introduce themselves to the soldiers around them. Suzuki was at peace. He had done it. They had all done it. The Mundanes were back together, and they had pulled something off with the Horsemen that had never been done. They had stormed the Dark One's defenses.

And now they were going back for more.

15

It was some time in the middle of the night by now, and most of the soldiers had retired to the makeshift tents the Mundanes and the Horsemen had managed to cobble together for them.

The tents were made from anything that the two parties could spare from their inventory: old leather armor that they had outclassed; extra tents that Wendy, the matron of the Red Lion, had sent with them just in case something happened; tents pitched from broken spears (out of the seven MERCs, none of them had any use for spears) and metal from shattered swords and axes.

Not one of the soldiers went unfed or unsheltered that night.

The soldiers would talk of the hospitality of the MERCs for years to come. They would tell their fellow soldiers in the military. They would tell their friends they wrote home to. Their children would be raised on tales of the night they were rescued by a MERC in the body of an imp and a MERC who looked like the walking embodiment of Jesus Christ himself, how they were brought to a cavern filled with the burning bodies of the MERC's enemies, how they had been greeted like old friends in a banquet hall that would have made Valhalla look like a steaming pile of shit.

Finally, the only ones still awake were the Horsemen and the Mundanes. The night had grown quiet with the rest happily sleeping, their bellies full of food and drink. The MERCs, however, weren't ready to dismiss themselves yet. There was too much energy, too much to revel in.

Suzuki had seen this at the Red Lion more than a couple of times. MERCs who had been out for weeks, months even, refused to rest after a night of heavy drinking. Suzuki was never one to want to stay up past his last drink. He usually excused himself early in the night to go shower and think— to meditate, as he had taken to calling it, for he was not merely obsessing. He was tearing through his thoughts, potential war situations, and battle tactics with the vicious-ness of an ogre. It was a battle meditation. Yet beneath him, the Red Lion raged. Dwarves, elves, humans, and halflings drank themselves merry, they gambled, they danced, and they lived.

Suzuki could see why now. They were celebrating life. Life was an abstract concept that philosophers spent their entire lives trying to understand. Suzuki had read their books, along with every fantasy novel that he could get his hands on. They were both about life, and, more importantly, they were concerned with death. Death was the reason that the MERCs celebrated into the early hours of the dawn, the time when the sun is just making itself known to a world swallowed in darkness.

He had experienced life.

Whatever he had felt after the missions he and the Mundanes had completed before paled in comparison to this feeling. It could not be said to be happiness, nor relief.

It was a deeper feeling that seemed to grow in his heart and flow all the way down to his feet, to flow through his hands and up to his neck, settling in the back of his neck, where his hair stood up on end. It was a feeling that only came from having your life plunged into the depths of impossibility, then to have it ripped away from the greedy claws of death and to have that life dropped back into your ignorant palms, to stare dumbfounded at all the glorious details of life that you had forgotten to pay notice to, all of the beautiful memories that now danced in front of your life with razor clarity, even though you hadn't thought of them in years. It was life. Amazing, glorious life.

The Mundanes and Horsemen had packed up the chairs, whatever had remained after they had been broken down for wood. All that remained of the hall they had created were the banners and the small campfires that filled the cavern with the smell of meat and wood. Sandy was adamant that they leave the banners hanging. It was a testimony of their victories, those past and those to come. She said that it was a proper spit in the face of the Dark One, to have robbed him of prisoners and sit beneath his mountain, feasting. Everyone agreed with her.

It was a pretty good "fuck you."

The fires burned brightly as if they were trying to catch up to how bright Suzuki's heart felt. He sat with the Mundanes and Horsemen around the fire.

They passed around a large plate of exotic fruits, savory meats, and stinky cheeses. A large bottle of ale was also being passed around. It felt like a small magical ritual to Suzuki. Most everyone was quiet, even Chip had been lulled into a deep, thoughtful silence, slowly smoking her loosely-wrapped cigarettes. Diana sat next to her, leaning her head on Chip's shoulder while she used her wand to draw pictures with the floating smoke: a dragon sitting atop a mountain, stars glittering above, the moon, huge and frightful with a face carved into it that looked ready to devour the world underneath.

José sat a little away from his party. He was staring into the fire, his dark brown eyes reflecting the intensity of the fire as he tended a few wounds Diana's magic had not been able to heal. He'd been struck by a magical arrow during his prison raid, and he wanted to make sure the wound would not become infected. The arrow had been suffused with magic to counter any healing magic.

"It's troubling," José said softly to Beth, who was sitting at his side, drinking liberally from the bottle of ale. "Orcs don't really do this kind of magic. They've never had the knack for it. Even being controlled by the Dark One shouldn't give them this kind of...talent. Maybe they're getting other people to curse their weapons for them."

Beth nodded, her eyes looking sleepy. Her hair had grown a little since Suzuki had last seen her. She had to keep moving her bangs out of her eyes while she talked to José. "Yeah, we noticed a lot of shit like that too. There were orcs with weapons that were far better than they should have had. I didn't get much of the clan distinctions when I was in training, there were too many to pay attention to, but I got the gist. There were red orcs invading villages that had weapons that were way too good for their tribes."

"It seems that under the Dark One, their tribal squabbles have fallen to the wayside. I've never seen that many orcs working together. It's still hard to wrap my mind around having to deal with red orcs and gray orcs at the same time."

Beth poked at the fire. "Tradition couldn't have been completely tossed out the window. I was captured by red orcs. They didn't kill us. It was almost like red orcs were sent just because they have a tendency to take prisoners instead of killing them. We had seen whole villages on the other part of the country completely decimated by gray orcs. Then we had a couple of our outposts destroyed by gray orcs, our more important outposts, the magical research outposts and shit like that, shit that the Dark One obviously would rather have destroyed than risk having used on him."

"It would seem that they still do have their traditions then. It's hard shit to make sense of, the Dark One controlling them and all. It seems he has so much control over them, yet not completely, and it's working toward his advantage."

"Yeah, having a loyal army that gives you the best parts of each race without any of their drawbacks seems to be working wonders for the guy. It almost makes you wish that we had something like that on our side."

Beth handed the bottle of ale to Stew and Sandy, who were sitting by her side, both of them leaning back on their hands. Sandy shifted forward, took the bottle, and took a long draught. She wiped her lips and handed the bottle to Stew as she took a couple of pieces of cheese and meat from the plate.

"I'm glad that we don't," Sandy chimed in. "It would be disgusting. Fuck that. I don't want to be fighting for the side that has to use fucking microchips to get anyone to do anything."

"Yeah," Stew echoed. "Fuck that. Where's the honor?"

Beth laughed sarcastically. Suzuki couldn't remember ever hearing Beth laugh like that before. It was a new sound coming from her. When she spoke, her eyes looked tired and heavy as if they weighed enough to fall right out of their sockets.

"Where's the fucking honor in war?" Beth asked. "War is people learning how to be terrible so that they can kill each other."

"Bullshit," Stew growled. "We aren't learning to be terrible. The only thing I've learned is how strong I can be, how strongly my friends love me."

"Is that what you're fighting for, Stew? A feel-good anime lesson?"

Stew looked hurt for a second. Then he smiled and took another swig of the ale. "Fuck, yeah, that's what I'm fighting for," he exclaimed. "The power of friendship winning out over a psychotic fuck who wants to enslave all of existence. That's exactly what I'm fighting for. That's honor as far as I'm concerned, being willing to stick your head out for everyone else. I'm not just some fucking meathead, you know. I remember why we all came to Middang3ard. We heard the whole lecture on how evil the Dark One is and shit, but none of us really got it. We came because we'd been playing a video game for seven years and this sounded like a fun, real-life adventure. Right?"

The Mundanes all avoided each other's eyes, but they nodded their heads in agreement.

Stew cleared his throat and went on. "So what? I don't think that's a shitty thing to admit. It sounded like a once-in-a-lifetime chance. Which nerd wouldn't have fucking gone for it? Then it was amazing at first. Boot camp was fucking ridiculous. Getting to do magic? Or watching you guys do magic at least." He laughed, pure and genuine, no edge or malice. "All that was fucking sick. When we first started to get out there, it was still sick and fun—the first few times, until we started to come up against some real life-or-death shit. That's when it clicked. This isn't a game. We joke and shit, but this isn't a fucking game. Sandy and Suzuki have pulled my ass out of the fire more times than I can fucking count. So, yeah, I'm totally gonna stick with being honorable. I'm not becoming a terrible person for the sake of a fucked-up war. I sacked up with the rest of my friends to come save your ass because you're our friend."

Sandy took the ale back from Stew and took a sip. "We slaughtered our way to you, Beth, because you're our friend. Our friendship is now built on the bones and blood of our enemies. And we'll carve our friendship into the Dark One's because it's honorable. Don't get me wrong. I'm still into death and carnage. It's kind of my thing..." she muttered.

Stew pounded his fist into his open palm. "Yeah, dude, fuck that whole enslaving the universe bullshit. Let people live. Besides, we gotta kill him on principle now. He fucked with one of the Mundanes. That makes him good as dead as far as I'm concerned."

Beth nodded and smiled. Her face had sharpened, and whatever pain had been floating in her eyes looked as if it had healed a bit. She wiped what could have been a tear from her eye and stared into the fire as she spoke. "I appreciate that. I didn't get to tell you guys how much I appreciate what you did for me! I thought I was going to die in that pit."

Sandy picked at the cheese and meat plate in front of her and shrugged her shoulders. "You're welcome, but you don't have to thank us. Never split the party, remember? We shouldn't have been split up from the get-go."

"How come we were? I know why Stew and Suzuki didn't get into the military. What was up with you?"

Stew's face went white, and he spat out his beer. "What do you mean, you know why I didn't get accepted? Even I don't know why!"

"Are you serious? José hasn't told you?"

Stew's face darkened as he glared at José. "No, José hasn't mentioned it."

José returned the glare, nearly as fierce as Stew's. His face eventually softened, though, and he looked around uncomfortably, an emotion that Suzuki could only recall seeing on his face once before when he spoke about Chip. "I didn't think that it was important to tell you. I thought you'd figure it out anyway."

"Well, what the fuck is it?"

"You're a berserker, and a pretty strong one from what I've been seeing. The military doesn't like to take any because...well, you guys are a little bit hard to control and kind of unpredictable. I haven't seen you go berserk—"

"Dude, I'm always berserking!"

"No, if you would shut up and let me explain, you—"

"Okay, okay, spit—"

"Will you shut up and listen?" José shouted.

Stew went quiet, but Suzuki could see Stew's mouth twitching to speak again. Instead, it curled into a shit-eating grin as he leaned back and popped in another piece of meat before handing the plate to Suzuki.

José took a deep breath and exhaled slowly. "It's kind of a big deal. MERCs accept berserkers but usually match them up with a veteran. You didn't get matched up with one. That's why I've been spending so much time talking with you. I've been trying to figure out if it was a fluke or not. You do have a habit of rushing into a fight, but that isn't going berserk. Like I said, I've been watching, and it's true."

"Okay, but you missed the most important part. How do I go berserk?" Stew asked, surprised there was more potential to his Leeroying.

"No one knows. It's different for everyone. I just wanted

to make sure that when it happened, you weren't the kind of person to kill your friends in a blood rage."

"Holy shit, that happens?"

José nodded. "All of the time."

"Shit." Stew turned to Sandy, grabbed her by the shoulders, and looked seriously into her eyes. "Babe, I'll never Hulk out and kill you. I swear on whatever weird gods the elves worship."

Sandy kissed Stew long, hard, and much longer than anyone at the fire thought was reasonable. "I know, Beef Cakes. I know."

Beth cleared her throat and mimed looking at a watch. "You still haven't answered the question, Sandy."

Sandy pulled out the Amulet of Elroz and dangled it in front of her face like a hypnotist. "Personality test did me in," Sandy explained.

"You're gonna have to give us more than that."

"It's nothing you guys didn't already know. My tests said I have intensely sociopathic tendencies and displayed a willingness to search for power above anything else."

The Mundanes all burst into laughter as the Horsemen stared warily at Sandy. "Oh, okay, you're right. It wasn't anything we didn't know." Suzuki laughed.

Chip raised her hand as if she were in a classroom. "Not to interrupt your lil family reunion, but that's just some old head doctor thing they be saying, right?"

Sandy shook her head as she tossed her amulet in the air and caught it in her right hand. "Nope," Sandy said nonchalantly. "I have an intense desire for knowledge at all costs so I can stamp out all of my enemies with that knowledge and spread their intestines through the streets of their familial homes. I like to think of it as a thirst for knowledge, not a thirst for power, but knowledge *is* power. Tests really don't see the difference, though. I just don't, *you know*, try to lead in with that when I'm getting to know people."

José laughed as he stood and walked to a corner of the cavern to take a piss. He shouted from his corner, "The fucking Mundanes, right? There isn't anything remotely mundane about any of you."

Suzuki picked at the cheese and meat plate. He was feeling embarrassed again. "The Most Mundane of the Mundanes?" Yeah, that was a title that he felt he was really earning right now. Beth had been a good-enough fighter to have been drafted into the military, and he had just found out the two others were too powerful for the military to control. The only reason that he hadn't been allowed to join the military was that he had the blood of an Englishman, something that generally drove giants into a state of frenzy. When Beth first got into the military, she had sent Suzuki an SD upgrade that allowed him to change his scent. That was how Suzuki had met the Chipmaster and, through Chip, José and Diana. It was a weird turn of events, sure, but not anything that made Suzuki feel more secure. Thankfully the Horsemen were more interested with Sandy's thirst for power at the moment.

Chip was prodding Sandy with a long stick, pretending to be afraid of Sandy exploding or something. "Heyo, so you're one of those dark mages who's always trying to suck up power to be the big bad infinite, eh?"

Sandy waved her wand at Chip's stick, setting the stick aflame and sending Chip scampering behind Diana, who laughed while Chip pretended to cower. "No," Sandy said, "nothing like that. I'm just pretty one-track-minded is all. I like magic, and I want to know all of it."

"Eh, with the way you seem to be gobbling up ancient artifacts that might not be too far down the line, missy."

José stood up and yawned, stretching his massive arms in a theatrical presentation of sleepiness. "All right, kids, I'm hitting the hay. We got a long-ass day ahead of us, and I doubt any one of us is going to enjoy all of it."

Chip and Diana did the same, both conveying the same general idea. Diana magicked away a few more of the needless items laying out, conjured another two bottles of ale that she placed by the fire, and swiped her wand to refill the food platter. "You guys have a good night and try to get some rest." She yawned as she turned to make her way to her tent.

The Mundanes sat together by the fire, alone and reunited for the first time in Middang3ard. Suzuki was aware of how much had happened, but this all seemed so normal, even more normal than when they had been playing VR together. Yet so much had changed. They were not the same people they had been when they had left earth. Everyone except for Suzuki, it seemed.

That didn't really matter, though.

Not really.

They were back together, and *that* was what mattered.

Stories flowed between the Mundanes for another two hours. They sat and shared everything that had happened over the last few months. Even though it felt like forever since they had all been together, they easily fell back into their old rhythm of things, sharing the same jokes and dynamics, but enriched by their separate experiences. Beth almost choked laughing about how Stew and Sandy finally figured out that they were dating. Sandy, Stew, and Suzuki listened in horror as Beth described the hellish conditions of the military boot camp. They all sat quiet for some time in honor of the dead MERCs and soldiers that they both had seen fall in battle.

Beth stood up and stretched, easily touching her fingers

to her toes. "This has been fun guys, but I'm fucking exhausted." She yawned. "Suzy, which one is your tent?"

Suzuki looked over his shoulder and pointed to a bright yellow tent a reasonable space from the rest of the crowd. He always liked to have a little more privacy than the rest of the two parties.

Beth walked past Suzuki and patted him on the shoulder. "Cool, I'll see you in a bit." She walked off toward Suzuki's tent.

Suzuki took a drink from the bottle and plopped another couple of pieces of meat in his mouth, staring at the fire. He noticed that Stew and Sandy had gotten very quiet. He figured that they were probably getting ready for sleep too. When he looked up at them, they both were staring at him, grinning very widely. "What the hell are you so smiley about?" Suzuki asked.

"Dude, you can't be that dense?" Stew smirked.

"Dense about what?"

"Beth just asked where your tent is."

"Yeah, I know."

"And she said that she's going to bed."

"Yeah, I know. And?"

"In your tent."

"Yes, in my tent."

"In your bed."

Suzuki's cheeks when red. "Oh. Oh shit. Oh, no, no, no, no. Oh, shit."

"It looks like someone might be having a hard time getting to sleep tonight."

"Shit...oh, shit."

Stew stood up and stretched, taking his time as if his limberness was somehow rubbing Suzuki's awkwardness in his face. "If you need any pointers, Suzuki, just let me know. I think Sandy can attest to my love-making abilities."

Sandy nodded as she finished off the last of the cheese and meats. "Yeah, Stew's a regular love machine. Even if he's a tactless jerkoff sometimes."

"Better to jerkoff than to not have jerked at all. Hey, wait, what are you talking about? How am I being tactless?"

"Suzuki's obviously nervous." Sandy turned to Suzuki. "Go take care of business. We'll see you tomorrow."

Sandy and Stew walked off without saying anything else, leaving Suzuki sitting by the fire alone. He knew that he had to get up and go to the tent. There was no choice. As he stood, he felt his legs trembling. He couldn't remember being this nervous in his entire life. There was too much buildup. Figuratively and literally.

Fuck it, Suzuki thought. *I can just sleep out here. I can tell everyone that I got too drunk and fell asleep. That's believable. Yeah, that's what I'll—*

Suzuki's HUD went off. It was a group chat message from Sandy and Stew. **Don't even think about pretending you got drunk and fell asleep.**

I better hear some booty clapping in there, Stew texted. **Like the real porno sound effects. But seriously, dude, just relax. Beth's probably just tired. That's so much more believable than her wanting to fuck you.** The text was followed by a variety of smiley faces. None of them helped him feel any better.

Suzuki texted back, **Fuck off, dude. Don't make me bring up the first time you and Sandy fucked.**

All right, all right. I'll leave it. See you tomorrow, dude.

Suzuki stared at the fire for a little while. His heart was still racing. He took a deep breath and turned to face his tent. Every step he took felt like it was going to be his last.

Orcs. Goblins. Dragons. Anything would have been prefer-able to this. Still, he made his way back to his tent. He opened it gingerly, the way one might peel off a bandage.

Beth sat in the tent. She was wearing a heavy bear skin robe and was sharpening her sword, her back turned to Suzuki. As Suzuki walked into the tent, Beth leaned forward, her robe slipping down one of her shoulders, showing a long scar that ran down her shoulder and under-neath her robe. She turned to face Suzuki and smiled as she brushed her bangs out of her eyes. "I thought you were going to make me wait here all night." She giggled.

Suzuki took a seat across from Beth with nearly enough space between them to fit a car. He crossed one leg over the other, coughed loudly, uncrossed his legs, and then crossed them again. "I was just having another drink before bed," he rambled. "You know, a nightcap. Some-times I have a hard time sleeping. Too much on my mind. You know, just the mind racing and stuff. Trying to figure out the whole day and shit. So, I was just going to drink a little—"

"And then pretend that you had gotten drunk and fallen asleep out there?"

Suzuki blushed and Beth broke out giggling. "I was not going to do that!" Suzuki shouted.

From outside, Suzuki could hear two other people giggling. "Y'all keep it down in there!" someone shouted.

Suzuki sighed softly. This was not how he was expecting things to go. In his mind, he had imagined that he would have rescued Beth and brought her back, sweeping her off her feet and carrying her into his tent like some barbarian god of olden days. Instead, he felt like a virgin being graced by the presence of a goddess of love. Aphrodite...

Beth stood up and pulled her robe close around her

body. She smiled coyly at Suzuki as she walked toward him. "Did you just call me Aphrodite?" Beth asked.

Suzuki hadn't been aware that he had spoken out loud. "No, no," Suzuki murmured. "I wouldn't have said that. You aren't anything like Aphrodite. I mean, not really. Not that you aren't beautiful. You are. You're really gorgeous. But I don't think of Aphrodite when I think of you. You don't really remind me of her. If you were a goddess, you'd be like Artemis."

Beth dropped her robe and it fell into a crumbled pile. Her body was covered with scars and small burns, the consequences of battle. Each mistake was imprinted on her skin. There was one scar that started at the base of her neck, snaked through her breasts, and ended right above her belly button. It could have been a tattoo in another lifetime.

Beth reached out and caressed Suzuki's cheek. "This is the part where most people say something really cool and sexy," Beth purred.

Suzuki wracked his brain. It was already working overtime. He could feel the outline of Beth's breasts against his thin tunic. Something sexy. Something sexy.

"Uh, you look...really hot naked."

"Honestly?"

"I mean, I love you."

"That's not what I was expecting...do you mean it?"

"I've loved you ever since I heard your voice."

Beth leaned forward and kissed Suzuki lightly on the lips, gently, almost as if she were afraid that Suzuki would melt away. He felt as if he would. When she pulled away, she wrapped her arm around Suzuki's waist and pulled him closer. "I love you too...and I want you inside me," she whispered in Suzuki's ear.

"Uh...I'd like that too."

16

Suzuki rose with the dawn, even though he couldn't feel its rays. He was smiling before he even pulled back his covers. Beth was sleeping beside him, her back rising and falling as she smiled in her sleep, a puddle of drool forming on her pillow. Suzuki covered her with the blanket when he stood. Her eyes flickered open for just a moment before she yawned, smiled, and rolled over on her side to continue sleeping. Suzuki grabbed his tunic and got dressed before leaving the tent.

Outside, the campfire was still going. Suzuki was surprised to see Fred sitting by the fire. The imp looked up at Suzuki when he approached and forced what could have been called a smile. For something with so many teeth, Suzuki was surprised that Fred could manage to be anything less than intimidating when he showed his teeth. At the moment, though, Fred only looked awkward, almost like a kid caught with his hand in the cookie jar.

Suzuki took a seat next to Fred and looked through his inventory for cooking supplies. A cup of coffee sounded amazing. He got to work getting the water boiling as Fred awkwardly fidgeted in his seat. "Is there something on your mind, Fred?" Suzuki asked.

Fred cleared his throat and scratched at his stomach. "I removed myself from your body last night to allow some privacy for your...activities," Fred explained.

Normally, that statement would have freaked out Suzuki. Not today. Today, Suzuki couldn't be bothered to give a shit. "Oh, well, thanks," Suzuki said as he poured boiling water over the coffee grounds he had set up to drain over a cup. "I really appreciate that."

Fred was still fidgeting awkwardly in his seat. Suzuki got distracted from the coffee that he was preparing and turned to face Fred. "Seriously, what the hell is up?"

When Fred finally met Suzuki's eyes, it was enough to shake Suzuki's happy glow. The imp looked sad. More than sad. He looked devasted. It was the only strong emotion that Suzuki had seen on his face other than murderous anger. Suzuki wondered if it were possible for imps to cry. He felt he was going to find out at any moment.

Fred pointed at the cup of coffee that Suzuki was making. "Your coffee looks about done."

"Seriously, I know we don't have *that* kind of relationship but what the fuck is up? I'm assuming you don't want to just sit here and mope in front of the fire all day."

"It is difficult to talk about, human...Suzuki. I left your body because of the complications of your feelings concerning Beth."

"There's nothing complicated about my feelings about Beth."

"Not yours...my own...not about her. About my family. About those I loved."

Suzuki weighed his next words carefully. He remembered that the last time Fred showed even the smallest amount of emotion, Suzuki had fucked it up by joking. He didn't want to do that this time. Even if he and his familiar were not as close as other MERCs and theirs, he still considered Fred to be a friend—a friend who was an asshole sometimes but, honestly, who wasn't?

"I don't mean to sound like a dick, but...I didn't know that eldritch creatures felt love. From what I know, it seems like you guys are pretty much into destruction and drowning the world in sorrow or chaos and similar shit. Love seems to be a pretty far cry from all of that."

"That is an understandable assumption. Although we are ancient, that does not mean we are incapable of love. We often love in a deeper way than most mortals ever do. The love of an elf lasts longer than the life of a human, much like how a dragon's love outlives the sturdiest elf. The love of an eldritch creature lives on for an eternity. Although an eldritch creature may continue on living alone, it never ceases to love those whom it has shared its life and hurt with."

"So, you guys just hate everything else?" Suzuki asked.

Fred laughed softly to himself. "No, we do not," he admitted. "It is mostly posturing. Maybe the oldest Elder Ones dreamed of swallowing the universe in darkness, but none of their children truly do, none of their grandchildren do."

"What about Ezekiel, that eldritch shit-head working for the Dark One?"

"He wants to honor his parents. You heard what he said. It was what his parents always wanted. In truth, us eldritch creatures are not that much different from any other mortal. We crave our parent's acceptance and we want to make them proud. We want to be loved and validated. I believe there are only two eldritch creatures that ever truly wanted to deliver the universe to chaos. In our stories, we speak of it as the First Madness. They came into this world, lost and frightened. There was nothing. So they tried to chase out their fear and created the universe. Now they watch and wait for a time when they can wash over us and create a new universe. To be honest, I don't even know if that story is true."

Suzuki drank his coffee, staring at the fire. "You know," he started, "you're really talking around the subject."

"I find these conversations uncomfortable."

Suzuki nodded. "That makes two of us. Let's just do the damn thing."

"Fine. Permit me to show you. It will be easier to understand."

"Go for it."

Fred stood and placed his hands on Suzuki's temples. Suzuki could feel Fred's cold claws against his pounding pulse. Then there was the smell of sulfur, and Suzuki was in a place he had never seen before. There was fire everywhere. A river of molten lava flowed near his feet. In the distance was a volcano, smoke brimming from its summit, covering the whole world in ash and black smoke. The ground was hot, but not too hot for Suzuki to walk.

The landscape was hellish in the very sense of the word, yet Suzuki felt welcome, almost comfortable. He figured that this was one of Fred's memories. It had to be. Only Fred would feel at home in a place like this, and Suzuki knew that he was picking up on Fred's emotions. Left to his own, Suzuki would have only been annoyed that this trip down memory lane involved walking through a literal Hades.

Suzuki wandered around without any direction for some time until he came to a bridge where he could cross the lava. Across the bridge, he found a small imp crying in a cave. He approached the imp slowly, watching it from afar for some time. The imp was an eldritch creature like Fred. Even though it was only a child, Suzuki could tell the imp belonged to the same category of imp as Fred. There was something about the imp that reminded Suzuki so much of his familiar. Suzuki got closer to the cave. He figured that this was only a memory. He must be safe.

As Suzuki got closer to the cave, he felt a gust of wind from overhead. He instinctively covered his head. It felt like he had just walked under a plane as it was taking off. When Suzuki looked up, he saw that another imp had flown over his head to get to the cave. It was an eldritch imp as well, but not Fred.

This new imp held a small goblin in its talons. The imp dropped the goblin onto the ground and cupped its throat with its feet. Then the imp motioned to the small child, which had stopped its throaty cries by now. The small imp looked from the larger imp to the goblin on the ground until something clicked. It bent low and bit into the goblins throat, sending blood and flesh flying as it knelt lower, biting off whole hunks of the goblin's body.

Suzuki watched the bizarre feeding ritual as he become aware of Fred's presence beside him. "What is this?" Suzuki asked.

Fred walked a little farther to get a better look at the imps in the cave. "This is my family." Fred sighed. "My wife and my child."

"I didn't know imps would treat their young so...kindly. Somehow I imagined you just left them to fend for themselves."

"No, it's quite the opposite. Eldritch imps spend almost their entire lives with their families. We build entire social networks. Generally, we stay away from other kinds of imps, but occasionally we adopt them into our own and breed them into the eldritch bloodline. There used to be whole planets of us. But you are correct in assuming that this is not how we treat our young. My daughter should be hunting by now."

"Why isn't she?"

"Because the rest of the imps on the planet have been wiped out. The Dark One invaded and told us to serve, and we told him to go fuck himself. He wiped us all out. These are moments before the only eldritch imps other than me were ripped from the face of the universe."

"A genocide."

"I believe it is very important for you to see with your own eyes what is about to happen."

Fred pointed to the horizon. Just over its ridge, an army was rallying. Orcs, goblins, and giants were stamping their feet and pounding their chests. They war-whooped themselves into a frenzy and poured over the horizon, running toward the child imp and her mother.

"I loved them deeply."

The two imps took off into the air. They flew toward the army rushing toward them.

Suzuki looked at Fred, confused and alarmed. "What the hell are they doing?" Suzuki asked. "Why are they—"

"We do not run from fights. We never have, and we never will. No one has but me."

"You left them?" Suzuki asked.

"No, I am not a coward," Fred growled. "I was defending the Northern Perimeter. We thought that if I was drawing the Dark One's attention, the child would be safe. But the child grew hungry, and she needed to be fed."

The two imps flew over the Dark One's forces. They

rained down fire and brimstone. Orc after orc fell screaming, consumed by the flames.

One of the giants took aim with a giant mechanical
spear-slinger. The child imp flew low and collided with the
giant's face, clawing the giant's eyes out, then spewing fire
from its mouth as it tumbled to the ground. It tried to get to
its feet.

Another giant brought a club down on the child imp.
The ground shook from the force of the attack.

In the air, the mother imp turned and stopped. A spear
flew through the air and pierced her heart. She fell to the
ground, her wings folded around herself, like a wounded
eagle. She hit the ground with an unceremonious thud.

Fred turned and pointed. In the distance, there was a
speck in the sky. "That's me," Fred explained. "I was flying as
fast as I could. I saw the whole thing, but I couldn't get there
in time."

Fred's memory sped past Suzuki with enough force that
it tore the air open in a sonic boom as the imp broke the
sound barrier. He flew straight into the heart of the Dark
One's forces and stopped on a dime. The Dark One's forces
were surprised. They didn't have time to react. Fred
screamed, a soul-piercing sound, shot up into the air and
covered the entire army in flames.

Fred sighed as he watched his memory fly above the
Dark One's forces, vomiting a fiery death upon them. "I
killed every last one of them. It didn't change anything.
They were still dead."

The memory ended, and Suzuki and Fred were sitting in
front of the fire. Fred looked at Suzuki, his eyes filled with
more loss than Suzuki ever could have imagined the imp
would have had. "Shortly afterwards, I volunteered to join
the Dark One. I believed that I could infiltrate his forces and

kill him. I did not have an understanding of how vast his forces were, nor what he was trying to accomplish. Eventually, I defected and joined the MERCs. I knew that the military would not risk me. MERCs on the other hand—"

"I'm sorry, Fred."

"My first host died. It was not my fault, but everyone assumed that it was. I could not blame them. I sat in that fucking garden forever waiting for someone to take me out so I could have my revenge. When I saw that it was you, I couldn't believe it. I thought an idiot had chosen me, and I would spend my days helping you fulfill inane missions and my revenge would rot like fruit. But here we are. Every day, you're bringing me closer and closer to that dream. I believe that you and the Mundanes will end this war. And I am honored to be a part of this. I have not met a human who I respect in a very long time."

"Are you saying that you respect me?"

"You may infer what you wish."

"I'm going to kill him, Fred. I'm going to make him pay for everything that he's done."

Fred nodded his head as he rose. "If you are done with your carnal pleasures, I will resume my occupation of your body," Fred hissed.

"Done? Dude, I'm making Beth a cup of coffee and waking her ass up. I am far from done. That was just round one."

"Ugh...filthy humans."

Suzuki slid back into bed with Beth. He laid there, staring up at the ceiling of the tent for a little while, uncertain of what to do with his body. All of the bravado from speaking with Fred had burned away. This was still all new to him. Well, not everything, but it felt like everything was new. He was almost afraid to turn and look at Beth. It was as if she would vanish if he made the mistake of looking at her. Even thinking back to the night before, none of it seemed real. A dream—that's what it felt like, something mercurial and liquid that was going to slip out of his hands the moment he tried to grasp it. Maybe it was better for him to wait outside. People say that they love you all the time. This could have just been one of those near-death experiences, hormones all jacked up and shit.

This kind of thing could be fleeting. Hell, it could even be meaningless. He'd seen movies and heard stories all of his life. People say shit when they're horny. He knew that *he* hadn't been talking to talk, but still, what if...

Beth sneezed in her sleep and rolled over. She tossed her arm over Suzuki's lap and nuzzled her face into his side. She sneezed again and woke up suddenly, sitting bolt upright, her eyes bright and searching. "Suzuki!" she shouted.

"Hey, I'm right here."

Beth whipped her head around and she was face-to-face with Suzuki, only a couple of inches away from him. She grabbed him and kissed him, her mouth parting and melting into his and they fell back onto the bed, their bodies intertwined as they embraced. "Shit," Beth whispered. "I had such a fucked-up nightmare. And then you weren't here. Or I thought you weren't here. I thought you left in my dream."

"Why would you dream that I left?" he asked.

"I don't know...none of this has been easy for me, all of this emotional shit. It's not...I mean, it's not that it isn't me. It's just not something that I like to do."

"You mean the whole love thing?"

Beth shook her head. "No, fuck, no, that's not what I meant. It's...goddamn it, that's not what I'm... Fuck this. This is what I'm talking about. Talking about things. Trying to explain how I feel. It's not fucking easy. *You* try doing this shit."

"Fine. I love you. I was sitting here worrying about whether or not what happened last night was just a one-night thing, a whole marine 'I didn't die, I gotta fuck the first person I see' type of thing. I don't know, I got scared. I got real scared."

Beth nodded and kissed Suzuki again. "You know how you think about things forever. Just think about them every day, not quite obsessing, but it becomes a part of your life. That's kinda...fuck, this sounds so fucking stupid." Beth took a deep breath. Her hands were trembling, and she clasped them together. "You know, people leave. People say they're going to be around forever and shit, but they don't mean it. Everyone leaves. But you didn't. And, when I was locked up in that cell, I kept...I don't know, I kept thinking about you. Even before that. When we were playing in VR, I'd go to sleep thinking about you. And then I finally saw you and I almost couldn't keep from laughing. I thought you were going to be some dried-up dweeb. But you weren't. You were fucking handsome. You could work on maintaining eye contact but, other than that, it was a pretty impressive first look. I just...you know, you don't expect things like this to happen."

Suzuki laughed until his sides hurt. He had to double over to catch his breath. "Yeah, who would have thought that we would end up confessing our love and fucking underneath a hollowed-out mountain that's been converted to an orc prison for a dark lord who wants to enslave the universe."

"Well, when you put it like that, me being in love with you is definitely the most normal part of all that," Beth agreed.

"So, this is a real thing?"

Beth nodded. "It's been real for a long time. I was just afraid."

"Same here."

"But now we know."

"Yeah, we know."

"So...we should probably stop talking now..."

Beth threw herself onto Suzuki and kissed him. Outside, they could have heard the rest of the MERCs getting up, making breakfast, pouring coffee, and talking about what their plans were. But they didn't hear any of that. The outside world ceased to exist for a while.

Beth and Suzuki both woke up an hour or two later. They talked together while they dressed, talking in a way that neither of them felt they had ever spoken with another person before. For the first time, Suzuki heard Beth speak about her family, not as if she were putting forth an effort to inform him about her past, but more like the information was just flowing out of her. It was as if a dam had just broken. Suzuki saw Beth as he had never seen her before, in a way that he never could have imagined.

Outside the tent, the Mundanes and Horsemen had already gathered for breakfast and coffee. Some of the soldiers had joined them. Stew was slaving in front of the fire, cooking a small array of meats, filling the cavern with the smell of sizzling fat, the savory allure of campfire cooking mixed with excellent ingredients. Diana was standing next to him, coaching or critiquing his technique as Stew whined and disagreed. Sandy was by the fire, her nose in a book as usual, twirling her amulet around her finger. She looked up at Beth and Suzuki when they sat down. "I'm going to have to teach you dicks that sound dampening spell," she teased.

As usual, the mere mention of sex caused Suzuki to blush brightly, this time taking on the complexion of a red dwarf. Beth was unfazed, though, reaching forward to grab a cup of coffee and asking, "Why the fuck would I want to dampen the sound? From what I've heard, you and Stew have been fucking like rabid rabbits hooked up to a Frankenstein sound amplifier. It's about time someone heard the sound of a sweet dicking that wasn't you two douchenozzles."

Sandy looked up from her book this time. "Finally." She sighed. "The old Beth is back. It's good to see you still know how to talk shit."

Beth leaned forward and jerked a finger at the soldiers who were timidly making their plates of food. "You would think marines could talk shit, but these guys are a bunch of pussies. They can dish it, but they sure as fuck can't take it."

"Not like you took it last night, eh?"

"More like giving it to Suzy."

Suzuki stood up suddenly, his face still bright red, and walked over to where Stew was cooking. José and Chip had joined Stew, standing around him like ravenous beasts. They smiled at Suzuki as he walked up to the campfire. "Sounds like someone had a right-on enjoyable evening," Chip teased.

Suzuki raised his hand to fend off any further teasing as he knelt next to the fire. "I came over here to escape being embarrassed," Suzuki whined. "I can't deal with Sandy and

Beth, but you three, I can easily tell to shut the fuck up and let's get back to work."

José tapped Stew on his shoulder and, when Stew turned to see who had tapped him, Chip swiped a couple of pieces of bacon, stealthily sliding them into José's hands when Stew turned back around. When José spoke, it was with a mouthful of bacon. "I didn't think you'd be so prudish." José laughed. "However, we do have things that need to be figured out. We can honor your lost virginity another time."

"Good. So, where are we at?"

"Well, last time we talked, we thought it seemed like a good enough idea to raid the Dark One's fortress and swipe that human ringtone, along with anything else we can get our hands on."

Suzuki looked around the cavern and wrinkled his nose. "I, for one, would like to not spend the next few hours digging around in new tunnels."

There was a loud braying and Suzuki whipped around to see where it was coming from.

GB was standing behind Stew, peeking out from behind Stew's legs. "You mean, we aren't going to be digging no more?"

Suzuki lifted a calming hand. "No, I said that I don't *want* to be doing anymore digging, but digging underneath the prison and up into it still might be our best bet, especially if we're planning on bringing all of these marines to the fight."

Chip was fixing herself a plate and was being very liberal with the bacon. "I already sent out a requisitions request for weapons and armor," she chimed in. "It might not be as classy as our gear, but it should be able to get these sods ready to get all stabby and warlike."

"Good. I suggest splitting into two different-size groups: a small group to travel overhead and a larger group that can tunnel through to our location once we're ready. The small group can sneak in and get to the ringtone while the larger group pops out to thoroughly fuck up the Dark One's shit."

José motioned for Diana to hand him her wand. When she gave it to him, he leaned over and started drawing in the dirt, concentric rings with a massive, deep circle in the middle. "So, this is the set up that we have right now," José said, pointing to their position in the second circle. "We still have a little bit of a hike until we get into the final ring where the tower is. I'm with Suzuki. I think a small group pushing forward would go undetected from what Chip's recon shows. The defense rings past the prison section use local flora and fauna as a defense. There's the occasional defense party, but nothing serious. Shit doesn't get bad until the final ring. That'll be the toughest section to deal with."

"We'll go in with our familiars that way. It's been working—" Suzuki started.

José shook his head. "That was before you found out that the viceroy is actually here. You can't keep posing as one of her guys if there's a chance you'll run into someone who knows she's in there."

Suzuki stood. "It's a risk worth taking. We shouldn't have to wander around that long, trying to figure out where the fuck we're going. We know what we're looking for and it should be pretty easy to find. It'll probably be in an area similar to the research area we found in the prison, where most of the tech is."

"And if we come across the viceroy?"

"Kill her. Same as everyone else."

"Do you know anything about the viceroy?" José asked.

"No," Suzuki said, feeling somewhat defeated. He

wished that he had been able to glean more information from their first meeting. Everything that he knew, he had already told the Horsemen. She was some kind of commander underneath the Dark One. On their last quest, the Mundanes had found that the viceroy was organizing the birthing of an Elder One by using vampires as her proxy. Suzuki had come across her when he accidentally touched a communication device. That was when the Mundanes realized that whatever the Dark One was using to keep his forces organized wasn't magic. Now everything was coming together: the technological communication, microchips, soundwaves, and ringtones to control. There was something else, though...

"When Chip was busted up!" Suzuki exclaimed. "I completely forgot about this. The viceroy looked a lot like that. The same kind of...I don't know...internals underneath. But worse. So much worse. She looked like whatever technology was attached to her was killing her...or like the tech was killing her flesh. I don't know what it was, but that shit looked a lot like what Chip looked like when she was... falling apart."

José turned to Chip and cleared his throat awkwardly. "Any idea what he's talking about, Chip?" he asked.

Chip shrugged and looked down at her hand. Her fingers fused together, rounding out and separating until her arm was a plasma canon, complete with a glowing blue orb in the middle, radiating energy. "Looking something like this?" she asked.

Suzuki shook his head as he looked down at Chip's hand. "No...not quite," he murmured as he thought. "It looked...older. Much older..."

"No idea. I mean, honestly, I don't have any idea about anything. I think I'm just some half-elf fuckup from New

Jersey who liked to make things go boom a little more than necessary. I never quite took to thinking about myself as a *robot* half-elf manic pixie chick, but alas, my cliché even includes amnesia. I got nothing, boy-o. The most I can say is that if the viceroy is packing heat like me, ye might want to tread lightly."

"Then that's it. Nothing can be done about the viceroy until we see her. Hopefully, we can just avoid running across her."

Diana shook her head as she took her wand back from José. "I think that is being willingly naïve," Diana interjected. "You've been posing as the viceroy's lackey for the last few days. She's got to know by now. When you walk in there, you'll be a moving target."

"I will be for her and her higher-ups. The grunts aren't going to give a shit. Most of the orcs working in the prison only knew the viceroy as a name. It'll work."

José stood and brushed himself off. He grabbed another couple of pieces of bacon and crammed them into his mouth before combing through his beard for any scraps. "The Mundanes and I take the small dispatch position. We find a good spot and have the marines dig their way to us."

Suzuki shook his head. Something in the plan didn't quite add up for him. It needed a tweak. "How about after we get past the flora and fauna circles, we split. That many people are going to be too much to get past the innermost circle. So, Sandy and Stew will stay back at the halfway point and help organize a joint digging situation with the marines and the rest of the Horsemen. Besides, from what I heard, GB is a digging fiend. He should be part of that squad, and I don't know what the fuck Sandy was up to when she went all 'flower girl' and shit, but it seems like she's pretty decent at the dig too."

Diana hung her head and shook it. She looked worried. "You and me both," she muttered.

"What do you mean?"

"I've been at this magic game for a bit," Diana said. "Never have I seen such rapid development of magical power. I don't know what's going on with her, and I don't know if we should keep pushing her."

"That's her choice and not ours."

"I don't know, after what she said last night about power and knowledge...just keep an eye on her, all right?"

"She's a Mundane. Her life is my life."

José smiled and nodded as he put his hand on Suzuki's shoulder. "Well said, kid. Well said. So, what are we still doing standing around with our dicks and clits in our hands? Let's get moving."

The Horsemen all rose, Diana and Chip making their way to the Marines who were starting to congregate together. José and Suzuki returned to the rest of the Mundanes, who were in full roast mode. Sandy and Beth were flinging quips at each other faster than Suzuki could keep up with. He sighed and shook his head. This had the potential to be a very long trip. He had forgotten what the Mundanes were like when they were all together: a band of warriors who were known in VR not just for their skills, but for an excessive amount of shit talk. This was going to be just like the old days when they used to pour hours and hours into raids.

Suzuki gave Sandy, Beth, and Stew the rundown of the game plan. None of them had any objections, so they agreed to go forward with it. After breaking down the camp, they prepared to go topside. Earlier in the night, Chip had scouted back through enemy territory to retrieve the axbeaks they had had to leave behind when they went underground. She assured the Mundanes that they would be waiting topside, tied to a tree a little east of where they would exit.

The Mundanes packed up and headed topside. Suzuki was excited. It had been days since he had had a breath of fresh air. He had gotten used to existing in a constant state of claustrophobia. He couldn't imagine how the grimpons had evolved to survive underground. The thought of never seeing the sun was enough to depress Suzuki. He didn't want to think about what it actually would be like.

They exited the tunnel and found themselves in a lush garden. It looked far too beautiful to be part of the defense rings of the Dark One. The only things Suzuki had seen the Dark One cultivating had been dead looking stone or sterile technology. This lively garden looked like it belonged in a painting of the Shire. Perhaps this was an area of the defense rings that the Dark One hadn't had time to destroy, an oasis that managed to avoid his deadly grasp—or maybe the Dark One didn't feel the need to destroy everything. He was, in fact trying to enslave whole races, not destroy them. Maybe there was some part of him that valued life.

Near the exit, they found the axbeaks that Chip had herded for them. Once mounted the Mundanes and José made their way through the deceptively-alluring garden. The more time that Suzuki spent moving through the garden, the more he found its initial appeal to have been built upon deception. There was something rotten in the garden. It was hard to place his finger on it, but it started with the scents. Although the garden was filled with blooming flowers, there were no sweet or floral aromas. If anything, the closest you could say that the garden had to a scent was a hint of decomposing flesh. When the Mundanes stopped to water their axbeaks at a river, Suzuki knelt and touched the grass. He found that it was sharp enough to cut his skin with hardly a touch. He looked at the axbeaks' feet. Luckily, their birdlike talons appeared to have been made for this kind of terrain. Suzuki was horrified to think what would have happened to a horse's hooves, let alone his own feet.

While the axbeaks drank, José wandered around, looking at the different plants that made up the garden. He drew his sword and pointed it at a plant that was nearly his own size. The plant resembled a type of pot. It had a bulbous bottom that stretched up and tapered off like a pitcher. A large leaf hanging over an opening in its midsection secreted a horrid stench.

José prodded the plant with his sword. The plant's leaf suddenly flapped open and the plant leaned forward, a row of sharp fangs gnashing at José as its pitcher mouth snapped open and shut. José jumped back and laughed. "Guess that's why these are in the defense ring." José chuckled. "It's probably bait for steeds. I don't see a human falling into something like that, but a wandering horse, looking for something to nibble on? These things have probably taken their fair share of lives."

Suzuki led his axbeak away from the water, which he now considered suspiciously. If the plants were vicious, who was to say that the water wasn't poisonous? José saw Suzuki's worried face and laughed again. "You don't need to worry about the axbeaks," José said. "They're tough. That's one of the reasons they're reserved for only the elite of the MERCs. These things can eat and drink anything. Their skin's immune to most blades unless they're magically enchanted. You could feed those things cyanide biscuits and they'd just shit it out. It would probably make a handy grenade."

Beth walked by as she grabbed her axbeak and mounted it. She made a face of pure disgust. "You would throw axbeak shit at someone?" she asked. "What the fuck, dude. That's some straight-up primate shit."

José mounted his axbeak, along with the rest of the Mundanes. "I'm not above slinging my own shit if it'll keep me alive," José said. "The dead don't talk shit last time I checked."

Sandy looked up, her eyes were hollow as if she were looking beyond her compatriots beside her in the garden. "No..." she murmured, almost trancelike. "The dead do indeed talk shit." Her eyes cleared. She looked around like she was lost for a moment, before shaking her head as if she were trying to clear a fog. "Huh...that was weird."

Stew rode up to Sandy, slapping his axbeak in the back of its head as it tried to rear up and toss him off. "Babe, you okay?"

"Yeah, yeah. Totally fine."

As they continued forward, Suzuki noticed that the head of the orc necromancer that he and Sandy had killed earlier in their journey still hung from the side of Sandy's axbeak. Its eyes were wide open, staring ahead as if it could see into a world that Suzuki was yet to be made aware of. All and all, it was a little disconcerting. "Hey, Sandy, what's up with that head?" Suzuki asked.

Sandy looked down at the orc necromancer's blank head, staring off into the distance. "Oh, that? I don't know, I think it looks better out and about than collecting dust in my inventory. You, know, a little bit of that old pagan fear mongering."

Suzuki tried to avoid the gaze of the dead orc's head. He felt like its eyes were watching him, but that was the least of his concerns at the moment as they continued forward, following José's directions.

Chip had left him a detailed map of the next two rings of defense on which she had thoroughly mapped out each junction, enemy camp, and body of water. The plan was to move through this floral ring and through a swamp to pass through the final ring of defense unnoticed. There they would find the Dark One's main tower in the defense ring fortress. If the swampland was anything like the garden, getting to the final ring was going to be a piece of cake.

They made their way through the garden and watched as it slowly became more decrepit and fouler. The healthy greenery came undone before their eyes as the axbeaks' talons tore at the grass beneath their feet. Trees drooped, their fruit and leaves hanging like the appendages of an elderly man, crippled by age. Many of the fruits were still rotting on their branches. The grass was dulled and browned as if it had been scorched by an angry sun. The earth itself started to break, giant cracks spreading throughout the ground, the torn earth looking as if it had been stricken with a great hammer by some violent, vicious god of old. The air grew sourer.

Beth and Suzuki were riding beside each other. They did not speak much, Beth occasionally mentioning or taking note of the terrain around them. Her conversation tended to stick within the realms of their mission. She sometimes asked questions or pointed out potential situations that they could encounter. It was very different from Sandy and Stew, who couldn't have been any less concerned with talking about work at the moment. They were both horsing around, trying to outpace each other in a snail's race behind Suzuki and Beth. From what Suzuki could tell from the snatches of conversation he could catch, they were trying to see who could ride the slowest without their axbeaks losing balance.

"Are they always like this?"

Suzuki snapped out of his thoughts when he heard Beth talking to him. "What did you say?" he asked.

"Are they always like this?"

"Like what?"

Beth pursed her lips. "They don't seem worried about anything. It's like they're having fun."

"They *are* having fun."

"Hmm. Being out here with you guys is different. It's not like back in the military. No one talked out on our patrols. The commander would have been chewing them out for giving away our position. Things with the MERCs seem...a lot more relaxed."

Suzuki nodded. "Yeah, I would figure. We don't really have commanders, not even party leaders."

"You seem like you're leading the party."

"Maybe, but it's not a formal thing. I guess it's kind of like back when we used to play together. I wasn't really the leader, just the guy who came up with most of the plans. It's not like anyone has to listen to me or anything. Same with the Horsemen. Mostly, I've seen José coming up with plans and tactics and shit. But sometimes it's Diana, and Chip usually has something to throw in, here or there."

"It feels almost like I'm gaming with you guys..."

"Were there a lot of gamers in the military?" Suzuki asked.

"Honestly, a shit ton, mostly those pro-kids and shit. I guess that would be the big difference, that and you MERCs are out for the loot, right?"

"Well, that's their whole marketing thing, but I don't think that's all there is to it. Honestly, our loot was shit until we found out about you. We were only trying to find better equipment so we didn't end up dead out here."

"What about the whole killing the Dark One thing you were going on about?"

Suzuki shrugged. "That's part of the gig too. I guess we're just having a better time doing it. Not having someone barking orders at us kind of helps. The most we have is an annoying-ass dwarf who thinks that we're his proteges or some shit like that."

"Seems nice." Beth sighed.

Sandy's axbeak suddenly surged forward, nearly bucking her off of its back as it tried to push its way to the front of the queue, running directly into Beth. Both Sandy and Beth were thrown off their axbeaks. They rolled across the brown grass until they stopped in front of a giant plant that looked like a mix between a Venus flytrap and a rose bush.

The plant growled hungrily at the two women as they slowly stood. "We shouldn't make any fast moves," Beth suggested.

"Yeah... nothing too fast," Sandy agreed.

That didn't stop the plant. Thorned tendrils shot out of the plant's roots and wrapped around Sandy's feet, flipping her into the air as it opened its mouth, greedily waiting for its meal.

Beth drew her sword, shouting, "Sandy!"

The worry was pointless, though. Sandy spun in the air and conjured her staff into her hand. She threw it down sideways so the plant snapped its flimsy jaws on the staff and was unable to break it, its mouth stuck open. Sandy then conjured her wand, landed on her feet, and set the plant on fire, her staff shooting jets of fire from inside the plant, her wand shooting a thin bolt of lightning. The plant was reduced to ashes within seconds. "Goddamn it, Stew," Sandy shouted, "I said no fucking tickling. That's cheating."

The rest of the Mundanes and José hadn't bothered to stop riding. Stew looked over his shoulder, that boyish shit-eating grin resting smugly on his face. "Dude, I totally saw you trying to enchant my kilt," he called back. "I just got you better than you got me."

Sandy laughed and jumped back on her axbeak, punching it in the back of the head so the creature wouldn't attempt any further revolts. She almost rode off, but stopped and cast a glance back at Beth. "Hey, you coming along?" she asked.

Beth mounted her axbeak and followed after Sandy. "Were they about to leave you?" she asked.

Sandy shook her head. "Them? No. I mean, no one is going to stop over something that I can easily take care of, but I know they're watching out for me. We just trust each other, that's all."

"Looks like a lot of trust."

"I trust Stew and Suzy with my life." Sandy's eyes sparkled as she spoke.

"It must be nice."

"What do you mean?"

Beth looked away. "Nothing, forget about it."

Sandy and Beth caught up with the rest of the party and they snaked their way through the garden as it deteriorated into a swampland. This was nothing like the swamp that the Red Lion was built upon.

The Red Lion's swamp was lush, dark but still inviting. Trees hung overhead, covered in Spanish moss; pathways were built to keep you above the mucky waters mixed with treacherous mud. It smelled of life, of trees and vines, of greenery bursting with the desire to continue its own existence. There was something deep within that could not be explained, the very joy of life that the splitting cell has, that smell mixing with the fresh food cooking for returning MERCs.

This swamp was nearly the opposite. There was nearly no scent, the little bit that there was could only be called the smell of death. It wasn't the smell of decomposition nor the iron scent of blood that set your nose on fire. No, this was something else. It was almost the absence of scent. That was what Suzuki thought death must smell like.

José pulled his axbeak closer to Sandy. "I have a bad feeling about this place," José whispered. "How's that invisibility spell that Diana's been working with you on?"

Sandy wouldn't meet José's eyes, obviously embarrassed. "Eh..." she murmured. "I mean, I can cast it on myself, but I can't quite get other people right. They tend to turn blue."

Stew, who was riding at Sandy's side, nodded and grunted in agreement.

José waved away Sandy's worries. "Don't worry about it," he said before turning to Suzuki. "And what's your scent set to right now?" he asked.

Suzuki brought up his HUD. Unless there was a reason for it, he rarely checked what his scent SD card was set to. He didn't usually need to worry about it. His scent was always set as something other than "English Blood" so that he wouldn't attract any giants. At the moment, his scent was set to 120-year-old aged whiskey. He told José, causing Beth to laugh so hard that she had to cover her mouth, trying to stifle her giggles. "What's so funny?" Suzuki asked.

Beth put on a straight face, still trying to keep the giggles from bubbling over. "I was wondering why you smelled so good," she explained. "I thought it was a cologne but, I was like, where the fuck would Suzy be getting cologne from?"

Stew cleared his throat loudly. "Uh, could you guys keep all the PDA shit to yourself." He scoffed. "That's kind of a closed-door conversation."

Suzuki stared at Stew, his jaw nearly completely detaching from his skull. "Are you fucking serious, Stew?"

José cut in, putting the question on the back burner. "You should change it to something less conspicuous," José suggested. "Maybe something more in line with the natural scents of the swamp."

Suzuki flipped through his HUD, imagining what the best scent for this muggy swamp would be. Usually, he would have swayed toward something natural. But he had a feeling about this swamp, one that he believed echoed whatever José was picking up on.

Suzuki chose "Decomposing Flesh."

At Suzuki's side, Sandy waved her wand and cast her invisibility spell. Suzuki saw her slowly wave out of sight as if her body was nothing but a few ripples in the light spectrum. She turned wavy like a hallucination and then was gone. Suzuki thought it was a pretty cool trick, something that could come in handy when they were overwhelmed. If Sandy had the spell down well enough, she could easily double as a rogue.

That was something you didn't see often.

A mage-rogue.

That would give the Mundanes an insane edge.

While Suzuki was thinking, he raised his hand to scratch his nose. He stopped midway, his hand hanging in midair. Or, at least, he assumed his hand. His palm was nowhere to be seen. And the rest of him was slowly disappearing as well. He looked down as his entire body slowly vanished. Then there was a loud pop and he could see himself again. "Uh, what the hell just happened?" Suzuki asked.

José laughed as he disappeared and then reappeared with a pop. "Everyone has their talents. Mine usually goes unnoticed. I have a very strong, passive, rally buff going at all times. Unless it's being used like this, most people don't even pick up on it. But any spells or buffs that are cast in my vicinity are amplified to the whole party."

"Jesus fucking Christ, that explains so much!" Suzuki marveled. "That's how you were able to get all of those soldiers out. All you needed to do was find a few mages and you could—"

"Cover an entire army with this badass power. It's a Horsemen secret, though. Try not to let it get out, newbs."

"Dude, not a fucking problem. Your secret is safe with us."

"All right. Now let's check out this swamp. But first..."

José leaned over and placed a small stone on the ground. There didn't seem to be anything special about the stone. Then he tapped his HUD and a glowing beacon popped up beside the rock. He walked away without explaining anything. Suzuki figured that he'd find out when and if it was important. José didn't usually like to waste time with words or explanations. Hell, he'd only just told the Mundanes that he'd been passively enhancing their skills since they first left. Whatever the stone was for, Suzuki felt like he'd find out eventually.

The Mundanes and José rode farther into the swamp, leaving behind them the sickly, deceptive garden. The world grew dark around them as the ground become swampier and swampier. The axbeaks slogged through the swamp, the mud getting thicker and deeper. They were slowing down, struggling to get their long, spindly legs out of the mud. They weren't succeeding. After half an hour of trying to coax the axbeaks along, Suzuki suggested that they tie up the birds. It would be easier to just wade through the swamp themselves. The axbeaks would be able to take care of themselves. They were vicious enough.

Stew and Sandy roped the axbeaks together and tied them to a tree where they squawked and screeched until Sandy leveled her wand at the fowl. They shut up pretty quickly. Just for good measure, Sandy cast another sound dampening spell on them before leaving.

Then they set forward on foot, cloaked in the invisibility spell, reeking of decomposing flesh. They entered the swamp as wraiths. Up above, the sun grew darker and darker as the grossly abundant trees of the decaying swamp attempted to block out all light.

17

———

They had been traveling for nearly three hours and noon was quickly approaching. The temperature of the swamp had changed drastically from that of the garden. The balmy, breezy weather was gone, replaced with a muggy, sticky heat. The Mundanes and José slowly made their way through the swamp, responding to the heat that clung to them like an extra layer of skin. They were dripping sweat and their legs rose and fell with the weight of exhaustion. Still, they were making good time. They would be close to the final ring soon.

As they made their way through the swamp, they had come across a handful of sentries, mostly orcs patrolling through the swamp. Thankfully, Sandy's invisibility cloak and José's buffing had rendered them all invisible. The cloak extended further than just the eyes. It also masked them from magical awareness as well. This was an added benefit that Suzuki was extremely grateful for because most of the sentries were also outfitted with mages, more orc mages than Suzuki had ever seen.

José raised his right hand and the Mundanes stopped.

He leaned over to Sandy and whispered in her ear. Sandy raised her wand and with a flick of her wrist cast a sound dampening spell over herself. José's passive buff caused the spell to extend to everyone in the immediate area. José snapped his fingers, looking over his shoulders to see if the orcs a couple of feet away could hear him.

The orcs took no notice.

José nodded his approval as he turned back to the Mundanes. "I just wanted to make sure that we could talk as well," he said. "It doesn't make a whole lot of sense to be wandering invisible and mute. What do you think we should do about them?" he asked, jerking his thumb toward the orcs.

Suzuki shrugged his shoulder. "I say we leave them. We don't want a bunch of bodies piling up while we're sneaking around. It'll raise attention. Even if they can't see us, I wouldn't be surprised if they found a way to find us when they start getting suspicious."

"Good point. Let's keep pushing on."

They continued on their path, working their way around the orc mages that stalked through the dark swamp, the orcs holding hefty torches that cast a pale-yellow light across their path. The patrol was made up of three orcs, two of them mages, their bodies covered in some sort of ashen warpaint, their faces painted up like skulls with two beady eyes glowing in the dimness.

Suzuki pointed at the orcs as they walked past them. "What's with all of the mages out here?" he asked. "Aren't orcs that can do magic supposed to be super rare?"

Sandy nodded as she came up closer to Suzuki. "They are rare," Sandy explained. "Very rare. And those aren't even orc clan mage markings. They're something else. I've never seen anything like those before."

Beth laughed a little derisively. "Since when did you become an expert on orcs?" she asked.

"Books—I've been reading a lot about the different magical systems of the different races. There's a huge section on orcs because magic is so rare with them. It's almost like an aberration. They usually give their mages specific markings from youth so that the rest of the orcs know to stay away from the mage since they can be...volatile while they're growing up."

Suzuki laughed to himself.

He didn't want to say it out loud because he wasn't sure how Sandy was going to take it, but he could see that Diana was rubbing off on her. The way that she talked about magic and history really reminded him of Diana. He made a mental note to ask her more questions about the orc tribes later. He was very curious to know how magic worked with the orcs.

The Mundanes and José made their way past the orc sentry as the orcs were rounding a bend of trees. One of the orc mages stopped walking and stared out where the Mundanes had been as if he could feel some trace of what had been there before.

Suzuki stopped to watch the orc try and figure out what was going on. Fortunately, the orc wasn't able to sense anything definite. He turned back to his fellow orcs, and they lumbered off on whatever their mission was. Suzuki noticed the large microchips on the backs of their necks as they continued on in their search. He wondered if the microchips impacted the magical abilities of the orcs. If the Dark One was able to control the minds of those who were microchipped, what was keeping him from being able to control and influence other aspects as well?

Suzuki let his mind wander a little bit. It was a really

good question and one that was worth investigating. There were tons of benefits of having an army of willing slaves. But once you started playing with the mind, what else was possible? Suzuki knew that his body had changed so much when he came to Middang3ard. Bonding with his familiar granted him magic and also helped his body perform superhuman feats. He remembered when he first merged with Fred, he had told the imp that he felt like Captain America. If that was possible, to what limits could the Dark One push the bodies and psyches of his slaves?

Beth looked at Suzuki and saw that he was deep in thought. She gently pushed him, breaking his concentration. "What's up?" Beth asked. "You look like you're about to have an aneurysm."

Stew laughed from across the party formation. "That's just the way his face looks, dude," Stew chided. "You've just been away for a bit and forgot. He's got resting nerd face."

Suzuki ignored Stew. He knew that would get under Stew's skin more than if he had said something back. As he spoke, he noticed Stew's smile drop as Suzuki sidestepped Stew's teasing. "I'm thinking about what the mind control could be doing to the orcs," Suzuki said. "You know, breaking the mind down to control it...that's some heavy shit. I guess I was just wondering what else it would be capable of doing."

"Why?" Beth asked. "What does it matter?"

"What do you mean?"

"Fuck them. Who cares what it's doing to them?"

Suzuki shrugged. "Maybe we should. Were the orcs running raiding parties and killing innocent people before the Dark One enslaved them? How long have they been slaves?"

"Suzy, these are pointless questions. They're trying to

kill us, so we have to kill them first. That's just the way that it goes."

"I don't think it's that easy. There might be another way. Maybe we could—"

"The Dark One's forces are monsters, Suzy," Beth said.

Suzuki thought of what Fred had told him earlier, about Fred's family. "Yeah," Suzuki said. "Maybe they aren't monsters like we think they are."

"Maybe not, but they're still the monsters that are trying to kill us."

Suzuki couldn't think of anything more to say. He'd noticed that Beth seemed to have a much harder stance on what was going on in Middang3ard than he or the Mundanes did. It probably had to do with the fact that she was military. There seemed to be a level of finality that the military had which MERCs did not share. Suzuki had noticed it at the dinner the night before. Of course Beth had just been sprung from a prison where she and her friends had been tortured for weeks. It would be surprising if she had walked away from that without being somewhat changed. Suzuki couldn't imagine how that experience would have changed him.

He tripped over a root and faceplanted. By the time that he was able to pull himself out of the mud, which seemed to be trying to suck him under like quicksand, he was coated in it. He looked like a creature that had just risen up from the swamp itself.

Stew helped Suzuki get to his feet while Suzuki tried to shake the mud off his arms. "Dude," Stew started. "You look like a low budget Swamp Guy movie or something."

"It's called Swamp Thing," Suzuki grumbled as he wiped mud off his face. "If you're going to try to rip on me, you might as well get your facts straight."

Stew smirked. "I just like to call attention to how unbelievably nerdy you are."

"Stew, there's a new comic book movie every two weeks. There is nothing nerdy about knowing who Dr. Holland is."

"Dr. who?"

Suzuki let out an exasperated sigh. "Holland. Alec Holland. The Swamp Thing, you know."

"No, I don't. I think I was too busy not being a huge ass nerd to have caught that reference. Case and point. Check and mate."

"It's just 'checkmate'."

Stew gave Suzuki the biggest smile. "Oh, I know, dude. I know."

Up a bit ahead of the rest of the Mundanes, Sandy stopped walking. She looked over her shoulder and held her hand up to signal to the rest of the party to stop. They stood there in silence for a moment, while Sandy knelt down and stared at the mud. She walked back to the rest of the Mundanes. "There's something down there," Sandy said.

"What are you talking about?" Stew asked. "Like, under the mud?"

"In the mud, babe. And yeah. I didn't get a good look at it but it was swimming. Like this was water or something."

Suzuki nodded and pulled out his hand ax. "We should be good, though, right?" he asked. "We're still invisible."

"Yeah, we are. Whatever it was didn't stop when I got close to it. It just swam past, but I figure it's better to be aware, you know. Pointers from Chip and Diana: keep an eye on your surroundings."

"So, you're switching to a rogue now?"

"It never hurts to diversify," Sandy said as she pressed her amulet to her chest, causing her skin to turn pale gray and flake off until she was covered in a cloak of ash.

"That is so unnerving to look at."

Sandy's masked face stared back at Suzuki. "Yeah, but you gotta admit that it's pretty fucking badass."

Stew was running his hand through Sandy's miasma of ash like a kid fascinated with a new toy. Sandy waved Stew's hand away. "Cut it out, babe." She giggled. "That tickles. Come on, we should keep moving."

As they walked farther into the swamp, Suzuki noticed that Beth was staring at his ax. He decided to show off and tossed his ax into the air. He missed it, and his ax plopped into the mud. "Fuck," he muttered as Beth started cracking up.

"Were you trying to impress me?" she asked. "Because you failed miserably."

"Whatever," Suzuki said. He shrugged and kept walking.

"Wait, aren't you going to get your ax."

"Huh? Oh, yeah."

Suzuki absentmindedly held out his hand. His ax pulled itself from the mud and flew into his hand.

Beth stared at Suzuki's ax, her mouth hanging open. "All right, that was impressive," she admitted. "Where the fuck did you find that?"

Suzuki looked the weapon over. "The ax? Oh, probably our first mission or something. I actually can't remember where I picked it up."

"Are you serious? I thought you said that the loot you guys were getting wasn't that cool."

"It wasn't for a while. There wasn't anything special about the ax. I've just been working on my enchanting. I figured it would be cool to take something really simple and turn it into a badass little work of art. You know, make something that's just mine."

"Where did you learn how to enchant like that?" Beth asked.

"Just reading and practicing and shit. Sandy hooked me up with some books and I've just been tinkering away at it. It's like a hobby."

"Okay, that's really impressive. I don't know anyone in my platoon who can do anything like that. Honestly, I feel like we're all just grunts. It seems like you guys have a lot more freedom to, you know, figure things out."

Suzuki thought about what Beth had said. There did seem to be a lot of freedom being a MERC. No one told you what to do. You could learn what you wanted. The Vets seemed pretty interested in helping the newbs develop. Suzuki quietly thanked whoever was listening that he had failed to get into the military. Beth wasn't making it sound like a great place to be. Even though it didn't feel like it, Suzuki was thinking that the MERC was where it was at.

There was a sudden crash from behind, and Suzuki whipped around to see where the noise was coming from.

Stew was sitting in the mud, struggling to get back to his feet. Sandy was reaching over to help him back to his feet. "Not so easy to stay on your feet, is it?" Suzuki called back.

"Fuck off," Stew muttered as he stood up, grinning broadly. His smile vanished as he suddenly fell back down into the mud. Then he disappeared beneath the surface of the swamp.

Sandy reached down into the mud, grasping for Stew's body as she screamed, "Stew!" She stood up, empty-handed, covered in mud. "Where the fuck did he go?"

Something brushed against Suzuki's leg. He looked down, but the mud was too thick. He couldn't make anything out. Then he felt something else rub up against his leg. He jumped and yelped a little. Whatever had touched him had also shocked him. It was no more than a static electrical pop, but it still caught him off-guard.

A few feet away, Stew exploded out of the mud, flying through the air, screaming until he hit a tree, falling onto one of the branches. He scratched his head as he struggled to sit up in the tree.

Suzuki tried to run over to Stew, but the mud was impeding his movements. The rest of the group were also making their way to Stew. "Hey, dude," Suzuki shouted, "What the fuck was that all about?"

Stew looked down from the tree, his eyes widening. He was a good twenty feet off the ground and Suzuki remembered Stew once mentioning something about being afraid of heights when they had been playing together. "I don't know!" Stew shouted. "Something grabbed my leg and pulled me under. I thought we were invisible, Sandy!"

Sandy pulled up her HUD and looked through her status updates. "We are," she replied. "All of us, still pretty invisible."

"Well, something knows that we're here. And I have sneaking suspicion that it wants to eat me."

Suzuki felt a pressure around his ankles. Then there was a jolt of electricity, much stronger than last time. His legs went hot, and then his teeth clamped down as something in the mud pumped him full of electricity. Another shock ran through him and he went flying through the air, slamming against a tree and sinking into the mud. Once his strength returned to him, he scampered up the tree that he had been knocked into. Whatever had shocked him was in the mud, and Suzuki wanted to be as far away from that as possible. "Up in the trees, everyone," Suzuki shouted.

Sandy waved her wand and levitated herself up into a tree where she sat perched like some swamp spirit. José took a giant leap and landed gracefully in the branches of a tree covered in Spanish moss. Beth took the longest to get to safety. She had done a double take when Suzuki had shouted orders. Maybe she wasn't used to listening to anyone other than her commanding officer. Either way, she managed to get into the tree before whatever was slithering in the mud could zap her.

Now they were all in the trees, looking like some odd parody of a child's nursery rhyme. They hardly looked to be the rag tag group of adventurers that they thought of themselves as. *We must look so fucking stupid,* Suzuki thought. *At least we're invisible.*

Suzuki leaned over the side of his tree branch and stared down at the mud. He could see movement, something slithering back and forth. He couldn't tell how many somethings there were, though. "Does anyone know what the fuck lives in swamps?" Suzuki called out.

Sandy shrugged as she stared down at the slithering things in the mud. "I don't know, alligators?" she suggested. "I think maybe monkeys. Definitely leeches. I really hope those are leeches."

"Why the fuck would you want them to be leeches?"

"I don't know. I think they're pretty cute—all those fangs and thirst for blood. I'd like to catch a few. Maybe try some ritualistic blood play..."

"What the hell is wrong with you, Sandy?"

"I think you mean, 'How did you develop such a complex personality and interesting opinions?' Thank you for the compliment."

Beth was standing in her tree, sword drawn. She looked anxious. "Uh, so are we just going to stay up here all day?" she asked.

Stew was hanging upside down on his tree branch.

Apparently, what he had said about being afraid of heights had been something of an exaggeration. "Nah, I doubt it," he called. "Unless this suddenly became an episode of Naruto."

Sandy snapped her fingers and mimed a gun pointed at Stew. "And Stew with the references, coming for Suzuki's nerd champion status." She laughed. "You guys are tied. Now it's sudden death."

In her tree, Beth started laughing. Not the guarded, almost worried laughter that had been sneaking out here or there whenever she heard the Mundanes joking. This was the real deal, a straight up belly laugh that made Suzuki smile. It seemed like she was finally starting to warm, finally starting to remember what being a Mundane was like.

But that was enough joking around for now. Suzuki stood, balancing himself on his branch. He took aim at the slithering movement in the mud and threw his ax. It landed with a satisfying thud and whatever had been moving stopped. "Guess that was easy enough," Suzuki said.

"I doubt there's only one," Sandy said.

"Are you volunteering to go check it out?"

Sandy shook her head. "Nope. I'm pretty sure our Fearless Leader should take care of it."

Beth dangled her feet over the branch she was sitting on like a child on a swing set. "I thought MERCs didn't have leaders?"

"We do when it's convenient for someone to have to do the dirty work. Plus, Suzuki likes looking impressive and shit."

Suzuki leapt out of the tree and landed with a splash of mud. "That's not true," he said. "I just like getting the job done without looking like a jackass like some Mundanes I know."

As Suzuki spoke, he felt movement around his ankles. that same kind of slithering. There was more of it this time. It seemed to be dozens upon dozens of what felt like snakes rubbing up against him. "Sandy, is there anything that you can do about this mud? I can't see anything," Suzuki complained.

Sandy floated down to the ground, her wand raised high above her head. "I think I got this," she said as the holes in her masks began to glow. The cloak of ash covering her bones started to glow brightly and change color as blossoms and wildflowers covered her body. Her wand magically turned into her old staff, a hewn, crooked wooden thing, and she slammed it into the mud.

Suzuki stared at Sandy. She looked impressive. It was like every couple of weeks, she found a new magical path and mastered it. "So, what exactly is this?" Suzuki asked.

"The amulet lets me remember everything I've read, even stuff I forgot I read. I guess that crash course on alchemy really stuck. I'm still trying to get the hang of it, though."

The mud around Suzuki and Sandy's feet turned into crystal clear water. Suzuki could see to the bottom even though the water was the consistency of mud. He instantly regretted being able to see.

At first glance, it looked as if the water was filled with thousands and thousands of eels. When Suzuki looked closer, though, it was a little harder to determine what was slithering between his feet. They were too long to be merely eels. In fact, they looked somewhat like tentacles. *Fucking tentacles,* Suzuki thought. *I'm so sick of tentacles.*

The eel tentacles suddenly retracted, sending up a jolt of electricity through the muddy water, shocking both Sandy and Suzuki, who fell to their knees, the muddy water washing up over their faces.

Suzuki lay there, the mud washing over his face as his body tingled with the electrical current. It wasn't enough to knock him out, but it was enough to render him immobile for a moment. He rallied his strength and got to his feet. At his side, Sandy was already getting back to her feet. "Back to the trees," Suzuki suggested.

Sandy's eyes got a wild look to them. "Fuck that noise, I want to rip whatever the fuck that is to shreds. I wanna see guts."

"And how are we gonna do that?" José asked.

"Buff us."

"Got it."

Sandy raised her staff and the air crackled with electricity. But instead of shocking anyone, the electricity gathered in a series of small balls that floated over to each of them and settled into their chests. "Get your asses down here," Suzuki shouted, checking his HUD. It read 50% chance of success. 50%, high enough to go for it. Low enough that success wasn't guaranteed.

Perfect, he thought before saying out loud, "We're gonna have ourselves an old-fashioned tussle."

Stew was the first out of the trees, hardly able to contain his joy at an upcoming fight, followed by José, then Beth. "Do you think it's gonna be a big one?" Stew gleefully asked.

Sandy waved her hand and the water ahead of them cleared up, not as clear as what they were standing in, but clear enough to see the retreating eel tentacles. Suzuki and the group chased the tentacles until they came to a large, mossy cavern in the thick of the swamp. Heavy fog poured from the cavern's opening as the tentacles withdrew inside.

Stew drew both of his swords and twirled them. "So, how'd this shit figure out where we were?"

José stomped his feet in the mud.

An eel tendril shot out in his direction, nothing more than a mass of snapping jaws filled with teeth, electricity jumping from its body. José stepped to the side and grabbed the tentacle. A jolt of electricity ran through him, but he ignored it, taking time to observe the tendril before releasing it to return to the cavern. "That's how," José explained. "It can feel our vibrations. That must be how it uses its tendrils, or eels, or whatever the fuck they are."

Suzuki ran through his options, mentally taking stock of all the information that he had. There were hundreds of tendrils. The creature generated electricity, enough to shock, but not enough to kill. The mud was thick enough to keep the water from being super conductive. The creature was holed up in a cavern, waiting for anything to vibrate the ground.

"Sandy, can you do something about all this water?"

Sandy waved her staff and the water directly around the Mundanes rolled up as if it were being pushed away in a diameter around them. The circle of solid earth extended to about twenty feet. Flowers bloomed across the circle that Sandy had magicked.

"Stew, could you kindly make some noise?"

If possible, Stew grinned even wider than before. "Oh, hell yeah, I can." Stew crouched low to the ground and then exploded up into the air. He soared nearly higher than the highest tree.

Suzuki whistled, obviously impressed. "Now that is some fucking height. All right, everybody get ready. When Stew lands, those tendrils are gonna come for us. Everyone get a handful and we're yanking this son of a bitch out and taking care of this here and now. I don't want any more surprises while we're getting through this swamp. 'For honor'."

"For glory," Sandy shouted.

Stew landed with a heavy thud that sent a concussive shock wave rocking through the swamp. "For fucking XP!" Stew shouted.

Eel tendrils shot out of the cavern almost instantly. There were hundreds, each one ending in a small mouth that gnashed and sparked electricity while headed toward the group. Suzuki jumped out of the way, sliding underneath the volley of tendrils, and he wrangled an armful. He looked around to see how the rest of the troop was faring. Beth had managed to get a handful of eel as well. So had Sandy and José. Stew had too, but in his own way. He was wrapped up almost like a cocoon by the eel tentacles. His screaming was muffled through the tentacles.

"All right!" Suzuki shouted. "Pull!"

They all pulled as hard as they could. There was a loud screech from within the cavern, and the creature slowly was forced from its hiding spot. Out in the open, Suzuki could see just what kind of monster was before them. It was nearly the size of the cavern and looked somewhat like a massive toad, covered in warts and spots. Instead, there was the mass of tentacles that spread from its stomach, with some sprouting out of its back. It also had a large tree growing from its back, something old and gnarled, twisting toward the sky as if it were reaching for the sun. The mythical eel-sapo roared as it stepped out into the sunlight, its small eyes closing for a moment, only to snap back open as thousands of eyes opened up all over its body.

"Keep moving!" Suzuki commanded.

Beth whirled around and gave Suzuki a bewildered look.

"But it can feel us moving," she said. "Why the hell would we do that?"

"If it hears us moving, it knows we're out here and won't go back in the cavern. That way we can fight it on our terms."

Stew had finally gotten himself free from the tendrils. A mass of eel tendrils lay at his feet and he was swinging his axes wildly, trying to get himself a bit of breathing room. "Let me in, coach," Stew joked.

Suzuki ran his hand across his ax, thinking of his list of weapon enchantments. He cast a sharpening and fire enchantment so that his blade glowed with an unearthly heat. "Everyone balls in!" Suzuki shouted. "Sandy, containment!"

Sandy whirled her staff around and slammed it into the ground. The mud cleared away in a direct path to the electric frog/eel creature. More flowers and vines sprouted up from the pathway, ensnaring the monster in a cluster of vines as it screeched with rage.

Stew, Sandy, and José charged the monster. José raised his sword and prepared to bring it down on the monster's head, but he was snatched up by the creature's tentacles, a strong electric shock coursing through his body, the tendrils tossing him away. He hit the ground with a sickening thud and lay there for a few moments before he could move.

Suzuki leapt back, away from the eel-sapo, toward José. He helped José to his feet, and they turned their attention back to the eel tentacles flying toward them. José and Suzuki both chopped them down without wasting any time. From what Suzuki could see, it looked as if the eel-sapo was creating more eels. Almost like a hydra. Up ahead, Beth, Stew, and Sandy were trying to fight their way closer to the massive creature. Even with it being pinned down, it was still a formidable foe. "Flank it, Stew," Suzuki shouted.

Stew didn't take long to respond. He leapt through the air, easily soaring over the eel-sapo, landing on the other side, both swords already drawn. He buried them deep in the eel-sapo's back. Black blood squirted from the wound, covering Stew in its thick, iron-like mess. Then four tentacles sprouted from the monster's open wound, wrapping Stew up, shocking him, and throwing him into the mud. Stew rolled to his feet, slogging through the mud, pulled his throwing daggers and tossed them at the eel-sapo's eyes as he joined up with the rest of the party. "Anybody getting strong hydra vibes from this shit-head?" Stew shouted.

Beth flipped through the air, landing on top of the eel-sapo. She drove her sword deep into its warty head, sending blood and chunks of eel tentacles flying everywhere. Suzuki stopped what he was doing, his eyes glued to Beth. He hadn't seen her in full battle mood in a long time. She was a beast. Every one of her movements looked like they were divinely planned, the way that she flipped through the air, her muscles twitching as she twisted the blade of her sword before pulling it out of the eel-sapo's skull. It was a beautiful orchestration of pain and skill, which made the image of tentacles wrapping around her feet and slamming her into the ground all the more jarring. She groaned slightly as she picked herself up, rolling out of the way of a bundle of tentacles that came flying through the air.

Sandy stood back-to-back with Stew, slamming her staff into the ground, sending short shockwaves that shook the eel-sapo's balance, changed to her wand, and sent a steady stream of fire toward the creature before switching back to her staff, calling down a couple bolts of lightning from the sky to strike the ground around the monster. "So much for fighting it on our terms," Stew shouted.

A bundle of tentacles came at Suzuki, their mouths snapping with bloodlust. Suzuki cleaved them in half, threw his ax, and then recalled it in a fluid motion. "Can't you just go berserk and finish it off or something?" Suzuki asked as he noticed Beth flying through the air in his direction. He stepped to the side, opened his arms, and caught her.

Beth jumped out of Suzuki's arms, smiling. She looked like she was having a good time—as good of a time as you can have when your life is in danger at least. "Thanks, Suz," she said. "So, any great ideas?"

Suzuki swatted off some tentacles snaking his way. He looked at the eel-sapo. It was still growing more appendages, but no longer healing itself. It was covered in open wounds and the ground beneath it was breaking apart. "Yeah, I think I got one," Suzuki said. "Mundanes, all in!"

"Finally," Stew shouted. "Let's do this!"

Stew ran forward, pulling out his last two swords, screaming as he ran, Sandy right behind him, her wand glowing with bright energy. José followed closely behind as Beth and Suzuki charged the eel-sapo. Suzuki jumped and soared through the air, landing on top of the creature and Beth landed next to him. Sandy and Stew took the legs, along with José. "All right," Suzuki shouted. "You guys take out the legs and we'll take out the head."

The Mundanes attacked like a well-oiled machine. Each member of the party selected a section to hack away at, spewing black blood all over the swamp. Beth easily fell in with the group, standing atop the giant tentacled toad, nearly laughing with blood lust as her and Suzuki's steel cut through the coarse, oily skin of the eel-sapo.

The legs of the creature went out from under it, and in a

last-ditch effort, it rolled over onto its side, trying to crush its attackers. Sandy, Stew, and José were able to toss themselves out of the way and avoid being crushed. Beth and Suzuki leapt straight into the air. The toad exposed its stomach. Beth came crashing down on its soft under belly, slicing it open down the middle. As Suzuki fell, he recalled his ax and drove it deep into the eel-sapo's body.

All was quiet. The eel tentacles and the eel-sapo lay still, dead.

Stew cracked his knuckles as he leaned back and let the bones in his spine pop. "Now that was a fucking fight!" he exclaimed. "Do you see how big this son of a bitch is?"

Sandy had pulled off her amulet and was back to her regular, casual MERC battle robes. "Yeah, he put up a pretty good fight. Suzuki was right, it would have been a pain in the ass wandering around the swamps with that thing trying to take us down. Good call, Suzuki."

Suzuki nodded as he accepted the gratitude and compliments. He didn't think that it was that big of a deal. It was something that anyone in the party could and would have figured out. He just happened to be the first one to say something.

Beth and Stew were chattering with each other as José went to inspect the body of the eel-sapo. Suzuki was only able to pick up little snatches of what they were saying, they were talking so fast. Beth seemed excited. She was smiling and miming stabbing. She and Stew gave each other high fives. Suzuki did catch Beth saying that this fight was just like old times and she had forgotten how much she loved raiding with the Mundanes. "I haven't felt like this in forever," Beth said. "It was amazing...just like when we were in VR. Even better than we were in VR. We kicked the fucking shit out of that thing."

Suzuki walked over to join José while he appraised the corpse of the slain creature. José waved for Suzuki to come give him a hand. They both pushed up against the eel-sapo and rolled it over on its back. There was a large microchip attached to the back of its neck. "Figures," José said. "Even the wildlife around here is being put to use by the Dark One."

Suzuki pulled the microchip out of the eel-sapo's neck. "I didn't get a chance to grab one of these when we were getting out before," Suzuki said. "We should give this to Chip and see if she can get any information out of it."

"Why would she know anything?"

Suzuki looked at José, slightly confused. There had been an edge to José's question, almost as if he were afraid of something, or as if he did not want to give something away. It was the first time that Suzuki thought that he might have to be careful with how he was phrasing something to José. "I mean, she's good with tech," Suzuki explained, weighing each of his words for how they might be taken. "I'm not quite sure what exactly she is, but maybe she has an inclination toward understanding this kind of shit. I've seen the way that she tears up those HUDs. It's almost like she's doing it to relax or something. She'd probably be able to find something that we could work with."

José nodded, his face softening. Whatever had been there passed like clouds before the sun. His face was radiant again, almost cheerful. "Not a bad idea," he mused. "Not a bad idea at all. On another note, I've been watching you, kid. You've been pretty impressive this trip."

"You trying to flirt with me or something?" Suzuki joked.

"Also, I liked you a lot more when you were in fear and awe of me."

"Well, you know what they say about getting to know your idols and gods. They become painfully human."

José chuckled. "Which I am... and I'm feeling it a bit more than usual. I haven't had a quest this long in a while. I'm starting to feel it in these old ass bones. Like I was saying, though, I've been watching you. You're not a born leader, which is what makes this so impressive. When I first met you, I thought you were just some scrawny punk kid who'd gotten himself into something that was way over his head. I think that I was right, but I've been watching you grow. It's been something, to say the least. You're really coming into your own. You've got a good head for tactics and, even better, you know what's going on with your party."

"What do you mean?"

"Simple orders. Lots of wiggle room for them to do what they're best at, and you adapt your plans well to what they're doing. That kill move that you called for this son of a bitch was like watching a work of art unfold in front of me. You all moved seamlessly. Even Beth, and she hasn't seen you in a good chunk of time. Yet here the Mundanes are, fighting together better than most of our MERCs."

"It's mostly them, you know. I just make an occasional observation. Sandy's the one trying to get god level with magic; Stew's one hell of a scrapper; and you saw Beth. She's just a great all-around fighter, probably the best I've ever seen."

José waved a dismissive hand. "You really trust your party, and they trust you a lot. You've got a lot of good shit in you, kid. I'm excited to see how you bring it to the Dark One."

"Thanks, José. That really means a lot to me."

"Come on, we should keep moving."

"Yeah, you're right."

Suzuki and José joined up with the rest of the Mundanes. They checked around to see if there was anything that could be looted, but found nothing. Stew, determined not to leave empty-handed, cut off a couple of the eel tentacles and a hunk of meat from the main toad body. He sprinkled it with salt and stashed it in his inventory. The plan was to give some to Diana and Wendy at the Red Lion. The last few meals that Stew had been cooking with Diana had stirred his curiosity about different kinds of meats that he hadn't thought to try. Suzuki could understand why. He still occasionally thought of the giant insect that had been whipped up at their last big meal. Just the thought was enough to make his mouth water.

Once Stew was satisfied harvesting the remains of the eel-sapo, they got going again. Sandy tossed another sound dampening and invisibility spell over them all, letting José's passive buff take care of extending the range of the spells, just to be safe. They all checked their statuses and then moved to the trees for additional safety. It took longer to move through the swamp, but it was a worthwhile decision. Suzuki noticed more of the caverns beneath them, the mud disturbed by slithering eels. The trees allowed them to keep moving, albeit at a slower rate, without calling more attention to themselves. As they continued on, the swamp thinned until they could see where the swamp ended and a new defense ring began. The distinction was almost immediate. Massive buildings were in the distance, buildings made of sleek metal and constructed in bizarre ways that Suzuki knew he would have to get closer to fully understand.

The Mundanes and José stopped and stared out at the next defense ring. "All right," Suzuki said. "This is where

Beth and I are going to go on ahead. It'll be too risky if we all go. And you guys—"

Sandy sighed and leaned back against a tree. "We get to dig," she interrupted. "Sounds fucking great."

"Would you prefer to be sneaking into enemy territory under a disguise that the enemy knows about? Oh, don't forget the part about being hopelessly outnumbered. Or the part where you have to wait for your reinforcements to dig themselves to you? All while trying to find a fucking ring-tone? Like, what the fuck does a ringtone even look like?"

"O humble creature of the Shire, I do believe you will find it. Let the strength of love and friendship guide you!"

All of the Mundanes burst into a fit of giggles. "Fuck off," Suzuki said. "I'll let Find Your Target do that for me."

Stew shook his head as he folded his arms. "That's if you want to get caught casting that spell in there," he interjected. "That's a sure way to get everyone paying attention to you. Look here, an imp we've never seen before, wandering around, following a golden light like he's looking for something. You do plan on coming out of this alive, right?"

"Fine. We'll be sneakier. This would be so much easier if we actually had someone who knew how to sneak into places."

José laughed as he looked at the last defense ring. "They do make life a lot easier." He chuckled. "More difficult in some ways, but always worth it. You two haven't been doing too bad of a job so far."

"That's just because we haven't gotten killed yet."

"That is generally the criteria."

"All right. Well, guess we'll see you guys later. Try not to die of asphyxiation."

"Try not to get found out as a spy and have your intestines ripped out."

"Dude, not cool," Suzuki said as he closed his eyes and reached out to Fred. "You ready to do this?" he asked Fred.

Fred uncurled from behind Suzuki's unconscious. "As ready as I will ever be," Fred answered.

Suzuki felt his body slipping away, rolling down into the dark, struggling and grasping to find himself or to keep from losing himself. Even though he and Fred had switched bodies a few times already, the feeling of his physical form slipping away from him never stopped being disorienting. It reminded him of the time he had been teleported into Middang3ard and how sick it had made him. At least now he didn't feel like vomiting every time they changed places.

The switch was complete. Fred stood where Suzuki once had, and Suzuki could see through Fred's eyes. Could feel the imp's thoughts and feelings crashing against him like a wave. So much more this time around. It was as if Fred wasn't even bothering to hide them from Suzuki anymore. Maybe that wasn't an option. They had grown close, a lot closer than Suzuki ever thought would have been possible over the last few days. There were parts of Fred that Suzuki didn't believe could have existed. Maybe this was how Fred was all the time. Either way, the change was finished.

At Fred's side, Beth had also switched places with her familiar Ros'ten. The giant bee floated lazily next to the imp, its long tongue slithering out for a second to groom itself before flapping its waxen wings and rising into the air.

The Mundanes readied their weapons as Fred reached out and wrangled Ros'ten out of the air. It looked like Fred was trying to choke the life out of Ros'ten. Instead, Fred swung his foot over the bee's body and straddled it as one would a steed. "Apologies," Fred said, growing aware of the Mundanes ready to pounce on him. "It's a biological instinct. Imps used to ride... inferior creatures. We once bred bees specifically for transportation—and fun."

Ros'ten didn't seem to have a problem being straddled. In fact, its wings were beating even faster so that they were creating a gentle hum.

Sandy shook her head as she laughed to herself. "Even when they're in their familiars, Suzuki is still trying to get on top of Beth."

Suzuki was glad that he was within Fred at the moment because otherwise, he would have been blushing and fumbling with his words. In the back of his head, if you could call it that, he could hear Beth laughing. "Beth, is that you?" he asked.

"Yeah, yeah, I think," Beth said. "How are we talking to each other?"

"The familiars have their own psychic communication or something. I guess that when we're in their position, we can use it."

"This is weird, Suzy. I feel like... I don't know... it's just weird not having a body. I'm all floaty."

"You know, I wasn't trying to straddle you. That's all Fred. He's a little—"

"Suzy, don't worry about it. Straddle me anytime you want. That's what I'm going to do."

"Oh. Okay."

Back in the physical world, Fred and Ros'ten were ready to go. Fred reached out to Suzuki. *We are departing.*

All right, Fred. Let's get those ringtones and liberate some motherfuckers.

18
———

Fred and Ros'ten passed over into the final defense ring. The ground was cold, almost as if it were made of something other than earth. Even the air itself felt different. It sent a chill straight down into Fred's chest, and Suzuki could feel it all the way in the back of his head. It was as if this last defense ring had been lifted from someplace other than Middang3ard. As if it had been carved out of another world and dropped in the middle of this realm. Suzuki could feel Fred thinking, trying to figure out exactly what was off, but coming to no conclusions. Beneath Fred, Ros'ten's wings vibrated loudly.

Suzuki directed his thoughts in Beth's direction. *Hey, how are you holding up?* he asked.

Beth's voice bubbled up in Suzuki's mind. *I'm getting used to it. Still kind of weird, and a little freaky,* she said. *Ros'ten isn't much of a talker so this is interesting. There's a lot about Ros'ten I don't know.*

Yeah, I was surprised too when Fred and I first changed places. I've learned a lot about the guy.

What's there to learn about an eldritch imp? Beth asked.

Apparently a lot. It's just been a lot to learn about the different races in general. Like, I had heard that a bunch of the eldritch creatures joined up with the Dark One as soon as he started trying to fuck people's lives up. That's not what I've seen in Fred's memories. It's a lot more complicated than that.

They're still working for the Dark One.

Suzuki sighed. *The ones that didn't get wiped out. I'm talking multiple genocide.*

Fuck. I had no idea.

Neither did I.

Fred rode Ros'ten farther into the defense ring. They were getting close enough to actually see what was going on. What they saw surprised all four of them.

This defense ring was nothing like the ones that they had passed through before. The towers that they had seen in the distance were much taller than they had appeared. They were built from some kind of metal that looked to be in constant motion. White lights emanated from the windows of the buildings.

Orcs and goblins were everywhere, but very few of them were walking. Most of those who passed were riding in sleek hover cars with glowing blue pads that hummed softly, some kind of anti-gravitational field. They zoomed by as the orcs and goblins hurried along their ways to perform whatever command their chips were giving them. The entire first section of the ring had been almost barbaric in comparison to this ring. Everything was futuristic. It didn't look like it belonged in Middang3ard.

Suzuki could hear Beth reaching out to him. *What the fuck is this shit?* she asked. *This looks like something out of Blade Runner.*

I have no fucking clue.

Fred rode Ros'ten through the last defense ring, which

was bustling. There were almost too many different races to keep track of. The closest thing that Suzuki had ever seen akin to the sheer volume of bodies moving around, unconcerned with each other, was Times Square. The only difference was that no one looked interested in shopping: it was all business. The few orcs and goblins walking around wore visors that looked to be similar to the HUDs the military and MERCs wore.

It wasn't only orcs and goblins, though. The defense ring was filled with long-limbed elves and squat dwarves and halflings. All of them wore the visors as well. As Fred and Ros'ten passed by the mortal races, Suzuki noticed that they all had small microchips embedded in their necks.

Beth cleared her throat, an odd sensation that Suzuki felt across the back of his neck. Apparently, sharing a communication channel with her was somewhat similar to the type of connection he shared with Fred when they were talking to each other. *We should try to find a place to set up a Nav point,* Beth suggested. *Just in case digging out to the other section doesn't work out well.*

Suzuki nodded as Fred looked around, washing Suzuki with waves of trepidation. *Yeah, that's not a bad idea. Where the fuck do we even start?*

I'd say a central location, I guess, or someplace private, tucked away. It's your call.

I say private. We can get a good set up for an ambush.

All right. Let's get cracking.

Fred and Ros'ten moved through the crowded space dominated by bodies that seemed to be working for a single purpose despite not interacting with each other. As Fred was riding Ros'ten, Suzuki was able to get a better look at the vehicles that were being driven by orcs. They were small and similar to electronic scooters. The only difference was that they didn't have wheels. The vehicles floated a foot or so off the ground and were outfitted with pulse cannons that looked eerily similar to the hand cannon Chip had used. It wasn't the same tech, but similar enough. *Where the fuck did they get all of this shit?* Suzuki asked.

Beth shrugged. *Who knows? It makes sense, though. We already knew that the Dark One wasn't using magic for anything. Tech would be the next bet.*

Yeah, but from where? This is leaps and bounds beyond anything that I've ever seen on Earth.

I know. We'll probably find out soon enough.

They continued on through the defense ring, marveling at the tech that they were passing by. Suzuki noticed that most of the races they passed were also carrying firearms. They were not guns like any he had seen on Earth. These were long, metallic rifles and pistols that seemed to be made for beauty as well as function. The ends of each of them glowed with a dull blue energy.

The atmosphere of this ring was different from the others as well. It was almost cheerful. While in the pits of the prison, Suzuki had noticed the general disgruntled attitude of the workers until he had come to the research facility. The workers here were nothing like the grunts who worked underground. These orcs almost had a distinguished air to them. It was jarring, but Suzuki could almost see them wearing suits, rushing off to their next meeting. Maybe there were different variations on microchips and ringtones, depending on your station. All in all, the nuances that were part of the Dark One's mind control scheme were far beyond Suzuki's ability to grasp. There did seem to be more than met the eye, though.

Ros'ten grunted loudly and balked. Fred looked in the direction that Ros'ten was staring. There was a cluster of small, squat buildings that looked less impressive than the rest of the area. *That looks like a good place to get set up,* Beth said. *Let's check it out.*

Fred and Ros'ten tried to make their way through the sea of bodies that were moving by. It was worse than walking in downtown during rush hour. They kept bumping into the passersby, trying to avoid eye contact or apologies. None of the other races seemed to have a problem staying out of each other's way. As Fred and Ros'ten neared the end of the vast intersection, an orc reached out and grabbed Fred.

The orc was huge, larger than most orcs Suzuki had seen. He was painted with the traditional clan paintings of a chieftain or warmonger. The orc sized up Fred and Ros'ten, glaring at them with suspicious eyes. "Where you off to so fast, little imp?" the orc asked.

"Why's it any concern to you?" Fred fired back.

"Because we ain't used to seeing eldritch assholes in this neck of the rings."

Suzuki couldn't help but laugh to himself. Even with all the official air of this last ring, the orcs were still the same, surly and ready to pick a fight. Perhaps there was only so much that the microchips could mitigate.

"Where the fuck are you going?" the orc asked again.

"I am an envoy from the viceroy. I am here to review working conditions and report back to the viceroy. Do I have your permission to continue on in my mission, or should I relate to the viceroy that I was being held up by...what is your name?"

"You don't need to know it."

"The viceroy will."

"The viceroy is already here in this circle. What the fuck—"

"And do you think the viceroy has time to march

through every one of these shitholes, checking to see if things are up to the Dark One's standards? Do you think the viceroy has time to sit here and talk to an idiotic orc about what she is here to do and not do? Do you think that is a proper use of the viceroy's time?"

The orc said nothing, just stared at Fred, its eyes betraying nothing other than irritation and mistrust. "Where are you going?"

"Why do you have so many questions?"

"As an emissary of the viceroy, I believe that it is my responsibility to figure out why an imp is pretending to be in the viceroy's service."

Suzuki didn't have time to react. Fred grabbed Ros'ten, kicked the bee in the sides, and took off for the buildings they had been heading toward. The orc launched an immediate chase. Suzuki was glad Fred was the one in charge of their movements. Fred had made a genius decision running. Years ago, Suzuki had read in a game file that orcs have an unnatural desire to chase, almost like when a dog feels the need to run after a car. It was something primitive and primordial within them. As long as Fred kept moving, the orc would have almost no choice but to follow.

Fred veered Ros'ten to the side so that they flew behind the squat buildings. The orc was close on their tails. Fred jumped off of Ros'ten, who flew around the buildings at a breakneck speed, checking to see if there were any witnesses.

There was no one. It was as if everyone was too busy to have noticed.

Fred stopped running and backed himself up against the wall as the orc closed in, drawing out a blood-covered battle ax. "We heard about you a little while ago," the orc said. "We heard there was an imp running around in the tunnels, trying to free as many prisoners as possible. We lost a lot of test subjects because of you. So, who are you? One of those straggler imps trying to get revenge?"

"What straggler imps?"

"Don't play stupid with me. Now give me your name!"

"You do not need it. All you need to know is that you are dead."

"You would dare strike down an emissary of the viceroy in the middle of enemy territory?"

Fred turned to Suzuki and Suzuki connected his mind to Beth and Ros'ten. *We have to do this fast,* Suzuki said. *It's all you, Fred and Ros'ten. Just make it fast.*

Ros'ten moved first. He flew behind the orc and a pulse of electrical energy emanated from his wings, shocking the orc, who fell. Fred leapt, tackling the orc to the ground, sinking his teeth into the orc's neck. The orc didn't so much as shirk from the pain. He rolled, lifted his ax and brought it down on Fred, who neatly caught the ax in his hand. "Foolish," Fred said. Then he opened his mouth and spewed a stream of hellfire.

The orc was nonplussed, tossing Fred off of him with enough strength to dent the wall that Fred slammed into. *What the fuck?* Suzuki asked. *Aren't you practically an elder god or something?*

Be silent, Fred hissed. *I am fighting for our lives.*

Ros'ten circled around the orc again, but this time, the orc grabbed Ros'ten's wings. The bee tried to escape while the orc attempted to rip them off.

Fred rushed the orc and tackled him to the ground. He slashed at the orc's face, nearly ripping off its nose. Fred hissed under his breath as he bit the orc's neck repeatedly, trying to tear out his jugular. The orc raised his ax and brought it down on Fred's back. The imp screamed in pain as the orc got to his feet, holding Fred by his throat. "Who sent you!" the orc shouted again.

Ros'ten came up from behind, flying low and taking the orc's feet out from under him. Fred slid out of the orc's hands and crawled up the orc's back as he stood. He sunk his teeth into the orc's throat again, this time finding the jugular vein. He tore it out, sending blood squirting everywhere. When the orc fell, Fred jumped off his back. He stood there panting. Once he caught his breath, he covered the orc in hellfire, leaving nothing but bones. *That was...difficult*, Fred said. *Far too difficult.*

Fred rolled the body over and removed the microchip that was attached to the orc's neck. *These must be doing more than only controlling*, Fred said. *I have never met an orc that strong before. It must be the chips.*

Suzuki pushed up closer so that he could see better through Fred's eyes. *Higher grade chips and powers for those closest to the Dark One?*

Exactly.

Which means—

That every orc, goblin, and giant in this defense ring will be considerably stronger than anything we've faced so far.

Fuck. Why can't things just be easy for once?

19

Fred and Ros'ten had made sure to push the ashes of the orc they had recently killed to the side, hiding them out of view of anyone who might have wandered behind the buildings.

Then they set a nav point for the first group of diggers, the Mundanes and José, and another nav point for the second group, the rest of the Horsemen and the recuperating soldiers. Once that was done, they returned to the crowded streets of the final defense ring. Suzuki was more focused on what was going on around him now. The orc recognizing them had given him a scare. There was no telling how many agents of the viceroy were in the defense ring. They had to find the ringtone and get out of the middle of the viper's den as soon as possible.

One thing that caught Suzuki's attention now in a way that hadn't before was just how advanced the tech was that the different races under the Dark One's command was utilizing. It didn't just look futuristic. It didn't even look human. It was beyond anything that Suzuki had ever seen or read about outside the most utopian science fiction. There was no reason that it should have been here. The air was clean and smelled fresh as if there was nothing but clean fuel. The cars and trolleys that zoomed by hardly made a noise, yet no one seemed caught off-guard by them. Suzuki noticed that even the HUDs that appeared to be for the bureaucratic peons seemed to be more advanced than anything that he had seen MERCs with – and that was including what Chip had modified.

That brought Suzuki's mind back to Chip as they walked through the defense ring, both Fred and Ros'ten trying to be as inconspicuous as possible. The closest thing that Suzuki had seen to the tech being brandished by the Dark One was Chip.

Even then, it had only been for a moment.

Outside of seeing Chip torn nearly to bits, Suzuki hadn't gotten a chance to take a good look at her weaponry. Maybe Chip held some kind of tie to the Dark One. He remembered that he had initially doubted Chip's position with MERC. Those doubts had fallen to the wayside when he had seen her loyalty to her party and her willingness to help the Mundanes. But if MERCs could have spies as deeply imbedded in the Dark One's camps as Ansalm had been, what was keeping the Dark One from doing the same? Further, it didn't seem like free will was a part of the question.

Chip could be a spy and not even realize it.

Suzuki felt Fred turn inward and face him. *I know Chip and the tech are troubling you,* Fred started out. *But we don't have time for you to be lost in your thoughts. Even if you are not in your body right now, we need as many eyes as we possibly can get.*

You're right. I'll stay focused.

For all of our sakes, Suzuki, please do so. Beth and Ros'ten cannot do this by themselves.

Suzuki nodded. *Gotcha. Don't worry. My head's in the game. But there's some shit we need to talk about. I can't keep my brain from doing what it's got to do. We need to find someplace quiet to talk.*

Fred looked around. Besides the orc that had taken notice of them, it didn't seem as if anyone else was really concerned with who was around. *Maybe hiding in plain sight is the best idea*, Fred suggested as he guided Ros'ten to a bench placed in the middle of what looked like a small technological garden. There were no plants or trees. Instead, there were steel constructions that were made to look like foliage. Yet that was not it completely. The metal, much like the metal that formed the large buildings, looked to be alive, snaking back and forth, flowing as if it were water. Suzuki wondered what would happen if he reached out and touched it.

Again, Suzuki was surprised at the attention to detail and the beauty that seemed to run rampant in this section of the defense ring. It was almost as if the entire area had been lovingly built by an architect that had some message for the world. This garden radiated peace yet still seemed to push forward, toward the future, as if its entire elegant design was not something far beyond the simple machinations of humanity. Suzuki hadn't seen anything this well-crafted since he and the Mundanes had visited an elvish city.

Now that Suzuki thought about it, the design of the garden looked very elvish. It reminded him of a lot of the elvish art that he had seen in the VR *Middang3ard* as well. Chip *had* mentioned that she was half-elvish...

Fred took a seat on the bench and looked out at the

garden. Even though Fred was not directing any of his immediate thoughts in Suzuki's direction, Suzuki could still feel the appreciation Fred had for the garden, a feeling that Suzuki had not sensed from Fred before. However this garden had been created, it was made in a way that had touched all of them. This unsettled Suzuki greatly. Thinking of the Dark One as a force of evil had been easy in the abstract.

He had seen the damage the Dark One's forces had caused. He'd seen the tyrannical control the Dark One maintained over the different races. Yet here the Mundanes were, sitting in a beautiful garden crafted from the most illustrious materials Suzuki had ever seen, bathed in some kind of radiant glow, feeling a sense of peace that went down deep into their cores, almost as if it were ambient music being broadcast through speakers.

Suzuki felt Ros'ten and Beth connect to him mentally as they all sat in the garden and took in its delights. *They do this at Disneyland,* Beth mused. *The exact same freaky shit.*

Disneyland? What the hell was Beth talking about? *Care to elaborate a little more on that?* Suzuki asked.

Pump feelings into the air. You know, when you go to Disneyland, everything always smells so good all the time. It always smells like fresh popcorn or...I don't know...like savory foods and stuff. Not BBQ, but like something's grilling. You never know what it is. There's just this feeling. It's because they pump scents into the air. All over the park, they have all these vents that just keep flooding the air with smells of food. And you buy food. But it's not just that...it's weirder than that.

Are you talking Simulacra and Simulation?

Suzuki, I have no fucking idea what you're talking about.

It's a book by Jean Baudrillard. He talks about how Disneyland is—

Will you please just give me the Cliff Notes?

It's about how Disneyland is supposed to remind us of something that isn't real, but we wish it were. You know, like no place smells like great food all the time, and it's supposed to remind us of something magical, but there's really nothing magical like that...so it creates something completely new that we get lost in... and you don't even know it.

Like mind control that you don't even know is controlling your mind...like an alternate reality in your head that you don't even realize is nothing like reality.

Suzuki watched the crowds of orcs and goblins and ogres lumber through the streets of the last defense ring. They didn't look like tourists, but neither did anyone in an amusement park. Instead, the different races, specifically the races that Suzuki had always thought of as evil and barbaric, looked as if they were in a simulation imitating order, attempting to pass itself off as a machine with a heart and soul. Yet beneath the surface, there was a lie that was being carefully covered up. Suzuki did not know for whose benefit it was being covered up, though.

Fred interrupted Suzuki's thoughts. *Is this why we have stepped away from our mission, which I would like to remind you, is extremely time-sensitive? To talk about banal human philosophies?*

Suzuki remembered what he had initially wanted to ask Fred. *No, that's not what I need to ask you. I need to ask if you have any fucking idea what is going on here? This shit isn't normal, Fred. This isn't like anything that I've ever seen in Middang3ard. Do you have any idea, any clue as to where all of this advanced tech came from? Have you ever seen anything like this?*

Fred was hesitant to answer. Even when he spoke, Suzuki could still hear it in the imp's voice. *I...I have not seen anything like this,* Fred admitted. *I have seen many realms and I have never seen anything like this in my entire life. Nor do I believe many have.*

What do you know about the Dark One? Suzuki asked.

Beth broke into the conversation, her voice dripping with irritation. *Fuck, Suzy, he probably knows the same things that everyone else knows. The Dark One showed up out of nowhere and started enslaving everyone. How the hell does that help us now?*

Beth, we've been fighting this war, and we don't even understand what is going on. How are we going to beat something that we don't understand?

The same way that we beat everything else, Beth growled. *We stab it until it doesn't get up anymore.*

Suzuki shook his head. *It's not that simple. Nothing since either of us has gotten to Middang3ard has been that simple.*

Beth sighed. *All right. Fred, do you have any insight, whatsoever, that makes any of this make any more sense? That makes it any less important that we get that ringtone and get the fuck out of here as soon as possible? Do you have some kind of ancient understanding of the Dark One that you're only going to explain in riddles and weird ass stories?*

Suzuki could tell how frustrated Beth was getting but he didn't care. They were already grossly outnumbered in the defense ring. It really didn't matter how fast they tried to take care of their mission. If someone was going to catch them, it was going to happen. They had been found out within their first ten minutes. Suzuki needed to know. He could feel that Fred knew something. He felt it deep down and had been feeling it since their connection had been growing. Fred knew something important, even if Fred didn't realize how important.

Fred, what is the Dark One? Suzuki asked.

Fred paused before he spoke. The citizens—for that is what they seemed to be, not slaves, not workers, not mindless drones—walked past, hardly taking notice of the imp and magical bee sitting on a bench, admiring the liquid metal sculptures in the garden.

They are said to come from the stars, Fred explained. *But in my language, the dead language of the eldritch imps, it is a different sort of star. We have said for eons that the Elder Ones came from the stars. They were born in black holes and dying nebulas. For the most part, it's true. The first dragon was born of a red dwarf. I saw it myself. I watched him fall from the heavens to an unsuspecting world beneath him. For much of my time, I did not pay too much attention to the rumors spoken of the Dark One. If they were to come from the heavens, what of it? Many greater creatures did just that.*

What exactly are you saying, Fred? Beth asked.

The word that I heard for the stars that the Dark One came from was different. It did not mean stars as you know it. The word was yogasoreth. *It means the other stars. The stars which we cannot see. The stars which we cannot know.*

Suzuki considered this before speaking, *There are realms folded on top of realms. That was one of the first things that we learned about Middang3ard. It's just a realm resting on top of our realms. What's so special about someone who comes from a star when there's seven or thirteen different realms with eighty different races?*

Because the Dark One comes from the place where there are no stars, Fred said. *I believed it to be superstition when I was younger...for much longer than that, and for the same reasons. What difference would it make if a man came from space? There are dwarves that live underground, elves that slip and slide between the realms with hardly a thought, and dark gods that* dwell in places both seen and unseen. But what they said of the Dark One was much different.

And what is it? Just spit it out!

Fred fell into silence. It was as if he couldn't bring himself to speak what must be said.

Instead, Ros'ten spoke. His voice was deep and bubbly, almost like a curious river. *He's embarrassed,* Ros'ten murmured. *He thinks they be the tales of a child. He is not alone, though. I will say what Fred is afraid to. It is a story many of us hear when we are children. It's a nowhere place, a place where there is nothing but chaos. Not the chaos lovingly spoken of by the Elder Ones or the eldritch. A place of pure chaos, of pain and suffering that extends outside the limitations of space and time. It's not another realm, but an entirely other dimension. A place so foreign to us that we would not even comprehend it if we were able to see it. The realms are all different, but they are all the same. They have similar rules of existence. Things are born and things die. Some take longer than others. There is magic. Some know it more than others. But they are all the same, more or less. This realm, the dimension of the Dark One is different. It is outside our comprehension in its horror. And it is said that the Dark One was the only being in this dimension, among millions and trillions of planets, who was able to order the chaos, who single-handedly shaped the entire dimension into a form found to be pleasing. There is no god in any of our realms of such power.*

Suzuki still didn't quite understand what Ros'ten was trying to get at. *So, what are you saying? That the Dark One is a god? Like, a real god?* Suzuki asked.

I am saying that the Dark One was powerful enough to bend an entirely separate dimension outside our own to his will. The Dark One represents order, in all its potential perverseness, and he has come to spread that order to Middang3ard.

Beth laughed, and Suzuki imagined that she was

shaking her head. *Ros'ten, you know how to drop the bombs, don't you? she asked. What I'm hearing is that we're not facing a god, just a control freak. That sounds easy enough.*

Suzuki appreciated Beth's cavalier attitude, but he felt like it might be misplaced at the moment.

Whatever they were fighting was more than just a control freak. If what Ros'ten was saying was true, they were attempting to go up against a being that believed that he might be a purifying force of nature. He knew people of this sort. He had read about them throughout the world's history, different generals or leaders who believed that they had the answers to the issues of chaos. Their answers were always totalitarian and always deadly. They were never easy to destroy.

Outside of the internal dialogue that was taking place with the Mundanes, the crowd of orcs and goblins and other races had turned their focus to something that was taking place farther in the defense ring. The whole attitude of the citizens of the defense ring had changed. Before, they had been walking with an almost comically, leisurely pace. Now these same races were rushing toward something, their eyes alight with a kind of fervor and passion which Suzuki had not seen since they had entered the ring. "What the hell is going on?" Suzuki wondered aloud for everyone to hear him.

Fred was the first to answer. "It seems as if something has caught the attention of our enemies."

Beth chimed in next. "Now would be a good time to make a rush for that ringtone."

Suzuki weighed his options. Whatever was going on probably was enough to distract the majority of the defense ring based on how strongly this section of citizens was behaving. If there were to be an easy time to sneak into any of the buildings, this would be it. And therein lay the problem. There were multiple small buildings and moderately-sized skyscrapers. There wouldn't be enough time to search each one. They would be shooting in the dark. "We need more information," Suzuki finally conceded. "We have no idea where the ringtone is."

Beth scoffed derisively. "You suggest that we go ask someone where they're storing the ringtones?" she asked. "Is that before or after we get outed for impersonating the right hand of the viceroy, who just so fucking happens to be in the same defense ring as us?"

"No. I suggest that we keep blending. You said so yourself—this place is like Disneyland. Have you ever been to the Electric Parade? It's one of the few times in the whole day that the guests are paying attention to the assholes in costumes and the assholes in costumes aren't paying attention to the guests. It would look more suspicious if we weren't there."

No one could disagree. Fred and Ros'ten stood up and followed the crowd that was swelling around them. *Whatever this is it better be worth it,* Suzuki thought.

20

——————

The crowd of races under the Dark One's technological control were converging toward one of the larger buildings. A long, slender awning stretched out and curved as if to offer shade to what was beneath. Resting under the curve was an odd, monolithic structure. It looked like a giant black slab of concrete that was ten feet tall and roughly five feet across. From a distance, it looked thick and sturdy. Suzuki felt that he recognized it from some place before, like a movie or something. When he thought back, he was reminded of the monolith in the novel *2001: A Space Odyssey.*

He wondered if Myrddin, the wizard who had created *Middang3ard* VR, had been responsible for seeding the human consciousness with this idea as well. Suzuki couldn't remember exactly what the monolith was for, though. There was too much going on to distract him.

What Suzuki did notice was the odd energy that seemed to be coming from the monolith as he got closer. He wasn't sure if it was because he was outside of his body, much the same way that he had begun to think that was why both he and Beth noticed the odd "amusement park" feel to the last defense ring while their familiars hadn't brought it up. Suzuki apparently was more sensitive to energy at the moment.

Whatever was coming from the monolith was hitting him like a hammer over the head.

The crowd had gathered as if they were watching some kind of sporting event. Suddenly, a screen was projected from the building's pylon, directly above the monolith so that everyone had to turn to face the monolith so they could see the screen.

The image of a woman was projected onto the screen. She appeared to be ageless, and her skin was an odd yellowish color. Yet it was not her skin that called the eye's attention, not the color at least. It looked as if her skin were peeling, but not from being dry. Rather, it seemed that her skin was cracked and there was something underneath, desperately trying to force itself out. She seemed to have fiber optic cables underneath her skin instead of muscles and veins. Technology had infected her like a virus. She was missing an eye. It had been replaced with a red orb outfitted with circuitry covering her eyelid and most of her brow. The technological decay extended down to her arms and her chest. The viceroy's face was the only part of her that conveyed any semblance of being human. She was cloaked in a dark purple robe and sat on a sleek, hovering chair.

The viceroy smiled, an unnerving gesture that showed teeth which were immaculately straight and white, tiny pearls afloat in a strange and hideous sea. "Greetings," the viceroy's voice boomed. It was softer than when Suzuki had first heard it, weeks ago in the vampire's underground labyrinth, after accidently touching the communication device the Dark One and the viceroy used to keep in contact with their fleets across the realm.

"How I have longed to come among you, my brothers and sisters, to spend time walking beside you in the name of our Dark Lord. It has been far too long. I apologize. There are many camps which need attending. Our forces grow stronger and stronger by the day. Week after week, there are new bodies that promise themselves to us, new bodies which make the pledge of flesh. As we grow in loyalty, we continue to grow closer to our true purpose. For we all have a purpose under our most gracious Dark Lord. Many of us were unaware. Many of us were too low, too pathetic and vulgar to have seen it for ourselves, even though it was directly in front of us the entire time. Yet here we are. Elevated from our stations in life, our stations in birth, our stations in creation. Elevated by the sheer grace, love, and perspective of our Dark Lord. For it was the Dark Lord who looked upon us and saw our potential. It was the Dark Lord who so loved us that he crossed the stars, tore through reality itself, to reach down, tenderly..."

Here the viceroy stopped speaking. She appeared to be overcome with emotion, with a love and caring so deep that Suzuki had to ask himself what exactly he was watching. This couldn't be real. It was... too theatrical. The only way the crowd could be taking this seriously was if they had been brainwashed.

Beth flashed across Suzuki's mind like a wildfire. *Do you see this shit?* Beth asked, her voice almost frantic. *This is out of control. It's like a fucking rally or something.*

Why would they need to have a rally if they're being mind-controlled? What's the point of doing this if the Dark One already has control of them? Suzuki asked.

Beth agreed. *Maybe the Dark One is doing it for the Dark One? Talk about a fucking megalomaniac.*

On the screen, the viceroy was still struggling to find her words, obviously overcome by her adoration of the Dark One. She smiled tenderly and nodded her head softly, as if reminding herself of some deep truth. "It was the Dark Lord," she started up again, "who took it upon himself to remind us what we are. To elevate us."

The crowd of races cheered loudly. Above them, the viceroy smiled. The most disturbing aspect of her smile was how genuine it looked. Nothing was forced. As she smiled, the parts of her skin corrupted by technology glowed a dull blue as if her devotion was giving it strength.

Beneath the viceroy's image, the Monolith hummed loudly. Suzuki could feel it in...he wasn't sure where, but he knew that it wasn't just in his head. Except it *was* in his head. He didn't have a body to register the vibration. *The monolith,* Suzuki exclaimed. *That's where the signal is being broadcast from.*

When Beth spoke, it was with a solemnity that Suzuki hadn't recalled hearing before. *No, Suzy. Something else is coming from that...thing. Wyatt explained to me how the system worked before I left. There's a broadcast station in one of these buildings around here. Whatever the hell that thing is, it's broadcasting something else.*

What else would they be broadcasting? What more would you need than the mind-control frequency?

Beth shook her head. *I don't know. But I think that it might be worse. I've seen one of those before.*

Yeah, so have I. In 2001— Suzuki started.

No, I don't mean in a movie, Beth interrupted. *I've seen it in the field. We found a bunch of halflings in a village that had been burned to the ground. I don't know what had happened there, but there were bodies everywhere. The halflings had been microchipped. But it was how we found them. They were all huddled around one of those monoliths. They were bent forward like they were praying or something. At the back of their necks, their skin was breaking up just like the viceroy's. We didn't know about the microchips back then. I don't think it would have made a difference if we had known either way.*

What do you think it was doing?

I don't know, Suzy. But I think you might be right. I think this is much more complicated than we thought it was going to be. All of this, everything with the Dark One...

Up on the screen, the viceroy was now standing. She spread her arms, her robe hanging loosely like unfolded wings. "It is our Dark Lord who wishes to show us the power of his strength, of his command over nature itself. For there is nothing within us, which is natural. No, our very nature is unnatural. Thus, it is only in the power of the Dark Lord to bend us away from our natural corruption. It is only our Dark Lord who may feed us with his bright and pure wisdom. He is our nature, as it is intended. Even if we need a reminder on certain occasions."

There was a mighty roar that went up from the crowd. All of the races were cheering together. And amidst that roar, there was a sorrowful scream, a lamentation that sounded as if the earth itself were groaning.

The various races stepped back from the projection of the viceroy. Where they once stood, a ring forced itself up from the ground. An arena carved itself from the ground, all sleek and beautiful, an electric current running through the clear twenty-foot walls that rose out of nowhere.

The ground jumped. Fred and Ros'ten whipped their heads around to see what had caused the vibration.

Towering above the heads of all the races, two majestic,

massive creatures were being led, their necks chained, their hands and feet bound. Treeants, standing nearly as tall as the wall themselves, creatures of old and wise times, creatures of wood and leaf, a beautiful mix of the mortal races and the humble yet powerful composition of the most ancient of trees. These two treeants looked to be thousands of years old, their bark nearly gray now even though the leaves hanging from their branches were the brightest of greens.

Four orcs led the treeants to the invisible wall where an opening appeared. The treeants were brought into the arena. The orcs quickly removed themselves. One of the orcs pressed its hand to the invisible wall.

The chains that bound the treeants fell to the ground, and they were free in the strictest sense of the word.

Above, the viceroy's mellow voice bellowed over speakers which could not be seen. "Here is that corrupt and perverse nature which the Dark Lord wishes to wipe out," the viceroy exclaimed, her smile so sweet and loving. "Some of the oldest remnants of such a nature. They wish to appeal to you, to sway you from the infinite love and understanding of the Dark Lord."

One of the treeants, the oldest, it would seem, who had a beard of the finest apple blossoms turned to the crowd that surrounded him. He wrung his hands, pleading as he spoke. "Children of Dust, hear me now," the treeant shouted in his deep, sing-song voice. "Have you forgotten your ways? Have you forgotten the beauty of yourselves? You, fair elves? Have you forgotten the paths of light which you built among the most ancient of my herd? Dwarves, you children of stone and genius, have you forgotten the ancient halls which you carved for the sake of beauty and beauty alone? Orcs? The first born of the earth, those whose skin itself is the very nature of the earth you walk upon, who were born in the stomach of the world itself. Have you forgotten your pride? Have you forgotten your defiant ways? Have you forsaken your tribes, your family, your ancient traditions? You of all, how have you fallen so low? You, first born of Middang3ard, how have you lost yourselves?"

The crowd roared their abuse. They shouted profanities, in their own tongues. They were united in their hatred of the treeants, who looked on the mortal races, their faces long and weary.

The viceroy's voice broke out over all the noise. The crowd fell silent. Even the treeants turned to face the viceroy as she spoke. "That is the sound of your nature: clinging to falsehoods, holding fast to corruption, filling your minds with weakness and lies!"

The viceroy dropped her robes. She stood before the crowd. All of the skin beneath her neck was replaced with technological corruption. The farther down the corruption extended, the less like technology it seemed to be. Her body was mercurial, at moments extremely smooth and the next, breaking apart, nothing more than a combination of gears and cables, quickly working to pull itself back together, to rearticulate itself in some semblance of order, to dominate the chaos that threatened to break apart, to rip her body to shreds. She was inhuman, a tightrope balancing act between that which is and that which should never be. "This is our nature!" the viceroy proclaimed. "Let the Dark Lord wash over us with his purpose!"

At that last statement, the viceroy reached through the projection. She did not teleport. It was as if she merely stepped through the screen as if it had been a door. The curved pylon of the building behind her contorted itself like an appendage broken into an unnatural position by an opponent. A throne stretched from the pylon and the viceroy sat atop it, the throne sending small, connecting ports into her legs and breasts, sliding between her legs, attaching to her arms and neck as her fingers stretched and joined into the pylon. "Let us sing our Dark Lord's praise!" she sang as she opened her mouth, uttering a shrill tone that only lasted a second.

The monolith hummed, and the crowd screamed in jubilation until another sharp pitch rang out—and then there was silence.

The treeants turned to look at each other. The old wisdom had gone out of their eyes. They threw themselves at each other, their wooden fists slamming into each other's bodies. The sound of their fists hitting each other echoed through the dead silence hanging over the arena. One of the treeants, the old one, fell to his knees. His brother took his head in his hand. The younger brought his knee against the elder's head.

The elder treeant fell to the ground. A shockwave nearly threw all of the spectators from their feet. Then the younger treeant stooped to his knee. He brought his fists down on the elder's head.

There was the sound of cracking wood.

Then silence.

Then another crack.

And another.

The younger treeant's hand hung in the air, posed over the elder's, his knuckles dripping with brownish red sap. Beneath him, the elder's legs twitched as the wind blew through his leaves.

A shrill, gleeful, almost innocent laugh tore through the silence. The viceroy was leaning forward, her eyes wide and lustful. "Treeant! What is your name?" she asked.

The treeant looked up at her. It was hard to say what was in his eyes. "I was named Fahelth. By my father," he answered.

"And where is your father?"

"He lies beneath me."

"Bring me his head."

"As you wish."

Fahelth brought his fist down on his father's head once more. It sounded as if a tree's entire root had been ripped from the earth.

Sap flowed and collected in a dark pool beneath the treeant's body. Fahelth stood, holding his father's head loosely, the cherry blossoms of the elder wrapped in the younger's fingers, the elder's eyes wide in an expression of bewilderment, mouth ajar in frozen horror and pain as sap dripped from his head.

Fahelth placed his father's head beneath the viceroy, who smiled as she spoke, "There is no father and son under the Dark One. No slave, no free man. No elf nor orc. There is only order."

Another ring pierced the air. This time it did not come from the monolith or the viceroy. It came from behind her, from the building which she had attached herself to.

Ros'ten jerked at the sound of the ringtone, twitching hard enough to bump into Fred, who quickly turned around and hissed at him, "*What the hell are you doing?*"

Fred's irritation turned rapidly to alarm. Ros'ten was practically convulsing, his wings suddenly flapping and then going limp, his large eyes blinking as if he were drunk, his mouth jabbering as his mandibles snapped shut. *Beth,* Suzuki shouted in her head, *What the fuck is going on with Ros?*

Beth sounded frightened, her voice sharp and strained.

He's freaking out, she answered. *And it's getting harder to hold on. We need to get him someplace safe now. Right fucking now!*

Suzuki and Fred scanned the area. Everyone was still interested with whatever was going on in the arena. It was a perfect time to act.

Behind them, about twenty feet or so, was the row of squat buildings where they had fought the orc. They could easily slip into a building, lock the door behind them, and figure out what was going on from there. Fred grabbed Ros'ten and pulled him away from the crowd, toward the buildings.

The two familiars burst through the door.

There were large toilet stalls, each one easily big enough to fit a medium-sized giant. *You have to be fucking kidding me,* Suzuki muttered.

There was hardly any time for him to complain about the situation. Ros'ten ejected Beth from his body, sending her flying into the wall. She bounced off and scrambled to her feet.

Ros'ten started to foam at the mouth. He had fallen to the ground and backed up into the wall, his whole body vibrating as his wings flapped weakly.

Beth knelt beside him, whispering softly to him as she petted his head, running her fingers through his yellow, puffy hair, trying to calm him down. "Hey, Ros, chill out. I'm here," she repeated over and over.

Suzuki reached out to Fred. *Spit me out, too,* Suzuki told Fred.

Gladly.

Suzuki had the sudden feeling of being vomited out, of tumbling into the world. He skidded across the bathroom floor, vaguely thinking about how disgusting the floor must have been despite the facility's futuristic looks. Once he got to his feet, he hit his HUD, checked around the area for anyone, and drew his ax. There was no one in the bathroom.

Beth was still at Ros'ten's side, singing to him softly. The bee was calming down, calm enough for Beth to start going through his fur. Suzuki came over to help. They found a little bit of a microchip left, embedded in his skin. Suzuki took his ax and removed it. The bee instantly stopped convulsing. "I thought we'd already de-chipped him," Beth wondered.

Suzuki crushed the microchip in his hand. "Maybe they use more than one. Let's double check him."

As Beth and Suzuki combed through Ros'ten's fur, the bathroom door opened. Four orcs walked into the bathroom, laughing together. They stopped laughing when they saw the humans. One of the orcs chuckled as he looked at Fred. "What the hell are you guys doing in here? Getting kinky with some prisoners?"

The orc's eyes fell to the ax in Suzuki's hand. His eyes widened and he reached for the door.

Suzuki threw his ax, hitting the door handle, locking the door in place. "Beth, fight!" he shouted. "Fred, groom Ros'ten!"

The four orcs squared up against the two Mundanes. "Ain't nothing like a barroom brawl," Beth said as she cracked her knuckles.

Sandy, Stew, and José were crouched in one of the trees on the outskirts of the swamp. Stew looked extremely bored. He had taken to sharpening his swords. It was difficult to tell how many times he had sharpened each one. There was no joy in the way he held his whetstone. He was just killing time. Sandy wasn't looking any better. Even though she was reading, her eyes hardly retained what she had been looking at. She was glad that she was wearing her amulet. Knowing you didn't have to pay too close attention really took the pressure off of reading.

José, on the other hand, seemed to be far from bored. He was peering through a looking glass in the direction of the futuristic buildings of the final defense circle. Every so often, he murmured under his breath and adjusted his sitting position.

Sandy lazily looked up from her book. "What's got you so excited over there?" she asked, half expecting José to ignore her.

Instead, José handed Sandy the looking glass. She glassed the distance, trying to find what had held José's attention. It did not take long. Off in the distance was a treeant, and it was holding the head of another treeant. "They've been fighting for some time, those two," José said.

Sandy handed the spyglass back to José. "How come you didn't say anything earlier?" Sandy asked.

"It didn't look like something either of you should have to see. It wasn't natural."

Stew looked up from his whetstone and sword. "What's going on?"

"Two treeants just fought to the death," Sandy said with a morbid fascination. "One decapitated the other."

"Aren't treeants supposed to be peaceful?"

"They aren't supposed to be peaceful. They *are* peaceful. Even when their forests are threatened, they've always managed to handle things in a diplomatic way. I've only ever heard of treeants fighting in the direst of situations and never each other. No matter what. It's like an ancestral code that they have: never do harm to another treeant. Which, honestly, never seems like a problem since they're so goddamn easy going. They're the least disagreeable people in all of Middang3ard, and I just watched two of them beat the living shit out of each other. Correction, I just watched a treeant murder what could only be family."

"How do you know they're family?"

"They have the same buds...the only time that happens is when family members grow old together. They start to take on the same shape of the trees around them. It's beautiful. What I just witnessed was anything but that."

Sandy reached out for the spyglass and looked through it again. "What do you think is going on in there?"

"I don't know. What do you see?"

"The treeants are gone, and now there are dragons."

"Shit. Fucking shit. How many?"

"Two. Black and gray."

"At least they're the small variety."

"That's the small variety?"

"Have you heard anything from Beth and Suzuki?"

Sandy turned on her HUD. She shook her head. "I tried to message them earlier, but something's blocking our signal, even with all of the upgrades Chip performed. Niv can't reach them either. Wherever they are, they're radio-silent."

Stew stood up and reached for the looking glass. He glassed the distance and whistled. "This sounds like a good enough signal to me." Stew handed José the spyglass and then looked through his HUD. "They already sent us a nav point."

"No confirmation, though. We don't know if that's the final one."

"Knowing Suzuki, there's probably going to be five more and then a fucking paper ranking them by level of importance and ease. We should go. They're already silent, way fucking outnumbered, and probably too horny to think straight. There's a lot of pent-up sexual energy over there in a really weird way."

"Aw, babe, is that how you feel? Too horny to concentrate?"

"I've said it before, and I'll say it again. There are only two things to do, fuck or fight. Are we fucking?"

José sighed loudly and muttered under his breath. "Thank Christ, you aren't."

Stew slapped his hands together as if his point had been beautifully illustrated. "Then we should be fighting. Let's go save some douchenozzles."

Sandy jumped down as GB popped out from behind Stew, his ass's grin nearly as wide as his face. "I'll send Chip and Diana the rendezvous," Sandy said. "They'll be some way behind us unless they're already headed this way. It shouldn't be too long, though. They've got a small army to put to work. I can't believe we're fucking digging again."

Stew jumped into the pit that GB had already begun excavating. "Yeah," he admitted. "There are definitely cooler ways to get someplace. At least GB will do most of the work."

"I'd much rather be riding in on a pale horse or something."

"Maybe on a troll!"

"Yeah, that would be sick."

"*I* could give you a piggyback ride."

"Actually, that might be kinda fun. Let's give it a shot."

Beth was the first to move. She moved so fast that Suzuki

didn't even have time to check his HUD to see what their chances were.

She threw her sword through the air at one of the orcs, who stepped to the side, leaving the sword to sail past and impale itself in the wall. She was still moving, though, having already pulled out her shield, leapt through the air, and landed on top of the orc she'd attacked. The two scuffled across the floor as she reached for her sword, but the orc grabbed her and slammed her head into the floor. She lay there dazed for a moment as the orc stood.

Suzuki flew through the air. He hadn't ever been in a fist fight before and that thought slowly crossed his mind as he connected with one of the orcs, the two of them falling and rolling around the floor as Suzuki tried to figure out what to do with his hands. It didn't seem like any of the orcs were armed and, at the moment, neither were Suzuki and Beth. He couldn't risk recalling his ax or one of the orcs might slip out and try to get help, although at the moment, it didn't seem like they needed it.

The orc grabbed Suzuki and tried to lift him to his feet as Suzuki kicked the orc who was standing over Beth, giving her enough time to snap out of it and woozily climb to her feet.

Two orcs held Suzuki's arms while the third one punched Suzuki in the face. He could feel something break, a sensation that he hadn't felt since he came to Middan-g3ard. Whatever level the microchips were in this section of the defense rings, these orcs could hit. Suzuki felt blood dripping down his nose as he got rocked with another hit, his vision blurring, going black for a second. He fought to hold on, but the world was starting to spin and two more blows hit him in the stomach, driving all of the wind out of his lungs so that he was gasping for breath, barely able to keep on his feet.

At Suzuki's side, Beth was being tossed against the wall. The orc was in control. He smashed Beth's head against the wall, putting a noticeable dent in whatever bizarre metal the wall was formed from. Beth fell to her knees, and the orc took her head in his hands and slammed her nose into his bulbous knee before pulling her back up to her feet. He swung and Beth ducked, leaving his fist to connect with the wall. She swept his feet out from under him, and as he fell, she grabbed her shield, twirled, and drove it into the face of the orc beating the shit out of Suzuki.

One of the orcs holding Suzuki flinched, ever so slightly. It was enough. Suzuki tore his arm out of the orc's grasp and elbowed the orc in the face. He turned and slammed his fist into the other orc and then, as the orc struggled to regain his balance, pushed the orc back into one of the stalls. As the orc stumbled, Suzuki dropkicked the orc in the chest, sending him flying into the toilet. Suzuki rushed into the stall, closed the door behind him, and shoved the orc's face in the water.

The other orc flung the bathroom door open as Suzuki held his immediate problem's face under the water, the drowning orc flailing his hands as he kicked. The orc that had just come into the toilet stall hit Suzuki on the head.

Suzuki slumped forward but he didn't let up on the orc whose head was beneath the water. He held it there, even as the orc behind him pulled out a small shiv. Suzuki felt the blade hit his armor. What Suzuki couldn't see was how small the blade was and how it had been made specifically to slip in between the chinks of armor. Suzuki found this out soon enough, though. His back erupted in bright red pain as the orc worked the shiv into Suzuki's shoulder blades, drawing it out and shoving it back in, trying to cut Suzuki's arm right out of the socket.

In the toilet bowl, the orc finally stopped thrashing. Bubbles stopped rising to the surface.

Suzuki turned around, the shiv still in his shoulder and headbutted the orc. He was losing blood, and there wasn't a mage around to help. He didn't have time to look for a health potion. The only choice was to try to end this as quickly as possible.

Next to Suzuki, Beth was still facing off with her orc, who had produced a wand that he was brandishing curiously. It was almost as if he didn't want to set it off. "You gonna fucking use that or not?" Beth shouted.

The orc smiled. He waved the wand right as Beth lunged forward to grab it. There was a bright flash of light, blinding them both. When Beth and Suzuki's sight came back to them, they both saw that they weren't wearing their armor anymore. "Oh, fuck," Beth murmured as she backed up, raising her fists and spitting blood.

There were three orcs left. Each of them had pulled out a shiv.

Suzuki kicked the orc in the bathroom stall in the chest, forcing him out of the stall so that Suzuki could scramble out, backing up toward the wall with Beth. He pulled the shiv out of his shoulder, sending a fire up his back. He handed the shiv to Beth. "What the fuck am I supposed to do with that?" Beth asked.

Suzuki raised his fists and rolled his shoulders. "I'm assuming it works the same as a sword. The pointy part goes in their soft parts."

"You ever been in a knife fight without armor?"

"Nope."

"This is going to be fucked."

"Yep. Ready?"

"Ready."

Suzuki lunged toward the orc closest to him. The orc swung with his blade arm and Suzuki took the hit to the side. The shiv tore his skin open, but he didn't step back. Instead, he stepped in to meet the orc, bringing his arm up and then down in a quick burst of strength, snapping the orc's arm in half. The orc dropped the shiv, and Suzuki leaned low, brought the orc's head up in his hands as if it were a loving caress, and then brought his fist down on the orc's skull. When the orc went slack, Suzuki dropped to the floor to grab the shiv. It was almost in his grasp when he felt a blade sink deep into his back. He couldn't help but scream, the pain was so unbearable. And then another. And another. Suzuki wanted to cry. He'd never felt anything like this before. Each second, his skin tearing open again, the other wounds still so fresh and open. He'd seen movies of people being stabbed. It was nothing like this. He felt like he was dying. Still, he kept reaching for the shiv.

The orc on top of Suzuki brought his shiv down on Suzuki's outstretched hand. Suzuki screeched in pain as the shiv went through his palm. He pulled his palm close, as if he were trying to cradle it against his chest. Instead, he pulled the shiv out, threw all of his strength into rolling to the side, tossing the orc off of him. He jumped on top of the orc and brought the shiv down on the orc's face, puncturing his eye as the orc wrapped his hands around Suzuki's throat, trying to choke the life out of the MERC.

Beth was up against the wall, one of the orcs holding her throat, the other stabbing her repeatedly in the stomach as she screamed. "Fucking human scum!" one of the orcs shouted.

Suzuki's world started going black. He couldn't

remember where he was for a few seconds, and then there was a brief flash of darkness before he came back to the world. He could see Beth, against the wall, coughing up blood as the two orcs mangled her flesh.

No, he thought. *This isn't how it's going to happen.* Suzuki closed his inner eye. He concentrated as hard as he could on, tried to remember everything that Sandy had told him about magic in their late-night study sessions. He released the orc's throat, held his hand in the air, and imagined fire rolling through his body. His hand grew hot. Then he jammed the fireball resting in his palm into the orc's face.

The orc burst into flames, screaming as Suzuki rolled off of him and grabbed the shiv laying on the floor. He ran up to the orc stabbing Beth and grabbed him by the throat. He brought the shiv down on the orc's throat three times before the orc slumped to his feet. Suzuki plunged the shiv deep into the orc's throat, dragging it sideways, severing his jugular. That was all the space that Beth needed. She headbutted the orc that was holding her from behind, managed to slip away, turned and wrapped her hands around the orc's throat as she kicked his legs out from under him. The orc sputtered to breathe, and Beth only strangled him harder until his choked gasps for air passed away and he slumped to the floor with a broken trachea.

Beth bent over and grabbed her stomach before falling to her knees. "Thanks," she managed as she leaned against the wall.

Suzuki leaned up against the wall beside her, slowly letting himself fall to a sitting position, covering the wall he leaned against with blood. He pulled up his HUD and scrolled through the inventory. Two health potions. He handed one to Beth, and they drank in silence. Suzuki could feel the wounds closing themselves up. Their blood would be replenished as well. Nothing short of cosmetic surgery was going to get rid of the scars, though. "You okay?" Suzuki asked.

"Better now that I'm not getting shivved."

"I think that was my first fight."

"What are you talking about? You've been in battles before."

"Not like that. I mean, my first...I don't know, brawl. Every fight I've been in before I've had armor, at least two weapons, and a shit ton of magical help. This was...I don't know, first knife fight at least."

"Same here."

"That was fucked up."

"I know I'm not bleeding from every part of my body, but this shit still hurts. Remind me to never get stabbed again. I'm wearing only armor from now on."

"They didn't include any of this in the glamorous Middang3ard promos."

"If someone had shown me this, I would have run away screaming."

"Knife fights should be a part of the VR update."

Beth chuckled as she looked through her inventory. Her armor was still there. She selected it, and her military armor conjured itself back onto her body. Suzuki did the same. They both helped each other to their feet and walked to the back of the bathroom where Fred and Ros'ten were.

Fred stood up when he saw Suzuki. "I'm glad that you survived, Suzuki," he said.

Beth knelt beside Ros'ten, speaking softly in a language that Suzuki could not recognize while stroking the bee's fur. "Did you get everything?" she asked.

Fred nodded as he walked toward Suzuki. "I combed over his entire body. There's nothing there. They must have implanted more than one microchip on him. It makes sense. He's an old creature, older than orcs or goblins. I suspect he was harder to control."

Suzuki looked over his shoulder as he called his ax back to him. "We should get moving," he suggested. "This is hardly the safest place for us to be."

The smell of sulfur filled the air as Fred disappeared back into Suzuki's body. Then came the scent of honey and fresh flowers as Ros'ten disappeared without a word. "Fuck, let's get out of this shithole," Beth said as she walked toward the bathroom door.

The door burst open. Now there was the smell of smoke, of bodies burned for eons and eons. Fire shot from the doorway as a smoking beast nearly the size of a giant, all fire and brimstone, poured himself into the room. A balrog. It roared loudly as it forced its body into the bathroom. "God damn, I have a mighty shit within me," the balrog bellowed.

Beth and Suzuki stood still, holding their breath.

"What the fuck are humans doing in here!" the balrog screeched as it brandished its whip.

Suzuki retrieved his ax, and Beth drew her sword. Before they could move, the balrog flicked his whip and it flew across the bathroom, slashing them both in the face with enough force to move a mountain. Beth and Suzuki collapsed to the ground.

The balrog stood over them, its eyes bright with fire, watching them as if it were trying to design some infernal pain for them to experience.

Suzuki recalled his ax back to his hand. "Fuck this!" he shouted as he crawled to his feet. "We can take him."

Beth nodded and used her sword to get to her feet. "We got this."

The balrog roared loudly and cracked its whip. Then the

door opened again and another balrog stumbled into the room. Even though his face was a mass of flames and horns, he was obviously surprised by the scene he had walked in on. "Uh-Hagreth? What are humans doing in here?" the balrog asked as he reached for his whip.

"About to get fucked up," Uh-Hagreth said as he cracked his whip.

Suzuki rushed the balrogs, Beth right at his side.

The balrogs cracked their whips in unison.

The two humans hit the ground within seconds, both too spent to defend themselves from the balrogs' attacks. The balrogs bent down, grabbed the humans, and slung them over their shoulders. They left the bathroom and the bodies of the orcs staining the floor with their blood.

21

———

Suzuki woke up in a cell. There was nothing other than a toilet. The walls were cold and white, bright light shining from a single bulb. Beth was in the cell as well. She was sitting in the corner, her arms around her knees, staring straight ahead as if her mind had been vacated. "Back in a cell," she muttered. "Guess this is my new home."

It took a little while, but Suzuki was finally able to sit up. His sides were killing him. Both he and Beth had been lucky that they had had those health potions. If not, they would have bled out in the bathroom floor, not that it felt like it mattered at the moment. They might not be dead, but they were imprisoned. "What the hell happened?" Suzuki asked as he touched the side of his head, which was swollen and bruised.

"Two balrogs wrecked us. I was out for most of our trip here, but I came awake a couple of times. Guess who managed to make it all the way to the big, bad castle in the sky?"

"Are you serious? We're in the main building?"

Beth looked around. "That's what it looks like. Even the prison cells are fancier in this part of town."

"Any idea how long I've been out?"

"Nope. I was too busy daydreaming about kicking the shit out of those balrogs to notice," Beth admitted.

"We've gotta talk to whoever brews those healing potions and let them know they gotta start including something to kick up your stamina. I'm fucking exhausted."

"Even after your power nap?" Beth asked.

Suzuki lay down on the ground and stretched out. "Honestly, I could sleep for the next day straight."

"You seem unbelievably relaxed right now. I would have thought that you would be freaking the fuck out."

"I might be neurotic, but I'm not stupid. The balrogs could have killed us. They didn't. They brought us here. We're obviously in trouble, big trouble. And you know what problem bad guys usually have?" Suzuki asked.

"What would that be, Thucydides?"

"It would...wait, did you just—"

"I'm not reading Greek war tactics to impress you. It's just a little self-education. Beth chuckled. "Bad guys don't seem to have a good handle on real estate. If we're big enough trouble to get brought to the boss, we're probably just a hop and skip away from the broadcaster."

"You know, that's not a bad train of thought."

"So, I say we rest up until someone wants to come to interrogate us."

"You make it sound so easy to deal with," Suzuki said.

"I don't plan on getting tortured, Suzy."

"And you're going to avoid this how?"

"I haven't gotten that far yet, but I'm working on it."

"Well, when you figure out how you're planning on

avoiding that, let me know. I'd love some pointers," Suzuki said.

"Seriously, though, we should try to rest up. Whatever we're going to have to deal with is going to be rough. Did you hear anything from the rest of the party?"

"No. I haven't gotten any messages or anything. I hope they got our nav points. Otherwise, we're really fucked."

"'Fucked' wouldn't even be the word."

Beth scooted closer to Suzuki and lay down next to him, resting her head on his stomach. Even with the potential of impending doom, Suzuki still couldn't wrap his mind around Beth wanting to be close to him. Of all the insane shit that had happened over the last month, this was the most fantastical to him. Beth sighed and snuggled her head against Suzuki. "You know they're going to kill us, right?" she asked.

"That's not the first time I've heard that."

"Oh, so you're Mr. Tough Guy now, Suzy?"

"I'm just saying, people been trying to kill us for how long? And we're still alive."

"You know, Suzy, if I wasn't so sore, I'd fuck you—seeing how these could be our last moments together."

Suzuki's heart started to race. He cleared his throat and tried to speak in his deepest, sexiest voice. "Oh, yeah? You would."

Beth giggled and lightly slapped Suzuki's cheek. "Are you trying to sound sexy?"

"No."

"It's cute. Instant gushers down there."

"Uh..."

"You know what, fuck it. We're gonna be sore anyways."

Sandy, José, and Stew were making good time with their excavation. According to their map readouts of the different nav points, they were going to arrive within an hour or two. GB and Niv were taking care of most of the digging. GB had already shown more than a proclivity for digging, but Niv turned out to be nearly as stoked as the jackass gargoyle was.

José and Stew hammered at the rocks and dirt as Sandy floated behind them, flower petals swarming around her ashen skeleton, softening the dirt that the two MERCs and familiars dug into. It was helping a considerable amount. This time, Stew was hardly working up a sweat. "What do you think that we're going to find when we get there?" Stew asked.

Sandy levitated a sizable chunk of dirt out of Stew's way. "Probably pulling Suzuki and Beth out of the shitter," she joked. "They've been away from us for nearly a day. There's no way that they managed to stay out of trouble."

José leaned over to catch his breath. He took a drink of water from his canteen. "You two going to be ready to move when we get in?"

"Of course. I was only half kidding. Not even Suzuki and Beth could be lucky enough to manage to pull off something like this. It was the best plan, though."

"When life gives you lemons—"

"Beat life to death with them."

GB casually looked over his shoulder and smiled his goofy, lopsided grin. "Do you guys want me to dig faster?" he asked.

Stew sighed loudly as he threw down his ax. "GB, are you asking us if we want you to dig faster, or are you offering to dig faster?"

"I *could* dig faster."

"Why the hell didn't you say anything earlier?"

"I didn't know that it was an emergency."

"Goddamn it, GB, of course we want you to dig faster."

GB squealed with delight as he clapped his hands. "All right, digging maximum overdrive!" With that, GB tore into the tunnel, throwing dirt over his shoulder faster than any of the MERCs would have thought was possible. "I really hate you sometimes, GB," Stew muttered under his breath.

Sandy checked her HUD. There were two glowing blips. One of them was the nav point that Suzuki and Beth had sent earlier. The other blip looked like it could have been their current location. Whatever tech was blocking the HUD signals apparently didn't work well underground, or the blocking signal might have only been strong when in separate circles. From what Sandy could see on their map, they had already crossed into the last defense ring. Either way, she wasn't going to shoot the messenger. "Guys," Sandy started. "We have a new nav point for Suzuki and Beth. It doesn't look like they're moving either."

"Guess you shouldn't have been joking about them being captured so soon. You probably cursed them."

"Stew, that isn't how curses work."

"So, change of plan?"

"Yeah, let's bring the party to them. Diana and Chip probably are heading toward the first nav point anyway. Two boarding parties always work better than one."

Suzuki woke up to the chill of cold water splashing on his face.

He jumped up, spitting, eyes wide, trying to see who the

offender was. Beth was already on her feet. Her eyes were red, and she looked ready to snap.

An orc held her hands behind her back. Another orc stood over Suzuki.

The orc held a plasma rifle which looked as if it had been connected to his forearm somehow. "Real sweet, human. Spending your last few worthwhile moments in each other's loving embrace." The orc sneered.

Suzuki raised his hands as he stood. "Were you assholes watching?" Suzuki asked. "I don't know what's weirder, the way you act like humans fucking is the most disgusting thing in the world or that you can't seem to stop watching. Has it been a while since you got your cock sucked?"

The orc slapped Suzuki across the face with his plasma rifle. The rifle was so hot that it seared Suzuki's face as he fell to the ground. Suzuki wiped blood from his nose and stood back up. "Go fuck yourself, you hormonally-backed-up sack of shit. Is this the part when you take us to whoever's in charge? Because I can tell we're obviously not going to be wasting our time with you."

The orc aimed its plasma rifle at Suzuki, who did everything in his power not to look frightened even though he was terrified. All the tough talk was part of his plan, and he had been rehearsing his insults and tone of voice before he had passed out.

Beth, on the other hand, was going to play the part of the broken soldier, and Suzuki was honestly surprised that she was able to get her eyes so red.

The plan was simple. Maybe too simple to work.

Suzuki was going to attract everyone's attention and keep it on him by being as brash and edgy as possible while Beth tried to become invisible. When they got a chance, Beth was going to slip away and raise some hell. The small diversion would give Suzuki some wiggle room as well. The plan hadn't gone any further than that. The way that Suzuki and Beth figured, this was the end of the line. All they could do was stall until the rest of the Mundanes and reinforcements showed up. If Beth managed to slip away, she might be able to find the ringtone, but there was no way that she was going to be able to destroy it or sneak it out.

It was a suicide mission. Still, as Beth put it, at least they weren't going out like a bunch of punk asses. "If this is where I die, I want to take as many of these assholes with me as possible," she said.

The orcs herded Suzuki and Beth out of the cell and into a long, glowing hallway. There were cells on both walls with the same invisible energy barrier that Suzuki had seen in the arena outside.

Each cell held a different race, many of which Suzuki had never seen or read about. There was one cell that was filled with what looked like gas, occasionally brightened by eyes that popped in and out of existence, their colors changing rapidly as Suzuki walked by. He wished that he could have paid as much attention as he wanted to, but there were other things on his mind. First and foremost, he wanted to find the controls to open the cells. Beth was more than capable of creating a diversion by herself, but a room full of freed prisoners would probably attract more attention.

From the hallway, the two Mundanes were led into a vast ceremonial hall. There were more of the monoliths that Suzuki had seen outside. These were small, though, placed in two rows that mirrored each other, a long, red carpet between them, starting at the foot of the room and ending at a throne, which was empty. A large screen was above the throne.

The walls were covered with bizarre, ornate sculptures. Most of the sculptures were of races that Suzuki knew had already been enslaved: orcs, trolls, and ogres. There were others that Suzuki had only seen cursorily serving the Dark One, including elves, dwarves, and halflings. Then there were creatures, much like in the cells, that Suzuki had never seen before. The sculptures were constructed out of some kind of liquid metal which gave the illusion that the sculptures were moving as if they were in a constant state of flux. Or perhaps it was reality?

Orc guards lined the walls. Each of them carried one of the plasma rifles that the two guards escorting Suzuki and Beth held. It didn't seem as if any of the guards had the traditional weapons Suzuki had grown accustomed to in Middang3ard. None of the orcs paid particular attention to the two Mundanes. They stared straight ahead, almost as if they were statues themselves.

Behind the throne and the screen, the hall opened up to the sky, overlooking the defense ring and the small buildings beneath it.

The guards brought Suzuki and Beth to the throne. "Get on your knees," a guard grunted.

Suzuki sneered and rolled his shoulders so that they cracked. "Is this a customary kneeling or a subservient bowing?" Suzuki asked.

"What the fuck are you talking about?"

"Am I paying respect or being asked to play the bitch?"

The guard pressed its rifle to the back of Suzuki's neck. An electric shock flowed through his body, and he momentarily lost control of his legs. He fell straight forward, smacking his head on the floor. It was all that he could do to get back on his knees without trembling in pain.

Another shock racked Suzuki's body, and he screamed in

pain. The guard smirked and chuckled, a cruel irritating sound. "Which one do you think it is?" the guard asked.

Beth dropped to her knees without a word. Her bottom lip trembled, and she was fighting back tears. "Whatever you want, we'll do it," Beth whimpered. "Just tell us. We'll do anything just, please, don't hurt us."

The guard shocked Suzuki again, this time longer, until Suzuki was on the ground twitching, his eyes rolled up in the back of his head. He was gritting his teeth, trying to breath, trying to keep from blacking out. *They're not even paying attention to Beth,* he thought. *It's working...*

"Get up, maggot!"

Suzuki's guard reached down and pulled Suzuki back up on his knees. Suzuki spat blood, his head still swimming. "What are we doing here? You guys worship an empty seat or something?"

As Suzuki spoke, the screen above the throne turned on. There was a crackle of white noise and static, and the viceroy elegantly stepped through the screen, floating down to take a seat on the throne, crossing her metallic legs as she leaned back. "It is time that we were able to meet in the flesh," the viceroy purred. Her voice was deep and brassy, almost a rattle, much different than she had sounded when she was speaking to the crowd. It almost sounded fragile, as if the little bits of organic life within her were dying.

Suzuki spat and tried to pull away from his guard. "Are we getting the royal treatment?" he asked. "Or is this how you treat all your dignitaries?"

"Dignitaries, you say? From what illustrious land do you hail? Who is it that I am entertaining?"

"We're the Mundanes. No doubt you've heard of our exploits. They're pretty sick."

The viceroy smiled.

She was even more unnerving in person. An air of violence and hatred seemed to emanate from her despite her syrupy sweet smile. Suzuki didn't know what it was, but he became very aware that the viceroy wanted to reach out and tear him limb from limb. It was a bizarre feeling because, despite how repulsive she seemed, the viceroy also deeply attracted Suzuki. He felt as if he were being called to her every time she moved, her mechanical body breaking apart in some sections as if it could hardly hold itself together, only to reconnect even more beautifully than before.

"You are the human who disrupted the raising of our elder god, aren't you?"

"Guilty as charged," Suzuki spat.

"And she is?"

The viceroy pointed at Beth, who instantly burst into tears, shivering as she cried.

"The fiercest fighter of the Mundanes," Suzuki replied.

The viceroy laughed and clapped her hands together before resting back in her throne. "A truly impressive sight. How is it that a collection of sniveling children managed to destroy a horde of vampires and an elder god? Not only that, but also manage to infiltrate our research facility? Interesting indeed."

"Research facility? I don't see any research happening here. It's only a shitty torture prison."

"And this is the part where you expect me to tell you exactly what it is we are researching, I assume."

"Nope. You don't need to. I already figured it out. You're researching how to control the different races with microchips and ringtones to serve your stupid ass...god? Leader? I'm a little fuzzy on exactly how you're sucking on the Dark One's tits."

"Your insolence is refreshing..."

"Suzuki."

"Suzuki... you speak as if you are the one in control. Even though you are bound and at my mercy. What gives you such confidence?"

The viceroy was emanating a different energy now. This was more subtle. Suzuki felt as if she were imagining devouring him. The look on her face was one of intense hunger. Suzuki swallowed hard and tried not to cave to the fear that was threatening to engulf him. "I'm the best at what I do, bub," he spat, instantly regretting his choice of words. "And what I do ain't pretty."

The viceroy leaned forward, her eyes nearly undressing Suzuki. "Hmm... you aren't particularly beautiful. None of you humans are. You could use... improvements, to say the least."

"Like you?"

The viceroy chuckled. "Oh yes, much like me. The improvements are only accessible through our Dark Lord. He will start by carving that insolence out of your mind. Then he will start with the flesh. He will bend it to his will until you are a creature of beauty, of order. The experience can be exhilarating, beyond your wildest dreams of pleasure."

"Uh... if it's anything like what happened to you, I'd like to pass. You look a little... hmm... fucked up to say the least."

"You do not believe that. Neither you nor your friend. I can see it in your eyes, the way that you can't help but look upon me as if in worship."

Suzuki tried to think of something to say, but he was too caught off-guard by the viceroy's candidness. He looked at Beth, who was blushing and avoiding his eyes.

The viceroy laughed, her voice nearly angelic. "There's

no need to be embarrassed," she cooed. "I will teach you the beauty of order. Personally."

Suzuki jerked his head over to the guards who were standing behind him. "What about these guys?" Suzuki asked. "How come they don't get the royal beauty treatment?"

"It takes a special mind to accommodate the process. You two show promise. I've been watching your exploits. What you did with the elder god was...inspiring," she said as her body seemed to shiver, come apart, and reconfigure. "After speaking with the Dark Lord, he has agreed to have an audience with you before you are...reintegrated. It is customary for the Dark Lord's lieutenants to be greeted personally. Prepare your bodies."

The screen above the viceroy crackled to life, and a man stood in a nearly black room. He was not quite a man, though. Even from the screen, Suzuki could see that the Dark One was too tall to be a human, or an elf for that matter.

The Dark One stepped closer to the screen, farther into the light. He had extremely smooth, white skin. His blue and green veins could be seen beneath his skin like a sort of grid. That was all there was to see of his face as well. There were no eyes. No mouth. No nose. Only a blank, porcelain visage colored by veins so bright that their contents were nearly visible.

The Dark One was completely naked. Much like his face, there were no defining features whatsoever. No genitals. No muscles. He looked as if someone wanted to create a statue of a human, but had only heard vague descriptions of one. His entire body was as smooth and white as his face, and his veins shone brightly, his chest being the most luminous. He was not muscular; rather, he was extremely slim. If

Suzuki had seen anyone that size on Earth, he would have assumed the person malnourished or sick. Yet the Dark One seemed anything but sick. His body radiated strength even through the screen. When he took another step forward, it was as if each muscle, if they were in fact muscles, was carefully controlled. He moved with an inhuman gracefulness as if he were a dancer of some sort.

The Dark One spoke, but there were no words, nothing that could be heard. Yet each syllable ripped through Suzuki's head like a personalized migraine. Both he and Beth instinctively covered their ears as they screamed in pain. It felt as if the Dark One had ripped their heads open with his thoughts. "These are the humans?" he asked, his voice thundering as if it were indeed that of a god.

The viceroy did not seem bothered by the sound. She didn't turn to face the screen, only watched the Mundanes writhing in pain as she answered. "Yes, my Lord," she whispered as if in reverence. "These are the humans I have selected to break. They should give us the key to unlocking the proper tone for their race."

"They do not seem exceptional. They strike me as mediocre. Mundane, even. What makes you believe that they are capable of being ordered?"

The pain of hearing the Dark One speak had subsided. Suzuki could finally get his thoughts back together even though each word from the Dark One filled his mind so that he thought his brain would explode. Suzuki tried to direct his thoughts toward Beth. "Can you hear me?" he murmured.

Beth barely showed any sign that Suzuki's words were heard, but she answered, nonetheless. "Yeah. I got you."

"What do you think we should do?"

"Suzy, I think we're fucked. They're going to experiment

on us. They're going to make us... like her. And... I think I want her to. Part of me. I don't know what it is but... I want to... I want to touch her. I want to feel her."

"I know. I do too. We have to fight it, though. It must be part of their indoctrination process. We can fight it. That's why they want us—because we're strong."

"We deserve it. No... No, that's not right. Fuck that. I don't want..."

"Keep it together, Beth."

"You too."

The Dark One's voice tore through their minds again as he leaned closer to the screen. His veins were glowing a dull white. "Interesting. You are both very strong of will," he thundered. "Acceptable. Prepare their minds and flesh for me to unveil my full glory to them."

The viceroy stood, smiling, and turned to the screen behind her. She opened her arms as if ready for an embrace. Her back broke apart, three long, slender appendages slipping out from her shoulders, propping her up as electronic tendrils stretched from the computer screen, connecting her to the screen as the same tendrils extended from the Dark One to the screen. The tendrils burned bright blue, and the viceroy moaned loudly before settling back onto the ground, her back knitting itself back together, her organs visible for a brief second before her skin returned to its bio-mechanical nature. The screen above went black and the viceroy turned to face Suzuki and Beth, her face flushed, showing more color than it had seemed capable of.

Suzuki wanted the viceroy to scoop him up in her arms, to take him away to wherever she wanted. The techno-organic skin that had repulsed him looked so alluring now. He wondered how many different ways she could break his skin apart, what she could force out of him for the sake of beauty and creation.

As these thoughts crossed through Suzuki's mind, he became very aware that they were not his own. Rather, they were not his thoughts as he had grown to understand them. They did not seem to spring from his own mind, but felt as if someone had inserted a seed of them in his mind and was quickly trying to get them to grow and mature. Suzuki instinctively looked away from the viceroy as he tried to shut the thoughts out. As he turned, he noticed that the monoliths seemed to be vibrating. The motion was subtle, and he wasn't sure if he wasn't just imagining it. Whatever was going on with the indoctrination that he already felt slipping into his brain, he knew that the monoliths were a piece of the puzzle.

The viceroy took a step toward the two Mundanes, her body moving as if it were made of pure liquid, her skin opening and closing, showing the beautiful, ordered interplay of gears and tubes working together, and she was standing before Suzuki before he realized it. She leaned down and took Suzuki's head in her hand and pressed her lips to his. They were warm and firm, parted and inviting. Then she kissed Beth, letting her hand rest against Beth's cheeks, her fingers splitting down the middle and a thin cable snaking out and caressing Beth's head before she pulled away. "Take them to the reintegration chamber," the viceroy said as she stood.

Suzuki felt a shock rock his body, and the world went black.

When Suzuki woke up, he was strapped to a cold, steel

table. His hands, feet, and head were bound. He could barely move and it was difficult to breathe. Above him, there was a singular white light so bright that it was nearly blinding. "Beth!" he shouted.

Even though Suzuki could not see Beth, he could hear her voice. "I'm right here, Suzy," she said.

"What the fuck is going on?"

"They're reintegrating us."

"Have they done anything to you yet?" he asked.

"No, not yet, Suzy. Just talk to me. The viceroy's been in and out. But she's hardly said anything. She's just trying to be encouraging. I mean...fuck...I feel like there's someone else in my fucking head."

"It's the monoliths. They're pumping out some kind of brainwashing signal or something. We need to get out of here. Now."

"You don't think I've been trying?" Beth asked.

"How tight are you tied?"

"Too tight to move. You?"

"Just as bad."

"I didn't think this was how the first time you and me getting tied up was going to be."

"Now is not the time, Beth."

"If we can't joke before we have our DNA rewritten so that we look like one of our parents fucked a microwave, then when can we joke?"

"Good point," Suzuki said as he chuckled. "I've got a plan. It's gonna go by pretty fast, so you gotta—"

"Are you going to shit yourself?"

"Why would I shit myself?"

Beth smirked. "I don't know. Who would want to do any kind of operation if you were covered in shit?"

"Are you gonna shit yourself?"

"I don't need to shit. But I would."

Suzuki heard a door open, quickly followed by heavy, plodding footsteps.

An orc wearing a lab coat popped down into Suzuki's field of vision. "You should count yourself very lucky," the orc scientist said. "Many of us dream of being hand-picked by the viceroy to ascend to a more ordered existence. And here you are, granted that right out the gates. Very lucky, indeed."

Suzuki struggled against his bindings. "Yeah, I feel like I won the fucking lottery," Suzuki muttered as he tried to raise his hands. It didn't matter. He was strapped in too tightly. There was only one option. He had to time this perfectly.

The orc leaning over Suzuki pulled out what looked like a long, hot glue gun, but instead of glue, there was a dripping, blue liquid. A drop of the liquid fell next to Suzuki's head and he heard the steel of the table sizzling loudly. The orc held a large microchip in his other hand. "To think, this morning, you were only a human. Now you're the secret to an entire race's reintegration."

Suzuki tried to relax. He started counting from a hundred slowly as he breathed. Now was the time.

The orc wrinkled its nose. He looked down at Suzuki's legs. "What are you doing?" the orc asked.

"I have a weak bladder. Very weak. It's probably going to just keep going."

The orc pulled back in disgust, covering his nose with one hand. "Are you serious?"

"I think I'm going to need a change of pants, unless you want to continue the operation to the olfactory symphony that I'm creating."

"Disgusting humans. I can't believe the Dark Lord

thought you, of all people, were worthy to elevate your race."

The orc continued to mutter under his breath as he undid Suzuki's leg shackles. Once Suzuki's legs were free, he wrapped his legs around the orc's neck, squeezing as hard as he could, the orc's face shoved snuggly into his piss-stained crotch. The orc tried to scream, but Suzuki just squeezed harder. "You are going to unchain my hands now," Suzuki commanded. "You got it?"

The orc nodded his head frantically as he thrashed, trying to hit Suzuki's wrist shackles. He managed to get one of them undone and Suzuki raised his hand, concentrated, and waited.

Beth was laughing from her table. "What are you doing, Suzy? This isn't a time to be striking a pose."

"Hush, I'm concentrating."

Suzuki kept the image of his ax firmly in his mind. He hoped this was going to work. He couldn't remember the last time he had had his ax. Maybe in the bathroom? How far would the enchantment work?

The answer came soon enough. Suzuki's ax came tearing through the operation room right into his palm. He didn't waste any time and chopped off his last shackle, then brought the ax down on the orc's head. He got up and unshackled Beth. "Grab your gear," he muttered, pointing to the pile of Beth's armor and swords before he took his pants off.

Beth threw on her armor. She turned around, and her jaw dropped when she saw Suzuki, naked from the waist down. "Oh, my God, Suzy, did you really piss yourself?" Beth asked, trying to hold back her laughter.

"Yeah, yeah, this is gonna make a great story and everything, but let's concentrate on that later. We need to figure out what we're doing."

"How am I going to be able to concentrate with you butt-ass naked?"

"I'm going to do it. Fuck, it's cold in here. All right, we're in the research facility. This is where they—"

"You don't have any other pants in your inventory?"

"No! I don't usually pack an extra pair in case I piss myself. Now I know better."

"All right, hold on."

Beth scrolled through her inventory until she smiled. She selected an item and it materialized in her hand: a pair of bright pink booty shorts that read THICC on the butt cheeks. She tossed them to Suzuki. "This way, everyone doesn't have to see your cock jiggling while you run."

Suzuki put on the shorts and sighed. "I'm pretty sure everyone's gonna see that regardless. You ready?"

"Ready."

Beth kicked open the operation room door. She and Suzuki stepped out of the room and into what looked like a glass menagerie of races, creatures, and monsters. The walls were covered with individual, clear cells that stretched across the entire length of the wall and went up to the ceiling. It looked like an alien version of a zoo. "Are all of them being microchipped?" Beth wondered aloud.

Suzuki wandered to one of the closest cells and peered inside. A three-headed, golden lion paced. Suzuki noticed that the skin around the lion's manes was starting to decay, similar to the techno-organic decay the viceroy had displayed. "No, I don't think so," Suzuki said. "I think what they do here is a little different. We weren't just going to be reintegrated, we were going to be elevated. It's something more extreme than just being chipped. I think that's what the viceroy is."

"I can't believe I thought that psycho was hot."

"Same here."

"Is there anything we can do for them?"

"I don't know. If they're already microchipped and elevated, they might be beyond our help. But I don't know how any of this shit works."

Suzuki looked around the room. He noticed that there were three monoliths, smaller than the ones he'd seen previously. "Whatever is going on, though, I'm a hundred percent certain that those monoliths are making it worse," Suzuki said as he cast a fire buff on his ax. He threw his ax as hard as he could at one of the monoliths, and it shattered into thousands of perfectly shaped black pieces. His ax came flying back to him and he threw it at another monolith as Beth charged the last one, knocking it to the ground and shattering it into fragments.

The occupants of the cells hardly seemed to notice. If the monoliths were doing anything to the prisoners, they probably weren't even aware of it.

A voice thundered through the facility. It was the viceroy. "Bring the humans to me, either dead or alive. Their will to live will decide if they are elevated or buried. Release the dragon."

Beth and Suzuki looked at each other. "The dragon?" Beth asked.

One of the cells opened with a deafening pop as the invisible barrier disappeared. The ground rumbled as something massive took its first step out of the cell. Slowly emerging was something red and long. Smoke billowed from its nose and mouth as it let out a roar that shook the entire facility.

Ashegoreth, the Red Death, stepped out of her cell, a microchip planted firmly in her forehead, the techno-organic decay already spreading from the microchip down the dragon's spine and wings.

Suzuki and Beth were frozen with fear. They slowly backed away, each step feeling as if their feet weighed thousands of pounds. "Oh, no," Suzuki muttered as he checked his HUD. It didn't read anything. The orcs must have messed with it. That, or something here was fucking with its ability to calculate percentages. "This is bad... this is really bad... we need to get out of here."

"Oh, my God..." Beth whispered. "That's a...a...drag—"

Ashegoreth roared loudly again and then spewed a funnel of fire in Beth and Suzuki's direction. The two Mundanes threw themselves to the side, only narrowly escaping being burned alive. Suzuki scrambled to his feet and grabbed Beth's hand to help her up. "No more plans," Suzuki shouted. "Just run! Just run!"

Beth and Suzuki took off, running the opposite direction as Ashegoreth, nearly avoiding another flaming vortex of death sent their way. As Suzuki ran, he tried to see if there was anything he could do to open the cells along the way, but he couldn't see any discernable control near the cells. There were no buttons or pads. The walls were all seamless steel and there were hardly any tools or controls around the metal tables that Suzuki ran by. Suzuki wondered if the whole facility was operated by some Wi-Fi signal sent out by the viceroy, but the screech of the dragon pursuing him shattered his train of thought.

As Suzuki turned a corner, two armed orc guards stepped out of the corner on the opposite side. The guards gave each other a bewildered look briefly before unslinging their plasma rifles and opening fire. Beth jumped to the side, the bolt of crackling plasma passing by her and tearing a hole in the wall. Suzuki wasn't so lucky. One of the blasts hit him square in the chest and sent him flying through the air and skidding across the ground.

Beth wasted no time moving.

She threw her sword like a spear into the guard on the left as she bolted, shield raised, deflecting another plasma shot, and jumped onto the other orc, lifting her shield and bringing it down on the orc's skull. Then she grabbed both of their rifles and tossed one to Suzuki when he finally caught up. "I think our weapons might be a little outdated for this fight," she said as she looked down the sights of the rifle. "You know how to use one of these?"

Suzuki looked at the gun with disdain and mild frustration. "I haven't shot a gun since I was twelve at summer camp," he admitted.

Three more guards popped out from a sliding door that seemed to have opened up from nowhere. Suzuki instinctively turned, aimed, and squeezed the trigger, sending a hot bolt of plasma at one of the orcs, tossing the orc through the air as it screamed. Suzuki and Beth took cover behind the corner they had just turned as plasma bolts went screeching past them. "Looks like you remembered the important stuff!" Beth shouted.

"The boom part makes things go dead, right?"

Beth laughed as she leaned around the corner and fired off two shots. One of them hit an orc in the chest, and he crumbled to the ground. "You think they would have invested in armor that would keep them alive," Beth murmured.

"Who gives the grunts a good set of armor?" Suzuki shouted as he rolled out of cover and fired, nailing the final orc. He pumped his fist and turned around smiling before his face dropped at the sound of the roaring, pissed-off dragon on their tail. "Fuck, completely forgot about the winged death trying to burn us alive."

"Okay, I know we gotta keep running, but where the fuck are we going? Out of this building, there's a whole defense ring waiting to rip us to shreds. The viceroy is somewhere in there, and I don't want to get in a fist fight with her. And outside of that, we got, four, five, fuck it, how many more defense rings to get through?"

"Maybe there's a way that we could un-chip some of these guys. The same way that we did Ros'ten. Better actually, seeing how we missed one of the chips."

Another roar from the red dragon interrupted their conversation. It sounded even closer this time around. "Run and think, run and think," Beth shouted as she took off down the hallway.

Suzuki followed close on her heels as he reached out to Fred. "Hey, buddy," Suzuki broached, "I think I got a special mission for you."

Fred hissed in Suzuki's head, voicing obvious irritation. "You do not need to pander to me, Suzuki. I assume whatever it is will be dangerous."

"Sneak out of me with Ros'ten and go un-chip some of the big bads in their cells. Thank you can handle that?"

"And how is it you presume that I accomplish that?" Fred hissed.

"You're the wise, eldritch creature. Figure something out. Our lives kinda depend on it."

"Well, if *your* lives depend on it, I'll see what I can do."

Sandy, José, and Stew stood in their tunnel. GB had stopped

digging and was looking up. The tunnel had gone from straight forward to arching upward and now they all stared at the bit of ground above them as if it were an attic door.

Stew poked the thin layer of dirt. "So, this is where the nav point comes up to?"

GB nodded emphatically, his donkey tongue hanging out of his mouth almost like a dog's. "Yep, yep!" GB exclaimed. "This is where we were supposed to dig."

"It's not too far from the first nav point that they sent us, is it Sandy?"

Sandy conjured her wand and poked at the dirt as well. "Yeah. Diana told me that the reinforcements are coming up at the last nav point. This one is all ours. We're the cavalry."

Stew drew his swords, as did José. "All right, well, let's fucking do this then. For honor!"

"For glory!"

José looked at both of the Mundanes blankly. "Am I supposed to say something?" he asked.

Stew sighed, his enthusiasm deflated. "Dude, it's not that hard. We say it all of the time. For XP."

"Gotcha. For XP," José muttered.

Fred and Ros'ten split away from Suzuki and Beth, barreling down the hall in the direction of Ashegoreth. They flew high up to the ceiling, barely slipping by the dragon, who was on a war path toward the two Mundanes, far too drunk on bloodlust to pay attention to the small familiars.

Ashegoreth exploded out of the hallway, skidding as she tried to grapple with the slippery floor. Her eyes were empty, not the eyes full of love and wisdom that Suzuki had seen before. These eyes were devoid of any intelligence. They were singular and dead, focused and driven on one thing and one thing alone: the Mundanes. She spewed another jet of fire down the hallway, roaring, which sounded more akin to screaming, a painfilled sound that was also mournful as if somewhere, deep in the recesses of her mind, she was aware of how lost she had become.

Farther down the halls of the research facility, Suzuki and Beth were still running for their lives. They had no idea exactly where they were, nor how long they were going to have to run for an opening. There was a surprising lack of guards for there having been an announcement to bring their dead bodies to the viceroy. Suzuki thought this was odd, but he wasn't going to look a gift horse in the mouth. With his current luck, the horse would have tried to bite his nose off.

Beth grabbed Suzuki's arm as they rounded a corner and pulled him in the opposite direction that he was running. "I think it's this way," she suggested. "To get back to the throne room."

Suzuki blinked his eyes as he tried to understand what Beth was saying. "Why the hell would we want to go to the throne room?"

"If the viceroy is out looking for us, it should be abandoned, and it overlooked the entire defense ring. We could just jump out. It'll be easier than just running around. I still haven't seen an elevator, and I know we can't be on the first floor."

"Good enough for me."

Suzuki followed Beth down the hall. She was right. It ended in a double door that opened to the throne room. Beth shot the doors open and Suzuki kicked them down.

The throne room was filled with orc and goblin guards, armed to the teeth. Some of them wore multiple rifles slung over their shoulders. Others carried glowing plasma pistols. And yet there were still more with upgraded versions of the typical Middang3ard weapons: swords, axes, and spears. The weapons lacked blades. Instead, there was a black energy blade that hummed slightly as it projected its energy.

A plasma blast shot past Beth and she ducked for cover. "Fuck," she shouted. "Are you fucking kidding me?"

Suzuki took a deep breath and leaned over the corner of the wall to see what they were up against. There were at least twenty guards in the room, and there was a dragon behind them. "Beth, you know defensive spells, right?" Suzuki asked.

"Just the basic shit."

"We have to get through them. That's our only way out. You ready?"

Suzuki cast Stoneskin on himself, and Beth did the same. Then he enchanted his ax with a defense charm, almost completely reducing its offensive stats so that it was more like a shield or a baseball bat. He grabbed Beth and kissed her as if it were the last time that he would ever feel his lips against hers. "I love you," he said.

"I love you too, Suzy."

"Let's fuck some shit up!"

Suzuki rolled into the throne room. He fired five shots without aiming to clear some space. One of the plasma shots caught one of the orcs in the chest, sending him flying and searing his skin.

It was just like Suzuki had thought. The orcs weren't armored at all. They had no magical defenses. That's why the blasts that Suzuki and Beth had taken hadn't killed them. They had armor and an additional amount of magical protection imbued in their armor.

With defensive spells, they would at least be able to stand a chance.

A plasma shot came rocketing toward Suzuki. He pulled his ax from his side and batted the plasma shot away, sending it careening into the side of the wall where it tore through the liquid metal wall, leaving a hole that quickly healed itself as if the walls, the building itself were alive. Suzuki placed that in his mental folder of things to think about later as he whipped his unwieldy rifle over his shoulder and fired again.

Beth was blocking plasma shots with her shield, slowly pushing forward and taking ground. When Suzuki saw what Beth was planning, he fired at the closest guards near her to give her a little more breathing room.

They weren't going able to take the room in a flurry of scattered shots, but if they kept their shit together, they could slowly force their way into the room and clear out the enemy.

Suzuki rolled over to Beth and hid behind her shield. He reached out and took it from her so that she could devote her full attention to the rifle. He had noticed she was a better shot than he. They didn't need to speak. Beth poked out from behind the shield and fired three quick shots at the guards, each one landing and searing through their chests. One of the guards dropped a plasma pistol that skidded across the floor. Suzuki dropped his rifle and picked up the pistol. It was lighter, a much better fit for what he had in mind. "Don't bother covering me," he said. "I'm gonna try to take out the left flank."

"You don't have a shield, douchenozzle!"

"Hopefully, I got reflexes."

Beth went to the right and Suzuki to the left. Outside of the cover of the shield, he was an easy target. The guards turned their attention to Suzuki, firing off a few rounds of steaming hot plasma that came jetting toward his face. Suzuki sidestepped a few, knocking away the rest. He threw his ax through a plasma bolt, fired off three rounds that landed two headshots, and recalled his ax. He leapt through the air as he enchanted his ax with a sharpness charm and landed on a goblin, swinging his ax and decapitating the guard before spinning around and narrowly avoiding being blasted by an orc.

Beth was still making her way toward the throne in her methodical fashion. She was growing frustrated with how slowly it was taking her to move forward. There had to be a better way. The rifles did damage, but they took too long, and Beth knew how to use speed better than anyone.

A plasma bolt sizzled past Beth's head, and she lifted her shield. Her foot touched something hard, and she looked down.

Two of the plasma swords were laying on the ground. She slipped her foot under their hilts and flipped them into the air, dropping her shield to upload back into her inventory, and catching the two swords.

They were light in her hand... just what she had been hoping for.

She sprang forward, faster than the guards could take aim, slid on the sleek floor, turned and sliced out the legs of three guards before rolling back to her feet, sprinting to another guard, leaping over him and slicing him down the middle. Another guard turned to face her. He fired two shots and Beth sliced through each one. If Suzuki's ax could knock plasma away, it only made sense that plasma could cut plasma. Beth tossed one of the swords into a guard's chest just as a plasma bolt hit her in the back, sending her flying through the air, smashing against the throne.

The orc that shot Beth ran at her to finish the job.

Suzuki's ax flew from across the room, landing square in the orc's back. The orc dropped to the ground.

Beth scrambled to her feet and picked up the orc's sword. She sliced through two more shots fired at her and hid behind the throne. "Almost there, Suzy!" she shouted.

Suzuki tossed his ax at a goblin, severing the guard's head, recalled it back in time to knock away a plasma blast, turning to fire his own plasma bolt that burned through an orc's chest. "We got this!" Suzuki shouted.

The positivity was cut short by an ear-splitting roar.

Ashegoreth plowed into the throne room, sending chunks of wall flying as she broke through the small opening. She leaned back in all her terrible glory, her red scales burning brighter red as she let loose a cloud of sulfur, a forewarning of the flames which quickly followed, torching the entire ceiling, creating an inverse of hell as she turned her flames toward everyone in the room.

Beth cowered behind the throne, trying to make herself as small as possible behind the one thing that didn't seem as if it were melting.

Suzuki, on the other hand, was running as fast as he could to avoid the flames on his heels.

He ducked behind one of the monoliths and prayed that it would be strong enough to keep him safe. If these monoliths were any weaker than the ones that he had destroyed earlier, he knew that he was fucked.

The fire abruptly stopped.

Suzuki peeked out from behind the monolith. Ashegoreth was staring at him, her eyes black and wounded, filled with a deep despair and emptiness that almost broke Suzuki's heart. "Ashegoreth," Suzuki started. "Ash... it's me. Do you remember me, Suzuki?"

Ashegoreth charged. Fast. Faster than anything Suzuki had ever seen.

The force of Ashegoreth's body was beyond anything Suzuki had ever felt before.

His brain shut down to block out most of the pain. He didn't quite know how it happened or exactly what was happening, but his body was weightless and he was floating through the air.

He saw Beth as he was rising. She looked scared. It didn't really matter, though, because she looked like she was safe.

Beth was safe.

When he moved his head to try and see what else was happening, it seemed like all of the world had slowed down. It was kind of funny that there was a dragon right in front of him, spewing fire every which way. He would have laughed if his ribs didn't hurt so much. And now he was flying through the air, the dragon above him, gnashing her teeth as he raised his hands (he didn't know why he raised his hands), trying to fight her off.

Then the ground and black-eyed pain rushed up to meet him.

22

S uzuki lay on the ground, his body wracked with pain, trying to look up at the sky.

He couldn't open his eyes.

Every muscle in his body converged, attempting to pull his eyelids open. It did no good. He accepted that he should probably lie down for a bit.

Take a nap.

He'd wake up feeling better if he could just sleep off this headache that was drilling into the back of his head.

Above the sleeping Suzuki, the dragon, Ashegoreth, spread her wings, descending slowly, breathing flames hotter than those of hell itself, as orcs and goblins and ogres flooded the arena Suzuki had landed in. Many of them were either holding plasma rifles or plasma swords. They were chanting in unison together, their voices melding into a nonsensical smattering of words and syllables, of lustful grunts and shouts. The sheer cacophony would have been too much for Suzuki to handle if he had been awake. Everyone in the arena wanted him dead.

Beth stood at the top of the building which Suzuki had

fallen from. She could have made the jump, but there was a dragon between her and Suzuki. She could try and take the dragon out, but even she knew that was hoping for a lot. Her heart was racing, and she felt like she was going to vomit. Now wasn't the time, though. She had to keep her shit together. This was what she had been trained for.

Ashegoreth landed in front of Suzuki. She reached her head up toward the sky and roared before unleashing a torrent of flames skyward.

The pawns of the Dark One cheered with glee.

Ashegoreth leaned over Suzuki, her teeth gleaming as flames grumbled within her stomach, her eyes filled with hunger.

Beth took aim. She had to execute this perfectly. A slight misstep would end up with her splattering on the ground and Ashegoreth would have two meals.

Ashegoreth opened her gaping jaw, her teeth dripping saliva as she slithered toward Suzuki.

Suzuki's eyes cracked open slightly. All that he could see were teeth. Teeth everywhere, surrounding him, engulfing him. *It won't be too bad,* Suzuki thought. *At least it'll be fast. It could be worse.*

"Hey, Fuckface, get the fuck away from our friend!" a voice shouted from behind the crowd.

Ashegoreth stopped in her tracks. As did everyone else in the arena, Beth included, looking from above at it all.

Sandy stood at the outskirts of the arena. Her staff was raised high.

Stew stood beside her and José beside him.

Behind them stood the military prisoners, along with Chip and Diana.

The soldiers were all armed and armored, their shields

and helms and swords gleaming in the mid-afternoon sunlight.

Above, black clouds gathered, nearly blocking out the sun. Thunder boomed as the air turned cold.

Diana walked up to stand beside Sandy. She raised her wand and pointed it at the sky. More thunder crashed as Sandy floated into the air, her ashen cloak spreading like a miasma of unforeseen pain and suffering.

"Let my enemies flee before me!" Sandy shouted. "Let them go crying and sniveling into the darkness that we cast upon them. May none live today! May we bask in the river of your blood! No one fucks with the Mundanes!"

Sandy slammed her staff onto the ground as Diana whipped her wand forward. Four massive bolts of lightning skewered the sky, striking the ground around Ashegoreth, one of them hitting her across the back, the other three sending a ripple of electricity through the ground, throwing many of the orcs and goblins through the air.

Ashegoreth keeled over to the side, screaming in pain as the Dark One's forces scattered.

Beth could see that this was her chance. She leapt from the building's alcove, landing a few feet behind Suzuki. She scooped him up in her arms and took off toward the Mundanes and Horsemen. None of the Dark One's forces paid her any attention. They were too busy trying to muster themselves around the dragon that screeched in pain, attempting to stumble to her feet. When Beth made it to Diana and Sandy, she collapsed and laid Suzuki down at their feet. "Help him!" she screamed, her eyes filled with the tears she could no longer hold back.

Sandy knelt down beside Suzuki. Flowers bloomed across her bones as her staff disappeared, replaced with her wand. She pressed her wand to Suzuki's forehead and sang softly as Diana knelt beside her and did the same.

A golden aura appeared over Suzuki. He finally managed to open his eyes all the way. The last thing he could remember was thinking about teeth. He wasn't sure if they were his teeth or someone else's. But teeth seemed very important. He was slightly disconcerted with everyone standing over him looking worried, but he figured there was a good reason.

"Did I die?" he asked.

Diana laughed as Beth helped Suzuki sit upright. "No," Diana said. "But a couple of minutes longer, you would have. You have your friend to thank for that."

Suzuki stumbled to his feet, swaying to the side as he coughed up blood. He raised his hand and his ax flew across the arena, going straight through two orcs before it arrived in Suzuki's hand. He spat more blood and swayed to the side, stabilizing himself by using Stew's shoulders. "I'll thank everyone after we're finished." He coughed. "First round is on me, all right?"

José couldn't help but smile as he patted Suzuki on the shoulder and offered him a healing potion. "Spoken like a true MERC." José laughed. "If we make it out of this alive, none of us will be buying drinks."

"Thank God. My tab is already shot to shit," Suzuki muttered.

A dragon roar broke the MERCs moment of comradery. And then two more. Suzuki turned to face the Dark One's forces. Two more dragons had landed beside Ashegoreth. They were slightly smaller, but looked just as ferocious.

The full extent of the Dark One's forces had been brought out to the arena. There were more than just orcs and goblins. The Dark One's army was filled with ogres, trolls, giants, and centaurs. Elves and dwarves were stationed above on the high rises of the buildings, each of them aiming plasma rifles on the MERCs and the soldiers.

The two armies glared at each other over the short distance of the arena, the dragons scraping their feet against the ground in anticipation, the giants stroking their energy clubs as if they couldn't wait to bash open the brains of each and every MERC and soldier, the ogres pacing like prize fighters that couldn't be contained, who dreamed of nothing more than ripping their opponents to shreds. Yet they did not move. They only waited.

Suzuki knew what they were waiting for. He felt her down in his stomach and he wondered how many other of the soldiers and Mundanes were sensitive enough to feel her calling.

Beth did.

He could see it in her face. It was almost as if being chosen by her had connected her to them. Suzuki was hardly surprised when the large building above the arena leaned forward, pouring itself into the arena to create a liquid metal throne, which the viceroy built herself upon, the liquid steel snaking up like a reversed waterfall, her slim, godlike body forming into the throne itself. She smiled down on the crowd, her electronic eye glowing brightly.

The viceroy leaned back against the throne as she crossed her legs. "All of my missing prisoners. All in one place," she gloated. "It is only fitting that you would find yourselves in the most ordered of orderly places to finally be brought into the Dark Lord's grace and glory. Why waste so much life, though? You are greatly outnumbered. We have three dragons. Do you really wish to throw your lives away? Is this where you want to die?"

Some of the soldiers turned and whispered to each

other. The Mundanes and Horsemen did not take their eyes off the viceroy. Suzuki could feel her words tugging in his head. He knew better, though. The feelings weren't coming from him. They were complete separate, some product of the monoliths which made him wish to be closer to reintegration, to elevation. But they were not his thoughts, not his desires. They were an artifice of the viceroy. When she died, the feelings would stop.

The viceroy's voice boomed again. "I propose a simple solution. Two champions each. I choose your two. You choose two of mine. And do not delude yourself, I will do you no insult by choosing your soldiers. You choose the champions, as will I. They will meet in the arena. If you win, I will let you walk free. If you lose, you will cease this needless attempt to sow the world with chaos. You will come into the Dark Lord's fold. You will allow us to show you the beauty of order."

The two parties looked at each other. José shrugged his shoulders as they all turned to talk to each other. "We're assuming that she's going to play fair," José said. "She's assuming that we're going to as well, which we aren't. So, what's everyone thinking?"

Diana looked over her shoulder at the viceroy's forces. "They have three dragons," she noted. "In a straight skirmish, they'd have air superiority. Sandy and I could probably manage to take down one or two, but not all three."

Suzuki nodded in agreement. "That means we'd take a shit ton of casualties. It looks like we've got nearly as many ground forces. Their rifles give them an advantage over us long distance, but our armor seems to stack up pretty well against it. Once we close that distance, they'll be fucked. We're at a disadvantage right now. I know the viceroy is going to attack if we don't choose one of those dragons to fight. That'll give us the chance to take at least one of them out."

Chip stepped forward, smiling as she pointed to her HUD. "We got another trick up our sleeves, loves," she said. "This whole defense ring is jam-packed with tech for my grubby, nimble little fingers. Gimme a little time and I can rig up something to get us home, all our bits and pieces separate too."

"Everyone?"

"Everyone. We're sitting on a gold mine of parts to be bent to my genius."

"All right," Suzuki said. "So we select one of the dragons. We take it out, along with whatever else their champion is. Expect her to be a sore-ass loser. Sandy and Diana will take out the two other dragons. Beth, José, and Stew will lead the offensive as a distraction while Chip gathers what she needs to zap us out of here. How's that sound?"

Stew clapped his hand on Suzuki's shoulder. "Not too bad for someone who just woke up from getting the shit knocked out of him," Stew said.

"You're going to have to bring it to them hard, Stew. We're going to be counting on you."

"Don't even worry about it, dude. I've been looking forward to killing these assholes all day."

"So, we're all agreed. This is the plan. Let's do it. José, would you do the honors?"

José turned to the viceroy and cleared his throat before shouting, "We accept your terms. I choose Ashegoreth the Red Dragon as the first champion. Second, I choose that really big giant, the massive, ugly one with the warts and fucked-up eye."

The viceroy nodded her consent. "I choose Suzuki and Chip. You may now enter the ring."

Chip looked up at the rest of the Mundanes and Horsemen, bewildered. "How does she know my name?" Chip asked. "I've never seen or heard of this techno-broad in my life. How'd she get my particulars?"

Suzuki shrugged his shoulders as he pulled out his ax and approached the arena. "Don't worry about it, Chip," he assured her. "The Horsemen are famous. She'd be a shitty evil lieutenant if she didn't know your name."

"I don't know, Little Fearless Leader. Something don't seem right."

Suzuki and Chip stepped into the arena. Ashegoreth and the giant were already waiting for the two MERCs. A plan was brewing in Suzuki's mind. He knew that it was a long shot but at this point, everything seemed like a longshot.

He looked at Chip, who smiled at him uneasily as the invisible walls of the arena closed down around them.

23

———

The air around the arena was electric.

The two armies stood at opposite sides of the arena, each glaring at their enemies through the arena or cheering on the appointed champions. From inside the arena, Suzuki marveled at what the viceroy had built in honor of the Dark One. It was almost a Roman coliseum. And nearly everyone watching was a pawn to the Dark One's foul machinations. There wasn't much time to wonder about it, though. The red dragon and giant were patiently waiting for the viceroy's command. The viceroy was perched in her throne above the arena, smiling smugly.

Suzuki also noticed that the monolith beneath her was vibrating strongly.

When Suzuki looked closely at Ashegoreth, he could see that the techno-organic decay had spread farther down her wings. The monolith was definitely responsible for causing the change. The microchips were for control and the monoliths for elevation. If he got out of this alive, those distinctions could be the key to destroying what the Dark One had created.

The viceroy lifted her hands, electronic tendrils and cables stretching from her fingertips, hooking herself into the throne and building behind her. "Let the battle begin!" she shouted.

Ashegoreth took to the air instantly, screaming and spewing fire at the arena below.

Suzuki ran, dodging the jet of fire as it came for him. He recalled his ax and pulled out his plasma pistol, firing three shots at the red dragon. The plasma shots bounced off the red dragon's chest, obviously causing no harm. *Fuck,* Suzuki thought.

Chip had rolled to the side, both of her arms converting to a plasma cannon. She fired two shots at Ashegoreth. The plasma blasts were huge and brimming with energy, tearing up the ground as they rocketed toward Ashegoreth. The dragon swooped out of the way, letting the plasma blasts hit the invisible barrier and dissipate.

Across the arena, the giant was barreling toward Chip. She turned just in time to see the giant's energy club nail her across the chest. She went flying and landed in a heavy heap beside Suzuki, who ran to her side and helped her up. "Come on, Chip, we got this. We just gotta plan it. Avoid Ashegoreth, take down the giant, and then we'll deal with the dragon. I'll get the giant's attention and you flank him. Then we close this down fast, all right?"

Chip nodded as she stood and her arms returned to their normal state. Suzuki tossed down his plasma rifle and ran his hand over his ax, imbuing it with fire. Then he scrolled through his HUD and set his scent to one thousand Englishmen. He watched as the giant's eyes clouded with an uncontrollable hatred.

The giant sprinted toward Suzuki as Ashegoreth dived at Chip from above. Chip jumped out of the way, rolling across the ground, her arm exploding as it rearticulated itself in a cannon, and she fired a shot that hit Ashegoreth square in the chest. Instead of following up with another attack, Chip took off running around the outskirts of the arena.

The giant was closing in.

Suzuki decided it would be better to bring the fight to the monster. He leapt through the air, his ax raised high above his head. The giant raised his club and Suzuki connected with the black energy shot out of the club. He could feel the energy blowing back toward the giant, but the holy fire was hardly enough to compare. The giant dropped the club, reached out, and snagged Suzuki from the air. He held Suzuki high up, Suzuki's arms in one hand and his legs in the other.

The giant pulled, trying to tear Suzuki in half. Suzuki screamed in pain as he felt his arms and legs being ripped from their sockets. He tried to wiggle away, but the giant was too strong. Instead, Suzuki focused on his ax, which came instantly to his aid. He focused on the ax impaling the giant's skull. Suzuki heard the giant scream in pain. His ax had cut through the giant's hand. *Close enough*, Suzuki thought as he grabbed his ax and sank it into the giant's other wrist.

Suzuki fell to the ground and scrambled to his feet just as Ashegoreth landed next to him. The dragon shot a ball of fire toward Suzuki, who rolled to the left, throwing his ax at the Dragon's eye. The ax sank deep in Ashegoreth's eye and the dragon screamed. Suzuki recalled his ax as Ashegoreth stumbled back, holding her eye. When Ashegoreth slashed at Suzuki, the MERC noticed that the techno-organic decay seemed to be spreading from Ashegoreth's open wound. Suzuki threw his ax again, but this time the dragon knocked it away. He raised his hand and the ax returned. Suzuki turned and ran as the giant swiped its club at him, barely ducking in time to keep it from taking off his head.

Two plasma blasts ripped past Suzuki and connected with the giant, knocking it off its feet as it roared in pain. Suzuki turned around and saw Chip next to the giant. She fired two more shots that connected with the giant's back, burning through its skin, and it fell to its knees. Suzuki turned, picked up the giant's club, and cracked it across its head. He then summoned a fireball in his free hand and launched it into the giant's face. The giant hit the ground with a heavy thud. Suzuki climbed atop the giant and brought his ax down on the giant's neck. He raised his ax and brought it down on the giant again, severing the giant's head from its body. He reached down and picked up the giant's head, raising it for the crowd to see.

The soldiers and MERCs sent out a deafening cheer.

Suzuki tossed the head to the ground. "I told you we got this," he told Chip. "Now, watch my back. Don't do anything unless it looks like Ashegoreth is going to rip me apart, all right?"

Chip shook her head, eyeing Suzuki suspiciously as if she didn't trust that he had thought his plan through completely. "At this distance, it won't be much help," she said. "You'll be blocking me from getting a good shot."

"All right. I'll try not to get ripped apart then."

Suzuki walked toward Ashegoreth as she pulled herself back onto her feet and he threw his ax to the ground.

Then he removed his helm and tossed that to the ground as well.

He raised his hands as he walked to the dragon that towered over him, smoke curling from her serpentine nostrils as her mouth hung open, the smell of sulfur and death rising from her gullet.

"Ashegoreth, Red Dragon, Bringer of Ash and Death, it is I. Suzuki. The Most Mundane of the Mundanes. It is I who approach you. It is I who found you in a cave, hiding as a child would from the Dark One as your brothers and sisters were lost to his mad cravings for power. It is I, Suzuki the Bane of Giants and Krampus, the Freer of Men, who beseech you! Remember yourself!"

Ashegoreth leaned forward and sent a jet of flames at Suzuki, who ducked and rolled out of the way. His hair and eyebrows were singed and he was covered in soot. He took a deep breath and looked up at Ashegoreth. He was close enough that she could have killed him in one swipe of her claw or swallowed him whole. Yet she had not moved. She only stared at him, some vague recollection perhaps in her eyes. Suzuki hoped that was the gleam that he saw meant as he stood and cleared his throat. "I... uh... I was a child when I heard the tales of dragons, of the fearsome creatures they were, of the proud creatures that they were. Yet here you are! Cowed by a microchip!"

Suzuki hit his inventory and stashed away his chest armor. He approached the dragon in only his tunic. "Have you forgotten your pride? Have you forgotten your strength?" Suzuki reached under his tunic. He pulled out the giant hawk feather that Ashegoreth had given him when she relayed her story of her lost love. "Have you forgotten your love, Ashegoreth the Red? Have you forgotten your anger? Have you forgotten the hatred that burns in your ancient heart for the Dark Lord?"

Ashegoreth screamed in rage. Then she spoke and when she spoke her voice was low and stunted, as if it took all of her being to utter the words. "I... I have forgotten nothing, Suzuki..." she muttered.

"Then why do I see a pathetic worm in the place of a dragon?"

Ashegoreth slammed the ground with her claws and tore into it, gnashing at it with her teeth before leaning back on her hind legs and screaming in pain and agony, sending a torrent of fire that reached up to the top of the arena so that it seemed that the sky itself was on fire.

Sweat poured down Suzuki's head. It was so hot that he felt like he was going to pass out.

He held onto his consciousness, though.

Ashegoreth reached forward and grabbed Suzuki in her claw. Suzuki could feel his organs threatening to pop as she squeezed him and brought him eyelevel. He tried to draw enough breath to speak as the hawk feather around his neck rested on the dragon's red scaled hand. "You sent me off to find my love," Suzuki managed to wheeze out. "I found her. We came back to fight the Dark One. Have you forgotten why we fight? Have you forgotten what is lost?"

Ashegoreth stared at Suzuki. Deep in those black and red eyes, Suzuki could see the dragon that he once knew. A tear rolled out of Ashegoreth's eye, instantly evaporating. "Let me free you," Suzuki said.

The dragon stared at Suzuki for what felt like an eternity, enough time for Suzuki to realize that he might have bet far too much on this plan.

Ashegoreth opened her hand so that Suzuki sat in her palm. "Please," she said through tears. "Release me."

Suzuki recalled his ax and jumped onto the dragon's shoulders before she had a chance to change her mind. He raised his ax and brought it down into the dragon's neck, right into the microchip between her shoulder blades. Hot blood squirted out onto Suzuki's face, so hot that it nearly burned straight down to the bone, but he did not stop. He kept cutting and cutting until he'd removed all of the microchip and a five by five gash was left on Ashegoreth. He watched as the techno-organic decay around where the microchip had been turned gray and burned away, giving way to Ashegoreth's natural red scales. "Now, Ashegoreth, Bringer of Death and Ash," Suzuki shouted. "Now will we burn the Dark One to the ground."

Ashegoreth reared on her hind legs, causing Suzuki to scramble for something to hold on to, and roared loudly as the invisible barriers broke down. She turned to face the viceroy uttering a low growl.

The viceroy leaned forward. Her face was grim, and she did not look entertained by the recent developments. "My understanding was that this was a fight to the death," she said. "You did not kill the dragon."

Suzuki shrugged and smiled. "I think we reached an agreement," he said.

"Unsatisfactory. Chip, kill the boy and the dragon."

Chip looked around, confused. She pointed to herself and laughed. "Wait, are you talking to me, your Shiny Holiness?" she asked.

"I never forget a project, even one as old and useless as you. There was a time that we attempted to grow order from organics, before we knew better. Regardless, you will still obey."

Chip shook her head. "Are you shitting me? Are you saying I'm one of your ruddy fucked experiments?"

"One of my first playthings, a lost toy. That was all you ever were. Whatever you have deluded yourself into thinking you are, you are not. You are a tool, and one I intend to use right now."

"Pish, well, you can kindly fuck off."

"You have obviously forgotten your training—and your

potential. Even our most flawed experiments yield some kind of beauty. Let me remind you."

The viceroy leaned back and opened her mouth. Her jaw disconnected like a python's, dropping nearly to her chest. A loud, high-pitched ringing came from her gaping maw. In the arena, Chip fell to her knees, screaming as she held her head. Her skin started to break apart, showing the technological mutation she was underneath, her head splitting down the middle. Her bizarre steel skeleton twisted and churned into liquid before her face seamed together down the middle. She collapsed into a shivering mess on the ground.

José pushed through the crowd and ran into the arena, screaming, "Chip!" He knelt at her side and helped her to her feet. Chip looked at José for a second. Then she back-handed him, sending him flying through the air. She slapped her hands together and they combined, breaking apart at the palms, the fingers bending back to create a plasma cannon. She fired at Suzuki and Ashegoreth, the sheer power of the blast pushing her back a few feet.

Suzuki ducked, trying to hide from the blast. Ashegoreth, on the other hand, spread her long, leathery wings and took to the air. The plasma blast whizzed past the dragon and the MERC, burning a long scar into the floor.

Ashegoreth flew to the other side of the arena, landing in the front row of the MERCs and soldiers. She breathed fire as Suzuki stood on her shoulders. He threw his armor back on and raised his ax, preparing for battle.

The viceroy leapt from her throne, landing beside Chip. Her legs split into four and she stood a foot taller than Chip, like some technological bastardization of a scorpion. She opened her mouth again, and a ringing screech tore through the air. "Kill them!" she shouted. "Kill all of them!"

Suzuki looked at the Mundanes and the Horsemen. "The ringtones are coming from the viceroy. We take her out, we take out the army, so stick to the plan?" he asked.

Beth nodded as she drew her sword. "Quick change. The viceroy is mine."

"What about Chip?"

José stepped forward, his sword raised. "I'll take care of Chip."

Stew drew his ax from his back. "All right, let's show them how the Mundanes fucking party!" Stew charged at the Dark One's army.

Sandy reached out, trying to stop Stew. "Wait, Stew!" she shouted. "Oh, fuck it!" She took off after him, raising her staff and calling black clouds as Diana ran behind her, whipping bolts of crackling energy at the Dark One's forces, who had already started firing, bolts of plasma whizzing past them. The Dark One's forces advanced, the two dragons taking to the air, breathing gouts of fire.

Ashegoreth took to the air as well, Suzuki still standing on her shoulders. She went straight for the other dragons, attacking the larger black one first, their claws tangling as their jaws lunged for each other's throats. Suzuki climbed to the top of Ashegoreth's head and slid down her snout, trying to keep his balance. The black dragon glared and tried to snap at him, but Ashegoreth slashed the dragon across the face. Suzuki took aim and threw his ax, blinding one of the dragon's eyes before recalling his ax. As he raised it again, the black dragon swiped at him, knocking him off Ashegoreth. Suzuki fell through the air, the ground quickly rushing toward him. He closed his eyes, ready to feel his bones shatter on the floor. Then he felt himself steady. Ashegoreth had swooped underneath him. He got back to his feet as a bolt of lightning ripped through the air, connecting with the larger dragon as the smaller turned in the air and sent a fireball at Ashegoreth.

Below the battling dragons, the soldiers connected with the Dark One's forces. It was pure chaos. The air was hot with plasma, and the ground was already growing slick with blood. Stew was in the midst of it all, his ax swinging wildly as he took down orc after orc. His blood was hot, and he could not tell whose blood covered his body. A giant pushed through the crowd of orcs and swung its hammer, connecting with Stew, sending him flying through the air. Stew froze mid-air, then descended, with his feet softly touching the ground. He turned and saw Sandy, holding her wand in his direction. "Thanks, babe," Stew shouted.

Sandy turned, whipped her wand into her staff, knocked back a row of Dark Forces with a fiery concussive blast, and gave Stew a thumbs-up with her other hand. Then a plasma bolt ripped through the air and hit her in the back. Her bones scattered in the miasma of ashes and Sandy was gone.

Stew's eyes went wide with horror and his scream could be heard through the entire battlefield. Those near him from both sides backed away, terrified by such pure, distilled rage. Stew clutched his chest, his eyes glowing red and his muscles heaving and growing. His body swelled to nearly twice its size as he grew an extra foot, now nearly the height of a giant. He foamed at the mouth as he grabbed an orc next to him in the steadily growing circle around him. The orc screamed as Stew ripped it in half, dropping the body and squashing the head. "Sandy!" Stew screamed again as he picked up his ax and tackled a giant. His ax hit the giant in the head, splitting it straight down the middle. "Sandy!" he bellowed again.

A blast of lightning struck beside Stew, flinging orcs and

goblins into the air. When the smoke cleared, Sandy was standing next to Stew. "Yeah, babe?"

Stew grabbed Sandy, her body dwarfed by his hulking Berserker form. "I thought you were dead!" he said through his tears.

"No, dude. I was just reforming. It's easier than dumping all my mana into defense stuff. Also, you look really hot when you're this big. Glad you figured out how to go all Bruce Banner."

Stew laughed, his voice booming. He dropped Sandy, picked up the club of the giant he had just slain, and smashed a goblin into jelly. "Leeroy Jenkins!" he shouted.

The Dark One's forces tried to back away from the deadly onslaught Stew had become as Sandy menaced them with elemental magic. That was the ground side of the battle. Above, Suzuki and Ashegoreth still fought the two dragons, with lightning bolts from Diana and occasionally Sandy narrowly missing both the smaller, faster dragons. José was leading the troops against the Dark One's forces, but they were still outnumbered and outgunned. Even with José's passive buff flowing through each of his soldiers, the battle was still being lost. For each one of the Dark Forces that was cut down, two or three soldiers died. Beth saw this as she cut her way to the viceroy.

Above, from the building that the viceroy had formerly been plugged into, Fred made himself visible. He and Ros'ten were flanked by a host of mythical creatures, almost the entirety of what had been imprisoned in the research cells. Fred raised his hands and pointed at the battle beneath them. "Now is the time to strike back against your oppressors!" Fred shouted before he leapt from the top of building into the thick of battle. The creatures and Ros'ten followed him, the flood washing over the Dark One's forces.

A bolt of lightning skewered the sky, striking the smallest of the dragons. The dragon screeched in pain as its body fell to the ground, where it split open on impact. Flames burst from the dragon's carcass, scorching whoever was around. Beth narrowly missed being smashed, only to block the attack of a giant before her, sliding under its legs, and cutting them out from underneath it. She saw José in the corner of her eyes. "Where's Chip?" she shouted.

José ducked to avoid a plasma shot as he headbutted a screaming goblin. "Can't find her! How about the viceroy?"

"Working on it!"

"Work together?"

"Get your ass over here then!"

José cut a path through whoever was in front of him until he was next to Beth. Together, they pushed their way through the screaming bodies and the dead that covered the ground. It didn't take long to find that Chip and the viceroy were still in the main arena.

The viceroy had not strayed far from her throne, her electronic tubes and tendrils still hooked into the liquid steel of the throne. Chip was standing by her side, her eyes glowing bright red.

José pointed his sword at Chip. "You need to snap out of this shit!" he shouted. "We don't have time for you to be brainwashed too!"

The viceroy laughed as she sat up in her throne. "This is not mind control," she lectured. "There is nothing to be controlled. Her mind was created by the Dark Lord. It was his to begin with. She merely forgot that. All I have done is to remind her."

Chip fired her hand cannons at José, who jumped to the side to avoid being burned alive. "Chip, come on, stop!" he shouted. "Don't you remember me! Don't you remember who I am?"

Chip smiled and took a step forward, her skin already showing the signs of techno-organic decay. "I haven't forgotten who you are," she hissed. "I only forgot who I was, what I was made for. I was—"

Chip was cut off by Beth flying through the air and tackling her to the ground. Beth smashed her shield into Chip's face as the android attempted to shoot her, sending five hot plasma bolts into the air, where above them all, one of the bolts hit the second dragon in the wings, giving Suzuki enough time to jump onto the dragon's back and bury his ax deep in the dragon's microchip. "Two dragons for us," Suzuki shouted as he leapt back onto Ashegoreth's shoulders. He looked down to see if he could make out anything in the chaos. "Hey, Ash, can you see anything down there?" he asked.

"Your friends have made their way to the viceroy."

"Sweet. Let's bring the party to her as well." Suzuki opened his channel to Stew and Sandy. "Hey, we're all converging on Beth's position. She's got the viceroy. Give support. If we take down the viceroy, we've won."

Suzuki flinched when he received Stew's reply. It was nothing but static, the screams of orcs, and Stew's blood-rage-filled shouts. Sandy replied quickly afterward, "I'll try to wrangle Stew over there. He's kind of...in a mood right now."

Stew's voice broke through again. "I'm gonna rip your fucking cocks off and skull-fuck you until you shit out your own babies!"

Sandy sighed. "Yeah, he's having a time."

Suzuki couldn't help but laugh as Ashegoreth descended, the smaller black dragon following her. The closer Suzuki got, the clearer he could make out the scene beneath him. José was battling with Chip, narrowly avoiding her plasma blasts, while Beth was fighting off the snaking tendrils of the viceroy, who still had not left her throne.

Ashegoreth hit the ground with enough force to make the forces on the battle ground stop dead in their tracks. She roared, a sound so piercing and fear inspiring that several of the Dark One's forces turned and ran, only to be mowed down by the soldiers. The black dragon landed beside Ashegoreth and both dragons shot fire at the viceroy, who leapt out of the way, finally leaving her throne.

The viceroy struck back with the tendrils from her back as Chip fired at the dragons. Suzuki launched a fireball from atop Ashegoreth that hit the viceroy flat in the chest as the viceroy's tendrils wrapped around Beth, tossing her into the air. Stew's voice could be heard roaring as he leapt over both dragons, landing in front of the viceroy. He grabbed her by the chest and slammed her into the ground three times before kicking her, sending her sailing. The viceroy skidded across the ground, landing next to Chip, before screeching, her tendrils and legs tearing up the ground around her as she ran for Stew. She connected, sending them both sprawling across the ground as her tendrils opened up, sending beams of plasma dancing around her, slicing anything that got near.

Beth managed to slice off one of the tendrils. It didn't matter; there were too many tendrils streaming piping-hot plasma. The Mundanes and Horsemen backed away as the viceroy carved out space for herself and Chip. The two techno-organics stood backed up against the throne, greatly outnumbered. "I am tired of these games," the viceroy said as she stretched her arms outward, her tendrils propping her up. Around her, the air started to distort. Large, black portals opened up and a ghastly sound came forth. "There will be order," the viceroy screamed.

Out of the portals stepped creatures composed of pure black energy. Their bodies didn't seem to be ruled by space or temporality. Some of them blended into each other, only to rip apart the next second, their immaterial bodies slithering and contorting much as the liquid metal the viceroy and Chip were composed of moved. These demons had bright white eyes that glowed like dying stars, and their whole bodies lit up like constellations. It was difficult to tell if they were living, tech, or something far more disturbing. Sections of their bodies were covered with armor that looked as if it had been cut from the same cloth as the viceroy's. They also wore HUDS that looked far more advanced than either the Mundanes' or the military's.

The demons melded together, flowing like a river of hot lava. They piled onto the two dragons, nearly drowning them in some kind of dark energy. They did not stop coming from the portals. The arena was quickly filling with their bodies as they poured into the fight.

Suzuki leapt from Ashegoreth's back and landed next to Beth. "We need to end this!" he shouted.

Beth grabbed Suzuki and looked him in the eye, her face determined and grim. "Get me to the viceroy, and I'll end this."

"Mundanes, we're taking the viceroy down! For honor!"

"For glory!"

Stew plowed through the mass of demon bodies, tearing into them with his teeth and swinging his ax as he shouted, "For XP!"

The Mundanes advanced, Stew leading them, knocking aside anything in his way as Sandy backed him up with quick bolts of energy to dispel whatever Stew hadn't killed.

Suzuki and Beth stayed near the rear, pushing forward when they had a chance, their blades slicing through flesh and whatever the demons were made of.

The viceroy's tendrils snaked out and snatched Stew, pulling him into the air where his struggling meant nothing. It took nearly all of her tendrils though, and Suzuki saw his chance. He ran toward the viceroy, ready to land the killing blow.

Chip stepped out from behind the viceroy and fired three shots. Each one of them connected with one of the Mundanes. Suzuki, Beth, and Sandy fell to their knees, smoke rising from their chests, all of them gasping for breath as Chip walked up to them. Stew was still held above them all as he struggled and screamed. Chip pressed her cannon against Suzuki's head, and he could feel the muzzle burning a ring into his forehead. Chip stared blankly at Suzuki.

José tackled Chip to the ground, knocking her over and rolling on top, trying to pin her hands to her sides. "You're not touching the kid," José shouted as he struggled with Chip.

Chip's face twitched and her jaw came unhinged and stretched open. A plasma cannon pointed at José. She fired.

José slumped to the side. Blood poured from what was left of his neck.

Chip's face rearticulated and she got to her feet. She looked down at José's headless corpse, and the side of her face twitched as she blinked rapidly.

Beth grabbed Suzuki's hand. "Now," she whispered.

Suzuki was in shock.

He couldn't block out what he had just seen.

But it didn't matter.

He saw Beth moving.

He would mourn José later, and he knew José would be proud of that decision.

Both he and Beth ran forward, past Chip, who was still staring at José, blinking as if she were trying to refresh herself. Beth and Suzuki slid past the few tentacles that were not occupied with Stew. Suzuki threw his ax, and it landed in the viceroy's chest. She screamed in pain as Beth leapt through the air and thrust her sword through the viceroy's head. Then Beth reached into her pocket and pulled out what looked like a small USB drive. "Fuck your order!" she screamed as she slammed the drive into the viceroy's head.

The viceroy froze, her tendrils went limp, and Stew fell to the ground. The techno-organic skin started to drip off of her like melting ice. She fell to the ground, convulsing as she threw up liquid silver technology, her entire body shaking as she screamed and coughed blood.

Chip's scream drew everyone's attention. Suzuki looked over his shoulder to see that Chip had fallen to her knees and was cradling José's body in her arms. Tears rolled down her face as she screamed, a sound of pure loss and anguish. For a moment, everyone on the battlefield halted and listened to Chip screaming and crying. There were no words to describe the sound. It was as if she had just seen a piece of herself hollowed out, dead, and bare for her to witness in all its fragility.

The sad serenity did not last, though. Demons were still pouring through the portals. Suzuki pointed to the viceroy's body and shouted at Stew, "Grab her! Now!" Then he turned to Beth. "Find two soldier's HUDS and give them to the dragons!"

Beth turned and ran toward the two closest bodies she could find as Suzuki sprinted over to Chip. He grabbed her by her shoulders.

Chip's face was crushed. She was blubbering and repeating, "I didn't want to. I didn't want to." Her whole body was shaking, and she finally stopped speaking and sat there and screamed until her throat was raw and there was nothing but a harsh whimpering escaping her lungs.

Suzuki shook Chip. "You need to get us out of here!" he shouted.

"I killed him," Chip wailed. "I killed him!"

"Chip, get us out of here now!"

"I didn't want to!"

"If you don't get us out of here right now, you'll kill all of us! Do it!"

Chip's eyes cleared for a moment. She looked at Suzuki, and there was no doubt in his mind that whatever had happened to Chip before had been out of her control. She was back now. "Please, we need to leave," Suzuki pleaded.

Chip nodded, pulled up her HUD, swiped once, and hit a button.

Suzuki felt his stomach turn inside out as he was sucked into a space that was not a space, and then everything around him faded into darkness.

24

―――――

S uzuki felt himself spilling out into reality.

He was dumped on the ground, completely disoriented. It was soft and grassy. This wasn't the swamp, nor was it the caves that they had been in. Something must have gone wrong with Chip's transportation. Perhaps she was still under the Dark One's sway. Suzuki struggled to get to his feet as fast as he could. He raised his hand, and his ax jumped from his waistband into it. Even though he couldn't see anything, he conjured a fireball in his hand as he swung his ax, trying to get his bearings. He heard voices surrounding him. *The Dark One's forces were surrounding him. He was going to have to fight his way out.*

"You're never going to fucking take me!" Suzuki shouted as he waited for a sliver of his vision to return. He didn't want to hit any of the Mundanes or soldiers. They couldn't have been teleported too far from him.

A voice came from the darkness. "Please, Mr. Fletcher, calm yourself." The voice sounded familiar.

Suzuki lowered his ax. It wasn't out of trust. He had just

realized how tired he was. More than tired; he was beyond exhausted. His body felt like it was going to collapse beneath him, and his mind felt fried. Hopefully, whoever the voice belonged to wasn't planning on killing him.

As Suzuki's eyes began to focus, he could make out the shape of a tall, older man. The man wore white robes tailored in military fashion. He looked to be very regal, but his bearing was not the consequence of his clothing. Regality was imbued in him from his poise and facial expression. Myrddin, the wizard and the architect of *Middang3ard*, stood calmly before Suzuki, his hands folded neatly over each other while he waited for Suzuki to compose himself.

All around Suzuki, the remaining soldiers were struggling to get to their feet. Their numbers had been significantly reduced. Captain Wyatt was among them. A little farther away from the soldiers were the Mundanes and Diana. They were all still trying to keep from vomiting as well. Chip sat away from everyone, José's body still clutched in her arms as she rocked back and forth, sobbing quietly.

Myrddin took a step closer to Suzuki and extended his hand. Suzuki took it and practically fell into the old man's arms. "You and your friends have accomplished something phenomenal today. We need to debrief you immediately, you and Beth."

"Give us a minute," Suzuki muttered. "Wait, Chip!" Suzuki turned, ready to walk toward Chip when he felt an invisible binding seize his body. He was unable to move.

Myrddin walked over to Suzuki and placed his hand on Suzuki's shoulder. "We will be quarantining Chip until further notice. She still might be a risk. Now come with me, please."

The wizard raised his hand and Suzuki felt his feet leave the earth. As the wizard walked away, Suzuki floated after him. Beth's body also rose as the wizard passed her, and she floated along with Suzuki. Captain Wyatt followed at a distance, trying to compose himself and keep from vomiting. There really wasn't much of a distinction at this point.

The four of them made their way through a military camp.

The tents were emblazoned with the military sigil, and there were guards everywhere. They went to one of the larger tents in the center of the camp. The tent was decorated with odd trinkets and curiosities, the sorts of things that only wizards and mages tend to find fascinating. Myrddin waved his hand, and four chairs conjured themselves into existence. Suzuki felt his body being led to the chair, and he was thankful, if a bit reluctant, to sit down. Beth was beside him, shaking her head and trying to make sense of what was going on.

Suzuki cleared his throat. He still had an odd amount of reverence for Myrddin, even if he hadn't seen the man since he had been brought to Middang3ard. "Where are we?" Suzuki asked.

Myrddin smiled sweetly as he poured himself a cup of tea. "Tea?" he asked, waiting a second before he went on to explain himself. "You are in an unnamed military camp on the outskirts of the Middang3ard realm."

"How the hell did we get here?"

"Chip's teleportation was redirected here by our technicians. That's one of the faults of tech; it can be very easy to hack if you know what you're doing."

"Why did you bring us here?"

"That was the plan all along."

Suzuki blinked his eyes as he tried to follow what

Myrddin was saying. He heard the old man talking, but nothing was making sense at the moment. "What do you mean, the plan?" Suzuki asked.

"Please allow Captain Wyatt to explain."

Beth had finally come around. She was sitting up straight, stretching her jaw out. She had a black eye and a few cuts on her face. Suzuki didn't even want to think about what he looked like.

Captain Wyatt cleared his throat. When he spoke, it was with the efficiency and formality Suzuki had started to unconsciously attribute to the military. "My platoon was captured in an attempt to infiltrate the Dark One's largest reintegration encampment. We were chosen because we are the best. But that wasn't all. We were also counting on you and one of our most promising private's relationship with you, Suzuki. Through you, we hoped to draw the Horsemen to the encampment to deal with the issue of the viceroy as a distraction we could use to upload a virus into the Dark One's mainframe, effectively disabling the ringtones being used to control multiple races."

Myrddin poured Suzuki and Beth cups of tea. Suzuki could feel the grip Myrddin had on him relax. He took the tea and sipped it quietly as he tried to understand what he was being told. "The mission was an overwhelming win for us against the Dark One. Not only were we able to sabotage the Dark One's mind control, but due to your creativity, we were also able to liberate a goodly number of creatures who would have made all of our lives difficult."

Anger was welling up in Suzuki, but Beth was the first to speak. "Are you fucking serious?" she shouted. "You've been manipulating us the entire time?"

"Not manipulating. We have been planning. The Dark

One's influence stretches too far for conventional tactics. Suzuki would understand."

Suzuki was too livid to speak. His mind was racing with all of the implications of Myrddin's meddling. "I would never throw away anyone's life," Suzuki finally said.

"Neither have we. You do not win a war without sacrifices. The higher the stakes, the higher the gamble."

"You knew about Chip? About what Chip was?"

"I have always known what Chip was. I have made a minor hobby of watching her. It took considerable attention and effort to guide her to the situation she found herself in."

"Considerable attention to guide her to killing José? What the fuck is wrong with you?"

"José's loss was an unforeseen tragedy. We were aware that Chip was a piece of the Dark One's old tech, old experiments he deemed failures for some reason or other. We could not have foreseen Chip being used to kill José, though. That was, as I said, an unfortunate tragedy. But it was unlikely that you would have been able to make it as far into the defense rings without the aid of Chip's...technological advancements."

"Why keep all this a secret?"

"Loose lips sink ships, Suzuki. Just as we have spies within MERC and MERC has spies within the Dark One's forces, we are not immune to treachery."

"What else do you know that you've just been waiting for us to figure out?"

"I believe you can answer that yourself, Mr. Fletcher."

"The Dark One...he's an alien from an entirely different dimension."

"Yes, we are aware. We have been working on a craft to invade his dimension and end this war once and for all. We believe your efforts would be better applied within the constraints of the military. You Mundanes have proven yourselves to be extremely reliable. The amount that you have grown as fighters is unsurpassed by any MERC party. You four are exceptional. Within the military, you would have more resources. You could turn the tide of the war with the Dark One."

Suzuki sighed and hung his head as he handed Myrddin his teacup. "So, you're saying you knew that the Dark One was an alien? You knew Chip was built by him? You willingly jeopardized the safety of my party and used us as unknowing pawns in your war games? And you want us to follow your orders now?"

"Suzuki, this isn't about whatever you think is right or wrong. We are fighting a war. There is more at stake than single lives. The Dark One threatens the very fabric of our reality."

Suzuki stood and cleared his throat. "I respectfully decline, sir. I understand what you are trying to accomplish, but I don't agree with your methods. I'm a MERC, not a dog of the military. Please return my friends and me to the Red Lion so we can continue our service."

Myrddin smiled as he leaned back in his seat. His face was warm and understanding as he sipped his cup of tea. "I assumed you would say as much," Myrddin said. "Though it doesn't hurt to ask. I will return you and your party—"

"Chip and Diana as well. And I want you to transport Ashegoreth back to her homeland."

"Are you making demands of me, Mr. Fletcher?"

"No. I'm merely asking you, as another enemy of the Dark One, for a favor. We've spent the last weeks doing them for you."

"Well said, Mr. Fletcher. I will return the dragon to her home, as well as your fellow MERCs."

"Good. Next time you need help, how about you just fucking ask?"

Suzuki stood and stormed out of the tent. He hoped that Beth would come with him, but at this point, it didn't fucking matter. She was safe, and she knew where to find him. He couldn't be around any of the military right now. It had taken everything for him to watch his mouth. In reality, he wanted to drive his ax into Myrddin's smug face. But that wouldn't have solved anything. Instead, he went back to the Mundanes. Sandy and Stew were finally on their feet. "We're leaving," Suzuki said.

Stew had returned to his regular size and Sandy had removed her amulet. They both stood when they saw Suzuki. "What's going on?" Sandy asked.

"The military's been using us. You probably already figured it out by now."

"We kinda figured that much when we ended up here."

"They want us to work for them."

"Fuck that."

Stew laughed callously. "Yeah, fuck them. Let's go home. What about Beth?"

"What about me?"

Suzuki turned around. Beth was standing behind him. She had removed her military armor and was wearing a plain tunic. She carried her sword and her shield. A military mage was standing at her side. "We ready to go?" she asked.

"Almost, just give me a minute. Go get Diana. Tell her we're taking Chip home with us."

Suzuki looked around. It didn't take long to see Ashegoreth, hidden by shadows, crouched low as if she were afraid of the humans walking around her. Suzuki went to her and knelt beside her foot. The dragon leaned forward, her face partially illuminated, her bright eyes dancing in the night. "Hello again, Suzuki, the Most Mundane of Mundanes," she whispered.

"Hello, Ashegoreth."

"I cannot thank you enough for what you did for me."

Suzuki nodded. "I believe you would have done the same for me."

"I'd like to think I would have, although I know I would now do anything for you."

"We have to go. I spoke to the guys in charge here. They're going to send you back home. You'll be safe."

"I don't want to be safe, Suzuki. I want to fight the Dark One and rid the realm of him."

"Well, I'd say come with us, but I doubt you'd like the Shire. It's a little swampy."

"Give me your hand, child of dust."

Suzuki held his hand out for Ashegoreth. "You say you are the most Mundane of Mundanes, yet today I have seen a human with the heart of a dragon, a heart that holds my own. I will always be yours, Suzuki. I am glad that you found your lover, and I am glad that she is safe. You are both lucky to have each other. There is little I can do to thank you for granting me my freedom. This, I believe, will be a reward."

Ashegoreth took her claw and sliced Suzuki's hand. He tried not to flinch, and he held his trembling, bleeding hand in his other one. Then Ashegoreth took her finger and ran her claw across it, cutting her scales open. She pressed her wounded finger to Suzuki's palm, and he felt fire consume his hand. He fell to his knees, quaking in pain, but he did not pull his hand away from Ashegoreth. The open wound sealed itself in fire and the pain passed.

"There are few things more sacred to a dragon than its blood. There are fewer things children of flesh lust after as well. Now my blood flows through you. Now you are a human born of the fire. Each boon has different qualities. We can never say how you will show the true nature of your blood now, but you will. You and I will forever be connected. Whenever you need me, I will come. No matter why. No matter how far."

"Uh, did you just marry me?"

Ashegoreth laughed, a hearty sound that filled Suzuki's entire body with joy. "Dragons do not get married." Ashegoreth chuckled. "But you are family now. As close as my brothers and sisters and lovers. And now I will name you. It will be the name that will be uttered for all dragons to hear. Wear it proudly, Suzuki the Dragon Blood, Born of Fire, Tamer of Dragons. Now go. Go to your friends. I will see you again."

Suzuki bowed, not knowing what else to do. Then he hugged Ashegoreth's paw and turned before there was anything else that would need to be said. He ran over to the Mundanes, who were all watching, mesmerized. Beth was the first to speak. "Suzy, did that dragon just marry you?" she asked.

Suzuki shook his head and smiled. "No," he said. "I think I kinda got adopted or something."

Stew clapped Suzuki on the back. "Dude, that dragon still totally wants to fuck you." He laughed.

Beth smiled as she took Suzuki's hand and looked at the flame-shaped scar in his palm. "I know I should probably be jealous or something, but that is really fucking cool," she said. "You told her you're taken, right?"

"I am?"

Beth wrapped her arms around him. "You're goddamn right you are, Suzy."

"She already knows, trust me. She said she's glad we're together again. *All* together again."

"Me, too. Now can we get the fuck out of here?"

Suzuki looked at the military mage waiting for them. The mage nodded and raised his staff. Reality started to blend and swirl, and Suzuki felt that familiar fishhook in his stomach. The Mundanes were finally going home.

25

———

It had been one full week since the Mundanes returned to the Red Lion. José's funeral had been carried out the next day, with all the MERCs showing up for the funeral.

Many of them hadn't believed José had died in battle until they saw his body in a casket.

Diana had insisted on an open casket.

She believed it was best for the MERCs to see what the Dark One had taken from them. Even the MERC they all respected the most, who they thought was incapable of dying, could be taken from them.

His body was burned at midnight.

Suzuki was chosen to carry the torch that reduced José to ashes, allowing the wind to take him to the stars.

Few of the MERCs saw Chip.

It wasn't that they were trying to shame her or that they didn't trust her. As it was said around a good many tables, if MERCs stopped trusting each other every time they fell under mind control or got bewitched and tried or succeeded in killing their friends, there wouldn't be any MERCs left to fight.

Stew, Sandy, and Suzuki raised many glasses to that toast. Still, Chip kept to herself in her room, no doubt trying to understand the role she had played in the fall of the Dark One's rings.

Diana, on the other hand, seemed to be everywhere, connecting with different MERCs, trying to help plan as many assaults on the Dark One's various camps as possible.

That was the way she handled her grief.

Suzuki could not recall ever seeing her cry, yet he had noticed that something had gone out of her eyes since José had passed. She moved slower than she had before, almost as if age was finally catching up with her. Often, toward the end of the night, she would sneak up to Chip's room with a few bottles of mead and lock the door as quietly as possible.

The dour spirit hung over the Red Lion for a few days. Of course, the MERCs drank to José and toasted to him every day. Soon the mood changed. Slowly but surely, as MERCs went on their own quests and missions and returned by the skin of their teeth, they sang their battle songs and drank deeply, their glasses raised high, their songs dedicated to José.

Ballads were composed by the halflings and dwarves honoring José, too many to count. And they sang deep into the night until many of them were drunk, telling stories of their time with José.

José was not the only one for whom ballads were composed.

It was not fitting for them to be sung until the fifth night, as was the custom of the MERCs. A ballad had been written for each of the Mundanes. One, dedicated to Sandy, told the tale of the ghost mage who wore the entrails of her enemies as if they were robes. Another detailed the exploits of the raging Berserker Stew, who ripped giants limb from limb in the middle of the Dark One's perverse arena. Even Beth, although a relatively new MERC, had received a ballad, lauding her as the woman who had fought her way from the bowels of hell, only to drive her sword through the head of the viceroy. After a couple edits, the dwarves admitted that sword was a much better poetic device than USB drive. But the ballads that were sung the most in the halls of the Red Lion were these two: *The Tale of the Mundanes*, and *Suzuki, the Most Mundane of the Mundanes*.

It was the fifth night of mourning and the Mundanes were sitting at their table, which had once been the table of the Horsemen. They had not bought a drink or a meal since they returned, and Wendy, the bar owner, assured them that they would not be doing so for some time.

The Red Lion had lost the Horsemen, but it had gained the Mundanes.

The table was quiet.

Neither Beth nor Suzuki joked or spoke very much. Nor did Sandy or Stew. It was not that they did not enjoy each other's company. Rather, each of them had seen so much pain and suffering, had seen themselves stretched as far as they believed possible, and they had all come back together. There was no need to speak words that needn't be said. Yet tonight was the fifth night of mourning and, according to the elves, it was bad luck to continue on in somberness and sobriety any longer.

Surprisingly, it was Diana and Chip who brought the Mundanes their first round of drinks and food for the evening. Chip placed a pitcher of ale on the table (Wendy had decided to change to pitchers because the dishes were getting out of control), and Diana brought round a plate of Wendy's bizarre culinary delights. They squeezed themselves into the table with the Mundanes, and it did not take long before they were all doing shots together while racing to see who could suck the most venom pits out of a pile of black lightning beetles.

Suzuki stared down at his hand after he had finished his ale, looking at the flame that had been carved into his palm. He felt like his whole body was scarred. In truth, Sandy seemed to be the only one of them who had walked away from the last few weeks without looking like she'd been repeatedly cut and burned, a point she often brought up. Now Suzuki was looking at his hand, thinking of José, wondering where he was, if he was, in fact, anywhere.

Chip was talking quietly to Sandy. She was crying softly but trying to wipe away her tears before anyone could see. "It's not your fault, Chip," Sandy was saying.

Chip nodded, reaching for a napkin on the table with one hand and a shot with the other. "I still pulled the trigger," Chip said. "I'm gonna make that son of a bitch pay. I'm gonna make him pay."

Diana reached over the table and took Chip's hand. Stew put his hand on top of Diana's, and Sandy's, Beth's, and Suzuki's followed. "We're all going to make him pay," Sandy said. "We're going to send that interdimensional sack of shit straight to hell. That's why we're the fucking Mundanes. All of us. You hear me?"

Chip and Diana looked at Sandy, their eyes watering. Sandy smiled at Suzuki. "Right, Suzy?" she asked.

Suzuki stood and raised his glass. "To the Mundanes! Let us never split the party!"

The six Mundanes cried in unison, "Never split the party!"

As Suzuki prepared to sit down, his vision went black. He was no longer in the Red Lion. He was outside time and space. He felt himself growing older and younger at the same time. He looked down at his hands as they decayed into ash and reformed as a baby's. "What the fuck is going on?" he asked aloud.

There was a light in the distance. It looked to be a burning bush of some kind. Then the bush contorted and the branches fell off.

José was there instead.

Burning still.

The dead MERC stood up, his eyes bright and alive. "Hey, there," José said as he pointed at Suzuki, then everything vanished.

Suzuki was standing in the Red Lion once again, surrounded by his friends. He sat down quickly and threw back his drink. *Must have drunk too much*, Suzuki thought.

"Well, look who's become local celebrities?" a voice shouted from behind Suzuki. Just the sound of it was enough to make Suzuki wince. The voice belonged to Milos, the surly dwarf who had been responsible for the Mundanes' first missions. "Bet y'all got your heads so far up your asses now that you forgot you're supposed to be here fighting the Dark One's legions, not getting drunk and fat every night."

Sandy laughed and poked Milo's stomach with her wand. "Honestly, you might want to remember that yourself from time to time," she joked.

Milos turned red and cleared his throat loudly as he pulled his gut above his belt. "Aw, shut up! I'm not here for jokes. I'm here to let you know there's a new mission for y'all. Extra high-level shit, something that only the best of the best can handle. Y'all keen to get started again?"

Suzuki looked at the Mundanes around the table. He could already see the answer in their faces.

The most Mundane of the Mundanes tossed back his

drink before slamming the stein on the table. "Hell, yeah. For honor..."

"For glory," they all shouted. "For XP!"

"For José," Suzuki added, looking at his party. "All right, Mundanes, it's time to get back to work."

AUTHOR NOTES RAMY VANCE

AUGUST 29, 2019

There is rarely an Edinburgh morning when their early morning squawking doesn't wake me up. And when we're out and about with my four year old, I have to diligently watch any food he might be eating, lest he put it down and some enterprising seagull swoop down and steal it.

To date, my son has had two partially eaten muffins and half a sandwich stolen from him.

But then I moved into a new apartment in West Edinburgh. Our flat is the top floor, and because the building is taller than any of the surrounding buildings, I get to survey my neighbors' roofs (often standing at the window in a power pose, arms akimbo, as I survey my kingdom).

I was in one of those power poses when I noted a seagull laying two eggs on the roof across the road. Because I'm interested in stargazing (and not at all because I'm a perv), I got out my telescope to get a closer look at the little gull family and over the following weeks, I watched in wonder as one of the eggs hatched and a baby seagull emerged.

That hatchling almost immediately started walking, and I was smitten from minute one, dubbing the newborn Little Bob. Here are his first baby pics:

Over the coming weeks I watched little Bob grow, while the other egg (his baby sister, Emma) sat under his mummy's belly, waiting for the opportune moment to hatch and enter the world.

I started to take pictures of the Gull family, precariously lining up my phone's camera into the telescope's viewer and clicking. I posted those pics on my author Facebook group, doing daily updates on the adventures of Little Bob and his baby sis.

It was strange, because I truly hate seagulls, but these guys ... I knew them and could no longer lump them into the general bucket of ire with all other seagulls.

They were the Gulls. A family just doing their best to survive this world, just like my own family.

I really felt for them and looked forward to my morning routine when I would get a chance to check in on them.

By now I suspect you can see where this is headed. I *felt* for them. As in, past tense.

Things were going great, my daily updates were getting more elaborate, when one day I woke to find Little Bob missing. I immediately launched a search party (which comprised of me going into my neighbor's yard. "Who am I, Mr. Neighbor? Why, I'm the guy who lives in the apartment across the road. You know, the guy who has a telescope trained on your home...")

Little Bob was nowhere to be found.

And after three days, I had to assume the worse.

Little Bob was gone. And with his departure, I wrote the following eulogy in his honor:

It is with a heavy heart that I announce Bob is gone. He has been missing for three days and all efforts to find him (in my neighbor's backyard) has led to nothing.

I do not know what happened, but given the recent magpie activity near the nest leads me to the following conclusion. Bob died defending his unhatched sister, Emma, from their predatory ways. Knowing Bob, and all he stood for, I can imagine the magpies descending on the nest and the little seagull standing his ground, crying out in the way that all seagull do, "This is my home and you will NOT hurt those I love here. Not today. Not while I breathe."

The battle must have been fierce, with Bob ending the miserable lives of several magpies until he finally succumbed to his own wounds. And Bob being the hero that he was ... he left the nest so that Mama Gull didn't come home to her bloodied son's body.

So, go forth, little gull, go ... go to the Valhalla of Seag-ulls, where you will be met with open arms and the loud cackling of the gulls.

We'll miss you, Bob. Truly we will.

(On a side note, this October I will be releasing a story, co-written with Jenn Mitchell, where Bob the Seagull will be a character.)

If you'd like to read all about Bob's adventures you can join my Facebook group: House of the GoneGod Damned! (https://www.facebook.com/groups/495713834233271/) The Facebook page is dedicated to my other universe – the GoneGod World (series include: Mortality Bites, Mortality Bound and Keep Evolving).

Just search Bob.

He's the only one in there.

AUTHOR NOTES MICHAEL ANDERLE

SEPTEMBER 2, 2019

Thank you for reading our work. We appreciate it from the bottom of our hearts!

I'm presently typing this up as we cross the Nevada border on our way back home to Vegas. Jet lag (after a trip through Europe to China and finally back to the US) is a challenge at times. Yesterday I took an eight hour 'nap' all through the afternoon, only to run to find that the bulb I purchased to replace our outside front lawn light was the wrong type.

That left me twenty-three minutes to jump in the car and run to Home Depot to replace it.

Now, enough about my home-handyman foibles and more about the stories ;-)

One of the reasons I like these stories is, I'd like to think that all of the millions of hours we lose to video games could be turned into something that has value. My mind turned to saving the planet as the ultimate option that would provide the reason.

Happy trigger fingers of doom are needed. REJOICE!

Grab your game controller and sign up at the nearest Middeng3ard Recruiting Station!

Further, I like the idea that many of the authors, game producers, and other content creators are in a vast conspiracy to prepare the next generation to take the fight "out there," where you can fight for humanity, dwarves, elves, and others, and perhaps acquire magical treasure.

I'm (over) fifty, and I STILL think this sort of shit is cool.

Hey, perhaps they have healing and de-aging magical potions, and I could join the groups of magic users. In my fantasy life, I sling magic like a god, and orcs fear me joining the field of valor.

Because I'm over-powered in my stories and can lay waste to mountains.

I'd like to point out that the ease of destroying my foe has nothing to do with the fact that I've slept outside on the cold, hard ground in my youth, and know that I'd rather be finished with the quest in time to make it back to the inn.

I'm (very) spoiled with good mattresses vs aforementioned painful ground.

Look out for our short story, where some of your favorite authors join us in protecting Middeng3ard. If you don't find it...

I suggest you bug the crap out of Ramy, because it lets him know you care ;-)

Ad Aeternitatem,

Michael Anderle

OTHER BOOKS BY RAMY VANCE

Mortality Bites Series
Keep Evolving Series
Fatebound Series

BOOKS BY MICHAEL ANDERLE

For a complete list of books by Michael Anderle, please visit:

www.lmbpn.com/ma-books/

All LMBPN Audiobooks are Available at Audible.com and iTunes

To see all LMBPN audiobooks, including those written by Michael Anderle please visit:

www.lmbpn.com/audible

CONNECT WITH THE AUTHORS

Connect with Ramy

Join Ramy's Newsletter

Join Ramy's FB Group: House of the GoneGod Damned!

Connect with Michael Anderle and sign up for his email list here:

Website: http://lmbpn.com

Email List: http://lmbpn.com/email/

Facebook:
www.facebook.com/TheKurtherianGambitBooks